KT-374-257

I and the public know
What all schoolchildren learn,
Those to whom evil is done
Do evil in return.

WH AUDEN

This novel is entirely a work of fiction. The names, characters and incidents portrayed in it are the work of the author's imagination. Any resemblance to actual persons, living or dead, events or localities is entirely coincidental.

Published 2017 by Crimson
an imprint of Poolbeg Press Ltd
123 Grange Hill, Baldoyle
Dublin 13, Ireland
www.poolbeg.com

© Cat Hogan 2017
Copyright for editing, typesetting, layout, design, ebook
© Poolbeg Press Ltd

The moral right of the author has been asserted.

1

A catalogue record for this book is available from the British Library.

ISBN 978-1-78199-850-2

All rights reserved. No part of this publication may be reproduced or transmitted in any form or by any means, electronic or mechanical, including photography, recording, or any information storage or retrieval system, without permission in writing from the publisher. The book is sold subject to the condition that it shall not, by way of trade or otherwise, be lent, resold or otherwise circulated without the publisher's prior consent in any form of binding or cover other than that in which it is published and without a similar condition, including this condition, being imposed on the subsequent purchaser.

 www.facebook.com/poolbegpress
 @PoolbegBooks

Printed and bound by CPI Group (UK) Ltd, Croydon, CR0 4YY

Typeset in Bembo 12/16

www.poolbeg.com

Leabharlann
Chontae Uibh Fhailí
Class: FIR
Acc: 30013006433191
Inv: 00046462

About the Author

Cat Hogan is a bestselling international crime-fiction author from County Wexford. Her first award-nominated novel *They All Fall Down* was published in 2016.

Cat lives in her native County Wexford with her two boys, within spitting distance of the sea. Her father Pat, a lightship man, instilled in her a love of the sea and the stars. Her mother, Mag, taught her to read before she could walk. Cat drinks too much tea, cooks way too much food and never gets enough sleep.

She loves her creative life and is a real advocate for positivity and mental health. She facilitates workshops for adults, concentrating on reading and writing as a tool to foster positive mental health, and she teaches Creative Writing for Wellness to young teens in secondary schools across the country.

She also teaches courses in creative writing for pleasure and her favourite is 'Couch to 100k – Kickstart Your Writing and Go the Distance'.

With both a Law Degree and a Business Studies degree under her belt, Cat runs her own business in content and digital marketing. She runs workshops and gives talks up and down the country to creatives and entrepreneurs alike.

She has facilitated workshops and given talks at festivals including Write by the Sea, Kinsale Literary Festival Words by Water, Waterford Writers Weekend, Bray Literary Festival, and Wexford Literary Fest, Enniscorthy.

Acknowledgements

'*Words are easy, like the wind; faithful friends are hard to find*' – from *The Passionate Pilgrim*

This book would never have been written without the support and encouragement of so many friends, old and new. I'll never forget that and I'll always be grateful.

To you – the readers. It is with a humble tongue and a heart full of gratitude I give my thanks to you. You bestow on me the gift of confidence with every message, email, letter and word of encouragement I receive. Thank you for staying up all night and for discussing my characters as though they were your friends.

Gaye Shortland and Paula Campbell – you are formidable women. It's a privilege to work with the pair of you and I'd be lost without your advice and friendship. To the rest of the team in Poolbeg – thanks for always being at the other end of the phone, or email.

Tracy Brennan, my agent – thank you for your unwavering belief in my ability.

To Rick O'Shea, Liz Lyons, and all my fellow book-nerds. The Rick O'Shea Book Club is like a life jacket to me. There are so many of you I want to thank for the constant cheerleading, book banter, and recommendations. Sometimes, your kind words and your outstanding reviews were the only things that kept me afloat. Rick & Liz – your incredible support and wisdom is something I will always cling to. Ledgebags!

Speaking of book clubs, I have to mention my amazing

neighbours and the swishest book club I've ever had the pleasure to visit. Anne-Marie Kirwin, Celine Rossiter, Vivian Devereux Brady, Sandra Bates and the rest of the lovely ladies, thanks for the cake, the chats and the fun! Looking forward to another visit soon xx

To my friends, neighbours, and fellow creatives in Wexford. You have championed me from the start and, without you, I believe this book would never have been written. To the incredible staff of Wexford Library, the Arts Department and all in Wexford County Council – many thanks to you all.

Tom Mooney and Anna Hayes. Your support continues to be unwavering – I wish you all the success in the world.

To the rest of my fellow-writer friends: Margaret Scott, Liz Nugent, Mark Leggatt, Catherine Dunne, Sue Leonard, Nessa O'Mahony, Ann O'Loughlin, David Nicholls, Alex Barclay, Brian McGilloway, Carolann Copland, Patricia Gibney, Andrea Mara, Maria Hoey, Lorna Sixsmith, Caroline Grace-Cassidy, Terry McMahon, Mary O'Donnell, June Caldwell, Frankie Gaffney, Karl Parkinson, Colm O'Regan, Dave Lordan and more locally, Eoin Colfer, Billy Roche, Paul O'Brien, Peter Murphy, Imelda Carroll, Tina Callaghan, and Carol Long. Each and every one of you have inspired me. Thank you and thanks to some of you in particular for putting the plasters on my grazed knees when the going got tough – that will never be forgotten. Alison Martin – you're just a doll and a fountain of knowledge.

Jackie Hayden, my formidable friend. You have kept me on the straight and narrow since the day I met you. It's an honour to have your name and your words on my book cover. Here's to many more cups of tea and chats about mystery and mayhem.

Aidan Gillen. Thank you for trusting in me. Your generosity of spirit is something I will hold dear.

A special shout-out and thanks to all the book reviewers and bloggers who have shouted about me since this all began. Your help in getting my name out into the world has been invaluable. Every single one of you agreed without hesitation to help, again. My job would be infinitely more difficult without you.

Huge thanks to the John Hewitt Society and the Market Place Theatre in Armagh. The John Hewitt Society provides opportunities for individuals across Northern Ireland to explore issues of difference and identity through literature and creative writing. Inspired by the ideals and ideas of the poet and political writer John Hewitt, the Society's flagship event is The John Hewitt International Summer School, a six-day festival of culture, creativity and discussion. I had the honour of attending the Summer School as a bursary student and not only did it ignite in me a passion for poetry and politics but it gave me the space and the time I craved to completely submerge myself in the art of creativity. The lessons I learned and the wonderful friends I made during that week will stay long in my memory. A special word of thanks to Niall McArdle for introducing me to the School in the first place.

Thank you to the Arts Council of Northern Ireland and to the Irish Department of Foreign Affairs and Trade.

To the many wonderful professionals who listened to my outlandish meanderings and imparted their expert knowledge as to what goes on in the real world. Particular thanks to Clive O'Regan, Martin O'Neill and Olly Daly. Any inaccuracies in the story are wholly my own.

Lucy Moore and the wonderful crew that makes up 'Write By The Sea' Literary Festival in Kilmore Quay, Wexford. It has been an honour and a pleasure to watch the festival grow into something so magical in such a short space of time. A wonderful festival for readers and writers alike and an eternal source of pride for me. Thank you for giving me the opportunity to bring my stories home – home, by the sea xx

To my constant friends. I count my lucky stars to have you in my life. Mel, Sab, Cookie, Jason, Rachel, Seán, and Rosemary. Rosemary – thank you for bringing Fran to life. Seán – thank you for bringing poetry into my life.

To Fiona Kiernan, my lovely friend. To you and your family and all the good and bad times we've muddled through together. Our friendship is so precious and I'm sure Dominic and Betty are

ix

keeping a good eye on us still. They're never too far from my thoughts and I'm sure they're proud x.

To the dynamic duo that is Declan Dempsey and Lorna Colfer-Dempsey. Declan, thank you for being one of the first readers and for sharing your story with me — we'll all be out of a job when you hit the shelves. Lorna — thank you for restoring my faith in humanity (several times) and thanks for the unending supply of shortbread, tea, and free-range eggs in the Summer Kitchen. That's where we keep it real! X

To Illanon, Wayne, Owen, Lauren, and Ciara O'Neill. Thank you for being the loveliest neighbours of all time and for making Joey an extra member of the family.

To my extended family - the Kehoes, the Wrights, the Devereuxs, the Dennehys, the Keanes, the O'Connors and the Murphys. Like always, we'll stick together. X

To all my Newcastle family — Yvonne, Martyn, Susan, Peg, Baby Rowan, Auntie Mu and the gang, and Carol and the gang. Thanks for shouting about me in the Toon.

Dave — it's time to remember the beauty in the world and in your voice. Let it shine.

Mam, Sas, Fidelma, Paraic, Leslie-Ann, Michael, Emma, Ken and Mick. There's nothing more important in this world than family and I love you all dearly.

My two little boys — my firstborn Joey and my newborn Artie. I'll never be able to put into words the depth of love I have for you both. You are my sunshine.

Dad — you'll always be my lighthouse.

For my mother – Marguerite Hogan

And in memory of her beloved only brother, Uncle Tom Kehoe

Chapter 1

The acrid smell in Fran's bedroom didn't trouble me. The manic expression and the unmistakable waft of kif oozing from him was pathetic and only served to anger me. His girlfriend lay crumpled on the floor between the locker and the bed, naked save for the *khamsa* necklace at her throat. She was as superstitious as he was but the talisman of defence against the Evil Eye was no match for the junk that she had just overdosed on. She was barely breathing.

He was babbling and pacing, smoking and crying.

'Scott … I dunno how this happened, man. I only went out to get smokes. She was clean. What the fuck, what the fuck? I'm a dead m-man!' His voice caught on the last word.

I punched him in the stomach, with enough force for him to drop to his knees but not as hard as I would have liked. The cigarette rolled across the floor into a pool of vomit. The syringe lay on the rug and the rest of the paraphernalia was scattered across the locker. This snivelling wreck was beginning to cause me real problems. He never listened.

'I warned you about her. How many times did I tell you to steer clear of her?'

He remained on the floor, winded. He stared at me, beseeching me to help her and fix the mess. Saidaa, Fran's on/off girl, was a local from the bidonville — or, in layman's terms, the slums. To complicate things further, she was the sister of a volatile dealer — the bruises and scars on her sallow little arms told their own story. But she had a connection to this area. She would be missed. Questions would be asked. She was not like the others.

The air in the room was viscous. The scent of near-death settled on my skin like sand from the Sahara. We needed to get rid of her. It was coming up to sunset. The streets would be filled with tourists. I knew how to be invisible in this city — I knew the rhythm of this place as well as a mother knows the beat of her child's heart.

'Did anyone see you with her?'

'No. She came here.'

'Did you contact her?'

He nodded and grunted from the strain of picking his emaciated-looking carcass up from his position of prayer. Tall and gangly, with pasty skin even after all this time in the sun, what Saidaa saw in him I'll never know.

'You fool! Get rid of the phone. I warned you to stay away from her. Thinking with your cock as always!'

'We were ... she told me she had stopped using ...' He started to snivel and pace again, not original enough to do anything other than run dirty fingers through lank hair.

'I don't want to know.'

He continued, snot and spit on his face. 'I came back and found her like this. I'd no idea she had that shit with her. Oh man, she's really bad!'

'You don't say.' The contempt I felt showed in my voice. It sounded brittle. 'We will remedy this and that's the end of it.'

Incompetent, ignorant junkie — a nobody. He stood by, an imbecilic half-smile on his unshaven face. I think he thought I was

2

going to call for an ambulance. I knew what needed to be done. I owed him nothing – I would wipe that smile clean off.

I sought out an answer to the dilemma by glancing around the room. It was a large space looking down onto the courtyard of the riad, tastefully decorated, thanks to my good eye. The property had been easy to acquire nearly a year before – people don't ask too many questions when they are presented with crisp notes. Privacy was on the top of my agenda and the town house had offered just that. A resident could remain anonymous here, the opposite to Ville Nouvelle, the slick and modern new town outside the walls of the old city. I should have left the useless lowlife in Tunisia. I knew he would eventually bring trouble to our door. But I never envisaged it would be so quickly. It had been a weak moment and my first mistake.

'Pull yourself together and help me.' I gestured to the floor, a plan forming in my head.

We manoeuvred the rattan dresser off the large woven rug. No attention would be paid to a man wearing a djellaba carrying a carpet on his shoulder. This was Marrakech after all. Not an ideal remedy but there was no other way.

'Scott, what are you doing?'

'What does it bloody look like? I'm cleaning up your mess – as usual.'

Perhaps another punch in the gut would make him more compliant.

'Do as I ask. If not, I will disappear and you can do this yourself.' Insolent fool. 'Help me with this.'

The huge rug was heavy but it slid along the wooden floor over to the side of the bed.

When I enquired about distinguishing marks, he looked as though I had just asked him a trick question. The cheap trinket around her neck came away with one sharp tug.

'Tattoos? Birth marks? Anything that will make her body easy to identify?'

Again, the blank stare. I was beginning to lose my calm. I barked at him to grab her legs. We placed her face up on the carpet. She groaned like the dying animal she was and her sunken eyes fluttered.

'She's still alive, Scott! What …' His question trailed off and panic flashed across his face. He just didn't get it.

Now was not the time to rush.

'Give me that scarf,' I said as I removed my watch. An Omega Seamaster, it was expensive and I didn't want to damage it.

I slipped the gaudy pink fabric around her sallow little neck. The knot tightened and did the work on her windpipe for me. Even in her state, a survival instinct kicked in and her body fought the inevitable. It didn't last long. The scarf stayed put and, as I threw her clothes, the bedsheets and the drugs paraphernalia on top of her dead body, Fran dry-retched beside me.

'Your phone, Fran.' I held out my hand. He removed it from his pocket and handed it over without a word. I removed the SIM card, pocketed it to destroy later, and handed back the device.

I worked the rug around her good and tight, the thunk of her head on the boards dulling with every roll.

'Get a bucket and scrub that mess off the floor. We'll wait until after dark.'

I brushed myself down and turned to leave. I needed a drink and I needed time to think. 'Stay here. And don't open the door until you hear my voice.'

The second hurdle was getting to the car with the body. I kept a car outside the city walls but moved it regularly for two reasons: one, to keep the engine ticking over, the other to ensure it was never in a place long enough to arouse the attention of local thieves or the police. In my game, an exit strategy was prudent.

I felt nothing for this young girl. Another junkie mignotta – a whore. She deserved it and now the city had one less parasite. The ebb and flow of life. One was exterminated – another would take her place very quickly.

Darkness swept in over the Atlas Mountains and swallowed the voice of a muezzin. It was time. The network of alleyways surrounding the riads would conceal us. Clad in the local attire, hoods up, we looked the part and we knew the route through the alleyways. I originally envisaged Fran carrying the carpet by himself and me following behind, but he looked conspicuous straining under the weight of what was supposed to be flooring bought in the souk. We carried the carpet together, on our shoulders. Fran was in front.

Our destination was The Tanners' Gate and the quickest route was though the souks. It would take us less than ten minutes.

The labyrinth of laneways was a landscape of pure darkness save for the bare bulbs of street lamps casting sodium light on flaking plaster and clay walls. We zigzagged along the laneways, moving quickly but not so much as to be noticed.

'Turn right here.'

The souks were as easy to identify by smell as they were by sight. I liked to spend time down here in the markets. We entered Souk El Kebir. I knew it well and we weren't far from where we needed to get. The chant of the woodturners selling their wares was constant. The smell of cedarwood hung heavy in the air. We kept to our pace and didn't stop. By now the woollen djellaba was stuck to my back with sweat, as we swam, with our cargo, against a sea of bodies. We arrived at Kissaria Square. It was noisy, hot, sticky, smelly, and overrun with tourists. Even under the circumstances, the assault on the senses never failed to amuse and amaze me. Here was a riot of sound and explosions of colour from clothing and fabrics.

'*Vous deux, arrêtez – où allez-vous?*'

A tall merchant with dirty caramel skin blocked Fran's path.

He knew we weren't tourists but he also guessed we weren't natives – hence the French. The locals were used to all sorts living within the walls of their old city.

Fran could barely speak English.

'*Entrez, entrez, amis! Voulez-vous acheter? J'ai le meilleur haschisch de qualité dans tout le Maroc!*'

Fran was shaking his head and trying to sidestep him.

5

'We do not want to buy hash,' I responded in French.

'*Vous achetez! Vous achetez*!' He was insistent and had Fran by the arm.

'Keep walking,' I muttered.

Fran didn't move. He was swaying on his feet and sweat was staining the fabric between his shoulder blades.

'We do not want to buy. Move out of our path.' I spoke in French again, this time more aggressively.

'*Vous achetez! Vous achetez!*'

This plan was unravelling. We were faced with a potential scene in front of tourists, or worse again, the secret police that frequented the city – they spent so much time trying to look inconspicuous that they stuck out of the crowd. My eyes had become adept at spotting them. But at that moment, I didn't have the luxury or the freedom to move around and watch.

In front of me, Fran's shoulders were hunched and his legs were shaking. If he dropped the carpet, it was game over. The square was filling up. Crowds were pushing and jostling to get past us.

'*Move!*' I said.

He did not obey me. The merchant still had him by the arm. My eyes swept over the square. I needed an exit strategy. If it was going to go bad, I needed an out. The minaret of Ben Youssef Mosque was in my eyeline, just to my left. Go there and double back down the alley. Fuck Fran. I had no reservations about saving my own skin.

The merchant shook his head and muttered something. His arms flew into the air and he roared at me, in Arabic this time. Then, bored with the exchange, he turned his back and accosted a pair of backpackers.

Fran almost broke into a trot. That was close. Maybe we should have taken the longer route but it was too late to back out now. Bab El Debbagh was near – once we reached that gate, we should be out of danger.

We were in the very north of the medina – the old city. A sea of bodies was flooding towards the square for the evening spectacle of street food, storytellers, dancers, conjurers, and hustlers.

'Turn right, and head for the tanneries.'

The alleyways were more deserted here, save for the odd scooter or an old man and his donkey. Tourists came down here during the day, but never at night. It was a good plan to come this way after all. The vats were kept covered during the day because of the heat but the dark unleashed the smells. I didn't buy into the superstitions of the locals – it was the living I had to watch out for. The locals believed the tanneries were inhabited by demon spirits, the traces of hair, blood and the dirt under my feet adding weight to their argument. The tanneries were located on the outskirts of town and the rancid trade was one for the poor. On Rue Bab Debbagh, it was like stepping into medieval times. Stinking tanners, with their stinking children and their piss-pots. We wouldn't be bothered here. The smell of urine, dung and decaying flesh made my eyes water. The old traditions, still alive and well – the scraping and stretching of dead skin.

Weybridge Estate and the harbour flashed before my eyes. The 'old sod', Ireland, the green grass of home – an appealing vision while here in the bowels of hell. The heat was making me soft. Fuck Ireland. That thought, and the faces in my mind made my breath quicken. I imagined for a moment it was *her* broken body here with me in this place. That made me feel better. One of these days, I thought, Jen would get what was coming to her.

But I wasn't at liberty to fantasise – Fran was speaking to me over his shoulder. He could see the gate ahead, the russet tones of the carved pisé – the straw-and-mud walls enclosing the city – signifying the light at the end of the tunnel. That put a spring in his step.

Outside the city walls, the air was slightly cooler. Even though we could have done with a rest for a moment, we couldn't risk stopping.

The car was where I had left it. I had bought an old Mercedes – it was an obvious choice – the most common car in Marrakech. A fine layer of dust had settled on the bodywork and crude graffiti had been scrawled across the back. The car had once been wine in colour, now it looked sandblasted.

Luckily, Fran seemed to have got over the incident in the

market and was more alert. The boot opened after a groan of protest and we put the carpet in there. It took a bit of bending and pushing but it eventually fitted in.

I, too, was feeling calmer. The muscles in my back were loosening after the strain of our cargo and I was tempted to go for a coffee. She was in no hurry after all.

Fran looked as though he might start blubbering again. He was a sympathetic sort of fool when all was said and done. There was more to this story than he had told me originally – I would get that information from him, one way or another.

Things were different here in the Red City. I needed to be ahead of the game. Trust no one and always have an escape route. That was my code. Ireland was different, but the liberties and sway I had there were gone. My fault, I suppose, but that bitch Jen back there had pushed me to it. I wouldn't let go, I *couldn't* let go. Thanks to her, I now owed my boss and I was trapped here.

'Scott! Are you listening to me?'

'Yes. Get in the car. Let's get this done. You drive. Head south, on the main road. I'll tell you where to go.'

He did not object.

He was calmer now and driving well, I noted as we set out.

'Why couldn't we leave her somewhere in the medina?' he eventually asked.

I had pondered this while waiting for sunset back in the riad. Why not throw her into a dustbin and forget about it?

'We can't take the risk of her being found.'

I had other reasons too.

Fran was sloppy. He wasn't telling me everything. He had a big mouth and a penchant for kif. Not a good combination.

We drove for ten more minutes in silence and darkness bar the tunnel of light from the headlights. The sky was a shade of inky blue, with a smattering of bright stars. The dusty landscape was broken up by billboards advertising the Royal Golf Hotel Marrakech. Golf courses meant lots of space and a lack of houses.

Fran saw the billboard before I did. *La Maison Marie Rose.*

Another hotel. The white lettering and logo stood out against the backdrop of blue, the up-lights making the words pop out.

'What are the odds of that?' he said.

Fran was superstitious and this city suited him – they were all the same here with their talk of black magic, jinns and demons. It was nonsense and didn't hold sway with me.

'I don't like this,' he said.

I could hear the nerves in his voice.

'I've told you before, I don't believe in superstitious nonsense,' I said. 'Now keep your eyes on the road and take your next exit to the left. That's a dirt road into waste ground. That's where we need to go.'

It had been quite some time since I'd had any reminders of Ireland, or Jen and Andy. Now twice in the one night. An odd coincidence: a hotel in Africa sharing a name with Andy's trawler all the way back in County Wexford. I didn't believe in karma. Maybe I should have started right then.

The car skidded to a halt on the dusty earth. The air was fresh and cool. Except for a chorus of sheep competing with the song of the Berber toads, there wasn't a sound.

We were far enough off-road to be concealed by scrub and olive trees. To the north, the Atlas Mountains stood guard over our actions, their snow-capped peaks a light grey against the dark blue of the sky. Even I could appreciate the majesty and beauty of that sight. The scenery appealed to my sense of grandeur.

I turned to speak to Fran and realised he was still in the car, staring out the window.

'Get out and help me.'

He didn't make a sound as he stepped out into the night. The boot groaned at us again as I opened it and he sighed.

'Did you think she wouldn't be there? Did you think she had come back to life and escaped?' I laughed at my own joke. 'Come on!' I grabbed one end of the carpet and gestured towards the scrub to the left of us.

We carried her a short distance and laid her down behind some bushes.

Fran hung his head. 'This is wrong, man.'

'Oh, stop being such a fool! Do you want her brother to know she was back on the gear? He'll blame you. You didn't take care of his little sister.'

'I didn't kill her – you did.' He looked at me like a wild animal on the verge of attack.

'Don't bother, Fran. You wouldn't survive a day in this shithole without me. You need me, man.' I chortled and headed back in the direction of the car.

I wasn't afraid of that miserable junkie. But he would have to go. Loose ends and all that.

I heaved and spat onto the dirt as the petrol hit the back of my throat. I had never managed to perfect the knack of syphoning. Directing the flow of the hose from the car into the container, it struck me how easy it was to dispose of a body. All one needed was a cool head and a plan.

'What are you doing?'

'What does it look like I'm doing? We have to burn her.'

'We can't.'

'We have to.'

'Scott, no! The flames and smoke will be spotted for miles. Are you mad?'

Irritation shot through me. At myself, not at Fran. He was right. I'd been about to make an elementary mistake.

I went back to the boot of the car and pulled out a couple of short-handled shovels. Always prepared for every eventuality. In my game, you had to be.

'Get digging.' I flung one of the tools at him.

The ground was dry but loose. It didn't take long to dig a shallow grave.

He knelt at the head of the open grave like a chief mourner. Grief was etched on his face and for a brief moment I felt sorry for the fool. I could put him out of his misery – all it would have taken was one sharp blow to the back of the head with the shovel I still held. It was tempting. He was a liability but he had saved my life once before – that counted for something. I was a man of honour after all. He was also the last tangible connection I had to my old life and the harbour – I wasn't ready to sever that.

'Get back in the car.'

He stood tall and looked me straight in the eye. He was challenging me. Brave or stupid? I couldn't decide. Regardless of the circumstances which had led us to that moment, he didn't have the courage to try and kill me. He wouldn't last a day without me. We needed each other – for now at least.

I stood over the mound and admired my handiwork.

He watched from the car. That was my second mistake.

Chapter 2

Fran's insides felt loose. He tried to ignore the overwhelming rush of panic and concentrated on the feel of the steering wheel in his hands. The amber lights from the dashboard made his fingers look like they were covered in blood. Shame and guilt were a palpable presence in the confines of the vehicle, threatening to suffocate him. He wanted to digest himself, transform, break free of his skin and fly away into the night. But he was trapped.

Scott is losing his marbles, he thought. *You should have let him drown that night in Ireland. Your life sure would be easier now. He's out of control. He murdered Saidaa. You let him. You helped him. They're going to know it was you — you need to get away from here. But you can't.*

Scott looked as though he was meditating. The oncoming lights lit up his face. Fran saw how it had changed in those last few hours. His face had turned into a mask. Something barely recognisable. He was a monster.

'Keep your eyes on the road.' Scott shifted in his seat and looked at him. 'You need to toughen up. I did you a favour there. Stop looking so ungrateful.'

Fran wanted to slam on the brakes, like he had seen in the movies, and watch Scott's body smash through the windscreen and out onto the asphalt. He wondered if he would have the strength to drive over him, just to be sure.

'And whatever plan you are concocting in that backward brain of yours, stop it. You need me, Fran.'

'I don't need you. I should have let you fucking drown that night.' He gripped the steering wheel tighter and accelerated.

'You're just such a decent guy – a real pillar of society. You couldn't bring yourself to leave me there, could you?'

Scott was laughing and Fran wanted to punch the smirk off his smug face. Signs of life were coming into view – it wouldn't be long until they were back in the medina. Fran couldn't think straight.

'Take the left here and head for Bab Sidi Ghrib.'

Fran did as he was bid. The traffic was light as they drove under the arch of the city walls. The tourists would still be in the main square while the locals would be at home for the most part, eating after evening prayer.

'There. Park there.'

Fran indicated and eased the car into a tight space under a sad-looking palm tree. He killed the engine, got out of the car and walked away.

Scott called after him. 'Don't wait up! I'm going out tonight. *Ciao!*'

The bang of the car door and the fading sound of Scott's whistling was a relief.

He stopped for a while and watched two kids kicking a ball in the dirt, supervised by laughing mothers in bright clothing sitting on stoops. Saidaa had laughed like that when they talked about running away to Ireland. They were going to clean up their acts and just go. He reckoned she would have loved it there in the harbour by the sea and she'd asked him over and over to tell her about the beautiful curved beach and the lighthouse. She had never left the city and she had never seen the sea.

He had thought his heart would break as he unrolled that rug after Scott had left the room. He'd needed to say goodbye.

Scott had him pegged as stupid. He rooted in his pocket. It was safe to take it out now – the khamsa necklace he had bought for her, now the only reminder he had of her. He checked to make sure the phone was still in his pocket – he needed that now more than ever. The SIM card Scott had taken from him could be easily replaced – he had a stack of them in his room – tools of the trade.

He leant against a tree, clutching the necklace, and hung his head. The children's excited shouts wafted towards him on the warm night air. He knew he was as guilty as Scott was – not only for this crime but for what had happened in Ireland that night. He clenched his fists against his head as the feelings took hold. He rubbed at his eyes, wishing he could turn back time, and like Dorothy click his heels together and go home – in his case, away from the madness, away from the danger. He was in way over his head and it was all his own fault. The events of that night in Ireland flashed before his eyes as though he had been transported back there to the strand. He walked up and down the path, trying to block the story out before resting against the tree again.

A few minutes was all it took to change everything. That thought made him laugh – they always said that – a split second is all it takes to change a person's life. He had finally accepted that.

He should have listened to the warning feeling in his stomach as he walked up the hill in the harbour that night – all the signs were there. He'd remarked to himself about the sky – an ominous shade of grey – looking like it was trying to crush the village. He couldn't see the spire of the church on his way up the hill – the clouds had swallowed it. Flagpoles were banging out a whistling death march and the sea was battering the harbour wall.

He wondered now what would have happened had he gone into the Gale for a pint first, instead of staying outside for a smoke, or if it hadn't been too windy to light up on the way up the hill. He would never have seen the van go by, with Andy looking like he had the fear of God in him. If he hadn't seen his face, he would have found out like everyone else later that night. It was the look on his boss's face that changed his life.

Scott had been on the blower that evening in foul humour. Fran had known something bad was about to happen.

Fancied yourself as a hero, Fran, and thought you would save the day. Ran in the direction of the headland – the shortcut to Jen and Andy's – but when you spotted the three of them down on the strand you hid in the scrub like a coward. You knew all along that Scott had it in for Jen and you never did a thing about it – you just kept on smuggling his drugs in on Andy's trawler instead.

You watched your boss fight with Scott as Jen lay half dead in the water. Did you help? No! You watched as Jen smashed a rock off his face and you watched him go under the waves – but you knew – you knew if they caught Scott you were a goner, so you waited for your chance and pulled him out of the water. Being the big man, trying to save your own arse.

Scott had been badly injured in the fight but he was like a damn cat – always landed on his feet.

You weren't to know he had a back-up plan and you surely weren't to know he had already shafted you. He played you from day one, boy – he knew all about your ma and your gambler of a da – you were played, boy. And now you have blood on your hands. And here you are in this godforsaken hellhole with him.

Fran was beyond the point of crying – too late for that.

He pushed himself away from the tree, thrust the necklace back in his pocket, and headed home.

Chapter 3

Fran's weakness bothered me. Few can face a situation as well as I do and his whimpering and crying were laughable. I was too busy to deal with his broken heart.

I left him to his own devices when we returned to the city. I don't think he realised when we left that my intention was to rid myself of him as well as the girl. His grief had turned to loathing – that would eventually become a problem. I couldn't trust him. I would have to remedy my dilemma in time but for now he could stay. His presence kept my hands clean in the day-to-day running of the business. Fran didn't understand what was happening. It was all a game and I liked to win. Fran was weak. No competition. I was glad I hadn't let him in on the latest business dealings I was into – he wouldn't have coped. I had a better colleague with a vested interest and it was the perfect set-up.

Ville Nouvelle was my destination and I couldn't be late. Time is money as they say. I had gone straight back to the riad after we parked the car. I had needed to change and I'd needed a drink. I

16

looked good – I looked the part. Another one of my many talents of course. Blending into all situations. My French had improved significantly – this helped but on this job it wasn't so vital. Timing was.

I reached Club Jasmine and bypassed the crowd. The owner and his cronies nodded as I passed them in the foyer. The club smelled of money and class – the new town in stark contrast to life behind the old city walls. This was the Marrakech that surprised. The late clubs, the designer boutiques – it was the commercial hub and more European than African. This was where I wanted to be.

Greeted with a nod by security, another door opened and I sauntered across the marble flooring in the direction of a baby grand piano. That was the meeting point. They usually looked intimidated as they walked up the corridor to greet me – clutching the pass in trembling hands. Beautiful young women, chosen carefully.

She was taller than I expected but typically South African, with beautiful brown skin and her gait a confident swagger. This was going to be a challenge. Her eyes stayed on my face as she approached me with an extended hand.

'You are Scott?'

Her eyes immediately rested on the deformity under my eye. The beard hid it well but, intentionally, not well enough. I knew she liked what she saw. I was blessed with the sallow skin and dark Italian features of my mother but it was my eyes people noticed first: a startling shade of blue. I was beautiful – just how the ladies liked it.

'It's a pleasure to meet you, Leigh, and to welcome you to Club Jasmine.'

She didn't resist when I kissed her on the cheek. I could feel her open like a flower under my gaze. They fell for it every time. 'Let me take your shawl.' I clicked at the faceless attendant to my left and she scarpered away to the cloakroom while my companion smiled an apology to the back of her head.

'Do you address all people so abruptly?'

She smiled while asking the question, but I had the measure of her already. This was going to be interesting. I had to trust my contact knew what he was doing. He had never been wrong and up until then our business transactions had never brought us any trouble.

'My apologies, Leigh. It's been a very busy day. Shall we take a seat in the restaurant?' I put my hand on the small of her back, like gentlemen do. Through the silk, I could feel her heat. She was a young raven-haired beauty.

I pulled out her chair and she sat.

A waiter appeared. He asked if I would like the usual bottle. I nodded and sent him away before she had a chance to object to that as well. Usually, the women were flattered by this show but her face was impassive. I wasn't in the mood to pacify her.

The surroundings were beautiful and I watched as she took it all in. We were seated close to the stage – the show would begin at 10pm but for now only muted lights danced across the wooden floor of the curved stage. The mirrors reflected the story of the evening unfolding behind us. Silk dresses, well-cut suits and silver buckets sweating in the evening air. The light from the candles flowed over the glassware on the dark mahogany tables.

'What brings you here to Morocco, Scott?'

I was disappointed her accent wasn't stronger. That South African drawl tended to turn me on. Her accent was flat and her English perfect.

'My wife and son died nearly two years ago. There was nothing left at home for me.'

Usually they asked about it. She didn't.

'What brings you to Morocco?' I countered.

She pondered the question while the waiter and I carried out the ritual with a bottle of wine.

'My compliments on your choice of wine.'

She had deflected the question. I would have to turn up the charm. I liked to entertain them and to watch them fall for me.

'Thank you. Volubilia Gris. The rose colour appeals more than anything, but don't tell my wine-buff friends.'

In response, she smiled the first genuine smile since we had met.

'Yes, a quality wine produced in Morocco by Frenchmen,' she said. 'Discovered through a love of golf and the sandy soils of Meknes. The vineyard owners also make olive oil.' She swirled the wine in the glass and tilted it towards the light.

'You have done your homework, young lady.' It surprised me.

'My father was a wine merchant. We owned a modest vineyard near Walker Bay. I was a good student.'

'Why are you not at home with your father, crushing grapes with your feet?'

'He died. I sold the land and left – never to return.'

'And now you are travelling the world alone, trying to find yourself and spending your inheritance?'

'Cheers.' She raised her glass to mine and took a drink.

The waiter reappeared to take our order. She nodded at me to order for both of us. That was a good sign. I needed her to relax. If she left early, it wouldn't work. I quickly ordered, briefly checking that she had no objections.

'What happened to your wife and son?' she asked when the waiter departed.

'You're very blunt. I like that.'

'If you don't want to talk about it, it's no problem, but we *are* on the subject of why we are here.'

I sat quietly for a moment and looked at the table. When my eyes met hers, there was sympathy there. I enjoyed this part.

'They were killed in a car crash. I was driving. The scar on my face is a constant reminder. Every day I look in the mirror, I think about Jen and Danny. Danny was eight at the time.'

Interrupted by a waiter, she complimented him on the speed of the service while he laid our starters in front of us. Warm chargrilled zucchini with mint and tahini. Delicious. I had worked up quite the appetite with all the hauling and digging earlier. We eyed up our plates. I didn't really care about her opinion on how the starter looked or smelled. I needed to stay on track.

I pulled a photo out of my wallet and showed her the smiling faces of Jen and Danny sitting on the harbour wall with the islands in the background. I pointed at the gold band on my finger,

'I can't bring myself to let go. One day I will go back there, but for now I'm here. I can't bring myself to take the ring off just yet.'

She was sitting forward with her hand under her chin – listening to my every word.

'I'm so sorry for your loss.'

'Thank you.'

I allowed a silence build up long enough for her to think about my tragic story and to feel real empathy towards me. It also gave us a chance to eat. To my surprise, for a graceful-looking young woman, she ate like a pig – chewing with her mouth open, half-eaten remnants of courgette rolling around her tongue. I wanted to knock her out with a fucking punch right there. She had turned me off my food. I laid my cutlery down to indicate I had finished, hoping she would do the same. She didn't.

I continued on with the script.

'I work with Marco, whom you know. Aside from running the hotel, we work in the commercial district over on Plaza. Lots of wealthy European clients. Marco has been here for many years. I travelled a little after the accident and landed in this city a year ago. We are trying to expand the offices – hence the job advertisement you answered.'

'You like Marrakech, do you? Why not Casablanca if it's commerce you work in?'

'I love this city and loathe her in equal measure. The commercial district is growing at a rapid rate. Casablanca is saturated at the moment – it's where everyone goes. We are diversifying into import and export. Everything is a commodity here, you just need to know where your market lies.'

'Interesting. I was just passing through – I don't know people here. I like it that way but my mind might change. I thought perhaps getting a job here might be wise for a while.'

'Do you have family back in Walker Bay? A boyfriend? People who are waiting for you to come home?'

'There's no one waiting.'

I should have felt sorry for her. She was perfect.

'And you think you are suitable for a job with us?'

She laid down her knife and fork and sat up straight in her chair. She was about to deliver the elevator pitch.

'Yes, I do. I'm fluent in French and I have a strong background in business. I'd like to think I –'

I cut her off. 'Why not get a job in retail or in one of the many hotels here?' I couldn't be bothered sitting there and nodding while she ran through a rehearsed monologue about her attributes.

'If I don't get this job, I will.'

'The job is yours.'

I nodded to the waiter to remove the plates. I couldn't have cared less if she had finished or not.

'Thank you, Scott. I look forward to working with you.' She extended her hand for the second time that evening.

We shook hands and she relaxed back into her chair, now that the deal was done.

'We can point you in the right direction for property rental. For now, you can remain in the hotel. How is it?'

'It's basic. Clean. Food is terrible.'

That was the moment the waiter decided to appear with entrées. Lamb shank, presented with spiced pears and couscous. The smell reminded me of Christmas. The service was rushed – we had only just finished starters. I didn't complain as it suited me perfectly.

She took the liberty of topping up our wine and chatted the whole way though the meal about her travels and her experiences. She bored me. The conversation was all about her and the more wine she consumed the more animated she became. It was coming close to the time. At least her table manners had improved over the last course.

'*Deux thé à la menthe, s'il vous plait.*'

Our personal waiter nodded again and, with a click of his heels, disappeared with unread dessert cards in his hand.

'I presume you will take tea, Leigh?'

She nodded and grinned. Giddy from wine, money, and my company. She looked her age now. I knew from Marco she was twenty-three – ripe for the picking, so to speak. Her earlier demeanour was slipping. Swaying to the gentle music seeping from concealed speakers, she was just a young girl in a foreign country, having a good time. She trusted me. Silly girl.

The lights dimmed and curtains fluttered on the stage in front of us. A hush came over the diners and, save for the scraping of chairs being repositioned, there was no sound. I moved my seat just close enough for my arm to rest beside hers. She didn't object. It was a done deal. She was settling down for the evening in my company.

When she went to the ladies' room I sent Marco a quick text. He would do the rest. No trace of Leigh from South Africa would be left in that hotel room. The paperwork would show she had checked out early that same morning in time to meet her taxi to the central rail station.

She had reapplied her make-up and perfume in the bathroom. She returned to me like an old friend and in her pretty little head she had landed on her feet. I leaned in and tapped her on the bare knee.

'I'm not supposed to mix work with pleasure, but I like you. Let's get out of here, and go to a real party, shall we?'

Hesitation caused her shoulders to stiffen.

I removed my fingers from her flesh and sat back in my chair.

'If you prefer to stay here, that's no problem. But the real party is downstairs in the members' club. My friend, and your supervisor, Maria, is down there too. I think it would be a good idea for you to meet her informally before you start.'

This did the trick.

'Why not? I'd like to meet my new colleagues.' She angled her body to face in my direction and her smile was the brightest I had seen.

I nodded to the waiter and he placed two flutes on the table.

'Congratulations, Leigh, and welcome to the club.'

'Champagne. That's thoughtful.'

She was greedy and knocked it back. Exactly what I needed.

Her shawl materialised on the back of her chair. The waiter, who was on our payroll, knew the score. Champagne first – then shawl. I ushered her in the direction of the door beside the stage. The champagne had gone straight to her head.

Girls, in various states of pre-show undress, didn't pay attention as we passed through their changing room. They were employees. They knew the drill. By the time we reached the back corridor, her legs had started to give way and her eyes were unfocused.

She tried to stop and gather herself together but I dragged her along with me.

'Come on now, love – it's time to go to work.'

She was too far gone to realise her last drink had been spiked. Down here the corridors were darker save for lanterns burning on the walls. It gave it a medieval feel – added to the ambiance. A sharp knock on the last door in the corridor and Maria greeted me.

This was her office. She ran the show and got paid well for it. The girls that didn't sell at the auction were kept here to service the needs of the regular clients – those with plenty of money and a lust for young women. Leigh suited the age bracket. There were enough scumbags in the city dealing with the younger ones. We also could have simply lifted women from the street and sold them – but ours was a high-end operation. Big players with big money. The product offered needed to be top class.

We draped her across the cot. Maria was beautiful once – a long time ago. She had been a working girl but had a good business head and had worked her way up the ranks. This was what it was all about: business and money.

She examined the recruit as though she were a camel, blood-red talons splayed across the South African's dark face. She ran her hands down the length of the silk dress, lingering over her breasts and the tops of her thighs.

'She is a beauty. Well done. She will sell well. We have one hour.'

Having sex with prostitutes was never to my taste – they were beneath me – no pun intended. But Maria was in a league of her own – she liked me and she always got her way. The cocaine she presented on a small make-up mirror helped. I gratefully accepted her offering – I was on familiar turf and I had an hour to kill. Her robe slipped from her shoulders as gracefully as the circumstances allowed. She turned to the unconscious girl and pulled the skimpy dress down, revealing her breasts. Pushing Maria forward over a vanity chair, I took her from behind, where we stood, never taking my eyes off the younger woman.

As soon as we were satisfied, she pulled her robe back on and poured us a drink. I sat on the chair at the vanity unit and wondered, not for the first time, how an ageing local woman had come to be here. How deliciously perverted it all was. She reminded me of my whore of a mother. This was something I would never admit but it amused me. I didn't even know if Maria was her real name. Not that I cared at all. I had thought about changing my own name to the one on the latest passport but no, I liked being Scott. The great and mighty Scott Carluccio Randall.

A stir from the cot announced our guest was coming around. That was good – we needed her somewhat lucid for the next stage. Dazed and confused, she asked for water. Maria mothered her and the girl allowed her to.

She sat up on the cot and recoiled at her own semi-nakedness. Pulling her dress up, her eyes widened in confusion – before flickers of realisation began to spread in splotches across her face. Her eyes filled up and she began to shake.

'Darling girl, don't cry. You are safe here with me.' Maria laid her hand on one bare shoulder and tilted the girl's head up to look at her. It was a perfect act and the girl responded to her. The monsters are always the men, are they not? 'Put this on, my dear.' She glided over to a small wardrobe in the corner of the room and produced a cream silk dress. The girl cried as she removed her own dress and, as soon as she hid herself under the fabric of the perfectly fitting outfit, she tried to make a run for it. So predictable. Maria was strong and the force of her punch to the girl's stomach drove her back onto the small bed. She quickly straddled her and forced the vial of liquid into her mouth.

'Any more nonsense, you little bitch, and I will slit your throat and throw you out to the dogs! You silly girl! Did your mother never teach you to stay away from strange men?'

The drug took effect quickly. Now she was listless – not a sign of her earlier aplomb. How quickly one changes.

It didn't take Maria long to dress and, while she finished her drink, a rap came to the door. The disconnected voice informed her they were waiting for her. She opened the door a crack and took the envelope.

My job here was done. Curiosity never got the better of me and this room was the furthest I ever ventured. Had never gone down into the basement while the auctions were in session.

'Scott, my darling – a pleasure as always.' Maria kissed me on the lips, then proffered the envelope. 'Yours, my dear. Do come again soon.'

She hoisted the girl up. She was conscious enough to walk but, under the circumstances, lucky to be out of it. She had no idea she was being sold to the highest bidder. Her and all the others scattered on cots along this corridor. Everything was a commodity here – you just needed to know where your market lay. My payment was ten thousand euro. This was business and a lucrative one at that.

Marco would be paid his dues and he would continue to source the product. He was the scout and the cleaner. I was the negotiator.

Chapter 4

Even in Jemaa el Fnaa or, as the locals called it, La Place, the majesty of the Atlas Mountains wasn't too far away from the eyeline. Since I had arrived in the Red City, the beauty of those mountains was a constant – a barrier between the city and the expanse of the barren Sahara Desert.

Both Fran's mess and my own work had taken it out of me. I was wrecked. Much as I loved the modern atmosphere in Ville Nouvelle, and of course the wealth of it, I liked to spend time in La Place, back behind the walls of the medina. It was like nothing I had ever experienced in my life. The riads and the warren of alleyways were to the north of the square – back there it was easy to hide. Here, it was wide open, and as the call of the muezzin faded and the night came sweeping in, tourists converged on the marketplace like rats to a landfill – waiting to be transported to the mediaeval world of an old city, lost in time. The Square, lazy and languid in the searing heat of the day, held its breath – and when darkness fell it breathed out all sorts of magic and mayhem. Painted whores danced with storytellers and snake charmers. Stallholders competed for the attention of the infidels. Monkeys ran free and pickpockets ran wild.

I arrived down to the square to the usual sights. Fran was around somewhere − working. I needed to keep an eye on him − he was beginning to get sloppy. The last thing I needed was him getting caught with our merchandise. I ran a professional outfit and I didn't need that imbecile muddying the waters again. He was the link to the runners and spotters on the ground. I was too important to get my hands dirty with those low-lives. In Fran's defence, he had recruited well. I had sourced the drivers and the cross-border carriers, and the boss in Spain looked after everything from his end. It was a well-run operation, it paid all of us well, and neither of them needed to know about my side-line operation with Marco.

I could hardly hear the hypnotic beat of the mystical gnaoua musicians over the noise of the heaving crowds and the cattle-call of vendors. It was easy to observe the first-timers − they were too polite to the merchants as they were heckled into buying boiled snails and téte d'agneau − row upon row of steamed sheeps' heads laid bare under lights. The lights and the smoke from grills gave the whole square the appearance of a mirage. The heat shimmered under the roofs of corrugated iron and blinded backpackers as they stumbled into yet another groping and shouting merchant. The generators adding to the cacophony. This place was not for the fainthearted.

I took my usual spot on a bench to the south of the melee and watched. I knew a lot of the faces by then and a gap-toothed local with a weather-beaten frown thrust a coffee in my direction, along with a paper cone filled with succulent dates. The coffee was thick as treacle and sweet as molasses. I touched my right hand to my heart. He refused a coin before shuffling over to his friend, a snake charmer. I watched him pick the dirt out from under his nails with a silver file, bored and oblivious to the dancing cobra at his side.

I needed to stay on top of things. I needed to watch. For

competition, for potential employees, for secret police, and most importantly, for my enemies. I stayed ahead of the game, I liked to win. I had made this my patch and no one else was going to spoil that for me. Most of them didn't have the intelligence to compete with me. The few who had not heeded my warning – well, they learned the hard way.

Fran usually took a couple of hours to shift the merchandise. After that he would head in the direction of a bar somewhere – all of them out of sight, of course, from the Booksellers' Mosque. The idea of him getting drunk and maudlin bothered me. He needed to keep his mouth shut about his junkie girlfriend. I wasn't so confident he could do that when he had a bellyful of Flag beer and his daily intake of kif. I needed to keep a close eye on him.

The wall of bodies was as oppressive as the heat. They moved en masse between stalls and vendors, stopping only long enough to observe the musicians, the belly dancers, the snake charmers, the blind man selling water or the sinister-looking storytellers weaving tales of cruel sultans, evil jinns and foolish virgins – a melding and clash of language, noise, and music.

The mismatched smells fought with each other. Flesh charring on grills, bodies, sweat, oranges, flowers, animal dung, heat, mint – a melting pot to assail the senses. This was Marrakech, a city suspended in a long-ago era.

I pushed and heaved my way through the throngs, following the sound of hammers on metal. I wasn't in a hurry but I felt anxious. Stopping briefly to buy canelle – dried oranges with cinnamon – my favourite – I made it across the square and saw Fran, standing over a young girl, gesticulating wildly. This was not good.

'Evening, Fran.'

'Howya, man.' He tried to gain some form of composure but I knew he was agitated.

I looked from him to her – she was crying. She didn't make eye contact with me. I looked her up and down. Another dirty little runt, obviously from the same slum as his old girlfriend.

'Aren't you going to introduce me to your little friend?' I said.

She stared at me for a moment. Then she addressed Fran.

'I will leave now. We will speak of this again.'

Then she was gone.

'You want to tell me what that was all about?' I asked him. 'Do we have a problem here?'

Fran fumbled in his jacket for a cigarette. The lighter lit up his face — he looked older somehow. He exhaled blue smoke in my direction and coughed.

'They're all looking for her, man. Everyone. Her brother and his crew have been asking a lot of questions.'

I could see the tremor in his hand as he took another drag of his smoke.

'And why are you worried? You keep your mouth shut.'

'Mala knows Saidaa was on her way to see me. That was the last time she spoke to her. We have fucked up big-time, man. Saidaa never strayed from home — they're all asking questions, including her brother Tarek. I know them, man —'

'Now, you listen to me!' I grabbed him by the arm and hard. I wasn't going to take the fall for the mess he had made and I certainly wasn't going to have a scumbag druggie from the slums making any assumptions. Fran would try to save his own skin if something happened. 'You will keep your mouth shut and you will bring no heat to me, do you hear me?'

'It's not my fault they're asking questions, man.'

'Of course it's your fault, you *halfwit*! You made this mess and I had to clean it up for you.'

'You killed her, Scott, not me.' He pulled back and broke free of my grasp.

He was getting brave or stupid — I couldn't quite decide which.

'Keep your mouth shut and everything will be fine,' I said. 'We don't want you disappearing into thin air either, do we? It's a dangerous city here, especially when you're on your own.' The look on his face satisfied me. He was easy to rise.

'I've kept it shut. Told Mala she never came to our place.'

He knew I would never take the fall for his mess. I had the

upper hand — and always would have. He smirked at me as though reading my thoughts and disagreeing with them.

'Something funny, Fran? What has you so amused?'

'Not a thing, boss, not a thing. You are right, as always.'

'Don't be facetious — doesn't suit you. Let's go down to Café Clock. I'm starving.'

'Grand.' He hung his head and walked ahead of me.

I had won, again.

It didn't take us long to reach our destination. It was quiet and the black granite countertop cooled my arms as I leaned in to order. Fran had gone to find a table on the balcony — from there we could observe everything from the darkness. This place was the embodiment of everything Marrakech had to offer and, if you were that way inclined, it was always easy to pick up a bit of skirt. Travellers high on the heat and kif. I wasn't in that kind of mood and Fran was still in mourning, the black bags under his eyes more pronounced than usual. His grief, however, didn't prevent him from tucking into a bowl of roast almonds. I laid the beers down on the stone table and pulled a chair up beside him.

'We have another big delivery from our Algerian friends on Friday. I need you to be sharp. The route has changed and I need you in Oujda. Send your crew up there tomorrow. Choose wisely — this is a big one. No mistakes, you hear me?'

He nodded and took a mouthful of beer. It left a foam moustache in its wake. He wiped it away and mentioned a couple of loyal spotters up for the job.

He looked out into the middle distance and nursed his beer. 'Do you ever miss home, man?'

'What kind of question is that? Hell, no — I don't miss it. You know that.'

'I do. I miss me ma, and my family. I miss the harbour. I'm tired of this place.'

'You're only saying that because of what happened with your little girlfriend. You're not going anywhere. You can't go home — you'd be arrested.'

'Thanks to you.'

'You need me, Fran.' I grinned at him and lifted my beer but my gesture of merriment wasn't reciprocated – his glass didn't move. He was going nowhere. I had him where I wanted him. I pushed back on my chair and thought about the 'old sod'. I mused over where in the world I might be if I had never got involved in this business. Where would I be?

My chair was pushed forward with such force the drink rocked on the table. I tried to push back and stand up. I couldn't move. Big hands dug into my shoulders. I was pinned. I looked at Fran. He too had a pair of hands pressing him down into his seat. He also had a small blade held to his Adam's apple. Four men surrounded us. Then the fifth entered. I didn't need to see his face. Tarek.

'Fran. It has been a while. The bidonville not good enough for you any more?'

Two things surprised me about him as he rounded the table and sat opposite me: his calm air of authority and his fluency in English. That was unusual. It was the first time we were in each other's company. Perhaps I had underestimated him. He kept his dark eyes on me as he waited for an answer. I didn't break eye contact with him.

'I've been busy, man.' Fran's voice cracked with nerves.

'Where is my sister?'

'Tarek – what is this about? Why would we know where your sister is?' I was a reasonable man – I could sort this out.

'Shut up – I know all about you. Now, I ask you both – where is my little sister?'

Hands pushed harder on the tops of my shoulders and Fran started to pale.

'I don't know where your sister is, man. I haven't seen her.'

Tarek sat back in the chair and took two blasts of an inhaler. He slipped it back into his top pocket and resumed his interrogation. 'Fran. I think you are lying to me.'

'Tarek – call off your hounds and go,' I said. 'We don't know where your sister is. Perhaps she ran away with one of her clients –'

The openhanded slap from a goon came swift and landed on my bad cheek.

'Scott, I have heard the stories. I know what you are doing – perhaps your business partner, Marco, can unravel the mystery?'

The goon who had landed the slap was waved away.

'Who's Marco?' Fran looked from me back to him.

Imbecile.

'Ah, I see – you know nothing of your boss's activities over in the new town? Is this true?'

'Marco is my business colleague. He has nothing to do with this. We do not know where your sister is.'

'She told Mala she was going to see you, Fran. Then, *poof!* She disappeared.'

'She didn't come to my house. I haven't seen her.'

'I will find out.' He stood up and swept open hands around in a semicircle. 'This is my city and these are my people. I have eyes everywhere – you will not take a piss without me knowing about it.'

As quickly as they came, they were gone.

Fran had his head down and I think he was weeping.

'Pull yourself together, you fool!'

My hands were sweating. The exchange was very brief but it unnerved me. The goons troubled me. They had bloodlust in their eyes – I had come across men of their calibre before. This was getting messy and I needed a plan. It was only a matter of time before Tarek and his goons came looking for the pound of flesh.

Fight fire with fire – Marco would connect me.

Chapter 5

The pain clawed at his temples, his head pounded, sharp and heavy. Fran lay on the bed in a pool of his own sweat and tried to massage the headache away. Since the altercation in the bar he hadn't managed to eat or sleep. The light in the room hinted it was early morning. The fear was enough to make him dizzy and his headache was a side effect of his arrival in a strange dark place where nothing was familiar any more.

He was afraid. Of everything. Watching Scott, he knew he was getting loopier by the day – he'd never seen him so deranged. Once upon a time he was together about everything but not any more. Now, to make it worse, Tarek and his goons had triggered a mania in him and he had spent the rest of the night on the snow. Fran had laid off everything in the last few days. He needed a clear head – maybe the withdrawals were fuelling the monster in his thoughts. Scott was scared – that terrified him. Scott was furious when they had to leave the bar – the owner wouldn't give them another drink. He said something to Fran in French. He didn't understand it very well but he got the gist – he was one of Tarek's allies.

Things were getting out of hand. He simply wanted to go home to Ireland and forget about everything – but everywhere he turned he was facing consequences.

He turned the pillow over and lay on his side. The cool of the fabric against his face helped. He thought again about the harbour and the events that had led him to this place. He had made so many mistakes along the way – he had to acknowledge his own decisions had led him here, not just Scott's manipulation. He couldn't stop thinking about the friends he used to have. Their faces swam before his eyes.

He came back to the present as another lightning bolt of pain passed over his eyes. The more he thought about everything, the worse the pain was getting. He sat up in the bed and picked up the muslin cloth. He rubbed the little black cumin seeds together and inhaled. It was the only relief he could get – Tylenol hadn't made a dent in it. Scott was always taking the piss about his herbal remedies – perhaps he should have taken a leaf out of his book and stayed away from the chemicals. They were frying his brain.

On impulse, he got off the bed and went to the dresser. Rooting around, he peeled the phone off the back of the drawer and turned it on. He dialled the Spanish number – Scott had no idea he had a number for the Boss.

The phone was answered swiftly and Fran kept the conversation short. Vital facts only. The Boss didn't say much other than to make sure they were ready for the 'delivery'.

He hung up and redialled.

The long lonely note of the international dialling code summed up how he felt. He prayed he hadn't missed Marian – she might have left for work already.

'Hello?'

'Hey, sis, how are you? How's Ma?'

'Fran! Oh, thank God! I've been trying to get through but the phone was off. Ma is okay – she hasn't got any worse and hasn't had to go back in for any more tests yet. On the mend now, thank God. How are you? You okay?'

He never stayed on the line for long and it made him smile when she tried to get all the words out at once. It was the same conversation every time – trying to reason with him. Pleading with him to come home. He was loved somewhere at least.

'I'm grand, sis, never better.'

'You need to come home. Be a man and face the music, hon – it will be alright. We don't even know where you are. We're worried sick about you, Fran, it's not fair on Ma.' Her voice cracked.

'I know, sis, I'm sorry. Ah, that's good news about Ma, isn't it? Did you give her my letter?'

'I did. She needs you here at home, we all do. Will you at least tell me where you are?'

Fran knew she was right and his decision was made. The lump in his throat made it hard to speak. 'I can't.'

'Fran, are you okay? You don't sound great.'

'I'm coming home soon. I'll ring you again when I'm leaving. Don't tell Ma for now though.'

'You've told me that before.'

'I mean it this time, sis. I've had enough. Just don't tell Ma. I'll text you when I can – I'd better go. I'll ring you soon. Love you – give Ma a hug.'

He hung up before she had a chance to ask him any questions. He had no answers.

He loved to hear her voice but he always felt like crap afterwards. He needed to go home to his mother. Seeing her was more important to him than any of the consequences he would face once he got there. She wasn't well and he was afraid he would be too late. And it was all because of Scott. If that bastard hadn't opened his big mouth in the first place, Jen and Andy wouldn't have known about his involvement smuggling the shit in on Andy's boat. No one would have known about him being involved. It was Scott's fault and he blamed him for his mother being unwell too – all that stress did that to her.

He padded over to the dresser and put the phone back in its hiding place. He checked his other phone and a text informed him the crew were leaving for Oujda. Everything was good to go.

The headache had reduced itself to a dull throb behind his ears.

Then the solution to all his problems came in one swift and very simple thought. In that exact moment everything was clear. He knew what he needed to do and he knew exactly how he was going to pull it off.

Chapter 6

Marco wasn't answering his phone. I had been calling him non-stop all day. I made up my mind to go over there and see him. We had work to do and I needed his input in resolving my other problem – the shit-storm Fran had dragged me into.

Fran had scarpered off to his room after the previous night's altercation with the Marrakech hardy boys. He had finally surfaced from his pit after wallowing in self-pity all day. He now had a bit more of a spring in his step, so to speak. Wouldn't matter to me for much longer anyway. If he disappeared, Tarek and his goons would jump to the only plausible conclusion – he had killed Saidaa and done a runner. We had a job coming up the next day. Once the consignment arrived, I would have no further use for him. Useless fool. He was an easy problem to solve.

The ground was shifting beneath me and I felt unsettled. Last night, Tarek had intimidated me – *intimidate* is not the correct word, it's too strong, but he did manage to make me sweat. This wasn't my city, he was right about that, but he was conceited enough to underestimate me. I, too, had eyes all over the medina, and I paid more for information. Money is the root of all evil – it's a powerful motivator too.

Life was peaceful in the riad. The courtyard garden was, for the most part, my favourite location. It was beautiful and smelled of oleander and orange blossom. The lavender reminded me of home – suffice it to say, I hated that smell. I should have ripped the plants out at the root but sometimes we need a trigger to stoke our anger and keep us on our toes. Lavender reminded me of Mother. Funny how the olfactory senses can betray us at times – smells – a powerful and almost primitive memory aid. Mother wore Chanel like a fingerprint but her hair always smelled of lavender and cigarettes. *Mother* – she hated me calling her by that undeserved title – claimed it made her feel old. 'Scottie, darling, please. Can't you simply call me Livia?' she'd say. Mother and her garden parties. Ensconcing herself in the cream of society and so preoccupied with keeping up with the rest of the pretentious bastards she had forgotten I existed. She never had time for me. She was never a mother to me. A social climber and a whore is all she amounted to. Everyone knew she had trapped Father. She got pregnant, he got a life sentence. Her life consisted of organising, hosting, and recovering from events in Weybridge, or travelling to the same nonsense somewhere else. She liked spending Father's money. It was lonely growing up as an only child – she never wanted me. I was the means to an end and she wasn't going to lumber herself with another screaming infant, no matter how much Father protested.

I remember one day in particular. I was eight years old and was home from school for Christmas holidays. Father was away on business and Mother was entertaining in the drawing room. She smelled of brandy. There was nothing for me to do. I had grown bored of my toys and I was eager to impress her – if I did something worthy of praise, she would spend some time with me. I spent most of the afternoon painting her a picture of her beloved garden. My teachers in school praised me for my artwork – told me I was advanced beyond my years and I had quite the gift for drawing. I fancied myself as the next Claude Monet. Art is something I still love and hold dear – perhaps I should have studied it and chosen a different life. Anyway – I spent the whole day painting what I thought was a beautiful picture just for her. I felt very proud when I had finished. Without delay, I went to her in the lounge and proudly presented the fruits of my labour. In my excitement, I didn't remember to tell her the paint was still a little wet – they were watercolours, a Christmas present from Father.

The empty brandy bottle was perched on the silver tray. An empty glass and a waft of cigar smoke was all that remained of her guest. She was slumped beside the fire in the wingback chair, eyes closed and an unlit cigarette in her hand. She startled me by asking why I was disturbing her. I had brought her something and yet her eyes remained closed. I laid the painting on her lap. She reluctantly opened her eyes, straightened herself and looked at my offering. The first thing she noticed was a flaw in the picture – the second, the wet paint. She snatched it up from her lap. It had transferred from the back of the paper onto her skirt. Flinging it on the floor, she started to rub furiously at the paint, calling me a stupid little boy, over and over. She told me I had ruined her dress and that she wished God had blessed her with a little girl who perhaps would have had more of a brain than me.

I only wanted to do something nice for her. I had messed up. Stupid silly little boy.

I disengaged from the reverie and was overcome with a feeling of rage. Furious with Mother, furious with Fran. They were the stupid ones, not me. I would show them all. How *dare* that inferior, barely literate fool of a Tarek speak to me like that? He might not know who I was, but I would show him. I would show them all. No little junkie whore was going to ruin things for me – no matter how much her rodent of a brother sniffed around. *That's the spirit, Scottie boy, onwards and upwards. Don't let the bastards grind you down – you are a brilliant mind. You can outsmart all of them.* I felt quite pleased with myself. None of them could compete. And my whore of a mother? Well, she would eventually get her comeuppance. I would make sure of it. Jen and her – they were on my radar. I would win.

The garden was warm. I moved over to the shade of the fig tree and celebrated my good mood with a warm beer and a line of coke. Marco was on the top of my priority list – after that, I would take some time to myself. I gave myself permission to feel happy for a change – I had been stressed of late. A late afternoon tagine was the order of the day and I would take a trip to the hamman baths.

My phone rang and I thought about ignoring it – then decided to answer it – hoping it was Marco. Nothing could ruin my mood.

It wasn't Marco – it was a call from Spain. I answered on the second ring and was surprised to hear the Boss himself on the other end. This was very unusual.

I enquired about his health and the business and told him it was business as usual over here. Never anything direct – never anything that could be deciphered. He was more paranoid than I ever was, but he had a lot more at stake. 'Boss' – it was the only name I ever knew him by and it was only then it registered how odd that was.

We skirted around the small talk for another few moments and I assured him that we were organised for the next day's 'party'. I was confident he trusted me. And then he advised me that I needed to come to Spain for a 'board meeting' as soon as possible. That was the first time I had been summoned over there and I didn't like the implications. Had he heard something? Fran didn't have the clout or the intelligence to have even come onto his radar – the Boss didn't deal with the minions down at the bottom of the ladder – but someone was watching and reporting back. Why else would he ring this week? Coincidence? I think not. I smelt a big fat rat and I had a feeling the rat's name was Marco. But where was the connection?

I agreed to come for a meeting once everything was in order from my end. He finished up the call by telling me to come alone.

I needed another line and a beer – that exchange had sullied my mood. I would have to be clever in how I approached Marco.

I shook off the call and put it down to coincidence – there was no way the Boss knew about the other business. He didn't know about Saidaa either and, even if he did, he wouldn't care.

Or was he pre-empting me? Perhaps he suspected that I was about to branch out on my own – didn't want to lose me. Yes, he was going to offer me a promotion for sure. I could get out of this hellhole and away from Tarek. Fran could stay here – that would suit me just fine. I was tired of the baby-sitting. He had the IQ of an amoeba – I needed people around me who were as intelligent and clued-in as I was. No wonder I was feeling unnerved, bored and restless. Not for the first time that day, I felt pleased by my powers of deduction. I was sorting it all out and I hadn't even left home – progress!

I cleared the table of the empty beer bottles and went upstairs to get a towel and soap for the hamman. I moved quietly and quickly around the riad. Fran was back in his room and the last thing I wanted was his company. I needed breathing space and alone time. It was another part of the culture I enjoyed. The afternoon was quiet as I walked over to the street with the best baths in Marrakech. It was a hidden gem – rarely spotted by tourists. Perfect.

The short walk from the baths to Ville Nouvelle was a pleasant one. Avenue Mohammed V was the quickest route. The light changed once I got outside the walls of the medina of course – the shadows under the rust-red bricks kept the secrets in and the noise of traffic out.

Starbucks seemed a million miles away from the carnival atmosphere of La Place. I tried Marco's phone and stabbed the foam in my coffee cup with the useless wooden stirrer as it diverted to voicemail, yet again. I was going to give him a piece of my mind when I saw him. It was no way to run a business. I had to deliver a girl this week and I was dependent on him sourcing her. That had to change too – I didn't feel comfortable having to rely on him so heavily. The business model needed to be adapted – that way I would be in full control again.

I was never a nervous man by disposition and I never bought into the superstitious nonsense of the people here but I could not shake the feeling I was being watched. I could feel eyes travel over my face – but no one was looking in my direction. I jumped out of my skin when a taxi driver bamped at a pedestrian.

Leaving the detritus abandoned on the plastic table, I went in search of my elusive partner. He could only be in one of two places – in the hotel or in his apartment. He rarely ventured further. I never visited him in his place of work. We kept our business discreet but I needed his help and fast. Couple that with the fact that the moron wasn't answering his phone and I had no choice.

The hotel was of medium size and air-conditioned lobby air washed over my skin like a mountain spring. My shoes made no sound as I walked in the direction of the beauty with the manicured nails behind the desk. She smiled widely and asked me if I needed her assistance – I had that effect on all women, regardless of what continent I was on and, if I had the time, I would have showed her exactly how she could help me. I made a mental note to ask Marco about her as I asked to speak with him. Her face froze.

'One moment, sir,' she advised and scuttled into the little office space behind the graveyard of keys.

The hair on my arms stood to attention. I couldn't see who was in that office. I scanned the lobby – two exits. One to my left and the other the door I came in by. I didn't have time to study the people I shared this space with, but none of them were taking any notice of me. A concierge was stationed at the door – I wouldn't get past him. The exit to the left meant I would be running blind – it could be a dead end or an alleyway. Run – the only option.

I needed to move.

A suit appeared out of the dark cavern and, just as I was about to break into a sprint, I noticed he was rubbing his eyes. Was he crying – or making it look like he was?

'Sir, can you come with me?'

'No, I can't. Where is Marco?'

'Are you a family member, sir?'

We could have been, I suppose. We did look alike – the dark skin and hair. I would have been the older and wiser brother of course.

'No, I'm a friend. Where is he?' My throat had begun to tighten and I didn't really need to hear what this man had to say.

'Please, sir, I implore you – can you come with me, this way?'

I nodded and followed him into the back office. The pretty receptionist had fixed her make-up and was sipping on a glass of water, a tissue in the other hand.

'Back to work!' he barked.

She left.

He turned to face me.

'Sir, I'm very sad to have to tell you this sad news. Very sad indeed that you should hear this news from me.'

'Go on …' He was making a meal out of the damn thing.

'Marco met with a very unfortunate demise early this morning. He jumped from the top floor of our hotel. I am the owner, you see. This is how I know this. We think he may have been overcome with a terrible illness and slipped from the balcony or he ended his own life. I am very sad to tell you this news.' He wrung his hands together as though he was washing blood off them. He was also sweating profusely in the cool of the air-conditioned office.

'Thank you.'

I left without another word. The receptionist smiled at me sadly as I rounded the counter.

Fuck. Fuck. Fuck. The ominous creeping feeling of eyes on me was stronger and more present. What had happened? Who had got to him? Let's face it, in our line of work there was a list. He didn't fucking slip and he didn't throw himself off the balcony. It struck me as odd how the hotel was open and it was business as usual – I didn't see any police either. I had to remind myself I wasn't in Ireland. Clean the mess up and move on – I needed to take heed of that idea.

I walked quickly and crashed straight into an old crone with a bag full of fruit in her arms. I was glancing over my shoulder but

43

she was lucky I didn't punch her in the gut. I waved an apology as she plucked the oranges from the cobbles to her bosom, cursing and shouting at me in Arabic. I was under pressure enough without a hex from a mad old bat with a grudge.

Think, Scott, goddammit. I had no fear of anyone. I was too smart for most of them but I felt the reins slipping out of my hands – that couldn't happen. Maria! Of course – I must see Maria. Business as usual. I could find a replacement for Marco – this time I would pay less.

Chapter 7

Jen Harper could hear the sound of the bells coming from the church in the harbour. Sunset would come slowly and at this time of year a cold breeze blew in from the sea. She closed the kitchen window to the elements and went in search of her son.

'*Danny Harper! Get down here now and get your homework done! I'm not asking you again!*'

Jen turned away from the stairs and went back into the kitchen. She sighed and slumped into a chair. Mr Cassidy was scraping at the glass on the French doors, begging to be let in, away from the cool September evening. She stood up, let the dog in and cleared the table of dishes. Glancing at the untouched place setting, she checked her watch. He was late again. It was happening a lot recently – she couldn't blame him really.

'*Danny!*' This time she bellowed from the kitchen.

'Alright, Mam, calm down will you?' The ten-year-old walked through the door. 'I'm here.'

'Get your homework out, please. I want it done and out of the way.'

A barely audible 'Whatever' escaped from his mouth before he thumped his heavy bag down on the table.

'I have a note.'

'Not again, Danny, please!'

'It wasn't my fault. That stupid teacher has it in for me.'

Jen dried her hands on the frayed tea towel and reluctantly walked over to his work station. She watched a tsunami of red rise over his face before she read the short note.

'Detention – again.' She tried to keep her voice in check before she continued but the truth was she was at her wits' end with all of it. 'Danny, I have had enough of your behaviour.'

'Ah, Mam! He has it in for me!' He had no qualms about raising his voice.

The irritating tone of his defiance drove her nuts.

'You *always* blame your teacher. It's the *third* detention this month. If your behaviour in school is *anything* like your bad behaviour at home, it's no wonder your teacher has it in for you. I'm sick of it, *sick* of it, do you hear me? You are grounded until further notice and no TV for a week.'

'Whatever.' He snatched his journal from her hand and slammed it down on the table.

She caught the end of a whisper.

'*What did you just say?*' She was shouting now. She couldn't help it. Her patience had all run out, and she could have sworn he'd just told her to 'chill feckin' out, Ma'.

'Nothin'.'

'I'm making an appointment with your teacher. I've had enough. I'm ringing your dad too.'

'I wish I lived with him and my new baby brudder!' The child stood up from the table, his hands balled into fists at his sides, his little blonde curls framing a face of indignation. 'I *hate* you and Andy, and that stupid dog!' He swiped a feeble kick in the direction of the little mutt and ran out of the room in tears.

Jen didn't have the energy to follow him. She grabbed her box of cigarettes and went out onto the back patio. It was cool out there and the lazy sun was sinking low behind the horizon, casting its red-and-gold farewell all over the flowers bordering the garden. She muted the guilty voice in her head, sat down on the step and took a long drag from the toxic cylinder. The sea breeze danced with her hair across her cheek. The voice reminded her again how everything was so different. It taunted her and asked her where Happy Jen had gone. *Happy Jen means Happy Dan and Happy Andy, you know!* It said on repeat: *Where's Bulletproof Jen gone?* She twirled the wedding ring on her finger and wondered about that. A lump caught in her throat but, as usual, she didn't have the time to sit around and wallow in self-pity. *Stay busy, Jen, keep your mind occupied.* Avoidance, avoidance.

She crushed out her cigarette and threw the butt into the terracotta pot. Staring into the distance, she tried to allow her mind to go quiet for a while – but it didn't work these days. Popping a mint from her pocket into her mouth, she pulled herself up, took a breath and vowed to handle the constant conflict with her little boy in a more constructive way. She saw him through the glass, back sitting at the table, his brow furrowed in concentration. He never sulked for long. He was a miniature version of her. Sandy blonde curly hair with a face full of freckles and sky-blue eyes. They were alike in every way. She watched as he paused and looked around the room as though inspiration was about to drop from the ceiling into his lap. He stayed poised like that for a few seconds before picking up his pen again. She loved her boy, more than anything in the world, but she struggled to believe she was a great mother. She hadn't forgiven herself for not keeping him safe the night Scott attacked them.

Stepping inside and closing the door quietly, she stood with her back to it.

'Sorry, Mam.' He spoke to the floor.

Jen sat down beside her little boy and pulled him into a hug. He smelled of washing powder and cherry drops.

'I'm sorry for shouting, Danny – that's not fair on you. Just get your homework done and we'll talk about the detention later.'

They sat together and debated about fractions. The child usually won — he was quite the whiz kid when it came to maths homework. Irish grammar, on the other hand, was something he hated with a vengeance — Jen usually ended up doing that homework for him.

The screech of the French door opening made the pair of them jump right out of their skins.

'Jesus. I wish you would oil that door.' Jen turned around in her chair.

Andy smiled as he kissed her forehead and flung his jacket on the back of the chair beside Danny. 'Evening, Champ. How are ya?'

Danny responded with a grin.

Andy slipped a Mars bar across the table. Jen pretended not to see it — she wasn't able for another stand-off.

Danny was trying to give her the look. She nodded. Of course she wouldn't say a word about the note.

'Is dinner ready?' Andy ran his hands under the tap and scrubbed at the oil-stains. 'I'm starving.'

'In the oven. We have eaten.'

'Do you want a hand with your homework, Dan?'

'Nah, it's grand. I'm nearly finished — did most of it in school.'

He scribbled something into a workbook and fired his books back into his bag.

Jen would check it later; she was too tired to do it right there.

Andy grabbed his plate from the oven and sat at the end of the table. Danny asked if he could watch a movie — Andy nodded and told him to go ahead.

'How was your day, love?' he asked Jen. 'Did you get out and about?'

'Not really.'

'Ah Jen, you need to start.'

'I will.'

'Do you think you should go back to the doctor?'

'Maybe. We'll see.'

Even doctors and therapists can't help you, Jen, you're a failure.

48

She flicked on the kettle and took two cups from the press – an avoidance technique. Too tired for a deep and meaningful talk.

'How was your day?'

'Busy. Selling fishing tackle and fixing outboards. My life is complete.' He did that clap he did, like a seal. His sarcastic clap.

'I thought –'

'I'm joking. You know I love the yard.' He shovelled another forkful into his mouth. 'This is delicious – thanks, love. What's up with Danny?

'He got another detention today. Don't say anything though – he doesn't want me to tell you.'

'Ah – I knew something was brewing when I came in.'

'I don't know what to do – maybe I should take him back to counselling? All this conflict, be it here with me or in school with his teacher, is driving me insane.'

'Jen!' Andy laid his cutlery down on the plate and pushed his chair back with his legs. 'You know what Mr Moore is like. He was a grumpy old git back in my day – he should have retired from teaching years ago. I wouldn't take too much notice of notes home and bogus detentions.'

Mr Cassidy danced around, yapping and bouncing at Andy's feet. Jen nodded as Andy gestured to the leftovers in the pot. He hauled himself out of the chair as the dog jumped higher.

'No – it's more than that.' Jen poured milk into her tea. 'His behaviour has changed in the last while – you know that. And he has started to have nightmares again over the last few nights.'

Danny's nightmares had stopped but it had taken nearly a year. Woken by him crying out in his sleep over the previous few nights, Jen was worried. She couldn't understand why they had returned. He was terrified by them and it took him ages to get back to sleep after. The poor little pet, she thought, and immediately felt bad about the earlier spat. Maybe he was just tired in school? He loved his new half-brother and Will, his dad, had gone out of his way to keep him included in everything – it couldn't be anything to do with the adjustment there.

They watched in silence as the little dog circumnavigated his bowl with an eager tongue.

'Is something going on in school?'

'I don't know.' Jen fiddled with a crystal charm on the table. Miniature rainbows danced on the wall as she spun it around and around before stopping it with a slap. 'I'll ring them in the morning.'

'Do. They might have an idea as to what's going on.' He slipped onto the chair beside her and kissed her on the cheek. 'Maybe we should try again soon? Dan would love a little brother or sister here too.'

She thought of the pills she kept so well hidden. She was taking no chances. There would be no pitter-patter of tiny feet. No way.

'Maybe. I'm too tired to talk about it now though.'

'You're always too tired. I want to have a family, Jen. We've been trying for ages – nothing's happening. Maybe we need to go to a GP.'

'You already have a family.' Jen was panicking. She couldn't bring herself to tell him. Sighing, she stood up from the table, the weariness in her bones a weight she could barely carry any more.

'You know what I mean.'

The skin prickled on her arms with the feeling of his eyes on her, expecting a response. She had nothing to say. Stalemate. The conversation always raced to the same conclusion. She looked down at her hands and the symbol branding her a wife: the mark of eternity, togetherness. Her nails were destroyed from biting them – a nervous tic she thought she had conquered. Another failing. *You're a terrible wife and a terrible mother, they deserve better than you.* The voice in her head was right – she couldn't quieten it any more. She was a real failure.

'Give Danny a shout there, will you?' she said.

He shook his head and went out of the kitchen – a tattoo of boots on wood indicative of his mood. Stalemate.

Andy was right about one thing. She needed to go back and see her therapist at least. *Therapist* … that word amused her. How very

American, she thought. How trendy. All the rage now – people banging on about how it's good to talk and how a kind word can save someone's life. They hadn't a clue. Their saccharine smiles would never shut the voice up or the images of Scott's blood dripping on her face, or her little boy, white with terror, wetting the bed for months afterwards. They could take their balloons and their good intentions and stick them where the sun don't shine. Where were they when the splinters from breaking up a kitchen table gouged into the flesh on her arms as she tried to hammer the memories out of her brain with a bad temper and a lump hammer? Where were they when the resentment towards her husband boiled over and bubbled out of her, manifesting itself in midnight cleaning frenzies and rearranging furniture in a room to exorcise the ghosts of that night? Where were they when she betrayed her husband, stuffing a pill down her throat daily to ensure there would be no pitter-patter of tiny feet? Where were they when she wished herself dead but wasn't brave enough to go through with it? They were at home, knee-deep in their own shit and woes, hurling cups at walls or insults across keyboards with their cronies – beating down the few that were trying to make a difference. Mental health wasn't the issue: humanity was. Jen felt the weight of the world on her shoulders, bearing down on her, crushing her good days and her light thoughts. She didn't trust herself any more. She didn't trust anyone. How could he possibly trust her to become a mother again? It was totally irresponsible of him and selfish, putting her under that kind of pressure. He had gone as far as suggesting she sell the house and rid herself of the memories that clung to it – she'd put paid to that conversation quick. She wouldn't let *that* man win.

Like the shifting sands on the strand outside, her life was eroding. She needed to make a stand, she needed to get over it and move on. She had tried so many times – and failed. Scott's ghost walked beside her constantly. He was in her thoughts, waking and sleeping, but lately the feeling was stronger. A whisper on the breeze or a lazy creak of a gate in the wind made her think about him. She couldn't tell Andy – he was tired of all of it. He wanted the quiet life, he wanted to move on. A peaceful, gentle soul was Andy.

Her hand went to the scars on her chest and the hazy memory washed over her from childhood. The inquisitive four-year-old was no match for the scalding pot of broth. By a miracle, her face was spared but her chest and torso still bore the damage She had obsessed over keeping Danny safe as he was growing up – the fire drills, the pots with no handles on them, the safety drills. She had tried so hard to keep harm from him and she had failed. She couldn't keep her boy safe – and there was no way she would bring another one into the world while the great Scott Carluccio Randall was still alive.

The kitchen door burst open, startling her. Making herself look busy, she smiled as Danny came in, in his pyjamas, looking for Mr Cassidy. The dog knew it was bedtime and he knew by the imploring look on the little boy's face that he wanted company tonight in bed. The mutt hadn't slept in his own bed downstairs in weeks.

'I'm going to bed, Mam. Andy wants to read me and Mr Cassidy a book. Can I take him up with me?'

'Oh, go on then, the pair of you. I love you.'

'I love you too, Mam. So does he!' He swept the dog up into his arms and waved his paw at her.

'We'll have a proper chat tomorrow, pet, okay?'

'G'night.' He ran out the door and pounded up the stairs.

It was time for some music – her solace. Anything to break the silence. She skittered over to her vinyl collection.

Nina Simone would keep her company this evening. As the arm of the record player jerked into action, laughter wafted down the stairs. Danny loved when Andy read to him – he would do all the voices of the different characters. It had taken them months to read the first *Artemis Fowl* book. She was relieved they were getting on again. It had taken a long time to get them back on track after the night they were attacked. Little Danny had blamed Andy for all of it. Scott had come into their lives because of his friend Andy, and Danny couldn't see past that.

As her hands sank into the warm suds she allowed velvet tones to wash over her. The blind lit up every few minutes with the warm glow of the lighthouse. The kitchen was quiet without them. Once upon a time, she loved this part of the day – ten minutes of peaceful stillness after the sun set and Danny went to bed. A comfortable silence. It wasn't comfortable any more. She wished she could have those days back.

Chapter 8

The chill in the morning air took Andy by surprise. Danny hadn't taken a coat to school with him but he figured all that running around at lunchtime would keep the boy warm.

He pulled open the heavy green door of the boatshed and the familiar smell of diesel skipped out into the watery sunlight to greet him.

Every morning, without fail, he marvelled at the view. The harbour looked particularly beautiful this morning. To his right, the morning fog was shimmering up and away from the water as the gulls circled and cried out for breakfast. The islands stood watch over the harbour, guarding it from The Graveyard of a Thousand Ships. He could just about make out the stone statue of the embracing couple who kept vigil over the sea, watching and waiting in the memorial garden at the top of the curved beach. Like most of the locals, if he tried hard enough, he could probably recite most of the names of the souls lost at sea, and now carved into the walls of the memorial garden

To his left, he could see the harbour and marina, busy with life – where yachts and trawlers mingled and threw insults at each other day and night, the lifeboat a referee and voice of reason between the two. The chug of the engines competing with the gulls. He missed the roll of the sea under his feet and itched to run down the pier and jump on board. He had made a promise and wouldn't break it. He had made a vow to protect Jen and Danny always, and to keep that promise he needed to be on land.

'I'm stuck here with you,' he said out loud as he walked into the darkness. He flicked on the light over the workbench and put his flask in the right place.

Andy prided himself on his organisational skills and his workshop reflected that. The men who frequented his space eventually got tired of ribbing him over how tidy he was and how well trained the Mrs obviously had him. He liked order: it made him more efficient.

He picked up his well-thumbed diary and dialled a number. He informed the customer on the other end that the outboard was ready to be picked up and he would be there all day. He had plenty of room in the workshop and didn't mind if the owner was delayed.

He spotted a couple of loose rudders and was up on a ladder hoisting them into the loft when John came in.

'You'll do your back in, son. Hang on, I'll give you a hand.'

'Thanks.'

They managed to get the rudders up to the loft with the use of a homemade pulley. It took a bit of an effort – because of their cumbersome shape rather than the weight of the metal.

Andy came down from the ladder and took a bundle of rags from a three-legged stool. He gestured at John to sit and poured two cups of steaming tea from the flask.

'It's a grand day out there, thank God.' John fumbled with the sachets of sugar before watching it cascade into the enamel mug.

'It is, John – but I doubt you're here to talk about the weather! Not like you to drop in unannounced.'

He studied his father-in-law. Retirement suited him. He was fresh-faced and happy-looking, the couple of stray wisps of white hair over his crown the only clue to his real age.

'Can a man not drop in on his son-in-law for a chat now, ha?'

'John, you don't do idle chat. What's on your mind?' Andy pulled up a chair and sat beside him, facing the door.

'I'm worried about her, son.'

'Me too.'

'She hasn't been herself since young Sal left. Her mother and I were talking. Those two have been joined at the hip since they were little ones in pigtails. Inseparable. Best friends. She's lost without her, really. Cooped up in that house day and night. Ma and me think we need to stage an intervention.'

Andy laughed to himself over the choice of words. He and Jen found her parents' obsession with daytime chat-shows a constant source of amusement. They had turned into a pair of armchair psychologists.

'Okay, Dr Phil.'

'Don't joke. We're worried. I know you want to get on with it, Andy, but Jen isn't getting on with it. We need to do something. Far be it from me to tell a man how to look after his family but you are sweeping this under the carpet.'

'What do you suggest I do then?'

'Do something exciting, son. Take her out for dinner, charm her – go have a bit of fun, just the pair of you. Danny is feeling it too. Since the new baby arrived, the boy is a bit lost, I think.'

'You have a point there. I'll talk to Will at the weekend.'

'She needs to get out of the house more. We would be delighted to have Danny for a few days if you wanted to go away somewhere and treat her. You could go to Berlin to see Sal? I don't want to see my daughter depressed any more.'

And that was it. The case had been put forward and the subject quickly changed. They sipped their tea and talked about the weather for the coming week followed by the usual chat about quotas, the EU and all the other things the longsuffering fishermen had to face every time they tried to do their jobs. The landlubbers complained in sympathy. Everyone, and every business in the village depended on each other. That's the way it was. They were a tribe.

'Okay.' Andy stood and placed his cup on the workbench. He fiddled with a couple of glow plugs, hoping his visitor would take the hint. He needed to get some work done.

'I'll be off so. Thanks for the tea. Think about what I said.'

'Will do.'

Andy watched the old man leave and head in the direction of the pier. He knew he liked to walk the length of it in the morning time, chatting with the fisherman and shooting the breeze with the tourists – he was quite the authority on history and folklore. They had a good relationship. Granted it had started out a bit rocky, but he had come around.

That conversation was quite typical of John. He was protective of his daughter and always had her best interests at heart. Andy should have seen it coming. He was right about one thing in particular: Jen was lost without Sal in the harbour. Those two had always been inseparable. Maybe a weekend in Berlin would put her in good form. It would be nice to get away and spend a bit of time together. They could do the tourist thing while Sal was in work and spend their evenings with her. He missed Sal too – her positivity used to have a great effect on all of them, Danny included. Maybe they should all go? That's a great idea, he thought, and smiled as he fiddled with a spanner. Danny would love to bunk off school for a few days. Sal and Jen could do girl stuff while he and the boy went to Legoland or the zoo. He was pleased with himself – that was exactly what they all needed. Jen would jump at the chance to see her friend, surely? He would book a nice hotel for the three of them, a real treat. The thoughts of schnitzels and that Currywurst with Pommes Frites thing Sal was always snapchatting to Jen took the sting out of the conversation with her father.

That was that. He picked up his phone and started a text to Sal.

He wouldn't say a word to Jen or Danny – a surprise trip – that's if Sal could keep her gob closed about it. She wasn't great with things like that. He stole another quick glance at his diary. He had a couple of outboard engines to service and then he would get up the road for breakfast. The day was turning out well after all.

The bulk of a man in the doorway blocked out the sun and made the workshop instantly gloomy. Andy looked up from the half-written text. His heart sank.

He had changed slightly. His hair was cut tight and physically he was bigger and stronger. He stood with his hands in his pockets and his face to the floor, kicking the dirt with his shoe. For a few moments he stood there, mute, turning slightly as if to run away from something. Andy put the phone on the workbench and placed his two hands on either side of it.

'Hello, Doc.'

'Howyeh, Andy. How are you?'

The prodigal son of the harbour had returned and things were about to change.

Chapter 9

The sound of the doorbell breaking the morning's silence startled Jen. She wasn't expecting anyone and none of her friends ever used the front door — meaning it was someone selling either broadband or salvation through religion. Irritated by the interruption, she prepared her polite refusal speech for the intruder as she went into the hall.

She opened the door and froze momentarily.

'Hi, Jen.'

'Hello, stranger.'

Jen stood back and motioned for Tess to step into the hall. She closed the front door behind her, slowly, giving herself a chance to calm her heart-rate down. It had been a while. They had tried to stay in contact of course but when her husband, Doc, went to prison, Tess pulled away from everyone, including Jen.

'Come on into the kitchen.'

Tess didn't say anything. Her steps were reluctant as she followed Jen into the bright kitchen.

Jen watched as she fumbled with her coat and stood beside the table.

'Tea or coffee?'

'Coffee would be lovely, thanks.'

Tess scraped a chair over the tiles and Jen grimaced. Another pet hate. Lift the damn chair, she thought to herself as she filled the kettle from the tap.

'The place looks lovely. I love the new table and the —'

'This is quite a surprise, Tess. How have you been? What brings you here?'

'I wanted to see you. It's been too long.'

'That it has.' Jen flicked on the kettle and stood with her back to the cupboards.

She wasn't sure how to feel about Tess sitting in her kitchen. She didn't want to be rude to her — lots of water under the bridge after all — but they weren't close any more. The sound of water boiling took the tension out of the silence. She rooted in the fridge for cheese and olives and placed them beside the soda bread on a wooden board.

She made the coffee and sat down opposite Tess.

As they sipped coffee and nibbled at the food, they small-talked about the beautiful weather and the harbour. Tess was looking forward to things quietening down after a busy summer season in the Tea Room and, yes, thank God, her business was going well. The new house too. Jen let her rattle on about herself — she was good at that. Hugh was thriving in his new school in Wexford town and was nearly as tall as her. Jen felt a nostalgia for the friendship they used to have. It was another thing in a long list of casualties after that night and the chaos Scott had brought to all of them. Tess hadn't escaped either — Scott had used her business to launder money and Doc had ended up in prison for drug-running. The nightmare continued for all of them and the friendship had dwindled.

At last the small talk dried up.

Jen looked at Tess. This was not the Tess that Jen knew. Maybe she was thinking nostalgic thoughts too.

'Okay, spit it out,' Jen said. 'Neither of us are ones for small talk.'

'Doc is home.'

Jen laid the olive back down on her plate and wiped her hands on a napkin. Tess looked her in the eye. Jen didn't comment and stared back until Tess dropped her gaze and fidgeted with her bracelet.

'When did he get back?'

'Four days ago,' Tess sighed and took a sip from her cup.

'And where is he staying?'

She knew the answer to that question before she even asked it. She knew Tess had started to visit him when he was sentenced. Every Tuesday, without fail. At least she had the good grace not to drag little Hugh up to that awful place.

'He's staying with me – with us – at home.'

Jen suddenly felt sorry for her. What a shit situation she was in. Again.

'Does that mean ...?'

'I don't know what it means. This is not a situation I ever imagined myself to be in.'

Jen could see the strain all over her face. She admired her in one sense. She was always so strong – nothing could break her.

Tess addressed her cup. 'He needed somewhere to go. He's changed. I couldn't just turn him out onto the street – especially not after being in that place for the last eighteen months. He's different now.'

'Different? He's not a drug-running addict, cheat and lying prick any more then?'

'Jen, please.'

'Please? He cheated on you, he made a fool out of you. He was involved in smuggling drugs on my husband's trawler. Andy could've ended up in prison because of him. He cheated and lied to all of us and spent his time taking coke and drinking. We were the ones picking up the pieces with you, Tess, and when he went to prison you turned your back on all of us.'

'That's not fair.' Tess's voice cracked with emotion.

'Fair doesn't even come into it, pet.'

Jen didn't mean to sound so aggressive but the truth was she had to blame someone for how it had all panned out.

Tess stood up and removed her coat from the back of the chair. She managed to keep her calm and didn't raise her voice.

'I'm sorry. I shouldn't have come. It was a mistake.'

Jen knew that if she let her walk out the door, that would be the end of it. They had been hanging on to the threads of a friendship in a downward spiral which had reduced them to nodding and waving at each other from a distance. She missed her friend – she wanted that friendship back. She needed to resolve this once and for all.

'Sit down, please.'

Judging by the look on her face, Tess wasn't expecting that request.

'I'm glad you're here. It's about time we face this head on and try to fix stuff.'

'Okay.' She sat back down and they finished their coffee in silence.

'How is he?' Jen was curious. Eighteen months in prison was a long time.

'He's alright. He doesn't talk about that place much. He kept his head down, got clean and got out of there. What else can I say?' She shrugged.

Jen knew her well enough to know that this was how she handled stress. Trivialise, compartmentalise and move on.

'He knows what an absolute mess he made of all our lives, Jen. He's trying to put it behind him and make amends to people.' She looked at her for a moment before she continued. 'He's heading down to the yard to see Andy.'

'Ah, I see – a double offensive. Spring it on the pair of us at the same time.'

'We're just trying to put the past behind us and move on. We don't want any trouble.'

'What did you think I was going to do? Take him out or put a homemade bomb under his car? I did think about it for a while.'

Tess arched an eyebrow. The feeble attempt at a joke hadn't worked.

'Look, Doc coming home has stirred up feelings and memories,' she said. 'That's why I'm here. We are all victims here, Jen, not just you. We all fucked up in one way or another and we have paid the price.'

'But I'm the one losing my mind. I just can't forget, you know? As much as I want to, I can't leave it in the past. Scott's still out there somewhere and I know he will come back.'

'I never entertained the idea he would ever come back.' Tess looked stricken.

Jen sat up straight in her chair and shook her head in response. 'Of course he's going to bloody come back! I'm sure of it. He likes to win – have you not, in all your soul-searching, figured that much out? He won't stop and when he does return, he will fuck all of us up. You and Doc cost him a lot of money.' Maybe it *was* unfair scaring Tess like that but it felt good for someone else to share the terror for a change. Andy had stopped entertaining her musings a while ago – he would never admit it but she knew he thought she was being melodramatic. History repeating itself.

'Stop!' Tess put her two hands up in front of her as if to ward off an invisible force. 'You can't think like that, She. You will drive yourself insane.'

Jen studied her for a moment. They never listened. That's what caused all this in the first place. She was trying not to get agitated, but it was hard. She had to make them see.

'Do you trust your husband?'

'I don't know is the simple answer to that.' Tess's phone trilled in her bag, giving her the reprieve she needed. She rooted around for the device. Glancing at the caller ID, she silenced it and placed it face down on the table. 'I didn't divorce him. We will see what happens. Do *you* trust *your* husband?'.

'If I didn't trust him, I wouldn't have married him.'

Jen stood up and walked in the direction of the hallway. She came back with a silver-framed wedding photo and sat down.

'That's what we looked like on the day, by the way, just in case you were wondering.' Point-scoring. Resentment is a hard obstacle to get over. 'Do you ever wonder how different our lives would be, had you all listened to me from the outset?'

'That's a low blow, Jen. I am not going to go down that road. We can't change what happened. Life is shit and shit happens – no point wondering about the what-ifs. That's what keeps us in the past. Dangerous thinking. You get on with it and you do whatever it takes to survive.'

'Wow. How long have you had that line ready?'

'We either make the effort to salvage our friendship or we call it quits today. That 'line', as you call it, is my survival mechanism. If I stay in the past, I'm going to go insane. I have to move on, Jen, and I want us to be friends.'

'You weren't there on that strand – you weren't the one beaten to within an inch of her life so excuse me for wallowing in self-fucking-pity. It's hard to move on from that. He didn't try to kill your son.'

Jen was on her feet.

'You are right.' Tess didn't move from the chair. 'He didn't attack me or hurt Hugh, I'll give you that. He killed all three of us, slowly. I lost a baby, lost my home, my husband and my friends. I had to sell the pub, I had to sell the house and downsize to one just down the road and I had to open the Tea Room on a shoestring, it was either that or starve. My husband is a criminal now. Do you know what it's like to visit someone in prison?'

'Really? No one forced you. I'm living –'

'Do you know what it's like to hold your son in your arms as he sobs over being called names in school? I had to move him into town – that's how bad it got.' She kept her voice even and remained in a seated position. 'I was constantly waiting for the Guards to arrest me over the pub – waiting for the sale to fall through because of *that* investment. The constant rows in the house with a child who hated me for keeping him away from his daddy.

Over my dead body was he going to visit that stinking shithole. Doc wouldn't allow it either. Have you ever watched someone go through drug and alcohol withdrawals? You don't get to lord it over me any more, Jen. You weren't the only victim. Get down off your soapbox and have a bit of empathy for others. And while we are on the subject, I did see you on your wedding day. I was outside the church when you came out. I turned down the invitation because I didn't want you to have any reminder of that night. I thought I was doing right by you, ducky.'

It was Jen's turn to look stricken. Tess had laid out the facts – those points she herself had barred from taking root in her mind. She fired the cigarette out the door, sat back down opposite Tess and propped her head up with her hands. The fight was gone from her.

'I'm on anti-depressants,' she said. 'I keep thinking about topping myself. Andy wants a baby – I don't. I'm taking the pill in secret and lying to him as he thinks we're trying for a damn baby. Danny hates me. He's getting into trouble in school. I can't sleep. Not that you needed telling but I'm comfort-eating all around me – hence this,' she pointed at her muffin top, 'and I have trouble leaving the house. Dr Norval has named it Chronic Post-Traumatic Stress Disorder. I stopped going to him because he was getting impatient with my slow progress. I want to crawl under a rock and die. I'm sorry, Tess. I'm just angry all the time. No matter how many times I redecorate or change the furniture around in this room, I can't stop the flashbacks from that night.'

And there it was, laid bare. The first honest conversation in nearly two years.

'What a mess, ducky. What a sorry mess.'

They sat in silence for a while, neither of them sure how to proceed. Jen glanced at her friend. A few more lines had appeared on her face and the sparkle had gone from her eyes. *You are so selfish, Jen. It's all about you and your drama – you never think about anyone except yourself. You are a bad mother, a bad wife and a bad friend. People would be better off without you.* And so on – the voice continued – static in her head.

Tess's phone broke the silence. A look flashed across her face but Jen couldn't define what that was. She didn't answer it — instead, for the second time, she looked at it and again she placed it face down on the table and let it go to voicemail. She laced her fingers together and stretched. Placing her hands on top of her head, she looked at the ceiling and sighed.

'Doc insists on sleeping with the light on. No matter how hard I try, I can't get the image of him behind the glass in that dirty grey tracksuit out of my head. I'm imagining it, but I can still smell prison off his skin. They broke him.'

The tears tried to come but she wouldn't let them.

'Give him time,' Jen said. What else could she say? What a huge mess. All because of that rotten sociopath. He was off goodness knows where and they were all falling apart. Lives ruined — for what?

'I'd better go. Thanks for the coffee and the nibbles.'

'I'm glad you came, Tess, really I am.'

Jen walked her friend to the front door. Tess stood on the doorstep for a moment. Akin to the end of a first date, an awkward silence followed as they stood facing each other. Tess put her arms out and Jen stepped into them, reluctantly. A quick hug. It was a start.

'Come down for tea soon.'

Tess went to her car and sat into the driver seat. Jen leaned against the rowan tree with her arms folded as the car kicked up dust in its wake. The sun was warm on her face and she took a moment to breathe.

'It's a beautiful day for a walk, isn't it?' a refined Dublin voice wafted in over boxwood before a tall girl with chestnut hair came into sight.

She smiled warmly then bent to tie the lace on her walking boot. She pointed in the direction of the strand before informing Jen she was about to take a walk on the beach.

Jen was used to tourists around the area, even this late in the year, but something about this girl made her feel uneasy — as though she had been waiting behind the hedge for her to come out. *Go inside, Jen, quickly.*

'Enjoy your walk.' Jen waved dismissively and made her way indoors.

'I will, Jen. *Ciao.*'

She spun around. The girl was gone.

Jen slammed the front door and ran into the kitchen to check the patio door was locked. Her hands shook. Teasing a cigarette out of the box, she slumped into the chair.

Jen, you are losing your mind.

A box of incense winked at her from the windowsill. Andy hated her smoking in the house – she rarely did but she wasn't going out the back and she needed the nicotine. She lit up and stared into space for the length of time it took her to smoke half the thing. She laughed then at her stupidity – Scott wasn't the only person in the world to use that damn word. *Ciao.*

Crushing the half-smoked cigarette out onto a saucer, she started to clear the evidence of her earlier visitor from the table and lit a stick of incense to kill the smell of smoke. Talking herself down, she felt better and convinced herself of her own paranoia. The sandalwood scent swirled up from the incense in a line of smoke, dancing like a cobra from a basket. It soothed her until the niggling voice came back into her head.

You're not being paranoid – she knew your name.

Chapter 10

The men stood in silence and appraised each other. Andy kept his hands on the workbench and took a deep breath. He'd known this day would come. They used to be good friends but all of that had changed dramatically since Doc had been arrested and sentenced.

'If you don't want to talk, I'll go.'

'Come in. You're here now.'

'Cheers.'

Andy couldn't read him. He looked like Doc and sounded like him but there was something very different about him. He felt uneasy and glanced around for something he could use just in case.

'Jesus, Andy, will you relax? I haven't turned into a serial killer.' Doc dropped his head again and continued to scuff the ground with his boot.

'Sorry. I just wasn't expecting you. Sit down there.' He pointed to the stool he had cleared earlier and hoped Jen's dad wouldn't come back for more man talk.

'So – you're back.'

'Yep.'

'For good?'

'Yep.'

'You kept that quiet. Welcome back.'

The words were flat. The conversation was flat. Everything about this little meeting was flat and wrong.

'Did you manage to get yourself together while you were there, Doc, or should we expect more of the same bullshit from you, now you're a seasoned criminal?'

The speed at which Andy's voice and temper rose surprised the pair of them.

Doc sat on the stool and pulled out a pack of cigarettes.

'Unless you want to add arson to your repertoire, don't light that thing in here,' Andy said.

Doc put his bad habit back into his pocket. He didn't speak. He shuffled around on the weather-worn stool, trying to get comfortable.

'Come on – I need air – you can have your smoke out the back.'

Andy stomped through the workshop and swung open the side door. The bright sun stung his eyes and he gulped down the fresh morning air. Doc followed and sat on a rusted hitch. Lobster pots and a small punt with a gaping hole in a once white-and-blue hull were the only witnesses to the conversation. The cigarette smoke filled the space between the two men.

Andy eventually sat beside him.

'Why didn't you tell me about Fran?'

'I didn't know, I swear to god. Tess told me about him. I was picking it up from a go-between. I had no idea it was coming in on the *Mary Rose*.'

'Why did you get involved with drug running, of all the fucking things to get caught up in? Are you mad, like? Why, Doc?'

'For the money at first, but then ...'

'You have a *lot* to answer for.'

'I couldn't stop. It all got so insane.'

'Why should I even listen to you now?'

'I'm here to apologise, Andy. It's not going to change anything but I need to say sorry.'

'Clear your conscience, you mean.'

'Leave my conscience to me. I've spent the last eighteen months in hell – getting clean and facing my demons. My conscience will never be clear but I have to try and put it right.'

'What was it like?' He was angry with Doc but curious.

'Nightmare. Degrading. Life-changing.' He took another drag and pulled the smoke deep into his lungs. 'I'll never forget the first night in there.'

'What happened?'

'I realised what I had done. In a holding cell, on a massive come-down from drink and coke and I thought I was going to die. A few weeks later they doubled us up and my cellmate was withdrawing from heroin.'

'Jesus. And they left him in there with you?'

'Yes. It's prison. Not the Betty Ford Clinic.'

'Did he get better?'

'We were holed up together for two weeks. He was dying sick. I had heard talk on the landing about people coming off the gear. I had never seen it before and didn't understand it until I saw him. I felt sorry for him.'

'That's rough.'

'He never slept. Just paced up and down the cell all day and all night. He couldn't sit still for two minutes. If he wasn't pacing, he was blaring the radio and sitting on my bed talking over it. Up and down, opening and closing the window.'

'You had a window?'

Doc didn't gratify the stupid question with an answer.

'He was alright, you know. Decent enough – he just couldn't get out of it. Where he lived, they were all on it. He would go through this ritual until he got a visit from one of his mates, who'd of course smuggle in some stuff for him and then he would be back to square one. He eventually got clean. I was moved down to the main drag after a few weeks. Down there it was easier.'

'How so?'

'You had your own room for a start and you weren't locked up all day. We did classes in all sorts. It was easier.'

'Classes?

'Woodwork, horticulture, languages, cookery – you name it. I did mechanics training in there and I even taught a few cookery classes. I kept my head down, didn't get into any trouble. Steered clear of the big boys and got the fuck out of there.'

'And here you are.'

'And here I am. Trying to put my life and my family back together.'

'At least you cleaned up your act – got off the drugs like. It could have gone the other way. You could have been a lot worse off.'

'You haven't a clue.' He crushed the butt of his cigarette with the heel of his boot and clasped his hands together. 'When you see someone raking through their own shit to find drugs they swallowed at visiting time or look at their teeth crumbling out of their mouth as they eat lunch – it's the best advertisement of all to clean up your act and stay off the drugs, as you put it. You know any junkies or jail birds, Andy?'

'Apart from your good self? No, I don't. Funny that. But I could have ended up in there myself, thanks to you and your cronies.'

'You brought him into our lives in the first place, man. Don't forget that.'

'So, all this is my fault?'

'No. I didn't say that –'

'Well, what are you saying then?' Andy jumped up from the hitch and stood over him.

'Sit down, man. You're not a brawler. I've spent a long time dealing with my demons. We all must take responsibility for the situations in our own lives. I have made peace with the part I played – maybe you should look at your role in this. I'm here to apologise to you for the part my actions played in fucking up your life. I can't force forgiveness on you. When I'm finished here, I will go and see Jen. After that, I will work on my wife and my son.'

'Don't go near Jen.'

'Why not?'

'Because she's not able for it. She hasn't been very well since all of this happened. And Sal left for Berlin a few months ago. It hasn't been easy.'

'Fair enough.'

'Give her time to adjust to you being back. It's going to bring it all back up for her. She needs to deal with it her own way.'

'I'm sorry for everything.'

'You paid the price, Doc. I don't hold grudges.'

Doc stuck out his hand. Andy took it. It was an awkward exchange. Andy had played out this meeting in his head many times. A lot remained unsaid – but what was the point? The past needed to stay where it belonged – he spent his time trying to instil that in Jen's head. He couldn't be a hypocrite now. They sat back down in the morning sun.

'What will you do for work? Will you go back to music?'

'Nah – that's over. I need to stay away from the pub scene and all that goes with it. The quiet life for a while, I think. No one will hire an ex-prisoner. I'm not working for Tess. New leaf – college maybe.'

'You said you did mechanics training inside?'

'Yeah.'

'I could do with a hand around here. The basics of engines are the same. The pay is crap but the offer is there if you want it. You could start in a couple of days.'

'Thank you, that would be great.' Doc coughed and cleared his throat.

Andy didn't embarrass him by looking at him – he knew the man was nearly in tears.

'Come on inside – I'll show you around.'

He killed ten minutes showing him his workshop. Doc didn't ask about the *Mary Rose* and how he felt about working on dry land. He was impressed by the training – Doc, who never knew one end of spanner from the other, could distinguish between a drive-shaft adjuster and a retainer. Poor guy, he thought – he was in hell. He may have slain the monkey on his shoulder but the shit remained on his back. He needed a chance and people in the village needed to just let him settle back into his life. That would take a while.

He wouldn't mention it to Jen for now. He wasn't sure how she was going to take the news of him being back and, more to the point, the news about the job offer. She didn't necessarily have a problem with Doc – it was the association. The 'anniversary' of that night was coming up – things were volatile. Jen was fragile and Andy was tired – the less drama, the better.

'Andy?'

'Sorry. I was thinking.'

'I'd best be going, man. I want to get home.'

'Have you seen anyone since you got back?'

'No. Today is the first time I've left the house.'

'You'll be hot news for a few days and then they'll move on. You know what the harbour is like. If they weren't gossiping, I'd worry.'

'Thanks, man. I'll give you a call over the weekend about the job.'

'Sounds good. Mind yourself.'

He watched as his old friend walked away. It saddened him to see the slump in his shoulders, hands in pockets and eyes trained on the ground. Oh, how it had gone so wrong for everyone.

Chapter 11

I didn't allow myself to become paranoid. Perhaps I should have. Marco's death was a temporary blip. Bad timing is a side-effect of life and death is part of it. I felt inconvenienced by his passing. I did not mourn for him — he didn't mean anything to me. Yesterday's feeling of being watched hadn't left me, I simply chose to ignore it. Besides, I had more pressing issues to focus the mind — the impending meeting with the Boss in Spain. Something wasn't right about that and now Marco was dead. Something was seriously amiss.

I needed to focus on the task that was before me. The delivery. Two phones sat on the table beside me and I waited. The consignment of heroin was due to arrive in a warehouse in Oujda — Fran had left the night before to make the eight-hour journey to join his crew who were already in place. The merchandise was coming in over the Algerian border through a contact in Tiaret. From there, it would arrive in Oujda, where the load would be processed and split in half. One load was destined for Tangier then on for distribution in Spain. The other set for delivery to Marrakech. It all sounded simple enough – once the network was properly managed. That was my job on behalf of the Boss. I'd been the brains behind the whole operation and an important link in the chain. The distribution channel was fraught with perils – but the business was run accordingly. I never concerned myself with the lowly 'employees' or the competition for that matter. My concern was only ever for the money and the drugs. I steered clear of selling on the street – that was a job for the goons like Fran.

Fran was the middle-man and his crew were the runners. The closer the merchandise got to the consumer, the higher the mark-up. It's a product after all and one in huge demand. Fran had chosen wisely with his crew. None of them were users. They needed to keep their minds focused on the job and I didn't need the headache of having to discipline unruly staff. I paid most of them on a commission basis – they needed an incentive to sell. At each stage along the supply route locals were used, for obvious reasons. The status for them outweighed the risk – everyone was happy. As long as the demand was there, we supplied.

I was the perfect candidate for this role and the Boss counted his lucky stars the day I arrived in Spain. Of course, at that time, I was a little the worse for wear and needed recovery time but he knew what lay ahead. I had several identities in my travels between Spain and Africa – building the network and making it possible for him to do business in a new market. He owed me big-time: he was getting very rich from my intellect. My ability to charm, fit into any location and disappear into the crowd at a moment's notice was the explanation for his success. That coupled with my ability to hide money in various business interests and properties gave him the edge over his competition. It was about time he was told that. I was beginning to look forward to this meeting with him. Perhaps it was time to overthrow the Captain and take control of the ship. I was tired of being the navigator. I was the real brains behind the operation.

The first phone lit up, confirming that the driver had cleared the border. He gave details of an ETA in Oujda – less than an hour. The roads were clear. Spotters had made sure of that. Game on.

I picked up the second phone and punched in a message to Fran. He would, in turn, relay a message to his crew – they never travelled together, too risky. This was the part of the process where I was most alert. The first drop. The courier needed to keep a cool head and deliver the package. He would collect his pay and be gone. Then the next phase would kick in. Little and often was the key to supply but this one was a larger consignment than the last. The law of supply and demand. Demand had increased and we had to service the market.

A text from Fran confirmed everything was in place. The warehouse we were using for this drop was a new location from a reliable source. The local in question had come good on the last deal and I felt confident about his involvement. For now, I needed to be patient.

I also needed a distraction. My neck was sore from sitting over the desk looking at the phones and the muted light from the large brass lantern on the ceiling meant I had to strain my eyes in the semi-dark. My senses were heightened and the intricate blue-and-white mosaic tiles on the floor seemed to be shouting at me. I longed for the cool white walls and sleek leather furniture of my old life. I did of course enjoy the opulence of this place but, at times like this, the glass, the brass, the tiles and the richness of the décor was an eyesore. The kitchen area was cooler. I picked up the phones, and hoped for some respite from sensory overload there.

As I was watching my step on the marble staircase, another text came in.

Great! I relaxed a little more and the cool white walls of the kitchen area calmed me. A bottle of Jameson begged for my attention. Anything can be acquired here, if you know where to look. The clink of the ice against the side of the glass and the amber liquid sloshing around was a welcome sound. The melodic crack and swirl as the ice challenged the liquid was the music I needed.

I remembered the last occasion I had drunk whiskey with a friend and I felt heavy-hearted. It was with Andy in a hotel in Dublin. It was our drink of choice any time we were out. That was the last time I had any civilised contact with him – before everything blew up. I was sure on some level he understood my intentions. I was trying to protect him after all. He had made some bad choices in his life – particularly when it came to women. I wondered if he would ever again sit down and have a drink with me. If he was aware I was willing to forgive him about Jen, maybe then we could put the past behind us and move on. I was also sure he had got over me using his trawler to bring in the stuff. He would understand why I didn't tell him. I couldn't risk him being caught up with the police had it ever gone wrong. I was protecting him by not telling him. He must miss my company now and then. I should have made contact sooner – but I knew he was so busy with the wedding plans and the boatyard. I didn't want to distract him. I had several sources and contacts in Ireland still, as I liked to stay abreast of happenings. Mother of course knew where I was too, but she would stay loyal. I told her it was in everyone's best interest she kept my location to herself. She didn't seem fazed by that.

In the half-light of evening, the formula for my plan was simple. Every good businessman needed a plan to move forward. Fran would be disposed of, thus getting Tarek and his little band of henchmen off my back. There would be no retribution exacted from me for the disappearance of his sister – Fran could take the fall on that one. Tarek was suspicious but he had no actual proof – that's why he didn't hurt us the other night – he had no proof. I thought about going to him and orchestrating the story to exclude my involvement but unless I had something of value to give him, he might just get rid of me too. An uneducated, illiterate half-wit such as he couldn't possibly understand business or negotiation. He wasn't worth the time or the effort. But, this left me with the remaining predicament. I'm not a monster – so me getting rid of Fran myself was out of the question. I felt a real disdain towards the imbecile but I couldn't bring myself to dispose of him. The simple answer came: I would hire someone to do it for me. Much like the bottle of Jameson in my kitchen, anything can be acquired here. You just need to know where to look.

Filling Fran's position wouldn't be as difficult as finding a replacement for me. If I were going to take over in Spain, I would need someone here. All in good time. It was probably a blessing about Marco – I wanted out of that nonsense. It was a good money-spinner and quite simple to arrange. The downside was the tedium in having to entertain those women, all with a distinct lack of intelligence.

The whiskey tasted as good as ever. The liquid fire hit my stomach and reminded me to eat.

I only then realised I should have had a text from Fran via his crew, confirming the arrival. That was odd. I looked around the kitchen and the light had moved further down the wall. The clock told me it was ten past five. I was on overtime – that idea amused me. I would give it ten minutes before enquiring. Fran was nervy on the job – I couldn't risk alarming him if it wasn't necessary.

Ten minutes later, just as I picked up the phone to contact him, a message from him came through: **No sign.**

The courier should have arrived at the warehouse by now. I typed a response, advising him to send out one of his own spotters, not a local, and then proceeded to text the courier. I felt the urge to call him but I refrained. I enquired about his ETA. I got no response. My hands began to tremble and I took off my light jacket. There had to be a reasonable explanation for this. No need to panic yet. The third phone vibrated against the chair. I pulled it out of my pocket, knowing who it was. The Boss. I ignored it. I was up, pacing now. He needed confirmation that all was in order. The crew in the warehouse would also be getting restless. This operation needed to be carried out quickly – it would take a couple of hours to cut and redistribute the merchandise. No one needed the headache of a delay.

Calm down, Scott. This will be over in a couple of hours. Everything is in order.

I replenished my glass and forced myself to sit. My leg was bouncing involuntarily. I didn't allow myself to think of the worst-case scenario. That didn't bear thinking about. I visualised the route again. We had pored over the maps, choosing the routes over the border and into Oujda that were the quietest. We varied the routes each time. The van was nondescript – like the hundreds of others one might see on any given day. The crew was handpicked by our own network – everything was watertight.

Would the Boss be pacing at the lack of response? He would just have to wait. This was my turf, my operation – and he could go to hell. I was in control here, not him.

It would take the spotter Fran sent out an hour to do the round trip on the roads to the border and back. It was his job to act like a sweeper – making sure the road was clear and no one was lying in wait for our van full of heroin. I had to be patient and sit it out. I sent Fran a quick text advising him of same.

I had to hand it to the Boss. Morocco was a good place to do business. We had started with heroin of course, bringing it in from our contact in Algeria. The coke came from Spain into Marrakech – through us. That network and route was long established ... if it ain't broke, as they say. Our biggest win was securing the route from the growing fields in the Rif Mountains. The key was getting the farmer to transport it to our contact in Tangiers. We needed the right crew there to get it into Spain and Amsterdam but the icing on the cake came when we spotted the gap in the market. Some of the best hashish in the world comes from the Rif Mountains. Everyone was exporting it. We started a network to move it into the cities. That was where the big money came from. Our product was of a higher quality than any of our competitors. It was simple and it worked. This was the first time we had ever run into any kind of problem.

The courier had crossed the border without interference. This was an issue on our side. I checked the phones again. Nothing. Time was ticking on. If it didn't reach its destination, someone would pay a very high price. That someone would not be me.

The phone rang. It was Fran. What was he thinking – ringing me? I was on edge so I answered it. He was in a wild panic at the other end.

'Fran, pull it together. And be careful here.'

'*It's gone! It's fucking gone!*'

'What?'

'They found the courier – beaten to a pulp and dumped on the side of the road.'

'Where's the delivery?'

'It's fucking *gone*. Are you *deaf?*'

'Clear the warehouse and get back here.'

'It's too late. The filth are all over it. Cops everywhere. I gotta fucking go.'

This was a disaster. What was I going to tell the Boss? I drained the contents of the glass, refilled it and repeated the process, pouring two fat lines of coke out for good measure. *Fuck. Fuck. Fuck.* The shit was about to hit the fan. First Marco – now this. Someone was selling me out. I needed to find out who.

Chapter 12

There wasn't a light on at home. Andy knew what lay ahead of him. He killed the engine and rested his forehead on the steering wheel. It smelt of diesel and the ocean – reminding him of his former life and, at times like this, he longed for the roll of sea under his feet and the sting of salt in his eyes. The window didn't close properly in his beloved old van. The crack between glass and the seal allowed the cool tendrils of air to skip across the back of his neck making the hair stand on end. He suddenly felt nervous. Sitting up, he turned on the lights, startling the rowan tree. It stood to attention – tall and proud. He glanced over his shoulder into the dim red glow of the van's cargo space, expecting a pair of eyes and the glint of a knife to greet him. Instead, he saw coils of rope snaking out of boxes and a couple of abandoned takeaway mugs. He turned off the headlights and laughed at his own skittishness.

The house was warm and quiet.

'Jen? Are you here?' It was Friday – Mr Cassidy and Danny were down with Will. 'Jen?'

No answer. He flicked on the lights and the shine from every work surface and the floor nearly blinded him. The smell of lemon detergent made him gag and the chairs were stacked on top of the table. She had been on one of her frenzies. He checked the sitting room and the furniture had been rearranged – again.

Shaking his head and steeling himself for what lay ahead, upstairs he went. A sliver of light leaked out from under the bedroom door. He swung it open. She was lying on the bed, staring at the ceiling. She jumped and dropped her iPod.

'Jesus Christ, Andy, you scared me half to death!' She pulled the headphones out of her ears and flung them on the bed beside her.

'I was calling you.'

She picked up the iPod from the floor and brandished it in his direction by way of explanation.

'I was listening to this.' Her tone was impatient and he felt as though he shouldn't have come up to disturb her. That was the thing with Jen – her moods controlled the atmosphere in the house, all the time. By now he'd got familiar with reading his surroundings as an indication. The frantic cleaning was a dead giveaway.

'Have you eaten today, love?' He sat on the bed beside her.

'I was cleaning.'

'What happened, Jen?'

'Tess was here. He's back.'

'He came to see me.'

'I know he did.'

'How do you feel?'

She shrugged in response. The near-empty blister pack on the locker caught his eye. He hated when she took those things but he also hated when she didn't.

'What else happened?'

She told him about the earlier incident with the woman, how she appeared out of nowhere and how she knew her name. It all spilled out of her mouth like water out of a broken tap.

He pinched the bridge of his nose with his thumb and forefinger as a loud sigh escaped his lips.

'Let me get this straight. You went on one of your frenzies and popped a load of Zanax because some girl out for a walk knew your name?'

'You don't believe me. I was scared, Andy.'

'I didn't say that – I'm just trying to understand you here.'

'Can you not see why I was nervous?'

'Get into bed and get some rest. I'm going downstairs to make some dinner. Do you want some?'

'No, thanks.'

As she lay back down and scrabbled with the iPod, he left the room, closing the door with a bang. He plodded down the stairs and back into the kitchen. While he rooted around in the fridge for the makings of dinner, in his head he was composing a text to Sal. He had to get Jen out of the harbour, if only for a few days. He also toyed with the idea of ringing her therapist. It had been in the back of his mind for a while. He cursed Sal for leaving – but he knew she had to go – she had a job waiting for her. He then cursed himself for not being able to fill the void. Jen was unravelling, again, and he couldn't for the life of him think of a way to stop it.

I'm sick of her and her mood swings, I'm sick of her moods dictating how and when I can be happy and I've had enough of walking on eggshells. She can pull herself together or I'm out of here.

The internal dialogue stopped him in his tracks. His subconscious screamed at him to listen and that was the first time he had acknowledged it. He was tired. He was at his wits' end – but leave her? He couldn't do that. He loved her.

But do you? You loved your life at sea, and she made you walk away from it. You can walk if you want, you know.

'Shut up, Andy, and make your damn dinner,' he said aloud.

He opened a bottle of Tiger beer and put a bowl of leftover Thai curry in the microwave oven. The door of the microwave bounced back at him before he closed it again – gently. It was too warm to light the stove but chilly enough for the skin on his arms to feel tight. He pulled a blanket from the armchair and ignored the table. The chairs could stay there. He abandoned his boots at the back door and responded to the ping of the microwave. A Tiffany lamp in the corner of the kitchen–cum–living-room gave the illusion of warmth when it was lit and the glow of the TV he had just turned on sated his need for company. Images of abandoned shoes on Greek beaches and boats overflowing with displaced and terrified families assaulted him. Perspective, that's what he needed. In comparison, his were small problems. He needed rest and he would sort everything out after a good night's sleep. He thought about Danny and how loved he was. He was tucked up in bed in the other home that revolved around him. Everything was in place for a happy life – everyone together as one big, dysfunctional, happy family. All he needed was for Jen to see it. To see that she was loved and protected. All she needed to see was that the past belonged just there and once they moved past her issues together as a family, everything would be the way they wanted it to be. In time, she would come around to the idea that a baby in the house – their baby – would fill the void in her heart and replace it with love. She was a great mother and would be a wonderful mother again. She was strong. He just needed to remind her of everything she had achieved up until that night. He would convince her of it. He would save her from this dark cloud hanging over her head.

Or maybe you will leave her, Andy? She's never going to get over it. Get out now, while you can.

Chapter 13

Jen muted the iPod and remained on the bed, staring at the ceiling. No amount of guided meditations or chemical interventions could quieten the white noise in her head. The muffled monotone of a news reporter floated up the stairs.

She toyed with the idea of going down to join him or getting dressed and suggesting a drink in the Gale. They hadn't been there in months. The idea always remained just that – a fleeting thought. It was all too much bother and the evening would inevitably reach only one conclusion. Danny wasn't here; Andy would seize the opportunity. She needed to avoid that. It frightened her.

Doc's arrival back to the village had pulled the rug out from under her feet. She knew she was being dramatic but she was furious. They were all moving on, putting it behind them. They didn't care about what happened to her. She couldn't vacate that space no matter how hard she tried and Sal moving was a kick in the gut. Sal had moved on – on to bigger and better – while she was still here, stuck in a time warp. Tess had moved on too: new house, new business. She said herself earlier that she had moved on – that living in the past was dangerous … but now her words seemed a little hollow – lip-service.

She thought about Tess. She couldn't quite figure out how she had managed to sell the Gale, sell the house, buy a new home and get a second business up and running in such a short space of time with little or no capital. She always was a shrewd businesswoman but there was something really odd about it all.

After Doc was arrested, Tess had stopped calling. She spent less time in the Gale and before long there was a For Sale sign outside the pub and outside her home. Hugh and Danny spent less and less time together both in school and at the weekends. Tess always had an excuse for not calling with little Hugh at the weekends and Jen eventually got fed up of texting and calling to arrange play dates. She couldn't understand why Tess didn't want the boys to remain friends. It was nothing to do with the children. Little Hugh had his own issues, of course – his dad was in prison for Christ sake. God only knew what kind of impact that had on a child.

The communication stopped completely around the end of January. Doc was behind bars and Tess had closed the pub. Hugh transferred to a school in Wexford town, and that was that.

Jen often thought about Doc. At times, the seething rage she felt towards him was overwhelming – other times the pity was depressing. Technically she had no right to feel anything – he didn't do anything to her directly. It was more the shit-storm he was part of. He swore he didn't know the drugs were coming in on Andy's boat – she didn't believe him. And now he was back – a free man. He had done his time, atoned for his sins. A green card to move on and put the past behind him.

If you hear one more person telling you to put the past behind you and move on, you'll scream, won't you, Jen? It's all about you, isn't it? They don't have a clue. Your life has been ruined. Your son's life has been ruined. You failed him. You're a terrible mother. A failure.

She wondered how Doc's presence in the harbour would affect Andy. He hadn't told her anything about their conversation and he didn't stay long enough to hear what Tess had to say for herself. Maybe he didn't care? He didn't seem to be too bothered over the strange woman she had seen earlier. History repeating itself. If he had listened to her about Scott in the first place, none of this would've happened.

The realisation dawned on her then – had he listened to his first wife Sharon all those years ago she might still be alive. Scott had killed her but, after all, it was Andy's fault.

The knot of rage in the pit of Jen's stomach was unfurling and threatening to take over her whole body. Her mouth was dry and she clamped her hands over her lips to stop herself screaming. She tried the breathing techniques and the visualisation again. It didn't work. At least she had been spared the flashbacks over the last few days. They weren't as frequent but when they came they did in high definition and they were always the same. She would never forget his face or the voicemail on the night of her engagement, letting her know that not only was he still alive, but he'd be back, someday, to gut her and her little boy. He was alive – they were still connected in a twisted soulmate-type relationship. She could feel his presence – she knew he wouldn't forget. He would come back and he would finish what he started.

She wanted her power back. Her sanity, her self-esteem, her peace of mind. The only way she could get that was by focusing on the here and now. She needed to build bridges with the people closest to her. They were the ones who loved her and cheered her on every day, and yet she had spent the last two years in a bubble of anger, hurt, fear and loathing. She wanted Strong Jen back and she needed to put the past behind her. Let go, forgive herself for failing her son. Forgive Andy.

No. That wasn't it. That wasn't the answer. She knew what she needed to do. She was going to find Scott. Her first stop would be his mother. She knew where he was, of that she was sure. She would get it out of her.

Are you listening to yourself, Jen? You are pathetic. Who the hell do you think you are – Lara Croft? You are useless. You couldn't stop him when he was here and you sure as hell can't stop him now. Take another pill and go to sleep, you stupid cow! You are weak, you are a terrible wife and a terrible mother. Just take the pills and do everyone a favour. There's enough there, you know – that's how you make it all go away and at least if you are not around for him to come back for, you guarantee Danny's safety. Will can take him and then Andy is free. That's how you solve this. There's no other way.

The voice in her head was a claxon. She couldn't drown out the noise, the constant chatter and the static. It was relentless. Scott's face flashed in front of her and now he was standing outside her house with the woman from earlier. Andy was there too, shouting at her to put the past behind her and get over it. Her face stung from shame-filled angry tears.

She didn't remember getting up off the bed. She was pacing back and forth in front of the window – the intermittent glow of the lighthouse counting away the minutes of her pathetic existence. *Just take the damn pills, Jen, just do it.* They were right there on the locker. It would be easier. She knew this sickness was taking hold of her and there was no way out. She would be better off taking control now and giving in. The scars on her chest tightened with every breath and her heart felt like a hammer trying to break out of her sternum. *Just do it – then you will have your peace.* The adrenalin coursed down her limbs like lightning and her body shook against her will. She looked at the locker where the blister pack sat like an incendiary device. Time slowed down as did her breathing.

She dried her eyes and went to quietly turn the key in the door.

Sitting down gently on the bed, she slid the drawer of the locker open silently. She took out her jewellery box and popped open the lid. The dancing ballerina hadn't danced in years and the music box was silent. The rest of the blister packs were concealed in under its false bottom. One by one she stacked them on the locker and worked methodically until all the pills sat under the lamp like pebbles on the beach under the moonlight. She wondered would the sixty or so be enough? The water in the glass was cool in her dry, tired throat. It felt nice. She drained the glass of water and scooped handfuls of the little blue pearls into it. She listened for Andy. He was laughing at something on the TV. Danny would be asleep by now over at his dad's house.

She crossed the landing in her bare feet and stood in the bathroom.

The voice in her head was gentle now. *You are doing the right thing. There's no other way. There's no other answer.*

She felt another surge of adrenalin as she lifted the glass.

She banged the glass down with a thud.

'*Fuck you, you pathetic little monster!*' she yelled. '*Shut your mouth — there's always an answer and I will find it!*'

She watched the pills sink to the bottom of the toilet bowl.

'Jen? Are you okay up there?' Andy called over the noise of the water flushing away her fears and that voice.

'I'll be down in a second. It's okay — I'm fine.'

She looked in the mirror and smiled at herself. The voice was silent.

Chapter 14

Fran steadied himself before opening the heavy wooden door. He hoped Scott would be asleep. The long drive from Oujda had given him the time he needed to plan. He could put that plan into place all the quicker if he could get in and out of the riad undetected. No such luck – Scott was up and, judging by his appearance, he hadn't gone to bed at all. Empty beer bottles lay on the tiled floor and he sat with his head in his hands. A bag of cocaine spilled over the coffee table.

Fran stood in the archway. He had rehearsed his lines.

Scott looked up at him – his eyes were red from lack of sleep and too much alcohol. The room stank of stale beer and body odour.

'The wanderer returns. You have fucked up beyond all compare this time, old friend.'

Fran was uneasy now. Scott couldn't know anything.

'You're not pinning this mess on me, man. I did my part of the job.'

'Your part of the job? *Your* part of the fucking job? Are you kidding me?' He was on his feet now and swaying like a drunken sailor. He began to laugh. '*I did my fucking job!* Fran, you stupid, ignorant fool. We are both dead – do you hear me? Dead, dead, dead. El Bosso is going to send in the clowns and that will be the end of us. You better ring your mammy and say goodbye.'

The red mist descended in front of Fran. He sprang from the doorway and hit Scott square in the face with a punch. Scott's lip split open. The shock of hitting him caused Fran to take a step back and gather himself together. This was not part of the plan – he needed to get out.

Scott stood in the middle of the floor, blood dripping onto his crumpled shirt.

'You finally show a bit of balls, Fran – good on you! I didn't think you had it in you.' He was laughing, lurching around the room. 'I should have known you had a bit of bottle in you. Bottle, that's a good word for you. It took bottle to ring Spain and talk to the Boss.'

Frans heart stopped momentarily. How did he know?

'What are ya talking about, man?'

'That time in Ireland. After I left the country. You used my phone to call the Boss. Following me to Spain like that when it all went pear-shaped, that took balls.'

Fran could breathe again. He didn't know.

'We've had a great time really. Join me for a drink, have a couple of lines. It's our wake, after all.' He proffered a beer.

Trying to keep the situation calm, he took it.

'I need to sleep, man, I've been driving all night.'

Scott had sat back down on the couch and scraped at the mound of white powder on the small table in front of him with a card.

There was no way Scott would sleep anytime soon. Maybe he would go out somewhere. Fran wouldn't get to leave otherwise. He needed to be asleep or gone.

'So, tell me! What happened to the huge fucking consignment

we were supposed to deliver to the Boss? It just, what? Disappeared into thin air? Or did the jinns take it?'

'I've already told you. I don't know. The courier was found on the side of the road. The van was gone. It was your genius idea to make sure he travelled alone. The warehouse was raided and I got the hell out of Oudja. Your guess is as good as mine.'

The beer bottle missed his head by millimetres and he jumped when it hit the wall behind him.

'*What the fuck, man?*'

'We're dead, Fran, that's what the fuck! Look!' He handed over the phone. Dozens of missed calls on the screen from Spain.

'Why didn't you answer him?'

'I'm in the company of Einstein here, ladies and gentlemen.' Back on his feet, bowing to an imaginary audience. 'This is the genius I have been running my enterprise with. From Spain, to Amsterdam, to Tunisia to here. It's a miracle we have survived — luckily one of us had a brain.'

He snorted another couple of lines and washed it down with a beer. He was becoming more manic by the moment.

'Shall we sit here and wait for our assassins to show up, or shall we get high and do it ourselves — a murder-suicide-type scenario? What do you say, Fran?'

Fran couldn't deal with it. He wasn't going to die here today and he wasn't listening to any more of Scott's coke-induced bullshit. The Boss would want answers but not this fast.

'Scott, I'm going for some kip. Do what you like. You're a dead man either way — I couldn't care less.'

He went upstairs and into Scott's room. He didn't have to be careful this time — in the state he was in, Scott wouldn't be capable of climbing the stairs. Not sure of what he was looking for, he began to ransack drawers. Surely there was something there he could use against him if he needed it? There was nothing of interest in the drawers. He tried the wardrobe. It smelled of expensive aftershave and was home to a row of expensive shirts, trousers and jackets. He rifled through jeans on the shelf above.

Nothing. He was about to give up when he spotted a shoebox at the back of a line of shoes. He opened it and took out a small notebook and an envelope stuffed with euro notes. There was a list of names, dates, and nationalities. It didn't make a lot of sense to Fran until he thought about what Tarek had said in the Café that evening. The last entry into the book was the name Leigh Pelser. Why in the name of God would he keep a list – was it some kind of trophy list? There were also several passports in the box. Different nationalities, different names – all with one common denominator – the photos. Scott's impassive face looked up from each of them. He took the cash and the notebook, threw the passports back in the box and went into his own room.

He was relieved to find the phone still in its hiding place. Two messages waited for him. Both were from Spain. From the Boss.

'Marco has been taken care of.'

The second message was slightly longer: **'Your boss is not answering his phone. He needs to come back to HQ, asap. Make sure that happens.'**

Fran was tired and his head hurt. The messages struck him as odd for several reasons. The first message clearly stated what had happened. Scott had come back from the new town and had been agitated. It was also the same day he himself had made the call to Spain. If the Boss was so against the side-line business and Scott's involvement in trafficking – why not just get rid of Scott instead of Marco? Marco had no connection to him at all. He had seen him in action – the Boss had no loyalties – but Scott always got away with all sorts. There had been a couple of incidents in the preceding months when Scott's arrogance had brought heat down on their shoulders. He always got away with it.

Again, the second message – why weren't the goons on the way? Why wasn't the problem just sorted? Did that mean then, by proxy, that he himself was safe? He was past the point of caring. They weren't his problem any more – his decision had been made.

He responded to the messages.

'The delivery never arrived. It's gone, and Scott is too.'

Then he took the SIM card out and broke it in half.

He needed to move – there was no going back now. He bent down and fished out his old rucksack from under the bed. Stuffing the money and the notebook in at the bottom, he gathered up his essentials. He listened at the top of the stairs. There was no sign of life below. He was jumpy but, at this stage, getting home to his family was his driving force and for that he would die trying.

The other problem was more complicated. He had hoped, on his return to the city, he would be safe. He had traded fairly, so to speak. He was sure that by giving Tarek the delivery he would leave him alone and stop blaming him for his sister's disappearance. But someone had tipped off the police about the warehouse. Someone thought Fran would be there and all loose ends would be tied up.

He was in a desperate situation now but he had one card left to play.

Chapter 15

The bidonville was like a city within a city. Fran had been down to the slums many times but on each visit the landscape changed. Gaping holes appeared regularly where mud-wall huts with tin roofs had been pulled down in an attempt to shield the eyes of the tourists from the chaos of poverty. If they couldn't pull the huts down, they built walls. This of course was all done in the name of progress but it didn't feel like progress to the families in the neighbourhood. Thanks to the latest government intervention, the residents were on the brink of revolt. Every strange face was viewed with suspicion and foreigners didn't go too far without being spotted. He needed to find her and fast. He didn't have long – word would go out on the grapevine. They might find him quicker.

He kept the hood of the djellaba up, even though the heat of the morning made him dizzy. Thousands of square metres of mud, corrugated iron and chaos stretched before him and the only way to navigate was look up, find a tall building in the medina and plot the route from there. He spotted the mosque – he knew where he was going.

He stepped over the stagnant pools of water in the alleyways as smiling barefoot children scooted out of his way. No one knew for sure how many people lived in the bidonville – they were mostly local or immigrants from rural towns, moving to the city for a better life. There was a hierarchy there too depending on whereabouts a resident was based. He was heading for the housing units – the 'middle-class' area. The tourists' first impression of the slums was one of repulsion – they steered clear. They didn't realise that down there it was its own community and network – just like suburbia at home. The difference being down there in the slums, though, everyone looked out for their neighbour. Down there, you knew who your friends were.

He passed the hanout spice huts and old men frying harsha flatbreads. They paid him no heed. The air smelled of kerosene, spices, rust and heat. His pace quickened when he spotted the white walls of the buildings.

There was quite a bit of activity outside in the morning sunshine. Two men, leaning against a wall and smoking, spotted him first. Mothers were gathered around washing lines, laughing and gossiping. Children threw rag balls to each other and the younger ones made mud pies in the shade. It was safe – the children belonged to the community. Old men sat in the shadows, watching the next generation grow – silently praying the children would get further in life than the perimeter of the slum. Others sat and recounted generations of stories and folklore to them, passing them down as their grandparents had once done. Fran walked on with purpose and went inside the building. He tried to remember which door was Mala's – he'd been here a couple of times with Saidaa. Her little apartment was at the end of the passage on the right. He remembered Saidaa in a yellow dress, dancing the length of the corridor to her friend's place, hair escaping down her back from under a floral headscarf.

He stole a glance to his left and knocked on the flimsy door –

he could hear chatter inside. The door opened a crack and Mala's dark eyes were suspicious. He pushed the door back, stepped in and closed it quickly behind him.

'What are you doing here? You need to go. Tarek is looking for you.' She picked up her beautiful toddler from a playmat and held her tight.

'Mala. You need to listen to me.'

'Where's Saidaa?'

'She's dead. Scott killed her.'

A sound escaped from her mouth and her face crumpled. She sounded like a wounded animal.

'No! Please. You lie to me.'

'Listen to me.' He walked to her and put his hands on her arms.

Startled by a stranger, the child began to wail.

'Please, Mala. I don't have a lot of time. Things have gone bad and I need to get out of here. I have something for you – I need you to give it to Tarek. I loved her. I need you to do this for me and for her.'

She hushed the little girl and sat her back down on the offcut of carpet. Sensing her mother was okay, she ignored the stranger and went back to picking up wooden toys in her chubby little hands. Mala was still crying but he had her attention.

He sat down on the rickety chair, and opened his rucksack. He took out the phone and the jewellery.

He handed her the necklace. 'This was hers.'

'I know.' She took it and held it to her chest. 'She was my friend. Since we were three years old.'

'I'm so sorry, I couldn't stop him. You need to give this phone to Tarek. Scott needs to pay for this.'

'Why are you doing this? How can I believe you?'

'Because we were friends. You know me. I must disappear. I am in danger now too.'

She put the necklace around her neck and took the phone from him.

'I will help you.'

He told her where Saidaa was buried and how she came to be there. The weight of the situation made his hands shake and he cried bitter tears for her. He took the cup of water she offered him and smiled gratefully.

'I have something else for you. For you and the baby. I couldn't help her but maybe I can help you.'

Out of the rucksack he took a thick wad of euro notes. It was more money than she had seen in her lifetime. She tried to refuse but he wouldn't take no for an answer.

'This gives you a chance in life now, Mala. You can go wherever you want with the little one.'

He didn't want gratitude for the gesture – he didn't deserve it – he just wanted to do something to help this woman and her child. Money would help.

She took the money and hid it in a battered tin in a cupboard.

'I have to go now. I can't stay here. Make sure you give it to him.'

They heard voices and heavy footfall in the passageway. Word had gone out on the grapevine and fast. He knew that voice – it was Tarek – coming for him. She ran to the window and whistled in two short bursts. A filthy teenager came running out of the alleyway to the north of the housing. She spoke quickly in Arabic and he nodded.

'Go! Quickly, out the window. My brother will take you to station.'

He quickly hugged her and squeezed out the hole in the breezeblock she called a window. He spotted his guide slipping around the back of the bins. He glanced behind him and she was heading for the door. He ran after the boy.

The heat was intense and it was hard to keep up. They criss-crossed unpaved laneways. He lost his footing more than once on the dirt.

The boy had stopped running now and he took him down a narrow laneway. They were back in the heart of the bidonville. Bent over from heat and exertion, Fran looked up and all he could see was uneven walls and bamboo sticks jutting out the tops of makeshift huts. The lucky ones had curtains for doors, the rest had torn plastic. Eyes greeted him from doorways and old men stood out of their way. They knew this boy, it seemed. That was a consolation. He had to stop. The heat was overwhelming and the djellaba clung to him and weighed him down. There was no one behind him. Not for now at least but he was totally lost and at the mercy of this young stranger. He had to follow him – he would never find his way out otherwise. Nothing looked familiar and the heat rose in waves from the dirt. The boy handed him a dirty bottle of water.

The boy spoke again. Fran couldn't decipher what he was saying. The boy looked scared.

'*Rapidement!*' He tugged at Fran's sleeve and jerked his head forward. He watched as Fran straightened up, trying to knead out the cramp in his side.

The laneways began to widen into an open space. They ran up an incline. The smell of decay and rot hit Fran square in the face. The screech of birds was deafening. The ground became spongey and it was hard to keep a steady pace. The boy was ahead of him. He had a cloth over his nose and mouth. Fran tried to pull the fabric of his T-shirt over his own face but he couldn't manage it through the djellaba. He spat the taste out of his mouth and tried to stop breathing through his nostrils – easier said than done when running. They were on the edge of the landfill and, even in his hurry and terror, he slowed for a second to look at the mountain of decay. He spotted the odd digger through the birds and the bodies. Whole families were up there, picking and digging – throwing their loot into makeshift carts and trollies. Women, with children strapped to their backs, worked in teams, old men sat around, deflated from the heat. On they ran and the ground underneath his feet changed again. It became more solid and the putrid smell became hazier. He saw them up ahead and sighed with relief. Train tracks. Instead of going left down the tracks in the direction of the station, the boy took him right and straight over the interchange. They ran down an alley to the side of a large and ornate building and when they came out into the sunlight he was at the end of a platform.

'*Aller acheter billet!*' The boy looked at him.

Fran returned his look with a blank stare.

The boy proceeded to gesticulate wildly, pointing at the train tracks and then shaking a hand in front of Fran's face as if the fingers were clutching something.

The penny dropped. A train ticket.

'*Merci,*' he said, using up one of the few French words he had. He stuck his hand in his pocket and handed the boy a twenty-dirham note.

His eyes lit up and he touched his right hand to his heart, then disappeared into the swelling crowd.

Fran strode down the platform and into the terminal. His eyes scanned back and forth, back and forth, watching for anyone coming in his direction. The vendor didn't even look at him when he bought a ticket to Tanger Ville. He would need to get another train to the port and then onto the ferry.

As he made his way to Platform 7 his nerves were frayed. The sea of faces became Scott, Tarek, Saidaa and even Jen and Andy. He knew he would have to face them too – that was part of the plan. For now, all he wanted to do was get on that train and close his eyes for a few hours.

The last voice he heard as the train *clack-clacked* out of the station was the muezzin singing adhan – the midday call to prayer. The sun was at its highest point in the sky – many would welcome the shade of the mosque. *Allahu Akbar, Allahu Akbar* – Allah is great, God is Great – his mother used to say that too, once upon a time.

He was going home. Home to the harbour.

Chapter 16

Torrential rain hammered against the windows and the wind tried to lift the roof off the house. A distant rumble of waves battering the shore added to the symphony. On days like this, the briny smell seemed to penetrate the walls. Jen turned over in the bed and pulled the covers up around her. She loved this kind of weather, especially when she was curled up and warm with the heavy curtains drawn. Danny was with his dad and, for her, that meant a lie-in. She looked at the clock on the locker – midday. Perfect. A lazy Saturday.

Sounds wafted up the stairs from the kitchen. That's odd, she thought. Andy usually worked Saturdays. She threw back the covers and padded out to the landing. She was greeted with the sight of him coming up the stairs in sweatpants with tea, eggs Benedict and toast on a tray for them.

'Ah, damn! I wanted to surprise you.' He smiled at her and stood with the tray in his hand – not sure what to do.

'*Woohoo!*' She ran back into the bedroom and slipped back into bed. Fluffing up her pillows, she sat up against them.

'To what do I owe this lovely treat?' she asked as he followed her in and sat on the side of the bed.

He laid the tray down between them. He hadn't spilled a drop of tea from either of the mugs. That was a first!

'And why aren't you at work?' She bit a corner from her toast, stretched over and flicked on the lamp beside her. The door creaked from the draft – but they were warm and cosy together.

'I decided to take the day off,' he said. 'It's been far too long since we made time for each other. Dan won't be home until tomorrow so I reckoned you and I could do something for the day – that's if you're feeling up to it?'

She kissed him on the cheek. 'I'd like that, Andy.'

'What do you think we should do today, then? Stay in bed – the weather is wild out there.' He looked at her.

'Maybe we could take a drive up to Hook Head?' she said. 'It's the perfect place for this kind of day. We could grab dinner somewhere later?'

'Sounds like a plan to me.' His response was deadpan.

She knew she'd hurt his feelings again.

He picked up his mug and drank his tea in silence. It wasn't one of those comfortable silences.

She talked about banal things as she began to eat her eggs – work, was the sink fixed, the need to do a grocery shop and pay the car insurance. Small talk was familiar.

'Your dad called down to the yard yesterday.' His eyes were trained on a crack in the wall.

'Oh? Why didn't you tell me that last night? Was everything okay?'

'He only popped in for a chat. Nothing was wrong.'

'He popped in for a 'chat'? That doesn't sound like Dad. You don't think there's something wrong with him, do you? I hope –'

'Jen, will you stop with the negativity! I've never seen your dad look so good. It was just general chit-chat and a catch-up. Asked about everyone … he mentioned Sal and Berlin amongst other things and it got me thinking.'

'About what?'

'How would you fancy a family trip to Berlin? I was going to keep it a surprise but I know what you're like. Next month, for a few days – Danny would love to bunk off school and it would do you the world of good to see Sal.'

Jen was really excited about the idea. She knew Sal would be delighted to see all of them. They could book a hotel so as not to be under her feet – Sal didn't have room anyway. The usual feeling of anxiety crept in as soon as she started to think about airports and public transport. Hard pushed to leave the house most of the time, a big airport or a busy train would be a nightmare.

'Andy, I'm not so sure we should take Danny out of school at the moment. He's in enough trouble as it is – I could ask Will to take him, but I wouldn't feel right leaving him behind.'

'We'll go on a Thursday evening and come back on the Monday. That's only two days. He's missed more days that than with a toothache.'

She could hear the frustration in his voice and she didn't blame him. She was making excuses – she wasn't that anal over school. A visit to a foreign city would be a real education.

'Danny would love it, and it would be educational.' Andy echoed her thought. 'I wouldn't go without him either. Come on, Jen. We haven't been away since Disney. He'd love Legoland and think of the fun you and Sal would have catching up!'

'What would you do about the yard? You can't just close up, can you?'

He shifted his weight on the bed and cleared his throat.

'That's the other thing I wanted to talk to you about. I need you to hear me out on this one.'

'Hear you out on what? What's going on now?' She didn't like all the surprises being thrown at her.

'I'm taking on an employee.'

'What do you mean – for feck sake, you barely make enough to pay your own wage without taking on some spotty young lad! And why in the world would you take someone on coming into the winter? Jesus, Andy.'

'It's not a spotty teenager and, with respect, I run the yard – I could do with a hand down there. I could take on more work and it would be nice to have company. I do know what I'm doing with my own business.'

She laid her plate back on the tray and crossed her arms over her chest.

'Who is it?'

'Now don't kick off, I know what I'm doing.' He took a sip from his cup. 'It's Doc.'

She thought she had misheard him. 'Say that again? For a second I thought you said –'

'Doc. I've given him the job.'

She pushed the tray back violently and jumped out of the bed. She couldn't believe her ears.

'Where are you going?' Andy said. 'Will you sit down for a minute and let me explain!'

'You're taking *him* on? Doc? The guy who played a hand in ruining our lives? And you want me to sit down and hear you out? Are you losing your marbles? *He's a convict. A drug runner.*' Her voice was rising with every word. She felt a surge of anger crawl up from her feet to her face.

'You need to calm down, Jen.'

'Oh yeah, of course I do. Yeah – sure, that's just lovely, isn't it? All very cosy. Life goes on – isn't that what you always tell me? Sure, why not suggest I drop my CV in to Tess while we're at it? Lovely little foursome that would be, wouldn't it?' She knew she was being a bitch, but she didn't care.

'*I have had enough!*' His voice boomed across the room and the words bounced off the wall. He was on his feet, his face red with anger.

He never shouted. Ever.

'What do you want me to do, Jen? Isn't it enough that I have tried everything over the last couple of years to make you happy? I didn't go back out to sea – I stayed here with you – I married you. And you just keep pushing me away as if you are the only one that has suffered!'

'Oh, you're a real martyr, you are!'

'Well, it beats being self-absorbed. He's just out of prison, his life's a fuckin' mess and no one will give him a chance. How's the man supposed to get back on his feet if no one will help? I was trying to help him, Jen, and by me having someone there I have more time to be here with you and Danny. I was thinking of us too.'

Jen took a deep shuddering breath. She hung her head and sighed. Could he not see she was trying?

But you are not trying, Jen. He's right. You are a selfish cow. You only care about yourself. Why did you marry him at all? You need to get on with your life – put the past behind you.

'And what did Tess think about this?'

'I don't need her permission either. He's a grown man. He can deal with his own wife. Can't see why she'd have a problem.'

He grabbed a towel from the back of the chair and stormed out to the bathroom. He didn't even bother to close the door behind him.

The rain banging on the window kept time with her heartbeat. She hated fighting but she couldn't understand why he couldn't just see it from her point of view. Tess and Doc hadn't been part of their lives for quite some time and now, in the space of a few days, Doc and Tess were taking centre stage. She felt betrayed. Tess would have no objection – quite the opposite – she was too proud to entertain the thought of her spouse on the scratch. She probably put him up to it. Doc would be of no use to her in the Tea Room – even though he was a great cook.

Why did Andy always take on the lost causes? *He's still with you, isn't he? You should be grateful for his kindness.* He was a kind person – she had forgotten that somewhere along the way. Doc used to be a kind person too and she had been fond of him – before everything happened. If his own wife could forgive him, then maybe she needed to mind her own damn business. She could hear Andy singing – he always sang in the shower regardless of his mood. The rage against Scott and Fran and Doc pulsed through her veins –

that could have been her husband in prison. He could have been banged up for bringing drugs in on the trawler. The idea made her blood run cold as she imagined herself lining up with all the other inmates' wives, getting ready to be patted down and sniffed as she prepared herself to look at him in a nylon tabard across a table or through glass. Then she wondered how she would feel if Doc and Tess turned their backs on him when he came home. Doc had served his time and she could only imagine how he felt in there every night as the door was locked behind him. Maybe he did deserve a chance. Maybe everyone deserved a chance. Maybe it was time to move on.

Andy came back into the room. He smelled of cedarwood and mint. She knew by the little smile he threw in her direction that the fight had gone out of him. He wasn't the confrontational type and he never held on to an argument.

Before she could think about it, she crossed the room and hugged him.

'I'm sorry.'

He didn't respond with words – he simply hugged her back.

Those two words weren't said nearly enough. From today, she would try harder.

He stood back, and looked at her.

'Do you want to talk about Berlin then?' he asked.

'I will. Just let me think about it, Okay? We'd need to look at dates.'

'Okay. Maybe around the third weekend in October?'

'I'll text Sal later. But maybe we should wait for the long weekend at the end of the month? Danny would be off then anyway.'

'That's Hallowe'en though – Dan's already talking about taking his little brother trick or treating. We can't do it that weekend – the third one is our best option.'

She couldn't think of any other valid excuse to put him off. She couldn't run the risk of lying and saying Sal couldn't get off work or something – Sal and Andy were in contact too. She was terrified of the thought of travelling. It was so unsafe.

She sat in the chair in front of the mirror and watched his reflection. He was still gorgeous. A dagger of pain hit her in the heart – she never told him that any more. She never made any kind of effort with him. How could he feel loved when she acted like that – all for her own selfish reasons? She felt like she turned a real corner the previous night. Things would be different now. She needed to save her marriage.

'You're very kind to give him a chance. Not many would.'

He stopped drying himself and sat on the bed behind her. He talked to her reflection.

'It's only a trial. I have my reservations about all of this too, but I figure it takes one person in the harbour to give him a chance before others will do the same. I'm able to help. We'll see how it goes.'

Jen picked up the brush and ran it through her hair.

'No one likes aggro, Jen. The harbour is a small place – we all have to live together.'

'I know. Maybe it's time we buried the hatchet with the pair of them. Move on, as you say.'

The surprise on his face made her happy. She loved him after all – maybe all this upheaval was the final hurdle to overcome. She would face Doc and try to put the past behind her. Living on nervous energy all the time was draining.

'I'm going to go back to the therapist this week – for a chat.'

Surprise again – all over his face.

'That's good to hear, darling, a chat will do you the world of good.' He stood up and pulled on a pair of jeans and a sweater. 'I'm proud of you. I'll go make some fresh tea and then we can decide what to do for the day.' He walked over and kissed her on the top of the head. 'We will get through this together, like we always do.' He left the room whistling.

He was a good decent man and she had let the events of that night sully everything. He was right – she needed to put the past behind her. She needed to come clean about trying for a baby. It wasn't going to happen. Her biggest fear in life was not keeping her son safe – that nightmare had come true. There was no way she would bring another baby into the world while Scott was still alive. This was the only part of her life she had control over and she was going to exercise it.

The wind whistled through the window, making her jump. She felt uneasy. It didn't take much to put her in that frame of mind. She threw on her clothes quickly and the woollen cardigan wrapped around her like a hug. She ran her hand across the top of her chest. Her physical scars didn't bother her any more – she longed for that time when it was only them she had to worry about.

A plan began to form in her mind. She would text Sal. She needed to speak to Danny's teacher as well – she would ring the school and book an appointment. She could clear it with them. They wouldn't mind him having a few days off surely? That teacher of his would just have to suck it up.

She sent a text to Will enquiring after her son and he answered almost straight away. She laughed when she read it – he was on the PlayStation, ignoring his baby brother. Happy out.

She was relieved. A day with her husband was just what she needed – the weather was irrelevant. She busied herself by applying a touch of make-up and her favourite perfume. A road trip for the day was exactly what *they* needed. It had been too long.

They ran out to the van, laughing as the wind tried to whisk Jen across the driveway, the travel mug like an anchor in her hand. The trusty old van spluttered into life. Andy cursed the stereo as it deafened the pair of them. Stunned by the volume, it took him a second to whack the song on to mute. Turning the radio back on, he ejected the CD. It was a cheap blank disc.

'That's weird! Is that yours?' he asked.

'No? Why would I be listening to a CD in your van?'

Jen had begun to pale.

'Put it back on,' she said. 'I want to hear the song.'

Andy thrust it back in, looking puzzled.

The iconic voice started to sing the opening lines. Her heart quickened and her hands began to sweat. She hit the skip button and the same song started again, and again and again. It was the only track.

'What's wrong?' Andy looked at her as she ejected the CD with shaking hands.

'Are you sure this is not yours?' she asked.

'Positive. It could belong to one of the lads. They used my van to move gear yesterday.'

'It's the song.'

She felt as though the air had been sucked out of the van and the roof was about to cave in on them. She fumbled with the winder for the window.

'What are you on about now?'

'It's the song he picked for me that night at the dinner party'

'Who? What dinner party? Jesus, woman, what are you talking about?'

He turned on the wipers and the lights. The condensation in the van began to clear.

'"Sunshine Superman". That's the song. It's the song Scott picked for me, the night we had the dinner party here – remember? Doc sang them all for us?'

'Jen, for God's sake. Don't do this. It's a coincidence.'

'No! Remember that night – it was the game he suggested after dinner? He'd chosen the songs he thought summed up our personalities and Doc had to sing them? Remember? We were all singing and drinking?'

'We are going for a drive and we are going to have a good day, do you hear me? Forget about this bull. It's a coincidence.'

He put the van into gear and reversed out the gate onto the lane. He took the disc from her and flung it out the window.

Jen said nothing. She was afraid to. Her breath was catching in her chest. Andy put the van into gear and drove – and her fear was amplified when she noticed how his hand shook as he ran it through his hair.

Chapter 17

I woke up to a ferocious hangover and the whoosh of blood pulsing in my ears. The half-full bottle of beer on the table was flat but it quenched a raging thirst. The place was silent, meaning most likely Fran was out somewhere – I didn't care either way. It took quite the effort to stand up. I didn't know what time of day it was – it was still bright outside but the fog surrounding my brain made it difficult to decipher whether it was late afternoon or early evening. I couldn't remember what day it was – Saturday maybe? My phone was on the floor – drained of life. For those few blissful waking moments, I had forgotten. It didn't take long for everything to come back to me. *Fuck.*

I never panicked. I was certain I had the capacity to clear up the sorry mess I found myself in. The job had been royally botched – but that was fine. The Boss would understand. Those things happened.

Fran was such an idiot and he bored me to tears. The loss of the drugs was a real fuck-up, and what happened with Marco – well, that was all just odd. I wasn't sure how the two incidents fitted together but I would figure that out. My guess was they had no connection, other than bad timing. But the more I thought about it, the more I realised how little I knew about Marco's other enterprises. I knew he wasn't in the same line of work as I was – the drugs – but beyond that I knew nothing. I had seen some of his contacts though – dodgy types who didn't look me in the eye. His death could have been at the hands of any number of people.

The coffee and shower worked. I felt sharper and my brain was clearing of the effects of staying up all night. My lip was tender but I smiled anyway at the recollection of Fran taking a swing at me – didn't think he had it in him.

There was no sign of him in the apartment. He rarely went out in the afternoon, choosing to stay in his pit watching movies on the laptop. Fancied himself as quite the movie buff – it was possibly the only thing he had good taste in. I would never have pegged him as such but there you go – people can surprise.

I managed to do a tidy-up. I couldn't think straight in the mess and I needed a clear head to speak to the Boss. The inevitable couldn't be delayed much longer. I needed to put this thing to bed and see why he wanted me to come to Spain for a meeting. The promotion was hardly likely now after the mess in Oujda.

I'd speak to Fran one last time and then I'd ring the Boss.

I was certainly feeling a little worse for wear after caning all that beer and cocaine. I wasn't sure how long I had been drinking and snorting – maybe ten hours.

Perhaps if I hadn't been hungover, the penny would have dropped sooner.

My thoughts were disjointed and I was getting nowhere. Things were bouncing around in my head, making no sense, and all the while I felt detached. I had overdone it but, under the circumstances, I wasn't going to berate myself too much. Where was Fran? On occasions like this when my nerves were frayed from chemical overload, my thoughts were hard to follow. Jumping here, there and everywhere. Repeating myself. It was infuriating.

Fran was really irritating me. He should have been back by now. He was a stickler for his routine in the afternoon and early evening. Maybe something had happened to him? Tarek might have got to him after all but surely I would have heard something? I've said it more than once – I had spotters everywhere. Money talks.

I could have done with a joint. It might have slowed the thoughts racing in my brain. Where was Fran when you needed him?

I walked out into the evening sun and sat at the table under the tree. It was warm but my skin prickled. The sun hurt my eyes. I was agitated. I needed to walk the nervous energy out of me. The feeling of foreboding was making me restless. I needed to go find Fran, haul his carcass back here and find out the exact details of what happened with the consignment. Someone would pay for this and it would not be me. I needed to know where it had gone.

After that, I would have to get rid of him myself. I didn't have time to hire someone – not someone I could trust to do the job properly. I would have little or no problem disposing of him. No one would give a shit about his body showing up in an alleyway. He had the look of a junkie – one that had overdosed. That was how I'd kill him – a syringe full of heroin.

Sweating freely, my body smelled like stale beer – it was coming out of my pores. I needed to get out of the sun. Another shower – that would work. Track Fran down and take it from there. One large dose would do it. Simple.

Back inside, my thoughts bounced back to clarity. The silence in the riad was unsettling. I could hear my heartbeat in my ears as I ascended the stairs – it was racing. All I needed now was a cardiac arrest. Maybe that's why I was sweating so much. I was about to have a heart attack. I was driving myself insane. The comedown was a bad one – the worst in a long time and the best cure would have been a few beers and a couple of lines. I couldn't go there. I needed to be sharp. The anxiety would keep me that way.

The minute I went into my room, I knew something was off.

There was nothing obvious to arouse my attention but a tie had fallen out of the wardrobe. I would never leave a silk tie on the floor. I opened the latticed door and the clothing had been disturbed. I straightened them and then I looked down at my shoes – they were not aligned. I crouched down and black spots swam before my eyes. Then I noticed it – the shoebox had been disturbed. I pulled it out and took the lid off. The notebook was gone and the money too. *Fuck.* I pulled everything off the bottom shelf but to no avail. I knew it was a fruitless exercise but I had to be sure. He had the notebook. I shouldn't have let it out of my sight. What the hell was I thinking? I underestimated him – that's what I was thinking. Where was he? Had he gone to the police? I needed to get the hell out of there.

I ran into his room – not sure of what I was looking for. Rifling through his drawers gave me no clue. He had fuck-all in the way of possessions anyway

A dust-rimmed square on the dresser was the only reminder of the small laptop he owned. It was gone. Fran was gone.

Chapter 18

Fran had screwed me. He would pay dearly for that. I had messed up, leaving that notebook lying around – but it would prove nothing. The sensible choice would be to disappear but where was the fun in that?

There was only one place Fran would go – home to his mammy. Pathetic wretch. He had ripped me off but at least I could put my problem with Spain to one side – I would blame it all on him. He had made himself the scapegoat – the fool. The Boss would look for him of course – no one likes to be stolen from. He would find him and deal with him.

No! I would do it myself. It was all becoming very clear.

The money he stole from me wasn't a problem. I had plenty of it – stashed all over the place. Money was never an issue.

I needed to make that call.

I was sitting on the floor in front of the plug – the phone was on charge. I checked my watch, it was too early for dinner – I wouldn't be interrupting him, even with the time difference. The phone was answered on the third ring.

'*Si – digame!*'

'Put the Boss on the phone.' I wasn't in the mood to relay messages through one of his hired thugs.

'He busy.'

'This is important. I need to speak to him about yesterday. Tell him it's me.'

'Who?'

'Scott.' How dare he treat me like an insignificant servant boy! My name should make him listen alright.

I heard muffled voices in the background and the hackles on my neck rose. Under the circumstances, the Boss should have come to the phone straight away … unless … he already knew the line I was about to spin. No – I was being paranoid.

'Boss is busy. He says you are to come in Spain *sin retrasco*.'

I was sweating. And just like that, the penny dropped with me. He never asked about the delivery. He knew it was gone.

'Ask him if Fran has arrived yet?'

More muffled sounds.

I was a fool.

'He not speaks to Fran since two days.'

'I'll be there as soon as I can. *Gracias*.'

I hung up the phone and it all made sense. Fran, Marco – everything.

Fran was the fucking informant all along.

You stupid, silly, little boy! Your arrogance blinded you, Scott. You had him pegged as an imbecile. He got you!

I felt as though the proverbial rug had been pulled clean out from under my feet. I was on my own. If I went to Spain I was a dead man.

I needed to get out of Morocco and fast. The Boss wasn't stupid. He would send someone today. The Boss called the hit on Marco – of that I was now sure. Fran must have been keeping him up to date on what was happening after our run-in with Tarek. He knew about that too no doubt and he would be pissed off. He had warned us to steer clear of our rivals – it was easier doing business that way. This was a huge fucking mess and now the missing shipment of heroin was on my shoulders too.

I spent half an hour retracing my steps and retrieving the money I had hidden all over the apartment – in the end, I had a holdall full of money. That would be a problem too – but I'd have to take my chances and fly into Europe with a bagful of cash – no one would bat an eyelid at a businessman in a suit at the airport. I gathered up the last of my belongings and stuffed them into the bag, changed into local attire and left the riad for good.

It was quiet when I came out onto the street. I needed to keep my eyes open and my head down. Tarek was in the city somewhere and I didn't want to cross him. He would have his spotters out too.

The heat was intense. I left the car where it was. I couldn't take any chances. I needed a route that kept me away from Jemaa el-Fnaa and the slums. The easiest option was to head for the Grand Taxi Rank and go from there. The airport was ten kilometres from the city and I planned to take the first flight out of there.

Rue Mouassine was teeming with activity. Locals getting their wares and stalls ready for the coming evening. The heat was stifling. Terracotta walls closed in on me and the light bounced off corrugated iron doors, rendering me blind in the glare. I was feeling claustrophobic – the comedown and the nerves adding to it. The strap of the holdall cut into my shoulder. I needed a drink. I couldn't stop, it was too risky. Mobylettes lined the walls where chairs had been shifted around tables and brass ornaments shimmered in the heat. Not a breeze blew in the alleyway. It was an oven. Eyes peered out of the dark as I walked past archways. I was constantly paranoid about being seen but my heavy legs couldn't move any faster. It crossed my mind to take one of the scooters but I refrained. I needed to remain undetected. The carpets hanging high on clay walls and the intricate metalwork encasing lightbulbs near the ground gave an upside-down air to everything. *Alice in Wonderland* didn't have a patch on this place. It was overwhelming. The sweat ran freely down my forehead and into my eyes as black spots swam in front of me. I needed to sit down. I needed to rehydrate. Light bounced off the walls and slid down to heat the ground below. I had to stop.

On my left I was greeted by a pair of enormous, iron-studded wooden doors. It added to my sense of disorientation – I was stepping back into medieval times. But it was a restaurant – I didn't really care past that. Lanterns lined the hallway and a dirty red mat was thrown across the marble at the bottom of the stairs. My stomach grumbled in response to the scent of ginger and coriander wafting up from the kitchen. A bored-looking waiter informed me that the restaurant was closed but they were serving food on the rooftop terrace. No one knew I was here. I would eat first and then go to the airport.

The rooftop terrace provided a spectacular view of Marrakech, and welcome shade from the sun. Canvas awnings kept out the rays and a light breeze danced across the deck. The meal arrived promptly and I was grateful.

I was feeling more relaxed by then. The horrible hangover had abated and I began to think about things in a more logical way. It was inevitable really – I knew it would end up this way sooner or later. I realised now that the biggest mistake I had made was alerting Jen and her cronies to the fact I was still alive. I had been watching all along but when I saw her Facebook profile explode with congratulatory posts about their engagement, I was furious. How dare they move on in such a short space of time! It was because of her my life was upside down and I was bumming around Europe and Africa with the other fool at the behest of the Boss. She needed to be taken down a peg or two. Because of that stunt, I was now on 'the list,' meaning I was being watched for – a criminal. It made freedom of movement all the harder. We had to go to the trouble and expense of false passports.

However, here in the shade it was all becoming clearer. A plan began to unfurl in my mind and it made me smile for the first time in hours. They had all screwed me over – my darling mother, Jen, Andy, Fran and the good old Boss in Spain. He would be easy to deal with – an anonymous tip-off would bring his splendid career to a screaming halt. I knew where I needed to go. Home to Ireland with a quick detour to see an old friend in Germany. After that I would disappear. I had the means and I certainly had the stomach. I was going home to finish what I had started.

I was enthused by the prospect. I couldn't wait to see Jen's smug face when I surprised her. Maybe I would wait until the middle of the night and creep into her room, show her a good time before I cut her ugly throat or maybe I would call on her during the day. I would love to see her face if she went to the school and her darling boy had disappeared. Oh, that would be fun! I knew Andy was working in the pathetic boatyard. He liked to spend all his time down there. There was nothing I didn't know. They would all suffer – just like I had done after I left. Closure – isn't that the buzz words of the therapists? I needed my closure before I sailed off into the sunset. I would enjoy my little trip to the harbour. Then I'd empty all the false bank accounts and poof! Disappear.

The same bored waiter approached my table and enquired if I needed anything else. I ordered a small beer to celebrate my plans. Any feeling of anxiety had diminished – I wasn't in that much of a hurry. Yes, I needed to get to the airport but another hour would make no difference. I went to the bathroom, feeling very good about myself. I changed into the suit – the scorching heat had subsided and I wanted to be ready when I arrived at the airport. I chuckled at my choice of attire – it was the same suit I wore the night I sold the South African.

I returned to my table and my beer sat sweating on the table. It was divine. The few diners who had been in the room were gone. I had the place to myself. The bored waiter was behind the bar, playing with his phone. Very unprofessional, I thought, but who was I to judge? As though he was reading my mind, he looked over and gave me the most peculiar smile before walking to the back of the room. He opened the door for a punter and went out himself. The man came in and bolted the door behind him. It took a second for my brain to catch up.

It was Tarek. Tarek had found me.

Chapter 19

'Of all the gin joints in all the towns in all the world, Tarek, you walk into mine. Wrong Moroccan city of course.'

The quote was completely lost on him and he stood with his back to the door. I stayed in my seat. The only exit was blocked.

'I warned you this was my city,' he said. 'You can't hide from me.'

'I wasn't hiding. I have no reason to.'

He moved away from the door and swaggered over to my table. He was smug. I was grateful he didn't have his band of thugs with him – perhaps they were downstairs, but he had locked the door behind him, so it made no difference … for the moment at least. That said, he did have at least one foot and about 20 pounds on me. He was one of those pumped-up beefcake types. He swung his leg over the small leather stool and placed a gun on the table. That made me sit up. He didn't need his goons. I scanned the room for something – anything – I could use as a weapon or an escape route, knowing that it was a fruitless exercise. There was no way out. I should have kept going while I had the chance.

'You have been a busy man, Scott. Selling women, selling drugs, and of course you killed Saidaa.' He was too calm for my liking – it unnerved me.

'I did not kill your sister. The other elements of my enterprise are of no concern to you.'

'You come as a foreigner to my city and carry out your business and you tell me it's no concern of mine? That is where you are wrong. This is my city and I know everything.'

'Fran killed your sister, Tarek. I had nothing to do with it. Surely if this is your city and you know everything, you know that he is gone.'

He smiled and shrugged. That smug look on his beefcake face irritated me. How dare he sit there and try to intimidate me! I needed to think fast.

'Fran is gone. He killed your sister and he is gone. In the meantime, I'm down an employee and a delivery. I suffered a loss here too.'

He stood up as his features darkened. He had the gun in his hand as he wiped the sweat from his brow.

'You suffered? You suffered a loss? You buried my little sister in waste ground and you complain to me about loss?'

'I don't know what you are talking about. Your sources are incorrect. I do not know what happened to your sister and, frankly, I do not care.' Why admit defeat? Why tell him what he wanted to hear?

'Let me see your face as this reminds you.'

He reached into his pocket and took out a flip-screen phone. Fran's phone. I couldn't see the screen but I could hear the video. Breathing. He turned the screen in my direction and the video showed a man standing over a mound of freshly turned clay. It was dark and shaky but as the man turned in the direction of the camera, there was no denying it was me. I had to give it to Fran – it was a clever move and the one that had just signed my death warrant. I was a dead man walking. My time had come.

'Your arrogance blinded you to how much your friend hated you.'

I picked up the glass of beer from the table and drained it. I nearly dropped it from my hand which was slick with sweat. I reached into my suit pocket.

'Keep your hands where I can see them.'

I pulled out a handkerchief and dried my shaking hands. I didn't let him see the tremors of course. I wasn't going to give in. It would take a bullet from that gun to stop me.

'Tarek – this is a mistake. I have connections. I did not kill her – whatever that video is, it was not me who killed your sister.'

'Stop. And let me tell you a story. Your friend was tired with your lies and your arrogance. I know he was not involved in your trafficking of girls. He was too gentle a person for that. He was going to leave Morocco with Saidaa. He did not kill her – you did.'

He was strolling back and forth, back and forth, with the gun swaying in his hand. He wasn't in a hurry and he was relaxed. It was surreal. Did he even care about his sister?

'He came to me, through one of my many contacts, and informed me of the consignment coming to Oujda. I think he felt this might be payback for what you had done to her. I took it but I was not going to let him get away with it. It was I who arranged the warehouse raid – hoping he would be there. A Moroccan jail is a worse sentence than death for a foreigner. It did not happen that way.'

I couldn't believe it. Fran was the one who had made that call – oh, how I had underestimated him! He was cunning.

'When he realised this was not enough to clear his debt to me, he got the phone to me though Saidaa's friend and he left the country. You will pay for her death.'

'Tarek – I did not kill your sister. Fran has clearly played all of us. That video is a fake.'

'I do not care, Scott. You are going to pay for her life with yours. We will go now, to the place we found her and I will put you in the grave you dug for her. Poetic justice – I believe that is the right language you westerners use for such a situation?'

'Clearly, I have no choice here. You are the one with the gun after all.' I stood up and pushed the table out to allow me to move. 'As the last wish to a dying man, let us have a drink before we leave?'

He smiled at me – safe in the knowledge I had resigned myself to my fate. He knew there was no way out for me and he didn't object as I went in behind the bar.

'Is beer okay for you?' I stood with my back to him and looked over my shoulder.

He nodded. He was in no rush – he had all the cards. He sat back down on the stool.

I returned from the bar with two fresh beers. It was quite the surreal situation. I needed to stall him. I put the glass in front of him and resumed my position behind the table.

Now he laid the gun on the table, but kept it close to hand. '*Besseha w raha.*' He raised a glass to me and grinned. He drank most of the beer in one mouthful.

Arrogant fool.

'*Allah ya'teek a-SaHa,*' I said in response, matching the smile. I took a sip. I was in no hurry to leave here.

'I am impressed with your knowledge of my language.'

'As I am with yours, Tarek. You speak English very well. It seems we have underestimated each other.'

'Yes,' he pointed to the gun, 'but your arrogance has now cost you more.'

If anyone had glanced into the bar, I'm sure we would have resembled two friends enjoying each other's company. We sat in silence for a while. What are you supposed to say to the man who is about to kill you?

He began to cough. I knew he was asthmatic – I had noticed him using an inhaler after our last altercation in Café Clock. That suited me just fine. He produced his medication and took two swift puffs, then drained his glass.

'Are you having difficulty breathing, Tarek, my friend?'

He looked at me and nodded. An emotion flashed over his face but it was gone as quickly as it came.

'Let me distract you by telling you a little yarn, shall I?' I was the one smiling now – not him. I continued. 'Have you ever heard of the book *The Art of War*?'

He was beginning to blink rapidly and he was sweating.

'Okay, let me simplify this for you, quickly, as we don't have a lot of time. The text dates from 5th century China and at its most basic is a book about strategy. There is one chapter I would like to discuss. It's the text on "Disposition of Your Army" – it explains the importance of defending your position, the importance of recognizing strategic opportunities, and teaches how not to create opportunities for the enemy.'

He knocked over his glass and tried to stand up. His legs gave way.

'You should have never let me leave the table – you created an opportunity for the enemy.'

He slid off the stool and onto the floor, a look of sheer confusion on his face. He couldn't get up and he couldn't understand why. He tried to speak but the words were incomprehensible. I came out from behind the table and hunkered down beside him.

'I've laced your drink with a cocktail of secobarbital and benzodiazepines. It's the same cocktail I used on the girls before I sold them but I gave you four times the dose – just to be sure. You are bigger and stronger. As luck would have it, the vials were still in my suit pocket. My lucky suit. What's even more fortuitous is the fact you are an asthmatic. In about three to five minutes, your respiratory function is going to shut down, thus killing you.'

He was on his side and saliva ran down his cheek. He struggled to get back on his feet but by now his heart had slowed, dizziness had taken hold and he was as weak as a kitten. I straightened up and pushed him onto his back with my foot. He was gasping for a breath and the fear of imminent death showed in his eyes.

Checkmate.

I finished my beer and picked up my holdall. A quick search of the rooftop terrace gave me an escape route over a short series of descending rooftops. I would be out and on the ground in no time.

I turned back to him and by now he was on his final breaths. His face had taken on a tinge of blue and he had lost control of his bladder. He was the dead man. Not me.

'Say hi to your sister from me when you reach the Gates of Hell. She was a more enjoyable kill than you were. *Ciao*, Tarek.'

Chapter 20

I wasted no time in getting out onto the ledge and making the short leap over to the adjoining rooftop. It was easy — only a couple of feet between them. Not for the first time that day, my luck was in again. I had stepped onto the terrace of another restaurant. It was empty. I went down a flight of stairs and out onto the alleyway. In his haste to apprehend me, he hadn't brought any of his goons with him — at least there was no one out on the street looking in my direction. The street was teeming with tourists and hagglers. They were like an army of ants, darting and scurrying all over the place. I was swallowed by the crowd. My senses heightened and adrenalin still flowing, I was assailed with sounds and smells. Spices, sweat, heat. The smells of the city.

The alleyway opened on to a wider street — Rue el Gza. I was close to the Grand Taxi Rank. Nearly there and no one was following me. Shabby houses covered in crumbling stucco greeted me in the sunlight, along with the smell of exhaust fumes, from the cars and mobylettes. The sun was lower in the sky now but the glare from the plastered walls still blinded me. Fruit stalls lined the sidewalks and in the centre of the road were carts full of apples, strawberries and bananas. By now my body had returned to a state of calm. I didn't give a second thought about what had happened back in the restaurant – kill or be killed as it were and I had no intention of shuffling off my mortal coil any time soon. Tarek was a drug dealer and a scumbag – I was a businessman. Plain and simple – hierarchy and survival of the fittest. Brains always trumped brawn. I was feeling more than accomplished. I had a beautiful plan and it would all work out in my favour – of that I was certain. I was tempted to stop and buy some fruit. The oranges of Marrakech tasted like nothing on earth but on reflection I decided against it – my last diversion hadn't worked out so well. I would have all the time in the world to indulge when I reached Europe. All I needed to do was reach the general vicinity of the main taxi or bus terminal without any further interruption. I cared little about whether Tarek had been found but I imagined he had been. However, the waiter who made the call no doubt was long gone with an envelope of cash – so whoever found Tarek hopefully wouldn't know him. I needed time to be on my side.

But, alas, I should have known someone would raise the alarm. Out of the mouth of a dead man – he had eyes everywhere.

I spotted them before they saw me. It would have been comical if not for the gravity of my predicament. Two of Tarek's ugliest and beefiest goons were approaching my direction on a mobylette. The small bike was spluttering and protesting under their sheer bulk and, even from a distance, I could see they were carrying weapons under their clothing – what kind of weapon, I wasn't sure. Possibly steel bars or worse, guns. I needed to get off the street. They were like a noxious gas, spreading and infecting people as they passed. A word in an ear – the description of the infidel. Eyes began to scan and I was now in hostile territory, as one would say. I needed to get off the street – my suit made me stick out like a whore at a funeral.

The alley to my left was the only option. I had no idea where it would take me but I had run out of options. I took a sharp turn and broke into a trot. Old men on stoops looked at me with suspicion as I passed. The alley was getting narrower with every step – it meant the scooter bearing the two huge goons wouldn't easily fit down here but it also indicated I was heading in the wrong direction. Back into the warren of backstreets and away from my destination. I couldn't stop. If they caught up with me, it was all over. They would take their time with me and I would never be found. The sweat began to gather at the base of my neck and my shoes began to scrape away the skin on my heels, chafing in the heat. I needed to get the hell out of there, I wasn't going to end up in a hole in the ground. I had no idea what direction I was heading in and I couldn't see the skyline to pick a landmark. A left turn, followed by a right, another right. Had I just turned left? Children were oblivious to my plight as I stepped over them playing in puddles of dirty water. Old women beat on mats. The sound was like war drums. In my haste to put some distance between myself and the goons, I had got completely lost. I was furious with myself but had no time to think about it. I was sure there was a lynch mob coming down the alleyways behind me or, worse again, they were lying in wait up ahead, ready for me to walk straight into their trap. I grabbed a cotton djellaba from a peg on a door and pulled it over my head as I walked. At least I could stop worrying about my clothing betraying me. The holdall was Moroccan leather and common-looking.

I stumbled straight out onto the street I had fled from. Back where I had started – full circle. There was no sign of them but I didn't know who was on the lookout for me. I kept my head down and walked straight up the road. I needed to get to the end of the street.

The mobylette came out of a side street ahead of me and turned left onto the main road. They were just ahead of me but looking in the wrong direction. I simply had to stay calm. I reached the top of the street and I could see the yellow of a 'grand taxi' ahead. *Nearly there, Scott, nearly there.* I walked to the car slowly

127

and an old childhood feeling of sheer terror enveloped me, that feeling I got as I was about to put the key in the door of the house or as I climbed the stairs to bed. That feeling where the boogie man is about to snatch you. I wanted to cry out and run. I steadied myself.

I reached the taxi and jumped in.

'*Aéroport – maintenant!*'

'*Oui, Monsieur.*'

The taxi journey took less than twenty minutes and, for an extra twenty dirhams, the driver was happy to circle the grounds and front of the airport a couple of times. There was no welcoming party that I could see. I still had the holdall of euro notes to worry about but my main priority was catching the first flight out of that hellhole.

It was windy. Airports are always windy.

The airport was impressive in its architecture. I took a moment to admire the front of the building, immaculately white – the structure a giant honeycomb shape, stretching up over two floors. The polished porcelain and the beautiful women behind desks further soothed me. The flight board informed me the quickest departure to Europe I could take was a flight to Munich. Germany – excellent.

I freshened up in the gents', got rid of the djellaba and made my way to the desk. The stunner behind the Lufthansa desk happily confirmed that my luck was in and, yes, she had a couple of seats left on the flight to Munich. However, the gate was closing shortly and she inquired if I had any luggage to check in. No, I assured her – I only had carry-on. She handed me my ticket – booked under the name on the passport I had acquired for myself. The Boss couldn't trace this one as he had no knowledge of Professor M Leggatt. I liked playing the role of an academic.

The opulence of the architecture was deceiving – the airport was smaller than I first thought and before long I found myself in the queue for security and passport control. This was the final hurdle. My hands were sweating as I stood in line, keeping an eye on the burly security guard at the top of the line. An old lady stood in front of me, weighed down with a large bag on wheels and a pair of walking sticks. She was perfect.

'Madam, may I be of assistance?' I addressed her and she responded in perfect clipped English.

'Young man, that would be delightful. I'm not as mobile as I pretend to be, but don't tell my children. They would not let me out of their sight again.'

'Your secret is safe with me, my dear.'

She patted me on the hand as I picked up her case, leaving her jewel-clad hands free to straighten herself up on her walking sticks – amber tops on black ebony with silver collars. Clearly handmade and expensive. Her soft leather case was also handmade and bore the name AM Hastie embossed on the top. This was a lady who was used to travelling and money was no object.

We made small talk as we stood in the queue. It was moving too slowly for my liking and, as for my companion, she was struggling with the heat and crowds. Now was my opportunity. I caught the eye of a pretty steward coming in my direction. She smiled at me – as they always do – and I beckoned her over.

In my most charming French, I gestured to the old lady in my company and gently enquired if we could pass through security ahead of the crowd and could she be discreet about it as my dear old lady friend would be terribly embarrassed if we made a fuss. We could talk freely as the old lady did not appear to speak French. The young steward was obviously impressed with both my charm and my chivalry and without hesitation took the old lady by the arm and pointed to the express family check-through at security. I followed with the bags and chatted with her as she scanned them. When I enquired if she needed to pat me down, she blushed, looked in the direction of her red-faced, sweating pig of a boss, waved us through security and escorted us to departures. My travelling lady and I both happened to be on the same flight and we sat together in companionable silence until boarding. I, of course, employed the same tactic on boarding and we were brought through priority. I would repeat the process when we arrived in Munich. My Scottish passport would ensure no difficulty on the other side. As the air stewards went through pre-flight checks and safety demonstrations, the old lady snored softly beside me.

The plane taxied and hurtled off the runway into the clouds. I allowed myself to relax. I had done it. Got out of there unscathed.

As my eyes grew as heavy as my weary limbs, I thought about her. The only girl I had ever cared for and the only regret I ever had. I rarely allowed myself to think about her – I had made such a blunder with her. I wanted to see her. I had kept tabs. She was in Berlin. It was fate I was flying to Germany. As I drifted into sleep, I was happy to capitalise on the fortuitous omen. I needed to see her again. I needed to see Sal.

Chapter 21

As the ferry pulled out of Tangiers, Fran breathed a sigh of relief. He had got through passport control without any issue and this had given him a boost. He wanted to avoid airports and had figured if he was going home to face the music he would make his journey by sea as much as he could. It had been a long time since he'd felt the roll of the sea under his feet. It made him homesick. He had a long journey ahead of him when he docked in Barcelona, twelve hours by bus to Cherbourg, then home to the harbour through Rosslare. It would take days but he didn't care. He was homeward bound.

He stood on the deck and watched the African coast get smaller. The white houses built into the hill on the shoreline overlooking the colourful working boats in the harbour took on the appearance of a watercolour painting. The mosque stood proud on the skyline. As the ferry gently turned on course for Barcelona, he was just another tourist returning home to reality. He was going home to reality but what kind he wasn't sure.

The fisherman in him loved when the land finally dropped out of sight. It was a clear evening and the sea had a gentle swell. He watched from the deck as the gentle breeze and the inertia from the ferry sculpted the waves into shapes. They burst like fireworks into white foam before being swallowed up and the dance began again. He knew that the tides and the waves in the Straits would act like nothing he had ever seen before but he wasn't sure if he would be able to see it from the deck. How he would have loved to have a look at the bridge! He walked the length of the deck and allowed the saline air wash over him. It was the first time since he left Ireland that he felt any semblance of freedom. He was his own person again and, from here on in, he would make his own decisions. He amused himself by chatting with a pair of English backpackers. They regaled him with their tales of adventure and stinking hostels. A young fresh-faced couple full of enthusiasm and joy for life. He enjoyed their company and chatted with them into the evening. They shared a meal and a bottle of wine together before he eventually made his way down the corridor and into his bunk. He felt like he had already come home. The gentle vibration of the engine and the sway of the ship his lullaby, he slipped into a contented and dreamless sleep, safe in the knowledge he had done the right thing.

Chapter 22

Standing at the boatyard door with his lunchbox in his hand, Doc looked like a little boy on his first day of school. Tess was with him, leaning against her car.

Andy waved at them and parked the van.

'Hi, guys, sorry I'm late.' He locked the door manually – the central locking had given up the ghost long ago.

'Morning, Andy,' Tess said.

Andy half-expected her to lick her finger and smooth down Doc's hair. He looked uncomfortable as he clutched his thermos.

'You all set, man?' He shook Doc's hand and smiled at Tess.

She seemed like she was about to say something but then she stopped herself.

'I'll see you this evening so.' She kissed Doc on the cheek.

'Okay, love.'

'Thanks for this, Andy,' Tess said. 'We appreciate it.'

He could see it in her face. She was uncomfortable with the situation – knowing her husband was some kind of charity case.

'No need for thanks, Tess. I need someone and Doc has the skills to do the job. He's doing me a favour.'

She nodded and got back into her car.

'Sorry about that, man. She insisted on staying to say hello.'

'No problem.'

Andy unlocked the bolt on the big green door and gestured for Doc to step inside.

'I run a tight ship here – I expect things to be done a certain way. I've a good reputation down here and I don't want to mess that up. We clear?'

'Yes, boss.'

Andy didn't view his friend as a charity case and he meant what he had said to Tess. He was able for the job and he would be paid fairly for his work.

'You can fire your gear in that locker and there's a spare pair of overalls hanging on the peg there.'

'Thanks.'

He put his flask on the bench beside Andy's and stepped into the navy overalls.

'Okay – here's the routine.' He picked up the diary and went through it, explaining that bookings went on the left-hand side of the page – name, phone number and brief description. Enquiries went on the right. Anyone that needed to be called was called in the morning and work was completed as it came in – bar emergencies.

'You need to be flexible. Boat mechanic one day – repairing nets the next. Things will quieten down a bit, and mostly we will have the lads off the trawlers coming down for parts. The odd time that means a trip down the pier to fit – but we can go through all that.'

'Sounds good.'

'We need to fill out your paperwork. Do you have any certs from your training?'

'Yeah – I've manual handling and a cert for the mechanics training.'

'Okay, good. I've been looking at upgrading some of the diagnostic equipment. Won't happen overnight but we will see how it goes. If I do that, we will both need to train. But let's not worry about that for now. I'm going to check the diary – you just have a look around and familiarise yourself with the place.'

'Grand.'

'Your first task is to service that bad boy.' He pointed to the two-stroke outboard propped against the wall.

Doc's eyes lit up.

'Those yokes are like gold dust – can't be bought any more so the lads service them regularly. We even get the homemade ones coming in. It's a simple process – fuel drain, clean tank, check sparkies and starter, carburettor, pump, gearbox, oil, anode – make sense?'

'Does indeed. Great.'

'Okay, have a look around and then we can have a cuppa. Anything at all you are unclear about, just shout.'

Andy picked up the diary and the phone. He made his calls but was conscious of the other presence in his usual solitary workspace. He felt good about giving Doc the chance. Doc was examining tools and writing in a small notebook. He looked happy and enthusiastic.

By the time Andy had the tea poured, Doc had a selection of tools laid out on the bench – ready for his first job. Andy was impressed by his choice – it certainly looked like he knew what he was doing. Andy told him to take five minutes for a cig and a cuppa.

When Doc returned from the backyard he sheepishly arrived over to the bench with a box.

'Tess insisted I bring these with me. Forgot about them until I was outside.' He opened the lid and the smell overpowered the waft of diesel. Chocolate brownies.

'I could get used to this.' Andy picked up a square and saluted him with his cup.

'She was delighted, you know.'

135

'I know, man.'

'She just wanted you to know that this morning – that she appreciated you taking me on. Giving me a chance. She wasn't so sure she would be as charitable.'

'Doc, man. I know you are grateful but the pair of you need to stop treating this as though it's a charity case. You had a shit time of it – but you've done your time now and you need to move on. You have the skills I need, and I have the money to pay you – that's the relationship here, okay?'

'Cheers, man. Was Jen alright with it?'

'She didn't say much. She has little to do with the running of my business. She was impressed to hear about your training.'

Doc drank the contents of his mug quickly,

'Right – no time like the present. I'll get on with that service then.'

'Let me know if you get sumped …? Get it?'

Doc laughed as he stood up and went to wash his cup in the little sink in the bathroom, before clearing his workspace and fetching the small outboard.

They worked in companionable silence bar Doc asking a couple of questions when he wasn't sure but, before too long, the little outboard was purring like a kitten.

'Nice work, man. I wouldn't have done it any quicker myself.'

Doc looked well pleased with himself. He was a grafter with the bonus of being spotless while he worked. Andy was glad he had asked him – this would work out nicely.

The morning passed quickly and they chatted about all sorts. When the conversation slowed, Doc entertained the pair of them by singing quietly as he worked.

What a waste of a great voice, Andy thought, as he fiddled with an LED bulb.

'You ever think about recording your own album?'

Doc stopped what he was doing and looked at his mate.

'All the time, man.'

'Why don't you?'

'Because if I made an album, I would have to tour with it to make it work. I'm not in the right headspace to do that yet. It's a struggle every day to stay away from the madness.'

'You could think about just recording it for now though, surely?'

'Maybe. I miss it, you know? But my priority is keeping my head down and getting back on track.'

'Could you do something else – music-related, I mean? Teach or something. Just seems a shame to waste a gift like that.'

'Are you trying to sack me already, Boss?'

'No, not at all.' Andy kicked himself.

'I'm joking, Andy. There's loads of stuff I've thought about. Music was something they used in prison – for therapy. I never got involved – didn't want to, but maybe in the future I'll think about doing something like that. With teenagers or something – keep them on the righteous path rather than making a fuck-up of their lives, like I did.'

Andy was taken aback by the conviction in his voice. 'Sounds like you have thought about that.'

'A bit. Need to get myself right first. We'll see. That's the thing about being banged up – it gives you a lot of time to think. I remember my career-guidance teacher from school once telling me I'd make a good counsellor or teacher. Maybe I should have listened then. Who knows? I'll see if I can survive working for you before I make any career changes.'

'Well, you have successfully completed your first morning. Look at the time – grub. I'm starving. Come on, I'll take you for lunch. Don't expect this treatment every day though. It's just because you're new and I'm a great boss.'

Doc punched him in the arm and smiled. He was delighted.

Andy was fairly delighted with himself too. Things were looking up.

They locked up the yard and made their way up the hill for lunch in the Tea Room with Tess.

Chapter 23

Jen was really annoyed with herself. She wanted to make the effort for his sake but standing outside the Tea Room, her nerves were at her. She could see the pair of them through the leadlights hunched over steaming cups, chatting. She sat down on one of the brightly coloured metal chairs for a moment to steady herself. When Andy texted her, she had thought up a dozen excuses for not meeting them but she didn't want to be uncharitable. Move on – leave the past behind and all that. After the Saturday disaster, she needed to up her game. He was convinced she was overreacting to *CD-gate* but it had put her on edge. Of all the songs in all the world.

She needed to calm herself before going inside. It had been a while since she'd been down to the harbour – she missed it. Sitting on the chair she admired what Tess had managed to do with the place in such a short space of time. The local Council had been on her back of course when she first acquired the property. They were concerned about the 'environmental impact' and planning issues. She kept her word and had restored the large thatched cottage

138

beautifully. From the outside, it looked like something out of a fairy tale. The block ridge on the roof was finished with a scalloped design, matching up with the other cottages along the main street. The lead and glass windows had been restored painstakingly. The small courtyard out front was cobbled. Boxes made from railway sleepers edged the walls and were a riot of colour against whitewash. The bright red door opened into a porch and from the outside, except for the hand-painted sign, the house could have been home to a little old lady.

She stood up, squared her shoulders and went in. Inside, it was large and spacious with a small open kitchen at the back of the room. A door led to the bathrooms, the storeroom and the small backyard. The ceilings had been removed, giving the feeling of space — bare beams a feature — and cast-iron light fittings hung down. Two stained-glass skylights, panes in a nautical theme, added to the airiness. Her legs felt unsteady as she weaved around the oilcloth-clad tables and mismatched chairs — all strategically chosen to give the casual feel. It worked. All the tables were full and it was busy.

Tess spotted her before the men did. Her face lit up and Jen instantly felt guilty. She should have been more supportive of her friend's livelihood. Andy was the next to spot her. Doc was sitting with his back to her. As Andy waved and smiled, she saw Doc's shoulders stiffen. She wasn't the only one who was uncomfortable, it seemed.

Andy stood, kissed her on the cheek and stepped back, allowing her to manoeuvre into the seat beside the wall. Doc hovered, neither sitting nor standing, until she sat down.

Tess materialised.

'Jen, what can I get you? Do you want me to go through the specials with you?'

'I had a late breakfast so I'll just have tea and a fruit scone, thanks.' Her tongue clicked as she spoke. She reached over and picked up her husband's glass of water. The thought crossed her mind to fire it at Doc and she disguised a giggle with a cough.

Taking a sip of water, she hid her embarrassment – her habit of laughing in uncomfortable situations was never too far away.

Doc stared at his plate and fiddled with a knife. She looked at his hands for a moment, half expecting to see 'love' and 'hate' etched into his convict knuckles. *Jen, be nice. Say something.*

'So, you have eaten then?' she asked, gesturing to the plates. It came out the wrong way.

'Sorry we didn't wait,' said Andy. 'You took ages and we were starving. I had to feed the new boy.' He laughed but it sounded empty. Maybe this had been a bad idea.

'Not at all, it's fine. I'm just having a snack anyway.' On cue, Tess came back with a steaming pot and a scone with all the trimmings. Interesting: she was wearing her wedding ring again. She didn't have it on her the day she had visited.

'Thanks.'

Tess stood for a moment and chatted about the usual. The weather, the busy lunchtime etc. In the middle of her spiel, she was summoned by two old ladies. Tess was at home here – nothing fazed her, even the old woman clicking her fingers. Jen wouldn't have been so polite. The young girl waiting tables for the lunch rush caught Jen's eye and smiled. Each knew what the other was thinking.

'How have you been, Doc?' Jen asked. 'How was your first day?'

She felt Andy softly exhale and relax beside her.

Doc looked up and met her eye.

'Good, I think. Got stuck in and the boss is alright to work for – not too much of a slave-driver.' He took a sip from his china teacup. It looked out of place in his hands.

'Well, that's good.' That's all she could think of. It was weird. That was her old friend sitting in front of her but they were now strangers again. The relationship had changed – he was her husband's employee – that's the only way she could look at him. All the things she had wanted to say and planned in her head on the way down the road had left her brain.

'Don't mind him, Jen. He played a blinder. He'll be taking over the place in no time.'

Doc sat up in his chair and placed his hands on the table. He looked at Jen.

'I'm just going to say this.'

Andy quietly told him he didn't need to say anything.

'I disagree.'

Jen picked up her knife and began to saw at the scone. The crumbs went everywhere and she was in a flap trying to tidy them up when he addressed her.

'Jen. I want to apologise to you.'

She stopped what she was doing and laid down her knife. She met his gaze.

'I had a hand to play in all the shit that happened to you. I can never take it back, I can only tell you how sorry I am and hope in the future we can be friends again.'

Tell him, Jen. Tell him to stick his apology where the sun doesn't shine and there's no chance that you will ever be friends with a lying, cheating addict and jailbird. Tell him you wouldn't piss on him if he was on fire and you are disgusted with your husband for being stupid enough to give him a chance.

Before she had a chance to respond, he was speaking again.

'I'm in recovery now. It's been a long road but I understand the effect my addiction and my actions had on everyone. I'm a different person now.'

It all gushed out of his mouth like a tidal wave.

'I can't thank you and Andy enough for giving me a chance in the yard. I'm trying to get back on my feet and this is a lifesaver to me. Thank you.'

To Jen's horror, he started to cry.

Tess had picked up on the atmosphere and was making her way over when he waved her away. He blew his nose and coughed.

'Sorry. I'm sorry.'

Andy's hand hovered over the table as though he was going to put it on his friend's shoulder. He looked at Jen, now red in the face, and placed it back down on the table. She sat up in her chair. Enough was enough.

'Doc, if you expect me to tell you we are going to be friends – it's all water under the bridge and hurrah for getting your act together – think again. I'm not sure how I feel about you even working for Andy but that's not my decision to make.'

'Please, Jen. Not here.' Andy fixed her with a stare.

'Let me finish. You brought us here, so this needs to be said.' Her tone was confident but under the table her legs had turned to jelly.

Doc tore little pieces off the serviette and didn't meet her eye.

'I will accept your apology. It's not easy to do that but I appreciate the sentiment. As far as your being in recovery is concerned – it's about bloody time. You wrecked your own life spectacularly but, if your wife can forgive you for doing that, then it's not my place to hold a grudge.'

Andy looked as though he wanted to nosedive out the nearest window. 'Right. Should we order more tea?'

They ignored him. They were now looking at each other in the eye and the atmosphere dripped around them like sludge.

'Tess and I are working stuff out,' Doc said. 'It will take time.'

'Yes, it will,' Jen said. 'I haven't been dealing with everything particularly well and your return to the harbour brings up a lot.'

He nodded.

'I don't wish you any harm,' she went on. 'I know you've done your time and you paid a price. I just need to figure my own stuff out too.'

'Guys, I think we have said enough now, don't you?' Andy looked at the pair of them.

'It's okay, Andy, let her speak.' Doc was still staring at Jen.

'Thank you,' Jen continued. 'Things will be okay, Doc. They're just not going to happen overnight.'

'I know.'

'But, thank you for the apology.'

He smiled at her. She saw a glimpse of her old friend in there and her resolve softened. As she looked at him across the table, she realised the price he had paid. He had been in prison for Christ's sake. She had also noticed the looks in his general direction since

142

she had arrived. He had enough on his plate without her adding to it. They had been friends once upon a time, and Danny had always loved him. Jen knew he missed him, and missed Hugh.

'Do you have time for more tea before the pair of you get back to work?' she asked.

She looked around for Tess and she came to the table – her eyes darting to Doc and then to Jen.

Andy squeezed Jen's hand as she ordered tea for three.

Tess looked relieved and cleared the table.

The conversation returned to safe territory. The usual talk of work and life and kids. Everyone was a bit giddy with relief and at times talked over each other. Tess joined them for a coffee. The lunch rush had eased and by now half the tables were empty.

'We better make a move, man,' Andy said. 'Get back to it, eh?'

He stood up and put on his jacket. He took his wallet out of his pocket and offered Tess a card. She wouldn't take it and insisted lunch was on her.

As Jen began to gather up her phone and belongings from the table, Tess asked her to stay for a coffee. She declined but arranged to come down another day.

Tess walked with them to the door. Jen kissed her husband, shook Doc's hand and gave Tess a hug. She couldn't help but feel the barrier between herself and the other woman. It was strange. With Doc, she had felt that connection with an old friend – even though her anger towards him acted like a buffer. With Tess, it was different. Something had frozen in their relationship.

She walked into the church carpark to retrieve her car and, by the time she started the engine, she had convinced herself she was imagining it with Tess. They would be okay – they would find a way through all of this.

'Ah, crap!' she said out loud. The Mechanics Manual sat on the passenger seat. When Andy had texted her about lunch, he asked her to bring it down for Doc. Neither of them had remembered.

She eased her car out onto the road, the entrance barely wide enough to accommodate the width of the car, and turned in the direction of home. She cursed herself for not giving Andy the manual. She'd give it to Tess, save having to head down to the marina.

Luckily, as she approached Tess was still outside, talking to a tall woman. Jen slowed down and beeped the horn. Tess looked around, startled, then said something to the woman who turned and went into the Tea Room.

Tess came across the road.

'I thought you were gone?' She was breathless and flushed.

Jen stuck the big book out the window.

'Forgot to give Doc this, from Andy. Can you give it to him?'

'Sure.' Tess took the book. 'Sorry you had to come back.'

'Not a problem.'

With a wave and a small forced smile, Jen drove off.

In the rear-view she saw Tess look after her as she crossed back to the Tea Room.

Jen ground the stick into gear and sped up the road, heart pounding.

The tall girl Tess had been talking to – it was the chestnut-haired girl she had seen outside her house the previous week.

You're paranoid, Jen. You're paranoid. That's how she knew your name. She's a friend of a friend. Or a customer of Tess's. No big deal. She must live in the harbour. It's fine. You're being paranoid.

Her gut told her otherwise.

Chapter 24

Jen was trying to be positive and cheerful – it wasn't working. She should have weaned herself off the Zanax but she didn't have the patience for it – if she didn't do it in one fell swoop, she never would do it at all. She consoled herself by admitting it was a low dosage anyway and in a few days she would be over the worst of it. After researching it online, she knew what to expect and was working through it. The anxiety was back and she was feeling a little bit manic.

Breathe, Jen, just breathe. It will be okay in a few days.

She didn't notice Danny until he spoke.

'Mam, I'm hungry.' His head was in the fridge. He was growing fast and she couldn't keep up with his constant snacking and munching.

'You're only in the door from school, Dan. Have a banana – I'm not making dinner yet.'

'I just want a little snack, Mam.'

She could hear the impatience in his voice. It was like that all the time with them lately. They couldn't have a conversation without it escalating into an argument. She didn't have the energy to argue today.

'Oh, alright then, pet. What would you like?'

'A rasher and cheese sam-widge?'

He was pushing his luck. It was her turn to feel impatient.

'If you have that now you won't be able to eat your dinner.'

Breathe, Jen, he's a child. Stop.

'Ah, Mam, come on! I'll make one for you as well. And of course I'll eat my dinner!'

No doubt he would. She gave in. 'Alright so. I'll help you.'

'I'll do it. Will I make you a cup of tea too?' He got the rashers and cheese from the fridge and placed them on the counter.

'Yep – that would be lovely, but I'll make the tea when the kettle is boiled.' She sat down at the table and unfolded the local papers. 'How was school today, by the way? Do you have a lot of homework?'

He was pouring oil – too much – on the pan. She winced but said nothing, then tensed as he turned on the gas.

'Careful now, don't turn the gas up too high. You'll burn yourself.'

She stood up and hurried over to the cooker.

'Mam, I'm grand. I have done this before, you know!' He carefully laid the strips of bacon on the pan.

'Okay, okay.' He loved to be independent and help with the cooking. It made her nervous but sometimes she had to just suck it up and let him off. She went back to her perch.

'School was grand,' he said. 'I got a gold star for my English homework.'

'Well done, you – that's great news. I'm proud of you.'

The aroma of sizzling bacon reminded Jen she hadn't eaten since a scone in the Tea Room at lunchtime. She was ravenous.

Danny laid out the bread, buttered it and grated cheese onto it. She watched him closely while he worked in silence, a look of sheer concentration on his face. Eventually, he flipped the bacon over to make it crispy.

'Just how you like it, Mam.'

He was a good boy and she loved him so much. She forgot to tell him that sometimes and she had been so caught up in her own worries, she had neglected him. It was no wonder he was getting into trouble in school.

You are a bad mother. You just keep failing him.

She jumped up from the table, to get away from her negative thoughts. Over to the cupboard she went and fished out his favourite teacup – the *Star Wars* one he had got for Easter the previous year. She was surprised it had survived this long – bar the odd chip here and there.

Danny was singing a song to himself while he arranged the rashers on top of the bread and cheese.

She wet a pot of tea and brought it to the table, followed by milk, cutlery, ketchup and a roll of kitchen towel.

'Your sam-widge is ready.' He placed the sandwiches on the table and looked at her with the pride of accomplishment only ever evident on a child's face. The simple pleasures.

'Thank you, young man. It looks delicious.' Apart from the holes in the bread from too much butter and a heavy childish hand, it did look tasty.

They munched away in silence for a few moments, Jen gaping at the sheer volume of ketchup he was putting on his 'sam-widge'.

'So, Dan. It's been ages since we've sat down for a chat, isn't it?'

He nodded at her, his cheeks at bursting point.

She poured the tea.

'You're a good boy. I forget to tell you that sometimes.'

He stirred sugar into his mug of milky tea and stared off into the middle distance.

'Something on your mind, pet?'

'It's grand. Not important.' He took another bite of his sandwich and shifted in his seat.

The hall door swung open and in walked Mr Cassidy – no doubt the smell of bacon had roused him from his afternoon nap. Danny stood up, took the extra piece of bacon from the pan and put it on the floor beside the table. Jen winced at the thought of grease all over her clean floor. *Shut up, Jen. Let it go.*

He sat back down and looked at his plate.

'Mam, can I ask you something?'

'Fire away.'

'Do you think I'm a bad kid sometimes?'

'Oh, baby, of course I don't. Why would you think that?'

'Because I think I am … I love my baby brudder but sometimes I wish he wasn't here. Dad is always so busy and then he's tired and then he hasn't got time to play Lego or anything with me. I wish it was me and him again. And you have been so grumpy all the time lately. I feel like no one loves me any more. Except for Nanny and Grandad. They haven't changed.'

As her little boy started to cry, Jen thought her heart was going to break in two. Mr Cassidy knew something was amiss and he was over, licking Danny's hand.

'Danny Harper, you are the most important thing in the world to all of us. Your dad loves you so very much but at the moment he's a little bit distracted – new babies take up all your time and energy because they are so tiny and helpless – but that doesn't last for long. Before you know it, your dad will be back to normal and playing with you again. You just have to give him a little bit of time.'

'I know, Mam. I feel mean even thinking like that but I just get a bit bored with all the baby talk. He's grand like but he doesn't do anything except eat and poo. I thought he would be more fun.'

'Oh, he will be, my love, just you wait and see. And he's so lucky to have a big 'brudder' to take care of him and teach him things. You will be the best friend he ever has.'

'Okay, I do love him though.' He smiled at his mother while wiping the tears from his eyes.

Mr Cassidy went back to the remains of his rasher.

'Dan, I'm sorry I have been so grumpy lately too. I think I didn't realise how much I was going to miss Sal when she went to Berlin. But things are getting better now, I promise you, and we are going to have great fun from now on. You don't need to worry about a thing any more, okay?'

'Will you ever have a brudder or sister for me?'

'Never, ever, pet. You are the love of my life and I don't want to have any more babies when I have you. Besides, you already have a lovely little brother to take care of now — so that's that. I'm going to go into school this week and have a chat with that teacher of yours about all the detentions — everything is going to be fine.'

'And you are better now, aren't you? You are not afraid any more?'

'I'm better, pet — just you wait and see.'

'Love ya, Mam.'

'I love you too.'

He stood up from the table and wrapped his little arms around her neck. She hugged him tight, breathing in the smell that was unique to her little baby. Her little darling boy. She vowed in that moment that never again would he see her upset or would she react in a bad way when he had a tough day in school or he was in a pre-teen strop. For the longest time, she had stopped him from being a child — all the woes of adult life had coloured her perception. She needed to see her boy being a child again. Danny came first — above everyone. She needed to protect him and start being a mother to him — no distractions.

'Can I go play the PlayStation now? I'll do my homework before dinner. What are we having for dinner by the way? Can we have tacos tonight?'

Jen glanced at his plate. All that remained were crumbs.

'Child — you have just eaten! Go on, play your games for a while and you can help me make the tacos after homework.' She kissed him on the top of the head and watched him and the little mutt scarper out the door.

She cleared the plates into the sink. Checking her watch, she decided it was too late to call the school to make an appointment. She would go there in person in the morning — it had been a while since she ventured up to the school yard. If she left it until the last minute, all the mothers would be gone.

She walked over to the living room and put on the record player. Music was a balm to her soul and it always managed to steady her when she felt shaky. Auntie Pat had instilled that love in her and it never went away. She was the one who had given Jen the security she craved for her and her boy. She had given then their own home and she was also responsible for her and Andy getting together. She knew what she was doing leaving her the house with that particular lodger – Andy – in it! Jen wondered how she would feel now – looking in at them. All the peace and tranquillity shattered by the fallout from a sociopath. Tom Waits was the record of choice and, as his voice filled the room, she let out a sigh of relief.

She located her handbag behind the couch and pulled out her phone. Notifications told her Sal had been in touch via Snapchat – she would look at them later when she had the time. She always had a mixed reaction to those little snippets of her friend's new life. Sal was living her life to the full – as she should be – but a feeling of missing out always clouded Jen's brain. She was stuck here in the harbour being medicated for what Sal's fancy man had done.

Jen, stop – breathe. That's not fair.

The door screeched open and she nearly jumped out of her skin. She stood up and rounded the couch.

'Will you please put some oil on that damn door?' she said. 'It's going to give me a heart attack one of these days.'

'Will do, babe! How are you?' Andy came through the door with a smile on his face and two carry-bags in his hand, one quite large.

'You're home early!' She kissed him on the cheek and made a beeline for the kettle.

'You are very observant today, Mrs McClean, but not observant enough.' He waved the bags in front of her. 'I have presents for you and the boy.'

'Oooh, what's the occasion?'

'No reason – Doc is in the yard and it's quiet so I left him there to get used to the place. Wanted to do something nice so I went to Wexford and bought presents for the pair of you.'

He plopped the bags down on the table and roared out the door for Danny to come down.

Danny came clattering down from his bedroom and Jen wished he would be as prompt in his response to her calling him down for dinner or chores or homework. She carried the teapot over to the table, then found a packet of biscuits at the back of the cupboard and put them beside the teapot.

'Dan, Andy has a surprise for us.'

Danny sat down. 'Me first, me first!'

'No, Dan – let your mam open hers first. Then we'll see what you got.'

Jen was intrigued. Andy took her present out of the smaller carry-bag and handed it to her. She turned over the beautifully wrapped gift in her hands, feeling the weight and trying to figure out what was inside. That was her ritual when it came to birthdays and Christmas – trying to guess what was inside. It felt like a book. The parcel was hard to the touch but with the slightest give in it. She turned it over and unwrapped the paper, slowly, to reveal the contents.

'Oh! It's beautiful. I love it.'

'What is it, Mam?'

'It's a journal.'

The smell of leather was intoxicating. The leather envelope wrap on the journal was hand-dyed and waxed and the buttery cream paper was an expensive cotton-pulp mix. He had written a poem on the first page. It said:

There is a pleasure in the pathless woods,
There is a rapture on the lonely shore,
There is society where none intrudes,
By the deep sea and music in its roar.

'You remembered!'

'How could I forget you loved Byron? I thought the notebook would be handy for doing those wish-list things you like. You haven't done them in ages.'

'Andy, thank you so much. I love it.'

He squeezed her hand and turned to Danny.

'Right, boyo, it's your turn.'

Danny had the paper ripped off the box and all over the floor in seconds.

'Oh. My. God. Andy – this is so *cool!*'

Danny stood up and knocked over his chair in excitement. Jen shuddered and tried to block the images that flooded her mind. The sound of the chair hitting the tiles in the kitchen, the visions of Scott splayed across the floor, covered in blood and wine as they ran from the house. *Breathe, Jen, stop and breathe.* She forced the images from her head and concentrated with all her might on her little boy's face alight with joy.

'Can I fly it now, can I, can I?'

'Whoa, slow down there, boy, we need to charge it up first.'

'What is it?' Jen asked.

'It's a drone, Mam! Look! It's the best present ever.'

'Well, it's a present for you being such a good kid. I know you are a bit tired and fed up at the moment what with looking after your little 'brudder' when you are over with your dad, so I thought you could do with a reminder of how cool you are – and your brother is too small to play with it. It's all yours, buddy.'

'Thanks, Andy, you're the best.'

'You are the best. I'm glad you like it.'

'I don't like it – I feckin' love it!'

'Language, Dan!' said Jen.

'Come on, we need to charge it, fly it before it gets dark!' The boy was beyond excited with the unexpected gift. 'And there's a camera on it, and a video and, look, it has a memory card and a USB stick! We can be spies!'

Andy laughed and picked up the instructions. By the time he'd read the pamphlet, Danny had it on charge – informing him it needed to charge for thirty minutes and they would get ten minutes' flight-time out of it.

'Right so. You get your homework done while it's charging and then we'll go out and fly it – deal?'

'Deal.' The child bolted out the door to get his schoolbag.

Jen gathered up the wrapping from the floor and the table.

'Jen, we can get a takeaway tonight. Why don't you go upstairs with your journal for an hour and chill, or read a book? I can give you a shout when we're ready to order the food. Here, let me take that from you.'

He took the paper from her and headed in the direction of the recycling bin outside. She stood there, arms swinging, and looking out through the glass. Danny had come back in and was firing his schoolbooks out onto the table. She had never seen him so enthusiastic about getting homework done.

'Look, Mam. There's my gold star.' He proudly proffered the copybook with the gold star stuck over his exercise.

'Well done! I'm so proud of you.'

Andy returned and took up his position next to Danny, leaning forward to help with maths.

'Go on then,' he said to Jen. 'Take advantage of us men being busy.'

She walked out into the hall with the beautiful journal in her hand. As she climbed the stairs she could hear them debating over long division. Her bedroom felt alien to her at that time of day. She sat down on the edge of the bed and read the inscription again. She had loved Byron, all her life, and had memorised many an extract from *Childe Harold's Pilgrimage* – that piece in particular reminded her of the harbour and of home. She hadn't thought of it in a long time and hadn't been down onto Stony Strand in over a year. She couldn't face it. Maybe tomorrow.

She leafed through the beautiful paper in the journal. She wanted with all her heart to start making lists and planning for the future. She would but, right at that moment, the only thing on her mind was the smiling faces of her husband and her son.

You don't deserve them. You don't deserve them. You don't deserve them. Write that in your journal, Jen.

153

Chapter 25

No sooner had he hugged and kissed her in the car, but Danny instructed his mam to wait three minutes before she went in. She laughed as he got out and ran in the direction of his little friends, his schoolbag bouncing on his back. She kept her head down and waited for the bell to ring. A few frazzled-looking mothers ran in the gates with their darlings and before long all was quiet.

The receptionist looked surprised to see her. She had a kind face and once the appointment was booked for the following afternoon, they made small talk about the refurbishment going on with the new classrooms and how all the children were growing so fast.

Jen was relieved to be back in her car but at the same time she was happy to have gone in there.

Another step, Jen. The world didn't fall apart and no one was pointing or laughing at you.

On the drive home she thought about the previous evening. It had been the first normal night they'd had in ages. Andy, good as his word, had got a takeaway and they sat around for the evening playing games and just being a family. It was a welcome break from the usual tension in the house. Danny was happier than she had seen him in a long time – and she felt a surge of love towards Andy for being so intuitive about what was going on with her boy. They had decided to speak to Will about it – but they understood it was a delicate situation. Will would never do anything intentionally to hurt Danny and they did have a new baby in the house, but he needed to know how his son was feeling. Will would understand – there wouldn't be an issue.

She reached the turn-off for her house but kept going.

You really are on a roll today, Jen. Are you sure you want to visit her, though? She'll be busy in work – she won't want you under her feet.

She pressed the accelerator a little harder. It was now or never, Jen had been bothered by seeing Tess with that girl the previous day. Her gut was telling her there was something up but she didn't know whether she was being paranoid or not. Her saving grace was she felt steadier than before. The fog was lifting from her brain, thanks to her body being Zanax-free. She knew Tess of old, and she knew how to read her.

You can do this. You are making steps to put the past behind you. You are getting better. There's a reasonable explanation as to who this mystery woman is. Your positive voice suits you, Jen. You go, girl!

She parked outside and went in to Tess before she could change her mind.

There were no customers. Tess looked up from her workstation as the bell announced her arrival. Jen walked up to the counter.

'Jen! How are you?' Tess looked frazzled. It took a few seconds for her expression to change to a smile, but she wasted no time in coming out from behind the counter to give Jen a hug.

'Hi!' Jen took off her coat and pulled out a chair. 'I was just passing, could do with a coffee.'

'Latte? I'll join you. It's quiet this morning – you called at a good time.'

Tess went back to her workspace, busying herself steaming milk and grinding coffee beans. Tess glanced around the coffee machine a couple of times and smiled at her. There was no point in trying to talk over the noise of the steamer. Paul Simon filled the room instead, barely audible over the sound of coffee being prepared.

Jen was feeling calm. She had the upper hand here – she was a paying customer.

But why are you thinking in those terms? You came here to see your friend. Tess was your friend for a long time – isn't that what this visit is about?

Jen smiled to herself at the unfamiliar positivity of the voice in her head. This was a definite turn for the better. She picked up a tent card on the table. She was impressed by the professional finish on the cards – not like the usual flimsy shite in coffee shops.

Tess laid two coffees on the table and took a seat opposite Jen. She had a tea towel over her arm. She folded it and laid it next to her cup.

'So, how are things? It was good to see the three of you in here together yesterday.'

'All is good with me – how about you? How's business?' *Jesus, really, Jen? Small talk? This is painful.*

'I'm actually in the process of changing menus and the likes – downsizing a little after the busy season. The tourists have gone back now and I have to change tack a bit.'

'You always had great ideas for the Gale – I'm sure you will have the same for here.'

Tess winced slightly at the mention of her old business, her father's pub that she had to sell, but then painted a smile back on her face.

'Yeah, I have a couple of ideas banging around in here,' she said, pointing at her temple. 'I'm looking at the possibility of jazz nights, poetry evenings, gigs, that kind of thing.'

'Sounds nice.'

'There's a lot of talented locals around here and very few options in the wintertime. It might be nice to have a creative space in here for them.'

'What about Doc? Will he get back into music, now that he's home?'

'Not in pubs for obvious reasons but maybe here would be different.'

'That actually sounds really cool, Tess. It's a great idea – there's nothing to do around here that doesn't involve the pubs. It would be lovely to have an alternative. I'd definitely be interested in something like that. You could let them BYOB and just charge in on the door.'

'That's true – but I was thinking about looking into a wine licence too – we'll see.' She took another sip from her coffee and pushed the cup away from her.

'What's wrong?'

'*Yeugh* – that's what's wrong. I'm trying out a few new coffee flavours but this one is too strong – it's after burning the feckin' mouth off me!' She stood up and fetched a bottle of water.

She took a glug as she sat back down.

'What did you put in the coffee?'

'Tabasco! It's called a Tabatte!'

'Ah Tess, what are you like? Tabasco? Why?' Jen laughed.

'It's going to be all the rage – these new flavoured coffees. I made it up by accident. Driving to Dublin one day, dunked a Tabasco-flavoured crisp into a takeaway latte – it was delicious.'

'You're losing your mind!'

Tess laughed and shrugged her shoulders.

'Maybe so, but the TaMochas are lovely. Chocolate and chili are a classic combo. You'll have to try one, once I have perfected the recipe.'

'I'll take your word for it for now, thanks!'

'Do you remember the tea-a-chinos Louise used to make in the Gale?'

'They were brutal.'

They both laughed.

'How did she ever come to the conclusion that foamed milk in tea would be nice?' Tess asked.

Jen on the other hand was really enjoying her latte – it was delicious. In fairness, Tess always made great coffee – the milk was steamed to the perfect temperature. She always added the sugar to the milk before she steamed it too – divine.

'I've missed your coffee-making skills.'

'And I've missed your compliments.' Tess reached over and squeezed Jen's hand. 'Now please excuse me, ducky, while I throw that shite in the sink and make myself a decent one.'

Jen looked around the place and wondered again how Tess had managed to pull it all together. She wondered about money. It had to have taken a fair bit of cash to do the place up after buying it and she also had a part-timer on the books to pay. Before all the madness kicked off with Scott and Doc and everything else, she was under huge financial strain. Surely she didn't have a lot of money left over after the pub was sold?

Tess came back with a fresh coffee Just as she sat down her mobile began to ring from the pocket of her apron. She ignored it but looked distracted.

'Feel free to take the call, Tess.'

'It's fine. I'll let it go to voicemail. How is Andy getting on with having an employee?'

Rapid change of subject.

The door opened and it made Tess jump. It was one of the locals, in for the usual takeaway coffee before heading down to the harbour. He was a pleasant soul. Made idle chat about the weather and the peace and quiet in the harbour now that the Dubs were all gone home.

As he left with his coffee Tess took her phone out and came back down to the table.

Something was off for sure. Tess was jumpy and distracted.

'Where were we? Oh yes, Andy and Doc. How is Andy finding it?'

The truth was, Andy was delighted after Doc's first day. He had nothing but good things to say about him, but she was still struggling with how easily they had fallen back into a friendship as though nothing had happened.

Breathe, Jen, you need to leave the past where it belongs.

'He's delighted with him – said Doc's a really hard worker and knows exactly what he's doing down there. He's really impressed and I think he enjoys the company. How was Doc after his first day?'

'He was wrecked last night but wouldn't shut up about his day.' Tess smiled at her. 'It saved his life, Jen, if I'm really honest.'

'That's good.' What else was she supposed to say?

'I mean it. When he got out of that place, it was like he was broken. He'd conquered the drink and drugs but he was so terrified about how he was going to be treated in the harbour. Andy is very well liked and well respected – as you know – so for him to give him a chance, it was like a lifeline. He's very grateful to him, and to you.'

'Well, Andy is a bit of a perfectionist when it comes to that yard, so Doc must be good. I'm glad he's settling back in here. It can't be easy on either of you.' She surprised herself by saying that, but realised it was true.

Tears welled in Tess's eyes.

After a few moments she asked, 'Will you have another coffee?'

'Oh, yes, please.'

Jen picked up her phone and looked at the screen. Anything to distract herself. She felt like they had come to an unspoken truce but she couldn't shake the feeling that all wasn't well with Tess. She was shifty and that was the opposite to the Tess she knew so well. It wasn't just the clumsiness of the conversation, there was more to it. Tess was never one to be intimidated by another person. Something was off.

Jen stood up and went over to the counter where Tess was standing with her back to her.

'Tess, is everything okay with you?'

Tess spun around, startled. She dumped her phone on the counter, rubbed her hands on her apron and planted a smile on her face.

'Everything is just fine. I just had to text a supplier – running low on coffee syrup.'

'Maybe you should try and look in the boxes there then?' Jen pointed to the back wall and to the unopened box of *Monin* syrups sitting on the stainless-steel shelf. She folded her arms and kept a level gaze on Tess.

'I'm an idiot, ducky – how did I miss that? Thanks. Here – your coffee is ready.'

She picked up the two cups and walked past Jen to the table.

'Aren't you going to text them back?' Jen sat back down.

'Text who?'

'The suppliers.'

'I will do. I'll have my coffee first.'

Jen just looked at her. *What are you hiding? What's going on?*

She took the plunge: 'Tess, you know when I came back with the manual for Doc yesterday?'

'Yeah – he has that damn thing on the bedside locker. Spent half the night reading it.' Tess laughed

'Who was the girl with you in the porch?'

'What girl?'

'Tall, pretty – chestnut hair. Dublin accent. Around my age?'

Tess glanced sideways and played with her spoon. Then she stopped and looked Jen straight in the eye.

'Lucy. At least I think that's who you're talking about. Comes in here now and again. Nice girl. Don't know her terribly well.'

You are lying through your teeth, but why?

'Does she live round here?'

Tess shifted her weight on the chair and looked over Jen's shoulder as the door opened and two young women with a buggy came in.

Tess didn't move.

'She moved here a few months ago, works in Wexford Hospital as a pharmacist as far as I know. Why are you so interested in her?'

'No reason. I just keep seeing her around the place, that's all.'

Tess caught her eye and looked like she was going to speak. Instead, she stood up. Greeting the two women, she offered them menus – they declined the offer of food, opting for two teas and boiling water to heat a baby's bottle instead.

The phone was on the table. Jen looked over to the table by the door – Tess was in conversation with the women.

Don't you dare, Jen, how dare you even think about doing it. And don't pretend it's because you're worried about her.

She's hiding something – I know it.

Don't even think about it. You're mental.

Her own phone beeped with a message. Andy. Great timing as usual.

Tess came back over to the table. The women she had served were deep in conversation and there was no sound or movement coming from the buggy. Peace.

'I'd better get going – I've a few things to do.' Jen unfolded herself from the chair and rubbed the backs of her legs. Wooden chairs always made the backs of her legs ache.

It's your weight that's making your legs ache – not the damn chairs.

She shook her head, trying to get rid of the constant noise – she couldn't shut that fucking voice up. It hadn't taken long for the negative voice to come back.

'You alright?'

'Yeah, just stiff from sitting down.'

'Why don't you and Andy come over for dinner one night this weekend?'

Jen got the distinct impression that Tess didn't mean the invitation to come out of her mouth – one of those 'oh shit, I said that out loud' moments.

'That's really kind of you to ask, but you'll be wrecked after working all week. You have enough to be doing.'

'No, honestly, please do.' She sounded more convincing. 'It will be fun – that way, we could chat properly and it can be our way of saying thanks for –'

'You don't have to thank us, Tess. I'll ask Andy and get back to you. Maybe Friday night?'

'Great! I'll look forward to it. Do you want to bring Danny as well? It's been ages since he saw Hugh.'

'He's with Will this weekend. Next time.'

Jen put on her jacket and took ten euro out of her purse.

'On the house,' Tess said.

'No – you got them the last day.'

'Okay.' She took the money, went and rang it up on the till and handed her back the change. 'Thanks for dropping in, Jen – it really is lovely to see you.'

'Thanks for the lovely coffee.'

Jen lit a cigarette when she came outside and noticed the tremor in her hand – she didn't know whether it was from the caffeine or the company. She glanced in the window and saw Tess sitting at the table, head bent over the phone, texting. She looked angry and sad at the same time.

Something is not right. Something is rotten.

'Hi, Jen. Jesus, long time no see!'

She didn't have to look up to know who was standing in front of her – she'd recognise that voice anywhere.

'Hi!' *Pull yourself together, Jen, you're like a giddy fecking teenager.* 'How are you?'

Her eyes immediately glanced at his hand. So, the rumours were true – no ring. He was divorced.

'Good, thanks. Just out for a stroll. Beautiful day, isn't it? Are you coming or going?'

'Sorry?'

'I mean are you going into the café or coming out? Do you have time for a coffee?'

'No. No, sorry. I've had my fill of coffee this morning, thanks. Well, nice to see you – must get going.'

In the flurry to get away from him, she fell over the strap of her own handbag. She felt her weak ankle about to give. He caught her by the arm and steadied her.

Smooth, Jen, real smooth.

He was laughing at her.

'You should give them up.'

'What?'

He handed her back the pack of cigarettes she had dropped.

'Thanks. Yeah, you're right. One of these days. Sorry I can't stay – maybe another time.' *Cop the hell on to yourself, you're married.*

'I'd like that. See you soon then.'

'Bye, Tommy.'

She sat in the car and when she was sure he couldn't see her she lit up another cigarette. Tommy fecking Flanagan. Older than her by about ten years. Older and wiser, and grey and tall and gorgeous. She had a massive crush on him when she was younger – until he arrived into the harbour with his stunning wife and broke the hearts of all the teenage girls. He had spent a lot of time down in the harbour last summer and the summer just gone out. They had got to know each other a little bit and of course had made friends on Facebook. There was plenty of random late-night chatting. Innocent. *You keep telling yourself that, Jen – don't you worry about a thing.*

He had it all in spades – looks, charm, kindness, and money. He had built his empire online and made serious money – and now spent his time giving seminars and talks on all things cyber-related.

Her phone beeped again – a Facebook message. From him.

Put out that fag, you brat. X

She laughed out loud, turned around, and there he was, sitting on the chair outside the Tea Room with a takeaway mug in his hand.

She responded: **Eat my dust. X**

She drove past him, waving and laughing until she realised she'd have to go the long way home to avoid seeing him again. Tommy fecking Flanagan.

Jen, your life is upside down. You are married and mentally you are falling apart. Don't even think about it. Don't be reckless. You are in self-destruct mode. You need help.

She pulled the car over and picked up her phone. Her hands were shaking. *You are responsible for your own peace of mind, Jen, nobody else.* She scrolled through her contacts until she found the number. She looked out the window to the space where sky met sea between the islands. In the rear-view mirror, she could see the side wall of the boatyard. She dialled the number and it was answered promptly.

'Good morning. Sunnyside Therapy. How may I help you?'

'May I speak with Dr Norval, please?'

The disconnected voice told her that Dr Richard Norval was unavailable for calls as he was with a client.

'Can I make an appointment with him, please. I'm a client of his? My name is Jen Harper.'

'Certainly, Ms Harper.' *Ms Harper? You are Mrs McClean, Jen.* 'How does tomorrow at 11am suit?'

'Perfect, thank you.'

She rang off and laid the phone on the passenger seat of the car.

Time to take control.

Chapter 26

Darkness had fallen as Fran walked into the harbour. He stuck to the side streets and kept his head down. He didn't want anyone to know he was back – not yet. He was within spitting distance of home – he had done it.

The key was in the usual spot. He turned it in the lock and pushed in the door – his heart lurched as he was hit with the old familiar smells. Home sweet home. He dumped his bag and made his way into the parlour. He found his ma sitting in the chair by the fire with her back to him, snoring gently. He noticed how much smaller she looked and how the hair had thinned on her head. He wanted to cry. She looked frail and she had aged in the last couple of years. He didn't want to disturb her but all the while he couldn't wait to see her.

'Ma, wake up.' He laid his hand on top of hers. The skin felt like paper. He shook her gently and her eyes flickered open.

For a moment she looked as though she didn't know who he was before the light of recognition dawned. She sat upright in her chair.

'Sacred Heart of Jesus! Is it really you?'

'It is, Ma, I'm home. I'm really here.'

'Thanks be to the Lord above and his Blessed Mother! They heard me. Fran – my boy. My lovely boy!'

She stood up and they hugged for the longest time – both in tears.

'I knew you would come home, son. I never doubted you.'

'It's good to be home.'

She stood back and looked up at him.

'There isn't a pick on you, son – what have you been doing to yourself at all? Come on into the kitchen and I'll make you something to eat.'

'Thanks, Ma – that'd be lovely.'

'Does your sister know you're home yet?'

He shook his head.

'Will you ring her – she'll be only delighted.'

'I will in a while. I wanted to see you first.'

She shooed him into the kitchen and began to make tea. She kept looking over her shoulder to where he sat at the table and smiling at him – as if to reassure herself he wasn't an apparition.

'There were a lot of rumours when you left. Talk of drugs and all sorts, child. What in the name of God did you get yourself mixed up in? I couldn't even go to Mass for fear of bumping into the gossips – sure I didn't know what to be saying to them. You should have told me you were in trouble. The Sergeant was here looking for you one day as well – sure what could I tell him? I didn't know where you'd gone.'

'I'm sorry, Ma. All the rumours are true for the most part. I fecked up good-oh. Thought I was a big lad sure, and then it all went a bit mad. I should have stayed and faced up to it, but I ran.'

She placed a mug of tea in front of him and pushed the milk jug and sugar in his direction. After he had stirred his tea, she placed her hands on either side of his bearded face and smiled.

'You are home now, that's all that matters. Go on up now with your tea and have yourself a wash. The dinner will be ready by the

166

time you come back down. I'll give your sister a ring now and tell her to come over.'

'Thanks, Ma. Just don't tell anyone else I'm home.'

'I don't have anyone left to tell, son.'

He watched her potter around for a few moments and the full weight of how she had suffered because of his stupidity hit him. She simply got up one morning and her son had disappeared. It was weeks before he contacted them and she couldn't defend herself against the poison tongues – his departure so soon after the attack on Jen had set the rumour-mill into overdrive.

'Ma?'

'Yes, son?'

'I'm sorry for everything. I'm sorry for all the worry I caused you because I'm so stupid. I never meant for it all to go like this. I never meant to turn into me da.'

'Whist now, child. All in good time – you are not like your da at all. I love you, son, and we all make mistakes. Go on up now and have a wash. Things will look better when you are clean and fed.'

He got his bag and climbed the small stairs. He was greeted at the top with the burning lamp of the Sacred Heart – Jesus Christ's physical heart as a representation of his love for humanity. Fran had hated the thing all his life. It always gave him the creeps – years of sneaking in home in the middle of the night, being judged by the red glow pulsating at the top of the stairs – like something out of a Stephen King novel. His mother had always been deeply religious and, until they became old enough to protest, he and his sister had been dragged to church in the harbour every Sunday without fail to worship. It was all so creepy and he and his sister used to dread the daily gong of the bells at 6pm – after they had said the Angelus they would all be on their knees clutching rosary beads and banging out the Joyful or the Sorrowful or the Glorious Mysteries. What good did all that praying ever do his poor old ma? She ended up with an absolute waster of a husband and a son that was no good at all. His poor ma. Then again, maybe it was the praying malarkey that kept her sane all these years. She never had a bad word to say about anyone and she always had a smile on her face. She was a good Christian. He was surprised by the fact he could rattle off the Ten Commandments in his head – it had been years since he had learned them in school and he couldn't remember the last time he had seen the inside of a church. The fear of school was still there – if you didn't know your catechism, you got a belt. That was a great motivation for kids to learn alright – no wonder his generation was so fucked up. But then again, maybe he should start praying. He was going to need something to keep him sane. Images and thoughts about what Tarek might have done to Scott were never too far from his brain during the three and a half days it took him to get home – how could he forget he had sentenced a man to death? The question of whether he deserved it didn't come into the equation. Fran felt the weight of responsibility bearing down on his shoulders. He had taken another man's life – by informing on him and twisting the truth. That made him no better than Scott. *Thou Shalt Not Kill. Scott, Saidaa, Scott, Saidaa, Scott, Saidaa, Scott. Thou Shalt Not Kill. Honour Thy Father and Mother. Thou Shalt Not Bear False Witness.*

He felt like the walls were caving in on him. What had he done? The red light mocked him and he could have sworn the face of Our Lord was smiling at him – as if to say: 'You shouldn't have taken the piss out of me – I'll get my own back now.'

He went into his room and found it exactly as he had left it. His bed was made and a pile of laundry sat folded on the end of it. Like he had never been away – the room even smelled like him. Home sweet home. He stripped off the clothes he had been in for the previous four days. His mother was right – there wasn't a pick on him. He had faded away to skin and bone. He looked like a junkie – all hollow eyes and sharp corners. This was his second chance.

Come what may in the near future, he was home and everything would work itself out.

The water washed away the tension and his shaved face felt

refreshed under the heat. He would pick up the pieces. Scott was gone. Game over.

His mother laid a plate of dinner in front of him at the table and no sooner had he put the first fork of food in but the back door opened. He had hoped to have another hour with just his ma before the sister arrived – he was really looking forward to seeing her too but he just wanted that bit of time with his ma.

Except, it wasn't his sister. It was the Sergeant.

'Fran, Joe is here to help.'

Fran raised himself out of the chair and thought about pushing past him and legging it – back to the ferry or somewhere in Ireland where he wouldn't be found. He looked at his ma and knew if he went again it would kill her. He had come home to face the music – it was happening too fast though.

'Sit down and eat your dinner, son,' said the Sergeant. 'I'm here off duty. Your mother rang me. I want to help.'

He took off his light jacket and Fran's ma hung it on the peg on the door. 'Some books, Breeda,' he said and handed her a shopping bag. She smiled and patted his hand.

Fran did as he was told. The Sergeant and his mother chatted while Fran ate. He hadn't eaten properly in days and this interruption wasn't enough to kill his ravenous appetite. He finished the plate of food in record time, stood up, kissed his ma on the top of the head by way of thanks and dropped the plate into the sink. He sat back down and poured a cup of tea.

The Sergeant appraised him. Fran wondered how he looked to this man of the law. Joe had been Sergeant in the harbour for as long as he could remember and had watched them all grow up. All the kids had been in trouble with him at one stage or another. Not an egg could be thrown or a doorbell rung late at night without Joe finding out. He always gave the same speech over the years and was liked in the community for being a fair man – a kind man. The harbour never was the centre of any major crime – a bit of vandalism or young lads joyriding on the back roads was the worst that ever happened, but things had started to change and the lines of the Sergeant's face had become more pronounced in the last few years. He had seen more in the preceding five years or so than he had done in all his years working his way up to the position he now held. The same old thing was always blamed for the increase in the badness – drink, drugs, recession, and lack of respect for the elders. He was known as a kind man but no one took that as weakness – they had all heard the story of what happened when that group of Dubs were down for a weekend and they terrorised old Mr Kiely on his farm out on the back road. They got their comeuppance but the young lads never saw the inside of a cell. By the time Joe and his group of local vigilantes were finished, those boys hit the road back to Dublin and were never seen again. Nothing ever came of it and no one knew for sure what had happened – but his methods worked. Could never be proved either – it would go to the grave with all of them.

He smiled gently at Fran and took out his notebook.

'Fran, I want you to tell me your story in your own words.'

The door flew open and Fran's sister Marian and her daughter came flying into the kitchen in a flurry of excitement. She stopped dead in her tracks when she saw Joe's bulk at the table.

'Ah Jesus Christ, Ma, what have you done? He's only home for Jesus' sake! Did you have to bring Joe into this already?' She threw herself across the room into her big brother's arms and sobbed.

'Watch your tongue, young lady. I'll not have that blasphemy in my house. We are trying to help your brother here – not send him to the gallows. Hold your whisht and sit down.'

Her four-year-old granddaughter Orla looked from one face to the other. The situation in front of her was irrelevant to her little world. She gave her nanny a hug and tootled into the parlour to the television. Her nanny settled her on the couch with juice, a treat and *Paw Patrol* cartoons.

'Can we all sit down, please, and get on with this?' Joe looked at all three of them and they quietened down.

Fran's sister held his hand and cried silently. His mother poured more tea out of the bottomless pot.

'Fran, as I was saying — I need you to tell me your story in your own words. You are of interest to me as you were involved in all that carry-on that led to Doc Martin's conviction, the assault on Jen Harper, the disappearance of Scott Carluccio Randall and his connection to the bigger players in the drug ring he was involved in. As a family friend, I am telling you that the evidence against your involvement is very weak — circumstantial, as they say, and I would be surprised if you were convicted as a result — but there's always a chance.'

The family members looked at each other. There was relief in their eyes but they were uncertain.

'We need your cooperation. You are a very small link in a big and ugly chain and the information you know is crucial to us in finding Scott and the rest of his players. I have assured the big boys in Wexford and beyond, if I have any pertinent information, I will pass it on. If you are fair with me and play ball, I will plead your case against a conviction on the basis of full cooperation and the fact you never had a blip on your record before this. I need you to be completely honest and leave nothing out. Can you do that for me?'

'You want me to be a rat?'

'I want to keep you out of prison.'

Joe sat back in his seat and allowed Fran time for that to sink in. Nobody spoke for a few minutes. His sister went to say something but the Sergeant gave her a warning look. Don't open your mouth, missy, that look said. She stayed quiet.

'I can't go to jail, Sarge. I just can't. I came home to do the right thing by my family and the friends I had shafted here. I want to do right but I'm afraid of that crowd — they don't mess around and I know they will be looking for me now as well.'

'That's more reason for your cooperation. We can get to them before they get to you.'

'Fuck it, I'll tell you whatever you need to know.'

'Language, Francis!'

'Sorry, Ma.'

'Ladies, could you give Fran and me a bit of privacy to talk this through?'

The two women looked shocked at the request. They didn't want to leave Fran on his own and they were also curious to see exactly what had happened in the time he had been away.

'I don't mind if they stay. I'll be telling them what happened anyway.'

'I'll make tea,' said his ma. 'Marian, get up there and make a sandwich for Joe. And get a few biscuits down too.'

In times of crisis, hit the kettle, make tea, make sandwiches. Feed and water the masses. Fran watched Joe watching his family. He knew by his face he wasn't here to trick him. He was looking at his mother with real affection and Fran wondered how long they had been friends. He also wondered how his ma's life could have turned out had she married someone as decent as the man in front of him. Joe had never married, a real shame. Fran reckoned he would have made a good dad. Married to his work in the end – but he was near retirement age – what would happen to him then? *Fran, you have more to be worrying about now than Joe's retirement or his love life. Get your act together and focus.*

Joe caught Fran looking at him looking at his mother and he blushed. He cleared his throat and started to scribble in his notebook.

'Fran – the floor is yours. Tell us what happened to you in your own words.'

The truth, the whole truth, and nothing but the truth so help me God. Thou shalt not bear false witness.

Three hours and copious amounts of tea later, Fran had purged himself of the madness that had been his life over the last while. He had told Joe everything: dates, times, names, locations – everything. He told him he believed Scott to finally be dead but he had no way of confirming that and, if he was still alive, chances were he had left Morocco and was hiding out somewhere in Europe. When asked if he thought Scott would ever come back to the harbour his answer was an emphatic no. There was only one tiny part he left out. Something he hadn't told anyone. Jen needed to hear this from him and no one else.

'Okay, son. Thank you. Try and get some rest and I will be in touch with you by the end of the week regarding a full statement at the station. I have your word you will stay here with your mother? I'll give you a few days if you promise me you'll stay here?'

'I'm home now, Sergeant, and that's where I'm going to stay. You have my word on that.'

Joe shook his hand and told him he had done the right thing by coming home – no matter what was to come, he had taken the first steps in fixing the situation he had found himself in.

He kissed Fran's mother on the cheek and gave her a hug. She held his hand a little too long for Fran's liking. He looked from him to her and back to him again before his sister called him into the parlour.

'Goodnight, Sergeant.'

Fran and his family sat together in the kitchen – all too tired to hold a conversation but happy to sit in each other's company. The little one was long asleep and tucked up in her mother's old bed. It had been a long time since the whole family had spent a night under the one roof. One by one, they made their way up to bed – exhausted from the events of the evening.

Fran was very happy to be back in his own bed. This was where he always belonged – home in the harbour with his family. If he strained his ears hard, he could just about hear the waves lapping at the shore. His lullaby. As his body began to give in to sleep, his mind slipped back to Jen and Andy. That was another day's work. He needed to see them and had asked Joe to keep everything to himself until he had the chance to speak to them directly. Joe granted his request as a courtesy, but said if it wasn't done by the end of the week, he would have to do it himself.

Fran would do it, of course, but he needed time to rest and find the courage to visit the pair of them – and then he would deal with the other one.

Chapter 27

The waiting room in the medical centre was a carbon copy of every waiting room in the western world. Soft, unobtrusive music played from speakers hidden behind rubber plants and the morning sun spilled in through the window over well-thumbed magazines fanned out in a semi-circle on a glass-topped table. Jen hated reading in waiting rooms. What was the point of getting stuck into a great article in a two-year-old copy of *National Geographic* when you could be called in at any moment? Instead, she liked to sit and play with her phone – all the while people-watching. She wondered about the little old lady wearing a crochet cardigan over a baby-pink silk blouse. What was she in for? It was a therapy centre after all – everyone here had some kind of problem with the wiring in their brains. She looked too sweet and wholesome to have ever had a day's hardship in her life. The teenager two seats down from her looked more at home. Anger radiated from him like a bad smell and he bit his nails until they bled. He didn't have a smartphone in his hand – unusual for someone his age. The toys in the corner opposite the rubber plants bothered her too – were they for young clients or the offspring of older ones?

Jen didn't want to be here but she knew she couldn't back out now. After she had considered taking her own life, and after her overreaction to Tommy fecking Flanagan, she had sworn to herself she would make an effort to get better. This was a positive step. She had liked Dr Norval from the start and the only reason she stopped coming to appointments was because she knew she was wasting his time – she was broken and he couldn't fix her. No one really understood what she was going through. She was a failure at everything. She shifted her weight in the plastic seat and it groaned in response. Both the old lady and the teenage boy looked up at her – their expressions so very different. The old woman smiled at her, full of kindness and wisdom. Whatever ailment had brought her to that seat, she looked like she had the wherewithal to deal with it. The teenager looked at her with murder in his eyes. Her palms started to sweat – he made her anxiety levels shoot through the roof.

A receptionist walked into the room and smiled at her.

'Jen, Dr Norval will see you now.'

She jumped up out of the chair and followed the young woman down a long, tiled hallway – she didn't need an escort, she knew exactly where his office was. The click of the receptionist's heels on the floor irritated her and she wondered why she had to wear those shoes to work – she was sitting behind a desk for most of the day – why bother with the fancy shoes? It maddened her.

Breathe, Jen, just breathe. Stop transferring your shit onto the poor girl. Breathe.

Dr Richard Norval was a portly man, well-spoken with a kind face and white hair. Jen and Danny had both liked him from the moment they had met him. She had let his gentle manner and melodic Scottish accent deceive her into thinking it would be an easy run in his sessions – it wasn't. He was very good at his job and nothing got past him. His office was small and cosy and always smelled of cinnamon. As soon as Jen walked in the door she remembered that this office was one of the few places she felt safe – she shouldn't have stopped coming to the sessions.

'Jen, take a seat. It's great to see you again. It's been a while.' He extended his hand to her and she accepted it.

'It's nice to see you again, Dr Norval.'

'Richard is fine – let's not stand on ceremony.'

Jen sat in the leather chair and he took his seat opposite her, the walnut desk a barrier between them. She glanced around the room – nothing had changed in the months she had been away except the plants were bigger. There was a picture of him with a baby on the windowsill behind him. Her eyes lingered for a while on it. It was a little girl and she was adorable – looked tiny of course in his arms.

'Ah, you spotted my wee bairn then?' He looked at her and smiled.

Jen thought he looked like the type of man who should wear glasses but he didn't.

'She's beautiful. Congrats.'

'Thank you. That's baby Ella, our first granddaughter. The apple of Granddad's eye.'

'She's a little dote.'

'How have you been? How is Danny doing? The last time we spoke, his father's partner was pregnant.'

'He's fine. Well – he's not. He has struggled a little bit with the new arrival and he's getting into trouble in school. We've been arguing a lot lately. I'm a little worried about him – he has also had nightmares several times in the last few weeks.'

'Have you spoken to his father and to the school?'

'All in hand.'

'And you think his behaviour goes beyond that of a little boy his age?'

'Yes.'

'Do you think that could be your perception again, Jen? We spoke about this? Your ability for catastrophic thinking.'

'We will see what the school says.'

'Why did you make an appointment to see me now?'

She hated when he changed the subject abruptly. She felt like he was trying to catch her out.

'I'm not trying to catch you out. I need to know what triggered your desire to come back.'

'My life is unravelling again — something bad is going to happen. I can feel it. There's this girl in the harbour — I know she is out to get me. Sal left for Berlin and I feel completely on my own, and Doc is back, he's working with Andy. Tommy fecking Flanagan is back too and divorced. Tess is being a weirdo. Andy is putting constant pressure on me to have kids and I'm taking the contraceptive pill. And I'm taking the morning-after pill after we — you know — just to be sure. It's selfish of him. I don't want to have more kids. I'm tired of feeling like disaster lies around every corner and he's still out there.' Her voice broke on the last few words and he pushed a box of tissues across the desk at her.

'Do you remember when you came in to me first?'

'How could I forget?'

'Are you ashamed about being in therapy, Jen?'

'Yes.'

'Why?'

'Because I'm not one of those people.'

'Jen, you are suffering from chronic PTSD. When you first came to me, your symptoms were getting worse, you weren't processing the emotions surrounding Scott and the attack.'

She flinched at the mention of his name.

'When Danny came to me, we progressed very quickly — that's often the way with children. Adults tend to intellectualise the dilemma — approaching it in a manner that's flat and detached. You have done this — and it's a very normal reaction. I have told you that. Avoidance is your defence mechanism. We need to engage emotionally with the trauma in order to process the feelings and emotions around it. You need to acknowledge those feelings and emotions. Danny did that and he then moved forward.'

'How can I move forward when that man is still alive?' Jen sat with her arms folded across her chest. She didn't like the fact he was blaming her for not being able to get on with things.

'In our last session, I explained to you that how you were feeling was totally normal. You are completely normal and your reaction is normal. Our goal with the sessions was to normalise the symptoms that presented.'

'It's not going to work if he's alive.'

'And that just reinforces the message you tell yourself every day. You are weak. The world is a dangerous place. You are incompetent. You are a failure. How frequently are you having flashbacks or nightmares?'

His gaze was intense. Jen didn't like this scrutiny. She shouldn't have come back – it was a mistake.

'Judging by your body language – you feel as though you made the wrong decision coming back.'

She shifted awkwardly in her chair and tried to remember back to her psychology degree days, what signs he was looking out for. She planted her two feet on the floor, pushed her ass into the back of the chair and made her shoulders relax.

'Nice try.'

He laughed and she joined in. He knew her well.

'How about this then?' he said. 'We will go back to the points you raised in a moment. Let's go back and look at the triggers and we can deal with them one by one. Have you been down onto the strand yet?'

'No.'

'Okay. Have you been out of the house much?'

'No.'

'Are you working or engaged in any kind of community activity?'

'No.'

'Are you still taking your medication?'

'No.'

'Are you sleeping?'

'Most of the time. I get a lot of nightmares though.'

'Would it be fair to assume you feel the world is a very dangerous place and that you failed your son?'

'Yes.'

'Would it also be safe to assume that's why you take the contraceptive and the morning-after pill – absolutely ensuring you don't have any other children – hence, not having the responsibility of protecting them in this dangerous world?'

'Yes, absolutely.'

'Is it safe to assume you blame Andy for the attack?'

'What? No – that wasn't his fault really.'

'Does Andy know you are taking the pill?'

'No.'

'Does he believe you are actively trying for a baby?'

'Yes. Actually – we haven't – you know – in a while but he doesn't know about the contraceptives.'

'You believe he should have protected you and Danny from Scott. You mentioned in a previous session that if he had listened to his former wife Sharon, she would still be alive and you would never have met Scott.'

'Did I say that? I was angry with him at the time but Andy is a very good man – he is a good father to Danny and a good husband.'

'Are you punishing him for not protecting Danny by not having more children?'

'What? No – of course not.'

'You have made the decision not to have more children. You haven't discussed it with your husband. Of course, ultimately it's your own choice but how will your husband feel if he knows he will never have a son or a daughter of his own?'

He stood up and opened the little window behind him. He walked over to the water cooler and poured two glasses – he placed one in front of her and sat back down with the other.

Jen didn't know how to answer the question. He was the only person she had mentioned it to besides Tess and now that he had said it all out loud, she could see what a mammoth decision it really was.

'I haven't discussed it with him. It's not really a joint decision.'

'Do you think that behaviour is fair?'

'It's my body. My choice.'

'That is correct. I'm just curious to know if this was discussed before you got married.'

'Things change. People change. I'm entitled to change my mind.'

'And if Andy left you because of this – would that be a sacrifice you would be willing to make?'

'Maybe.'

'Will you consider the possibility that this behaviour is a direct result of your learned behaviour since the trauma and the avoidance techniques you use all the time?'

'Hmmm – I dunno.'

'Okay. And where does Tommy fecking Flanagan fit into all this? You do realise you have never called him by any other name?' He chuckled at this.

'He's a handsome distraction. He makes me feel good about myself.'

'So you would never actively pursue him then?'

Jen blushed. If anyone knew the thoughts she was having about him, she would be arrested. But she was also an adult and could easily exercise restraint. Fantasies were allowed. Once they stayed that way they were harmless.

'Gosh, no. I'm married.' She pointed to her wedding ring and twirled it around as though she was checking it would not fall off.

'This attraction to him isn't just a mechanism to secretly hurt Andy then? He's just a distraction from all the negativity in your life now?'

'We all need distractions, Doctor.'

'Yes, indeed we do but distractions can cause accidents. Remember that. Tell me about Tess and Doc.'

'They are in the harbour, getting on with things and expecting me to do the same.'

'Is that an unreasonable expectation for them to have?'

'Every time I look at Tess or Doc, I'm reminded that they did just that — they got on with it and I can't. I can't get on with it while he's still out there. He will come back, you know, and kill all of us. I know he will and no one believes me — again. You all think I'm mad. I'm not. I'll get over this when I know he's dead — not a moment sooner.'

It was her turn to get up out of the seat and walk over to the cooler — walk anywhere. She couldn't look at him — they all thought she was mad and no one understood how she was feeling.

'Need I remind you Doc spent time in prison and you mentioned Tess has a new business — so her beloved pub is gone. That's a lot for one couple to deal with.' He sat up straight and looked at her empty chair.

'You tell me, Doctor. How am I supposed to reduce my unrealistic expectations of harm as you would put it, when he told me he would come back for me and my boy? How am I supposed to deal with that, put the past behind me, engage emotionally with the experience — thus kicking in my natural processing mechanism that's so obviously out of kilter. You are not the only one here that can research PTSD or whatever the hell you want to label me with. I have read reams on the thing and the one question that keeps cropping up in my mind is this: how am I supposed to feel safe when he is still out there?'

'Do you not think that's a normal reaction to what you have been through? Come, sit down, Jen.'

His tone was so gentle and so caring that she did as she was bid and sat back down in the chair.

'I don't think there's anything normal about me.' She put her head in her hands and started to cry. Quiet tears — a release from the anger she had just felt. 'I'll be happy when he's dead.'

'Jen, I want you to do several things for me. Firstly, I would like you to come back in for another session next week. We had started our PE therapy sessions the last time but you stopped coming. I think we should pick up from where we left off. Secondly, I would like you to do a little bit of homework for me. Avoidance is something you are very good at and this is impeding your recovery. I need you to start dealing with your triggers and working through them and I would like you to start with a visit to Stony Strand for half an hour. Alone.'

'I haven't been on the strand since it happened.'

'I know you haven't. That's exactly why I want you to go. That's the place with the strongest associative connections for you. You have got past the association with the house – you told me yourself you can deal with the flashbacks now. You need to challenge the ways in which the trauma has coloured your thoughts, beliefs and expectations. My mobile number is on this card. You can call me if you need me when you are there. I think you need to do this, Jen, I really do. Then we can discuss the next step in the process.'

Jen was still looking at the floor. Her legs were shaking at the idea of going down there – back to the place where he had nearly killed her. Was that really a good idea?

'I want you to consider this for a moment before we go. Every victim of a trauma I see in here wishes the same thing that you do – they want their assailant dead, as that way they wouldn't be frightened any more. You need to kill the monster in your head, Jen, otherwise he has won. Please let me help you do that.'

Chapter 28

It's rather amusing how quickly one acclimatises to an area or a situation. I had grown very accustomed to Marrakech and now that I was in Berlin the differences were striking. I didn't miss Africa one little bit – walking there felt like wading through porridge. Here, the air was light and clean, although it was quite a few degrees cooler and I was yet to get used to the change in temperature. But, boy, had I missed the scantily clad girls with their beautiful bosoms on show everywhere I looked! Ah, yes, it was good to be back in Europe – no morals, no modesty. There were all sorts of offerings in the terminal, tall, short, fat, thin, dark, light, Asian – a real feast for the eyes but mine were drawn to the milky-white limbs and the Arian look of the *Deutche Mädchen*.

Munich wasn't anything to write home about. I booked into a stylish hotel when I arrived on Saturday night and slept soundly until late on Sunday evening. I cursed myself as I was eager to get to Berlin – but then I realised that I needed a couple of days to wind down and get the Marrakech experience out of my blood and my head before meeting Sal. I needed to focus on her now. Besides, no one knew where I was and no one could find me. I embraced the freedom of that and luxuriated in the feeling. What was the hurry?

So I spent the next two days relaxing, absorbing the ambience of a European city again, sitting outside cafés drinking and watching the women go by. Tempting though they were, I didn't try to make contact with any of them — it was enough to look. I also spent time hopping around the city buying supplies and pre-pay cards to hide some of the cash.

I took the nine-hour train journey to Berlin on Tuesday night. I slept for most of the journey though Das Hinterland — little did I care for history or landmarks — I needed sleep. In any case, on an overnight journey I would have seen little of interest.

I arrived into the Berlin Hauptbahnhof bright and early on Wednesday morning. It goes without saying the Germans know how to build things — this was a glass-and-steel work of art. Slick, clean, and oh so German.

I was feeling positively rested and cheerful as I sat outside the terminal in the morning air and planned out my day — just like any other tourist reading a street map while sipping on a coffee.

The excitement about seeing Sal fluttered in the out of my stomach. I was sure she would be delighted to see me too. There might be a disagreement over the little incident with her friend but she did know us both well and she would understand where I was coming from with Jen. Sal idolised me and if I hadn't slept with that awful Clara woman, perhaps now I would be here in Berlin with Sal. My line of work was one that could be taken all over the world. It was big business everywhere. But I was getting ahead of myself — scanning the crowd for spotters and touts — an occupational hazard. Find them, you have your foot in the door and you can work your way up the chain — all you need is a contact and plenty of cash.

Anyway, I digress. I was getting into character, playing the part of the tourist and I was enjoying it. I drew the line at sandals.

However, I was dressed appropriately. Good walking boots, three-quarter-length khakis, a linen shirt. To complete the look – a new pair of Rayban Clubmasters. I had replaced my cumbersome holdall with a tidier rucksack and a disposable mobile phone – for those just-in-case moments. I had the good fortune to wander into the Turkish Quarter while in Munich and I had them work their magic on the beard. I wanted to keep it – it was a good camouflage. That, added to the fact it suited me and hid the scar on my face which you could barely see. It was only here I noticed how dark my skin was. I was pale over there but, here, I really did look like a foreigner. I wondered if she would recognise me at all. That remained to be seen.

Mathematically competent and good with a map, I estimated it was just over an hour's walk to the Mondlicht Gallery on Liegnitzer Straße.

My scouts back in Ireland constantly drip-fed information about all my former friends. That said, people never ceased to amaze me when it came to their online activity. For obvious reasons, it had been quite some time since I took to Facebook under my own name but, under airy-fairy pseudonyms, I was on most of the social-media platforms. The lack of attention to privacy settings on their accounts made it very easy for me to piece together all the information I needed about any one of them. Yes, it is easy enough to find out about where someone works but I also knew where Sal lived – she was forever on that damn *Facebook Live*, on her business page, and had led me right to her front door. She lived in Neukölln – that's a big place but I also knew her apartment block was sandwiched between a pastry shop and a pharmacy. I knew the names of both, thanks to her videos and her constant updates. There were about four apartments in the building, judging by the size of it. Piece of cake.

It was a little early to make my way down to see her. I knew she met her friends twice a week in Lagari, a restaurant on Pfluger-Straße and today just happened to be one of the days. Perhaps I would surprise her there or maybe I would wait for her outside the apartment. I would just have to see what the day would bring.

It was no wonder the Germans liked to start their day with sweet pastry. One Splitterbrötchen pastry and milky coffee later, I was ready to take on the world. First stop was Tiergarten - Berlin's most popular inner-city park. A nice walk in the park to purge my lungs of the last of the Moroccan air – it had been a long time since I walked on lush green grass. After that – on to see Sal. This was going to be a delightful day – whether she liked it or not.

I reached my desired location – irritated. I had misjudged the sheer size of Tiergarten and spent longer than I should have trying to navigate my way out of the maze. It was nice for ten minutes – after that I quickly became bored. Too much green and too many families with their snot-nosed kids screaming and bawling all over the place.

Liegnitzer Straße was ugly. Graffiti assaulted the steel shutters and half the area was hidden behind metal arms of scaffolding and plastic sheets flapping in the breeze. Apartment blocks lined up on either side of the cobbled road and the so-called flowerbeds were akin to post-apocalyptic art instillations – maybe that was the point. Trees lined the avenue too – their trunks deformed. The smog and carbon monoxide seemed to have done a number on them. Nothing about this area of Berlin appealed to me – aside from a nightclub called Loftus Hall – that made me smile and think of good old Wexford. Somehow, I think the Loftus Hall here in Berlin was more haunted with lost souls than the one that kept watch over the lighthouse back home. Large and obnoxious dome-shaped bins dominated the sidewalks – not immune from the devastation of spray paint either. How in the name of art was this area a suitable venue for a gallery? I was disappointed with Sal's decision – I had believed in her and thought beauty appealed to her artist's eye.

But I shouldn't have doubted her. In a sea of industriousness and seventies-style apartment blocks, the Mondlicht Gallery was a welcome relief – visually at least. The walls were painted snow-white with black signage on the façade. Understated and slick – totally out of place here.

A small café was located on the other side of the street – with outside seating. Reluctant to disturb her in her place of work, I sauntered over to it. I swiftly made my way to a seat beside another flowerbox and ordered a cold drink. I needed an opportunity to sit after all the tramping around. The street was quiet – those persons responsible for the scaffolding and what-not must have been on lunch. I was glad. I didn't want to have to deal with the noise of hammers and drills.

The window of the gallery was in clear view. In the shadows, I saw two figures. One a lot taller and broader than the other. One male and one female. The tiny shape in the back of the room had to be her. I would wait until she came out onto the street.

I took a sip from the glass and reached over to the table beside me for a paper. *Die Welt*. I did not speak the language but I chuckled to myself as I sat there peering over it – I was certainly getting into character again – this time, not the tourist but the sleuth. Maybe I should have bought a hat? No, too cliché.

The door of the gallery swung open and there she was – laughing out loud at something the man had said to her. She hadn't changed much. Her hair was shorter but she still carried a handbag that was nearly as big as her. She looked radiant. The city suited her – she had always said she wanted to move to a big city. The rural life never was her thing. The man she was with needed a shower – his clothes were rumpled as though he had slept in them and dreadlocks hung down his back, resting on a dirty woollen cardigan.

They passed by and didn't give me a second glance. I drained my drink, threw some money on the table and set off in pursuit – paper under my arm and headphones completed the look. They weren't plugged into anything other than my pocket. I was just another pedestrian, out walking at lunchtime.

They weren't too far ahead and were still laughing. Without warning, she took the man's hand. He lifted hers up and kissed it.

They were lovers and, as they walked, their intertwined hands swung between them like a pendulum. This was not part of the plan at all. She hadn't mentioned anywhere online that she had a boyfriend. They were too comfortable-looking for it to have been a one-night stand and why the hell would he be in her place of work if that were the case? No, no, no. This was a relationship. What did I expect? Did I think she was going to wait for me? I hadn't contacted her. Things would change once she saw me. She was mine, not his.

By now we had taken a left onto a long street and were heading in the direction of the canal. A quick check of the street map told me we were on the right route to her usual restaurant. At least this street got more aesthetically pleasing as I followed them along it. I had to avert my eyes from their carry-on. What was happening to Sal? She was worth so much more than that. They didn't look good together – mismatched.

The strong waft of the Landwehr canal rose to greet me. We were close to the bridge now and then it wouldn't be too far. I hoped the restaurant was big enough for me to sit unnoticed and observe them, until I decided on the best course of action. He was a fly in the ointment but flies are easily exterminated.

The street at the foot of the small bridge was more in keeping with what I had expected from Berlin. Bicycles were commonplace here and the architecture was more what I had imagined. It was pretty and it lifted my mood.

They stopped at the bridge and he kissed her. I was close enough to hear them speak to each other but, unfortunately for me, they were speaking in German. He was laughing again at something she said. It was getting tedious – but then he turned left and strode off down the street.

She continued over the bridge.

I decided not to stop her on the street, preferring to wait until we got to the restaurant. Then we could talk.

She moved like a woman without a care in the world – head up, greeting passers-by as they met. A couple of times she stopped at vendors' booths – they knew her of course and at the last one she bought a bottle of water and the paper. Would she purchase a paper if she was meeting someone for lunch? Maybe not.

She disappeared through the door of a small building located on the corner of the street. The place was very cool – painted orange with artwork and leather seating outside. It was smaller than I expected but I was confident she wouldn't recognise me until I was ready to reveal myself to her. The sunglasses helped.

She took a seat with her back to the window and I went to a seat in the opposite corner of the room. She chatted with the staff before placing an order for Tex Mex Eggs Benedict with a small glass of white wine. I ordered the same. On inspection I saw, behind a curtained-off area, a small stage. A live music venue and a bohemian restaurant. She probably met that loafer here – it looked like somewhere he would be comfortable smoking hand-rolled cigarettes and drinking herbal tea. I picked up the paper and took off my glasses. I watched her for a while – no one joined her. She glanced in my general direction but showed no signs of recognition. I went back to my paper and tried to look uninterested.

Now wasn't the right time to confront her. Not here – not like this. Her friends could come in at any time. I needed her undivided attention – in her home, one on one. All I needed now were the keys. How I was going to acquire them was another question.

I pondered this over lunch. She ordered a coffee after her meal. I followed suit and twenty minutes later we were back on the street. I needed to get close to her in a crowd.

My opportunity came ten minutes later when she turned into a busy shopping centre – the playground for professional thieves and pickpockets. Pickpockets that were easy to spot, and to buy, if you knew what you were looking for. They hung out in groups and the particular gang I spotted were using the old distraction chestnut: the girl dropped her bag, everyone rushed to help and the gang of boys went in for the kill while the tourists were helping the poor dame.

I made contact, pointed her out and offered the ringleader 50 euro to deliver her keys to me. He took one look and smiled, knowing it would be the easiest job he'd have all day. He also knew I wasn't the law – these guys had a sixth sense for danger.

From where we were, we could see her huge handbag wide open with rolled prints sticking up like periscopes. Sal always was one of those 'trust the universe' types. She never saw bad in the world.

Shortly thereafter and 50 quid lighter, I was on the underground, headed in the direction of Neukölln – her home. If her crusty boyfriend was there, well, I would just have to deal with that problem. Her apartment was easy to find. I took the keys out of my pocket and opened the front door. The lobby area was empty and I was right in my estimation of only four apartments. The letterboxes had names and corresponding numbers on them. Really? Could it have been easier? I took the flight of stairs in strides and knocked on the door of apartment No 3. No answer. Good.

The key turned silently in the lock and I stepped into her space. A home takes on a strange stillness when the occupant is not there. It's like being in the eye of a hurricane – the silence rushes at you from all corners of the building – silent save the sound of a dripping tap or a ticking clock. Smells also rush at you – in this instance, I smelt art. Linseed, turpentine, and the distinctive smell of chalk. The passageway was small and rectangular with four doors. Two to my left, one to my right and one straight in front of me at the end of the hallway. The corridor was almost bare except for a coat-stand laden down with articles of clothing and a stool supporting a lamp.

The door to my immediate left was ajar. I pushed it open. Her bedroom. Small and functional, it looked as though she had been burgled. The bed was unmade and her clothes were all over both the floor and the back of a small chair beside her dressing table. I sat on the chair for a moment and picked up bottles of lotion and potion. Nothing fancy – practical. Swiping at mounds of fabric, I was relieved to see they were all women's – she lived here alone. A stack of books lay on her bedside locker, balancing precariously. The classics of course – Steinbeck, Woolf, Keats, and a stack of detective novels. Beside them lay a smaller pile of notebooks – her journals. I scanned through them, looking for anything familiar. Names jumped off the page and, as I got further back in date, the passages made sense – familiar names, places. All these feelings about moving away, missing friends, the harbour. No mention of me. I was certain there had to be older diaries there, and a lot of entries about yours truly but a search of the room proved fruitless. I made her bed for her.

Beside her bedroom, a small bathroom – nothing much to see in there. Women's hygiene products, painkillers, shampoo – nothing exciting. No uppers, no downers.

The room opposite was far more interesting and I gleaned more about her mental state than I could have from any diary. I was in her studio. The lighting was fantastic, thanks to two large skylights that practically took over the pitched roof. Her workspace stretched along the far wall and her work was everywhere. Oils, charcoal, watercolours. The charcoal drawings drew me in. They were all on the same theme – a beach in the background and either a woman or a child with various weapons in hand standing over a male. They were angry and they were brilliant – two guesses as to the subjects of each. My favourite was the one of the child with what looked like a scimitar in his hands, poised and ready to disembowel the man on the ground. It appealed to me – it was the only drawing in which the man's eyes were open. They were a piercing blue and it was the only colour in the piece. I was flattered she remembered. Photos covered a large corkboard on the end wall and I was greeted with smiling faces and a landscape I hadn't seen in a long time. All of them were there, smiling happy faces – on the beach, in the pub, on the pier. Her going-away party. The wedding – I noted Tess and Doc's absence from that one. Doc of course was banged up at the time. A picture of Jen and Danny, similar to the one I had, was framed and sat on a shelf. I took it out of its casing and rather childishly punched holes in their faces with a tack. I chuckled as I replaced the altered picture in the frame. The idea of punching Jen for real excited me and I felt the first stirrings of an erection. I would have liked to have pleasured myself right there or in Sal's bed but I was saving myself. I would take Jen this time, instead of just threatening, and I would enjoy every fucking minute of it. Andy could watch … he might even enjoy it. I should have done it last time – however, all good things come to those who wait. And I had waited long enough.

The room at the end of the corridor was a large rectangular space – a small kitchenette to my right and the living area in front of me. The first thing I noticed in there was the back wall. It had been wallpapered floor to ceiling in cut-outs from cookery books and beauty magazines – very kitsch. An old two-door walnut-and-marble sideboard sat against the wall with a beautiful old gramophone in the centre of it. I was surprised to find it worked and Ella Fitzgerald crooned at me in response to my curiosity. I made myself a coffee and a sandwich and settled down with a book. I was bored after ten minutes. *Critical Essays on Art* just didn't do it for me any more.

Without thinking twice, I went back into the bathroom and put the plug in the tub. The hot-water pipes shuddered and jumped into action and before long the room was steaming. I helped myself to her lotions and potions. Slipping under the surface of the hot water, I felt all my worries desert me. I could feel her presence purely through the smells enveloping me and I could no longer resist the urge to pleasure myself. Satisfied and thoroughly relaxed, I allowed myself forty winks.

The water had cooled significantly by the time I woke up and the light had begun to fade. I was slightly panicked as I didn't know if she had a spare key and I wouldn't like her to find me in her bath without permission – that would be weird.

I dressed quickly and threw the towels into the small washing machine. I washed my cup and plate and left them to dry on the empty draining board. Then it struck me. If I accosted her like this in her own apartment, she might get angry with me and send me packing. It would make much more sense to let her come to me – she needed to be the one doing the chasing if this was going to work. I didn't like Berlin and I couldn't live here. She would have to move. That was settled. Let her come to me.

I rooted around in my rucksack – I found the book in a side pocket. *Aristotle's Poetics*. Sal and I had spent hours discussing it. She would know straight away who it was from.

I wrote an inscription on the inside: *'I still don't believe in karma. Let's go back to the harbour – back to where it all began. I'll wait for you. Xx 0152 6443 229*

I didn't sign my name. If she was clever enough to remember the quote and the relevance of the book, she was good enough to be with me. She needed more culture back in her life and she wasn't going to find it here in the bowels of Berlin. As an afterthought, I took the creased photo of Jen and Danny out of my wallet and slipped it in between the pages. I didn't need it any more.

I took one last look around the little apartment and was glad that she would be out of here soon. We could go somewhere more suited to my taste. Vienna perhaps?

I closed the door behind me and retraced my steps to the Underground. I needed to get back to the gallery before it closed – I was a gentleman after all and it was my priority to return her keys.

I went back into the coffee shop opposite the gallery and the same bored waiter barely acknowledged me. I felt like giving him a piece of my mind.

'Excuse me, do you speak English?'

He reluctantly made eye contact and continued to polish the glass. Indifferent.

'Yes.'

'Could you please do me a favour?'

He looked suspicious as I reached into my pocket.

'My ex-girlfriend works across the road and I can't bear to see her. She's there right now. It's all too much for me.' Damn, I was good. On cue, the tears glistened at the corners of my eyes and his expression softened in sympathy.

'Can you return these for me?'

I handed him the keys. He nodded and offered me a coffee.

'No, thank you. I have a train to catch. Will you make sure to take them over straight away? She doesn't have another set. Tell her I'm sorry about Clara and she's the one that I dream of.' I nearly made myself vomit with the last line and, once I got over that, I found it increasingly difficult to keep the smirk from my lips.

The poor fool had fallen for my tale of woe – he looked as though he was ready to hug me – probably a faggot, judging by the tight top and the perfectly coiffed hair. Fucking hipsters.

'I am sorry for your hard times, sir. I will go immediately.'

'Thank you.'

We walked out the door together and he sprinted over the road – leaving the coffee shop empty. I took out my street map and ducked down a side street.

The alley brought me back out onto a wider street and, as usual, my luck was in. A taxi was coming up the street in my direction, the music made by tires on cobbles a welcome sound to my weary ears. I flagged him down He switched off the light on the roof and before long I was speeding through the streets, thinking about the challenge I had just laid down for Sal and ready for the last leg of the long way home.

Chapter 29

When Jen came downstairs, Andy was cooking breakfast. Danny and Mr Cassidy were out in the back garden flying the drone. Danny spotted her standing at the patio door and shouted to her.

'*Look, Mam, I can do stunts!*' He flipped the little drone 360°. In protest, it hummed like a swarm of bees.

Mr Cassidy took the liberty of relieving himself by a tree before he yapped at her as well.

'Good morning to you too, mutt. That's great, Dan. Have you packed your lunch?'

He nodded and continued to fly the drone in circles – not once did it plummet to the earth. It was nice to see him playing in the garden for a change, instead of on the bloody PlayStation. She would have been happier again had the toy of choice been a football, but, baby steps.

Andy had put a steaming mug of coffee and two slices of toast on the table for her.

'Thank you, Mr McClean!'

'You're welcome, Mrs McClean.' He stood in front of her and put his arms around her waist.

'I don't deserve you, Andy.' She hugged him harder and longer than she had done in months. He hugged her back and didn't say a word.

'I've something to tell you,' she said.

He pulled back and looked down at her. He always did that, no matter who he was speaking to — always gave them his full attention. It was nice — it made people feel listened to. Something she was not so good at.

'I've stopped taking my medication.'

His face remained impassive but she saw exactly how he felt in his eyes.

'Do you not have to come off those things slowly, though? It's dangerous to do it all at once.' He had done his research.

'I did it last Friday. I'm over the worst of it now and my head feels clearer. I constantly felt foggy on them and I don't think they were doing me any good.' She didn't mean for her tone to be so defensive. 'I did some research and I knew what to expect. If the withdrawals had been too much, I would have gone back to the doctor.'

He dropped his hands and looked at her.

'You didn't even discuss it with him?' His tone was sharp and he was trying to keep himself in check.

He rarely lost his temper but she could read all the signals. She knew he was furious.

'I went back to Dr Norval instead.'

'Really? When?'

'Yesterday. We had a good talk. When I told him about stopping the tablets, he said to see how it goes for now. He's also given me some homework.'

'What kind of homework?'

'Who has homework, Mam?'

Danny had materialised in the kitchen. Andy must have oiled the door — it hadn't made a sound as it opened. She looked at her husband questioningly.

'Yeah, about half an hour ago. Kept meaning to do it – maybe I shouldn't have.'

She laughed at that.

'What homework, Mam? Are you talking about me? Can I put the memory card into the laptop to see the videos I made?'

'You can do that this afternoon, pet. I wasn't talking about your homework. I was talking about mine – just something I have to do today – now go on up and brush your teeth.'

'But, Mam!'

'Go brush your teeth – you'll be late for school.'

He stomped off in the direction of the stairs. What was it about brushing teeth little boys had such an aversion to?

'What kind of homework, Jen?' Andy was standing with his arms crossed.

He liked Dr Norval but had questioned his methods on occasion. Prolonged Exposure Therapy was quite the commitment.

Jen always believed Andy thought there was a quicker fix than that.

'He wants me to go down to the strand and spend at least half an hour there. He believes that place holds the strongest association for me and, in a nutshell, I have to get to grips with the fact the attack was once upon a time and, by going down there, I'm not going to be attacked again. He wants me to process it emotionally rather than avoid the whole thing.'

'Do you want me to come?'

'Thank you for offering, but I have to do this alone – doctor's orders! I'll take my phone with me and, if it gets too much, I'll leave and ring you straight away.'

'Jen, I don't like this.'

'I need to stop thinking the world is a really dangerous place and I'm weak. The first step to putting this behind me was coming off those horrible tablets. This is the next step. I want to get back to normal, for all of us. It's been so hard on everyone, putting up with my lunacy. I want to make things right for all of us.'

'I'm very proud of you – I just don't want you to do too much too soon. When are you thinking about doing it? I can stay in the house if you'd like – that way you'd know I'm right there for you.'

'You are lovely, but no. Go to work. I'm going to do it this morning. I feel braver today and it's a beautiful clear day. I want to do this. I want to put the past behind us, once and for all.'

'Are you sure you don't want to talk about this a bit more beforehand?'

'Andy – I'll be fine. Just wait and see.' She leaned up and kissed him on the cheek before making her way to the door.

'Danny, get off that PlayStation and get out to the car. You're going to be late.'

A clatter of shoes on stairs – followed by the scrape of paws.

'Bye, Mam, I love you.'

'Love you too. Have a good day in school and make sure you have your listening ears on.'

'Yeah, Mam, whatever.' The front door shut behind him.

Andy was gathering up his things in the kitchen. He flung his jacket on, grabbed Dan's bag, kissed her on the cheek and was gone.

Have a cup of tea first, Jen, what's your hurry?

Her hands trembled and she ran them through her hair.

I can do this.

No, you can't.

Yes, I can.

She poured a glass of water from the jug and drank it in one go. The coffee and toast lay untouched.

'Right, let's do this.' She spoke out loud and clapped her hands together as though to steady herself. The sound ricocheted on the walls and the flashback came in high definition.

In her mind's eye, it was now dark in the kitchen. Danny sat at the end of the table, Scott on the long side and she was opening the bottle of wine. She stood and watched as though it were a movie.

'Run, Danny! Out the back!'

In slow motion, she watches as the heavy bottle connects with his face.

In the seconds before it does, surprise registers there and he braces himself for impact. In her peripheral vision she can see Danny running out the patio door. He's outside, that's a start. The force of the impact travels up her hands into her arms and she watches as his chair tilts backwards. The bottle is exploding and he is grasping at it as he falls backward. She opens her hand and the bottle falls to the ground. His head hits the tiles and she jumps over him in bare feet and runs in the direction of the door. Her breathing is fast as adrenalin and sheer terror course around her body. Her only thought is to keep her boy safe.

She snapped back to the present and continued to hold on to the chair. He wasn't there, it wasn't really happening. She was sweating and Dr Norval's voice came into her head.

'You need to differentiate between remembering the traumatic event and being retraumatised. Acknowledge the feelings and emotions but know that you are safe. It is a memory.'

Breathe, Jen, just breathe.

She walked to the now-silent patio door and lit a cigarette. It calmed her. She reached for her jacket on the back of the chair and put her phone in the pocket. She had stored the doctor's mobile number on it – she might need it yet.

She was tired of blocking and avoiding and constantly being scared. She needed to do this for herself and for her family. She couldn't avoid it any longer.

The images came.

She watches herself as she bounds out the patio door and shouts again to her boy who has stopped dead in his tracks. 'Run, Danny!' she screams. She catches up with him and grabs him by the arm. It all slows down again and she sees the look of fear in her little boy's eyes but also the trust in there that his mam can fix this and make the bad man go away. She is sprinting into the orchard half-carrying the child. She doesn't need to turn around to know he is gaining on them, she can feel his evil radiate towards her. 'Faster, Mam! He's going to catch up!' her little boy cries as his legs struggle to keep up with her dragging him along. Her heart is about to explode in her chest but she can hear him panting behind her. His boots thudding on the ground as he runs with all his might to catch them. I can't

199

let that happen, she is thinking now, I must get Danny to safety. He will not hurt my boy.

She hadn't noticed herself walking down through the garden and into the orchard. She was too busy concentrating on the three ghosts in front of her. She was the observer – the witness to what had happened. She watched as the woman pulled her son along with her and ran in bare feet, trying so hard to get away from the madman bearing down on them. She tried so hard but it was futile.

Jen kept walking in the direction of Stony Strand. She knew what was going to happen next but needed to see it from this perspective.

The force of the rock smashing into her back causes her to fall forward. They are on the strand now and as she goes down she tries to push the boy forward. He falls too. The man catches up with them and he is laughing. He grabs a handful of her hair and pulls – the little boy attaches himself to her leg with all his might – too frightened to run. He's only a little boy and he doesn't want to leave his mammy. He is whimpering. The man punches her in the face and her head snaps back with the force. The little boy shuts his eyes tight and clings to her leg even harder. Her hand slips down and rubs his face. It's okay, son, it's okay – her message to him in that gesture.

She hits the ground and he grabs the boy. Checkmate. She's going nowhere now. He doesn't even have to restrain her.

He speaks. The mania in his voice is clear and present and his words punch home like fists on her face. 'Quite the little fucking actress there, aren't you? Good try, honey, but now you are well and truly fucked …' The rest of his words escape her. He has a knife in his hand. He raises his hand to the boy's face and rests the knife against his cheek. The air rushes from her lungs and the terror makes her numb to the elements raging around her.

She knelt on the beach with her hand out in front of her, watching the drama play out. She wanted to scream into the wind to tell them to stop, leave this place and never come back but she was shouting at her own memories. She could see how hard she tried to get them away. Her only thoughts were for her son, not herself. Tears streamed down her face and she had the overwhelming urge to run back to the house and never set foot on the beach again. But she knew, if she did that, there would be no peace.

You are confronting a memory, Jen, a traumatic memory – that's all. You are safe. He's not here.

She felt the slim form of her phone in her pocket. If it got too much she would ring Andy.

Her vision is impaired as her eye swells shut but all her senses are on high alert. He has just threatened to gut her little boy. He will not hurt her boy. 'Please, just let him go. This is between you and me. Let my boy go.' He is excited by her fear, she can read it in his eyes. A damp patch spreads down over her little boy's jeans and feet. He is pale with terror. The knife has cut him but he doesn't move as blood trickles down his face. She feels a rage building in the pit of her stomach. He is ranting now and again she begs him to let the boy go. The wind has picked up. The waves crashing on the shore sound like a war cry. This is war. He has her boy. Something snaps inside of her. The fear is gone – survival kicks in. She spots something in the dunes. This is her only chance. She doesn't speak to him now, she speaks to her boy. 'Danny, listen to me. I love you. It's going to be OK.' The man mocks her and tells her to say her goodbyes. His eyes are dead. He has no conscience. She asks her boy if he remembers their game about who loves him most in the world – aside from his parents. Something flickers in his eyes. He knows. He knows. She feels a surge of hope and the boy roars out the name of his beloved dog. The little dog springs from the dunes. The little four-legged hero – willing to do anything to help his Danny. His teeth sink into the man's arm and he cries out in pain. The shock of the attack causes him to loosen his grip on the boy. 'Run, Danny!' she screams and launches herself at the man. She feels bone shatter under the rock in her hand. Her boy is gone. He's gone. He got away. He will not hurt her boy. She sees little Butch with a knife in his belly. The little hero is dead. He saved Danny's life.

She was still on her knees and her eyes followed the path Danny took on that night to get back to the house. She had saved her boy. She hadn't failed him. He had got off that strand in one piece because of her – and, of course, little Butch. What a little hero, she thought, and cried again for him.

She knows her boy is safe. All she needs to do is keep him on the strand long enough for Danny to get help. She screams at him again and now he is on top of her. His blood drips on her face. He punches her again and she feels herself slipping. He grabs her arm and pulls. Her shoulder dislocates — she vomits and slips further into the darkness. He is pulling her now, down to the water's edge. The stones rip at her flesh and the cold pierces her skin like a thousand knives. A fog begins to envelop her brain. Sounds become more distant and feelings desert her. All she is thinking about is her boy. He is safe. He is safe. Things are vague now and snippets come to her, like a dream. She feels water. Her lungs burn and her body slips into darkness.

Voices pull her out of the abyss. Her face is submerged again. It's cold. The weight on her neck is gone. She opens her good eye. Her lips feel strange. Voices. Andy. Andy is here. Shouting. She needs to get up. She needs to get out of the water. Survival. Legs beside her. Andy is in the water. The man is on top of him. Survival, protection, love is spurring her on now. She stands — legs like jelly. A rock in her hand. She summons every ounce of strength left and smashes it down. As darkness descends she sees a figure in the distance. Is it someone coming to help? The blackness comes again. More voices, shouts, activity, warmth, lights, clothing being cut, warmth, no pain, no fear. It's over.

The missing pieces of what happened that night had been told to her by Andy. She had very little memory of what had happened after Danny got free — flashes came to her all the time but they were vague. She knew Andy had saved her — he found them on the beach — but she had saved him too.

She was at the water's edge. The water was like glass. Calm and so beautiful. She imagined Andy lifting her out of the water and carrying her back home as her friends raced to help her and Danny. Her friends. They had suffered too — all of them. She imagined how they must have felt in the moments after they found out and that time in the kitchen when her dad said what everyone had been thinking. Little Danny was the other hero in all of it. He had been on that strand too and he managed to get over it. They had started counselling a few weeks after the attack and her son had made rapid progress. She, not so much. Maybe she liked staying in the familiar surroundings of victim mentality. She wasn't a victim – she was a survivor. Victims don't make it – she would. She would. He wouldn't hold her to ransom from this day forth. It was time to take her life back. She sat at the water's edge for another while and watched as two sailboats rounded the head of the harbour, making for the marina. She could imagine the scene down there, trawlers being unloaded as they landed. Trawlers being packed for a trip out, all the final checks being done. Andy in the boatyard with Doc, Tess in the Tea Room making coffee for the locals. Danny in school trying to stay still on his seat. Life went on.

It was time to put the past behind her. She took her phone out of her pocket. The lack of contact from Sal bothered her – it wasn't like her to be so quiet but maybe she was busy with this new boyfriend of hers. She would have to give her a bell later to say hi. She scrolled down through her contacts and found Dr Norval's mobile number. She prayed he wouldn't be with a client and would have time to take her call.

'Dr Richard Norval. Good morning?'

'Hi, Dr Richard, it's Jen.'

'Ah, Jen. Good timing, I'm between clients. How are you?'

'I did my homework. I'm sitting on the strand now. I saved him that night, Richard, both of them in fact. I didn't fail them. I survived.' She could hear the weariness in her own voice but, for the first time in a long time, she felt contented too.

'That you did, Jen, that you did. I want you to go home now and write it all down. Everything that came up for you today – all the feelings and emotions. Write them down. Make an appointment for early next week – if you would like to come in and chat?'

'That would be good, thanks.'

'Okay. I'm very proud of you, that was a big step in your recovery. As soon as you have it written, I want you to forget about it for the day. Do something nice for yourself – go to the movies or get a massage. We can work on it next week.'

'Thanks, Richard.'

'Chat to you then – bye!'

She didn't much feel like going to the cinema or making any grand gesture. She knew she had reached a real milestone but it wasn't over yet. Maybe a movie night with Danny and Andy would do the trick. That idea made her smile. She could pop to the shop for treats on the way back from school. Danny would love it.

Her thoughts were interrupted by the unmistakable yap of Mr Cassidy. She turned from the water and watched him bound over towards her. Andy was sitting at the top of the lane. She should have known he wouldn't let her do this on her own. He was a good man and she loved him. He stood and waved at her, reluctant to invade her space. She beckoned him over. He ambled over the stones, his boots crunching on the shale. Without saying a word, he sat beside her and took her hand in his. They sat there without speaking until the sun reached the highest point in the sky. Survivors. They knew that, it didn't need to be said. They would pick their way through the rubble and emerge blinking into the sunlight.

Chapter 30

'Pass me the combi wrench there, man, will you?' Doc was bent over a piece of machinery like a wilting fern and his brow was covered in a combination of oil and sweat.

Andy walked over to him and handed him the tool.

He took the wrench and resumed his position. 'This bitch of a yoke has my heart broken. She won't get the better of me, though, I tell you that now.'

'Coffee?'

'Yeah, cheers.' The wrench made quite the racket as it hit the concrete floor and Doc let rip with a couple of expletives.

'Leave it for now. You didn't go for lunch, did you?'

'Nah. I'm grand. I've sandwiches there.' He opened the plastic lunch box and the smell of tuna filled the air. He took a seat at the bench and pushed the box in his boss's direction. 'How was Jen?'

'She was alright, yeah.'

'Did she go down there after?'

'Yeah.'

'And?'

'I've never been a fan of Norval. I know he worked wonders with Danny but I've found his methods a bit – I dunno – off the wall, like, but I think she got over a real hump today.'

'What does he think is wrong with her?'

'Chronic Post-Traumatic Stress Disorder.'

'Oh, Jesus, man, that's rough.'

'It's been pretty hard to live with too – the mood swings and the highs and lows in her moods. It was like she was on hyper-overdrive all the time.'

'He did nearly kill her, Andy. She's not going to get over that in a hurry.'

'I know but it was like she saw danger absolutely everywhere. In everything – she barely left the house and little Danny couldn't put a foot right.'

'What a sad situation.' Doc had pushed his sandwiches to one side and refilled the coffee cups.

Andy rarely talked about his marriage – he felt good having a friend to open up to.

'Yeah. As soon as the search was called off for that prick, she lost it. She and Danny started counselling. Things were okay for a while – then that phone call came – that voicemail. She was back at square one. And then in January we went to Disney with Dan and my sisters.'

'So why did she stop going if it was working?'

'She got impatient, I think. Then she went to her GP and he put her on antidepressants. She was like a zombie for the first few weeks. Then we got busy with the wedding stuff. She was obsessed with Scott in one way but wouldn't really talk about him, if you get me. It was hard.'

'And she decided this week to go back? Why?'

'I'm not sure but we'll see what happens.'

'What about you two – you know, how are things between you?'

Andy sighed and puffed out his lips.

'Getting better, I think. Since she came off those tablets, she's in better form. Anyway, enough about me. What's going on your end?'

'Hmmmm …'

'Okay?'

'Well, it's Tess.'

'What about her?'

'I dunno – ah, maybe I am just being a big girl's blouse. It's been quite the adjustment for all of us in the last couple of weeks, but, there's something not right.'

'With respect, you are only out of prison. It's not like you were on a sabbatical in India or somewhere – and you are a recovering addict. That's bound to mess things up a bit.'

'Not like you to hold back there, Andy – anything else you would like to add to my recent list of achievements?' Doc looked at him and Andy could see the words had stung.

'Sorry, I didn't mean it like that. I just mean, there's lots for her to get used to.'

'When I was in there – I had two options. I could either stay in the shit-storm I had created for myself or I could avail of the resources available to me. I was shit-scared in that place – you've no idea.'

Andy didn't interrupt him. Doc was a man of few words and this was the first time since the day he got back he had mentioned his time inside. Something was bubbling up inside him and he needed to get it off his chest. He didn't want to interrupt that by throwing his oar in.

'For the first few weeks, I was on lock-down and the only times I got out of the cage was to shower, eat and exercise. That suited me. I was too frightened to be near any of the rest of them. Then that changed. I know I've told you all this before. I started the AA meetings and spent a bit of time talking to the counsellors in there. That's when I had the watershed moment.'

'How do you mean?'

'It all hit me. Like a punch in the face. My behaviour, man, because of the madness. I deserved to be in there. I had done the crime, and you know what they say… For a while I thought I was going dull altogether – it was bad enough being locked up but I couldn't get away from my own thoughts. I wanted to rip my head off – just to get away from the noise and the shame.'

'What happened then?'

'I faced my demons. I concentrated on looking at me and the realisation that it was *my* bad choices – no one else's that led me there. I had fucked up – all by myself. Sure – I could blame Scott, and Clara, but it was me alone that screwed up my life – and Tess's. And Jen's – I was a link in the chain that nearly caused her and the little fella to be beaten to death on the beach. I played a part in other kids all over the country becoming addicted to all the shit I was transporting. All the killings and all the madness from the time that shit leaves wherever it comes from and arrives on the streets here – I was a part of that. The drug lords and the gangland shit in the country? I played a part in that.'

'Doc, I think you're being a bit hard on yourself there. You were a small fish in a very big ocean. You can't blame yourself for all of it.'

'I had to face my demons to get over them, though – didn't I? That wasn't easy but with help I got to grips with it and here I am. A new man.'

He spoke with a clarity Andy hadn't seen in him before. He respected him for it.

'I know what you're thinking. You're right!'

'Eh, what now?'

'You're thinking about where smug Doc is gone.'

'Wouldn't say smug now, maybe arrogant would have been a better word for the old Doc.' Andy laughed in an attempt to lighten the mood but it fell flat on the floor.

'I was smug *and* arrogant though. I used to see them all the time round the harbour or at gigs. The stoner brigades, the pill-poppers, the acid-munchers, the cokeheads. The pill-poppers and the coke-snorters never hung around the gigs too long – the acid-munchers never really knew where they were anyway day or night. The same, no matter where you went. Glazed eyes and wouldn't have a word to throw to a dog at the start of the night. Give them a few beers and a fix and they were all down the back of a beer garden, talking about conspiracy theories and the universe like fucking prophets. All the while, they spent every penny they had on their poison of choice — and spent weekdays washing reality away with antidepressants and cheap red wine hiding behind closed curtains, burning bloody incense. They wouldn't get up off their holes and work for a living if their lives depended on it. I would look at them each night and thank my lucky stars I was going home to my family, our business and my impressive house. And for a while, that's what I used to do.'

Doc hadn't moved from his seat. His hands were wrapped around the mug and he had spoken his monologue into his coffee. He seemed to be startled when Andy moved, as though he had forgotten he was there.

'And, how the mighty had fallen! I got to the point where I would be waiting for the likes of them to come in. I'd get the gig over and done with as quick as I could before joining the circle and talking crap with them. Then Clara came onto the scene and it all spiralled out of control. The thing about being an addict is you can't see it yourself. You think you are the only one in the group that's okay — you know the rest of them are addicts and losers but you forget that they are thinking the very same thing about you.'

'But you did it, Doc, you got your act together.'

'It took a prison to get me there. I'd be dead or still out there if I hadn't been caught. That's the worst truth. I lost my wife, my baby and my home and getting banged up is the only thing that stopped me.'

He stood up and went over to his locker.

'I'm going for a smoke.'

He didn't look Andy in the eye when he said that.

Women were good at this kind of thing, thought Andy. Pouring their hearts out to each other and solving the most complicated problems over tea and hours of talk. Men didn't have that natural ability. They hadn't evolved that way. But Andy knew that Doc needed to be heard by someone. He was going to his meetings every evening and he had a good support network there. But there, he was Doc the recovering addict – nothing else. Here, he had a friend to talk to – someone who knew him before the madness began. Everyone needs that.

Doc returned from his smoke and set about getting back to work.

'Sit back down a minute, Doc. We've time. We've only a call-out to do this evening down in the factory. One of the machines is acting up.'

'Grand – more coffee so.'

'What were you going to say about Tess? What's going on with her?'

'Not sure but she's cagey as hell and her phone goes off at all hours. She leaves the house at strange times too.'

'Is she having an affair?'

'Maybe. Nah, I don't think so. Maybe I've got it all wrong. Eighteen months inside, AA meetings and counsellors make you look at life differently, I suppose. The old Doc became a master at hiding things and bending the truth. She's acting odd – like she has something to hide.'

'Aren't there meetings for families of addicts as well? Maybe she could go to one of them. I can't see her having an affair on you, she's too decent for that. And especially after the fallout from your affair with that Clara one.'

'Yes, I suggested Al-Anon meetings to her. She refused. Told me she wasn't going to sit around holding hands and drinking tea with housewives and men in cardigans. Can't force her.'

'Harsh. How's the young lad?'

'He hates me.'

'He'll come around. He's at that age.'

'I hope so.' He sighed and looked at the floor while he scrubbed at the oil on his hands with a rag. 'I feel like the enemy in my own house. They are always in cahoots and he has no respect for me. He won't listen to a word I say and I was close to giving him a good kick in the arse last night.'

'Give him time. Big change for him too – having you back like. I suppose he was the man of the house while you were away. And look at the effect from you going inside. He had to change schools. That's huge on a kid.'

'I know she's busy in work but she spends all her time in there. She's never home and when it's just me and Hugh he refuses to come out of his room. Stuck up there on that damn PlayStation, blowing the shit out of stuff. He's an angry boy. Anyway…' He looked at the kettle, following the steam as it made patterns on the little window over the bench. 'It will be grand. It will.'

Andy knew that wasn't directed at him. It was a wish.

'But they're all the same on that damn PS. I have threatened to throw Danny's in the sea I don't know how many times.'

They both chuckled at the vision of Andy, running full tilt down the pier with the machine under his arm, Danny in hot pursuit.

'On a lighter note,' Doc said with his back to his boss, stirring steaming water into granules, 'I've started an online course. Haven't told Tess about it yet – I want to see how I get on first. Study never was my strong suit.'

Andy spoke to the back of his head. 'Good stuff. What are you doing?'

'Addiction counselling.'

Andy was really impressed. Doc was a good man and he was trying extremely hard to get on with his life and to give something back as all the gurus would say.

'Best of luck with it, man. Do you not hate them though?'

'Who?'

'Addicts. After what you said there, I just figured you hated them all.'

'I don't hate them any more, Andy. I get them now. I am one. No one chooses that life for themselves. We forget to separate the addiction from the person. That's what I've learned over the last while and at the meetings. Addiction is a disease. People with a disease need help. That what I want to do – turn the shit around and give something back.' He finished the last sentence in his best Dr Phil voice and laughed at himself.

Andy had forgotten how good he was at doing impressions. He tried to think of a quip in response but he wasn't fast enough.

Doc handed him a coffee and went back to what he had been doing before lunch.

They mooched around the workshop for the rest of the afternoon in companionable silence, save for the odd tune from Doc. They made a good team.

Chapter 31

Fran was nauseous from anxiety. He had no idea how his visit would be received by Jen or Andy. The idea of phoning them first crossed his mind but he knew in his heart they would've refused to see him. He decided to drop in without forewarning, praying it was the right thing to do.

His nerves became more frayed with every quarter hour that passed while he sat in his ma's parlour, looking out the window and waiting for Andy's clapped-out van to pass by, pointed in the direction of home. Eventually his signal came and he set out walking. He took the shortcut down by the post office and across the headland. The memory of the last time he had taken this route rose up and stabbed him in the gut. With each footstep bringing him closer to Jen and Andy's, he wondered once again how his life would have turned out had he not walked that path that night. He got that 'sliding doors' feeling – but for a split-second decision, his life would be on a different trajectory. Scott would have certainly drowned had he not been there to assist him – but how many lives would have been saved by his death? The awareness threatened to crush him. His heart hammered in his chest and he fought for breath in the dying light. He was responsible for everything that came after that night. A quick apology and a cup of tea was not going to fix that – not by a long shot.

He reached the end of the lane that spilled out onto Stony Strand. Another two minutes up the beach and he could have cut up through the orchard into their backyard. He had done that several times in the past but felt he had lost the right to that familiarity.

The van was parked out the front beside Jen's car. All the lights were on downstairs. They were home. He had hoped for the opposite, the bravery receding with every forward step. If he didn't do this now, he never would. The rowan tree swayed gently in the breeze, welcoming him into the drive. He turned around and walked back onto the road. He lit a cigarette and tried to convince himself he shouldn't go in there – it would only upset things. He was stalling and he knew it. *Do it, Fran, this is what you came home for. To make amends and set the record straight.* He fired the cigarette onto the ground, stamped on it and marched up to the front door. Before he had a chance to back out, he rapped on the door three times and waited.

He stepped down off the step – in his head, a mark of respect – he didn't want to be on top of the person who answered the door.

Andy opened the door and, just behind him, Jen was standing in the hallway – a look of concern on her face.

It took a few moments. When Andy recognised the caller in front of him, several emotions passed over his face. Recognition, surprise, shock, anger, curiosity. He turned to Jen and told her to go back into the kitchen.

In that split second, Fran read in his face what he wanted to do. He took a step back and waited for Andy to swing a fist at him.

'What the hell are you doing here – get off our property now before I break your legs!' Andy had closed the door behind him and was trying to keep his voice even.

'Andy, can we talk? I need to explain.'

Andy grabbed him by the scruff of the neck. '*I don't want to hear your explanations, do you hear me?*'

He was shouting into his face – drops of his saliva landed there and Fran was too afraid to move. He had never, in all the years he knew him, seen Andy get angry to the point of violence.

He pushed him back and Fran fell onto the gravel.

The light from the front door shone behind him and Fran could only see his silhouette from where he lay. He wasn't advancing on him. He hadn't moved. His hand came out and Fran flinched.

'Get up.'

He took Andy's hand and pushed himself upright.

'I'm not interested in what you have to say,' Andy said. 'Go home and never darken my doorstep again.' He turned his back to him and walked back up the steps.

'Scott is dead.'

That stopped him in his tracks. He was frozen, like a statue, before he turned back around to face him. His outline was all that Fran could see.

'What did you just say?'

'I think Scott is dead. I was with him for the last eighteen months.'

'And you expect me to believe you, why?'

Andy came down the steps again but the anger had abated. He was beginning to listen.

'If you don't want to listen to me, ring the Sarge. I told him everything on Tuesday night, when I got home. That's why I came home – to put things right and try to make amends.'

'Today is Friday? Why did you wait for three days to come down if you wanted to make *amends*? Cut the bullshit, Fran.'

'I was afraid to come. Please, man, let me tell you my side of the story.'

Andy threw his eyes to heaven. 'Stay there for a minute. I need to speak to Jen.'

Fran lit a cigarette and waited for him to come back out. He wasn't sure what was happening inside, but he thought he could hear Danny protesting about going upstairs, followed by loud stomps. The dog was yapping too. He had finished the cigarette by the time Andy opened the door again.

'You had better come in and tell us the story, without any bullshit or embellishment. I want the truth, Fran.'

Andy walked into the kitchen and Fran followed him. Jen was standing by the table – she had changed greatly in the time he had been away. She looked older somehow and drawn, even though she had clearly put on weight. Her hair was scraped back and pinned up on the top of her head. He had never seen her looking so, well, dishevelled.

She nodded at him and Andy told him to take a seat. He was offered tea or coffee and he declined both in favour of a glass of water.

They joined him at the table.

The atmosphere was thick and heavy. Fran didn't know where to start. He had thought about it all day and now he was here he couldn't form the sentences in his head.

'You said you have been with him for the last eighteen months. Where have you been? How do you know he's dead? What's in it for you, coming back here now?'

Andy fired questions at him relentlessly and he was dizzy from the onslaught. He needed to start at the beginning. He took a deep breath and cleared his throat.

Jen hadn't moved a muscle or spoken a word.

'I was on the strand the night he attacked Jen.' He didn't look in her direction and addressed Andy. The man of the house. 'I was the one that dragged him out of the water while you carried Jen up the strand. I had been watching – he had drifted away from where you were. None of you could see him from the shoreline. When he went in, it looked like he had been swept out to sea, but he hadn't. He was swept away from you. It was choppy, he was being bounced around like a rag-doll. You were too busy looking after

216

Jen to see me. I had him out of the water before anyone else came down.'

'Why, Fran?' Jen asked.

'I had been working for Scott for a while. I know he told you it was me bringing in the stuff. He approached me with a job offer one night in the Gale – he knew that me ma was up to her eyeballs in debt because of me da and sold it to me as an opportunity to get money together to help her.'

Andy looked at him and disgust flashed in his eyes. 'Less of the excuses, I don't want to hear them. What happened then?'

'He had it all planned out in his head. There was a car over on Seaview Lane. He had it all worked out. He was going to kill Jen and leave the country before anyone realised but then it didn't work out like that and he knew, once the alarm was raised by the Guards, the ports and airports would be watched. He rang his boss in Spain and he sorted it all out for him. He was gone out of the country a few hours later.'

'What boss in Spain? What are you on about?' Andy's patience was running out.

'The Boss was running the whole operation. Scott was working for him. He was importing the drugs for him.'

'So what happened to you then? You were still here. Why did you leave?'

'The next day I had a visitor who told me you knew I was the one who was bringing the stuff in and, if I didn't leave, I would end up in prison and wouldn't be able to help me ma. This person knew it was me who got him off the beach and she knew he was still alive.'

'She? Who told you?' Andy asked.

'I don't know why that person did it or what their involvement is but I was shit-scared, man. Scott had played me for a right fool and then shafted me anyway.'

'Who told you to leave?'

The visitor called to Fran's door the evening after Jen was attacked on the strand.

He let her in and they went into the kitchen. His ma was there, fussing around and getting out the good china — she liked Tess and was only delighted to have her in the house. Ma liked an excuse to get the good china out. She insisted on sending him across the road to the shop for good biscuits too. They chatted for a bit about Jen and what had happened. Tess was acting strange. She was vague. Eventually she had to tell his ma she was there to talk to him about a job and asked if they could have a few moments alone. She was only too delighted to leave them to it. She picked up her Ireland's Own *and went through to the sitting room.*

He knew Tess wasn't there to offer him a job, He wasn't that stupid.

'You have been a busy boy, Fran,' she said.

She always made him a bit nervous when he'd be in the pub — she had that way about her. Authoritative — that was the word for her alright. She had the air of the boss and everyone knew it. He was sweating with nerves.

'What do yeh mean?' he asked and took a slurp of his tea.

'Cut the bullshit. We all know about you bringing the drugs in for Scott. Jen got home from the hospital this evening — I've just come from there. Scott told her last night it was you — Andy knows too. How did you get wrapped up in this mess, Fran? You were always decent.'

'Keep your voice down, will you, for fuck sake! My ma is probably listening.' She would kill him before anyone else got to him if she knew.

'I've been told you were spotted leaving the front of the Gale in an awful hurry last night, even before the alarm was raised. Where did you go?'

She was being weird. It wasn't like she was upset or anything. Her friend had nearly been killed the night before and she was acting like a nosey neighbour.

'I went to join the search.'

'No, you didn't. You left the Gale before anyone knew what was going on. Were you in on it with him?'

She was getting more agitated, and he was afraid Andy was about to show up. It was all too much for him. The story spilled out of his mouth like water out of a broken tap. He told her everything about getting Scott out of the water, off the beach and his passage to Spain. The story didn't take too long and it honestly sounded like he was making it all up.

She sat in silence for what felt like an eternity. He was panicking and wondered if he should just ring Andy and go explain everything to him. He'd have to ring the Guards too and tell them what happened. He was in so much shit and his ma's heart would surely break after this. He thought about his da — he did inherit the oul lad's dodgy genes after all. He couldn't go to prison — the thought of that was enough to make him start choking on his tea.

'Have you told anyone else about getting Scott off the beach?'

'Hardly. Do you think I'm that stupid?'

She made him feel like shit then, the way she raised an eyebrow and smirked. Snobby bitch. He'd seen her and Scott in the pub together a few times and the village grapevine had gone into overdrive when she mysteriously started all that work on the Gale. Scott was involved in that pub somehow and that made her no better than him. He'd had enough of her. He was in the shit no matter what he did, but he wasn't going to put up with her bullshit and gloating over him.

'What do ya want, Tess? Are you here to gloat or what?'

'I'm here to help you. This is all Scott's fault — he used you. You are going to have to disappear for a little while and keep your mouth shut. If people know you helped him out of the water and he's still alive, you'll be lynched. You surely have money in the house — enough to get away?'

He hadn't seen that coming and it made no sense.

'I have a bit of money, yeah, but I can't leave me ma.'

'You are no use to your ma if you end up in prison. At least if you're not locked up you can send her money and help her that way. No one can know he's still alive and no one needs to know you helped him.'

'What's in this for you, Tess? Why are you helping me and Scott instead of your friend?'

'I don't have any friends, Fran. I look out for me and my son — that's it. The rest of it is none of your business. If you're not gone in the next twenty-four hours, I'll bring the Guards here myself.'

'Why are you here, Tess? Why are you helping me?'

'Just get out of here. Before it's too late.'

His ma heard them in the hallway and came out to say goodbye. Tess had the cheek to be all smiles and said she would see her soon.

219

His ma grilled Fran after she left, about the so-called job — he had to fill her full of lies. He didn't want to leave his ma, but what choice did he have?

'Fran, man — who fucking told you?' Andy shook his arm.

'It was Tess.'

Andy's face fell. He looked from him to Jen and back again, his mouth gaping like a goldfish. Jen walked over and stood right in front of him.

'*You're a liar!*' she screamed. 'How do we know he didn't send you here to tell us all this? You need to get out, now. Andy, call the Guards.'

'Jen, hang on a minute.' Andy strode to her and put his arm around her. He guided her into a chair.

Fran couldn't decipher the expression on Andy's face but he knew something was beginning to click with him.

'You followed him to Spain? Why?'

'I thought Scott's boss would help me and I could lay low there until things blew over. Scott was a real mess when I arrived. You messed up his face good, Jen. He has a big dent in it now.'

She looked up and an expression of pleasure crossed her face.

'After a few weeks, the Boss told me he wanted me to go with Scott to keep an eye on him and report back. The weird thing was, Scott was forever not doing what he was supposed to do. Other people just disappeared when they pissed the big fella off — but Scott could do no wrong. We went around Europe, then into Tunisia, Algeria and Morroco — Marrakech. That's where the Boss wanted everything set up. Scott was up to no good with another fella and it all went mental fairly quickly.'

He choked up and struggled to control his emotions. Then he told them about Saidaa, Marco, Tarek and the drugs. And what he had done to ensure Scott's death.

Andy sat with his head in his hands and didn't speak. Jen was smoking out the patio door. Fran didn't know what else to say. He finished his glass of water and looked at the floor.

Jen came back and stood at the table. She was as pale as a ghost.

'Can you prove it? Can you prove he's dead?'

'No, but there's no way he got away from Tarek. He's dead. I'm sure of it.'

'Did you actually see his body?' she demanded. 'Did this Tarek guy tell you he had killed him? Where's your bloody proof – you can't be sure of it if you don't have proof!' She paced back and forth, back and forth.

Fran looked at Andy. His face told him he was searching for something to say but his lips didn't move.

'Andy – say something, will you?' Jen was getting hysterical.

'Calm down, Jen. What do you want me to say? I don't know what to say.' He thumped his fists on the table and rubbed at the stubble on his chin.

'*Are you for real?*' Jen was shouting.

Fran didn't know what to do.

'I'm glad he's dead – I hope he died roaring,' Andy said. 'But how will we ever actually know?'

'Tarek wouldn't have let him off the hook,' Fran insisted. 'He killed his little sister.'

'He's still alive, I can feel it.' Jen was looking out into the night.

Andy rolled his eyes and Fran dropped his head.

'We're never going to know the truth, are we?' Jen faced both men.

The oppressive weight of guilt settled down across Fran's back. He had ruined this woman's life without ever laying a hand on her. Why, oh why, did he take him out of the water that night? That was the turning-point for everything and the worst crime of all.

Jen grabbed the pack of cigarettes and strode out, slamming the door shut behind her.

'I'm sorry for everything, man. I got way in over my head – it's no excuse and I know I'm as much to blame as that nutter.'

'If you're looking for forgiveness you've come the wrong place, man. You *are* as much to blame for the madness as he is.' Andy was stabbing his finger in the direction of the door. 'Have you any idea what this family has been through while you were getting your rocks off with Scott for the last two years? Not knowing if he was going to come back. We weren't sure if he was dead or alive – if he was going to finish what he fucking started. You've no idea, man! You pulled him out of the water – this is on your head.'

'I'm sorry, Andy.' What else could he say?

'Danny ended up seeing a fucking shrink. He's a kid, man. You think about that one for a while.'

The colour drained from Fran's face and he felt the beginnings of a migraine. He hadn't thought this out at all. The wise choice would've been to let the Sergeant break the news to them. He would have come across better.

'I should leave. I've been here long enough.'

'Yeah – you're right. You should.'

Jen came back inside – Fran wasn't sure if her eyes were red from the breeze or from tears.

'Do you really think he's dead?' Her voice sounded hopeful, like this news could solve all her problems in one fell swoop.

'Yeah, yeah, I do. I haven't heard from him'.

'Well, you'd better pray he is dead then, Fran,' said Andy, 'because if you lead him back here I'll kill you myself. You need to go.'

Andy stomped out the hallway and swung open the front door.

Fran followed him and stood, hanging his head.

'I'm sorry, man. I have to live with it now as well. I'm sorry for all the harm I've caused.'

Andy didn't respond.

Fran heaved a sigh and left the house. He hadn't reached the bottom step when the door slammed behind him.

He stuffed his hands into his pockets. Gravel crunched under his feet and over the noise he could hear a car engine and the sound of the sea. Lights lit up the tops of the ditches and the car slowed on the approach to Jen's drive. It made him jumpy and his pace quickened. He got out the gate and dashed in behind a tree. He could just about see the front door of the house as the car swung into the drive.

The driver got out of the car in a hurry and banged on the front door. Andy's face was like thunder when he opened it, assuming perhaps it was him.

Then his face softened and he hugged her. She stepped into the hall and the yard was once again enveloped in darkness.

Chapter 32

Jen let out a squeal and ran to her friend. They hugged for the longest time, both of them in tears.

'It's so good to see you!' Jen cried. 'Why didn't you tell me you were coming?'

'There wasn't time.' Sal flung herself into the chair Fran had just vacated and Andy went over to the glass cupboard.

Danny appeared too – delighted to see his old pal had remembered to bring treats from the airport. He was chuffed to see her and didn't reserve the hugs – but didn't hang around long. He scarpered upstairs with the bag of loot.

A bottle of wine was procured from the fridge. Andy opened it and placed it on the table with three glasses. He had found take-away menus in the drawer but they were ignored.

'When did you arrive, Sal?'

'This evening. Flight got in a few hours ago – I hired a car and came straight here. We need to talk, Jen.'

Jen looked at her and her heart quickened. Sal looked tired and drawn. It was more than just the travel.

'Fran is back,' Jen said.

They sat at the table and Jen proceeded to fill her in on the earlier conversation with Fran, Andy filling in the blanks at the bits she hadn't heard or had chosen to forget. As she said it out loud, she began to believe in the possibility that Scott was dead.

'I don't know how we can know for sure. Maybe there will be an investigation or something. According to Fran, he's dead, Sal. I can't believe it. After all this time, waiting for him to come back – he's gone. But we've no way of knowing.'

Sal let out a deep sigh. 'When was all this? When did Fran leave Morocco?'

'I'm not sure,' Jen said. 'He got back to the harbour on Tuesday.'

Sal played with the beaded bracelet on her arm. She turned it around and around and wouldn't make eye contact with Jen. She mumbled something and, to her horror, Jen realised Sal was trembling. She wasn't sure if it was from fear or anger.

'What did you say, Sal?'

Sal spoke in a whisper. Jen had to strain to hear her.

'He's not dead.'

'What are you saying?'

'He's not dead. He was in Berlin.' The words came out like bullets.

'When? What do you mean? Fran said he died in Morocco.'

'Jen. He was in Berlin on Wednesday. In my apartment.'

Jen's mouth hung open. She felt something in the recesses of her mind – something closing off and hardening. First Tess, now Sal. It was escalating again.

Andy spoke up. 'You'd want to start talking fairly fast there, Sal – that was two days ago.'

By now Sal was on her feet and Jen was the one trembling in the chair. Andy was glued to the spot, hands flat on the table, trying to keep himself in check.

'I couldn't get here any faster. What did you expect me to do? Tell you all this over the phone?'

Sal dived into her handbag and pulled a copy of *Aristotle's Poetics* out. She slammed it on the table and pulled her hand away, as though she'd touched something dirty.

'This was one of our favourite books. We spent hours talking about it. I gave him this copy. I'd recognise it anywhere.'

Jen stared at the cover. It meant nothing to her.

'So?' Andy asked.

'I didn't see him,' said Sal, 'but he was there – in my apartment.'

'What the hell are you talking about?' Andy demanded.

'Wednesday evening I was in work when the waiter from across the road came in with my keys and an elaborate story about how my ex-boyfriend had been in the café, visibly upset, and had asked him to return my keys while apologising about Clara. I assumed he had the wrong person until he gave me my keys.'

'*What?* Clara as in *Clara*-Clara!' Jen all but shrieked.

'*Will you let me finish!*' Sal's response came out somewhere between a yell and a prayer.

Jen folded her arms and nodded. Andy stood up and leaned against the kitchen door.

'I hadn't noticed my keys were gone – Abe was in the gallery when I got back from lunch so I had no need to use them. But I had locked up before lunch and put the keys in my bag.'

'You think Scott stole your keys somehow from your bag?' Andy looked at her in amazement.

'That's exactly what I'm thinking. It was creepy.'

'So what did you do? Did you ring the police?'

'No. I just went back home.'

'Did you call Abe?'

'No. Abe knows nothing about all the bullshit that went on here – and he'll never know, if I can help it.'

'You went home alone?' Andy was aghast. 'Sal, are you demented?'

'No, I'm not demented, Andy. I knew Scott wouldn't be there when I got back. Why would he come and hand the keys into my workplace if that was his plan? In any case, I couldn't call the police as they would have thought I was crazy.'

'You couldn't have known he wouldn't be there. He could have made copies of your keys. That was a really stupid move,' Andy said.

'I know him. It's not his style to lie in wait like that. He thinks too much of himself. He was announcing to me that he was back. I knew he wouldn't come back to my place and that's why I stayed there. I knew he would have left some kind of riddle for me and he had. Asshole.'

'What note? What riddle?'

'That book was sitting on the coffee table. It wasn't mine. He had left it there for me with an inscription, a number to a German mobile and this …' She pulled out the picture of Jen and Danny from her wallet. 'I've no idea where he got it.'

Jen took the photo from her hand. 'He took it from here. I'd printed a copy of this for you and one for Mam and Dad, ages ago. I couldn't figure out where I'd put them. Now I know.'

Jen's mind was screaming at her. *He's coming for you, Jen, you were right again! He's coming for you.*

'Jesus Christ. So where is he now? Here? Berlin. What the hell like?' Andy now was the one who was pacing.

Jen could hear the alarm in Andy's voice. She knew what had to be done.

'Guys, he's nuts,' Sal said with conviction. 'We had spoken about that book on many occasions. He knew I would know. He made my bed. He had a fucking bath and he made himself food in *my* apartment.'

By now, they were all on their feet.

Jen looked at her friend. 'But why did you take so long to get here?'

'I couldn't tell anyone what had happened, including my boss. What was I supposed to do? Just fuck off out of there and leave them to it? I have a life over there, Jen, and like I said I left all this madness behind me. I came as soon as I could.'

'We need to call the Guards.' Andy pulled his mobile out of his pocket.

'*No!*' Jen snarled at him and they looked at her as though she had finally lost the plot. 'We can't ring them yet. We have no proof he's even in Ireland. If he's here, he will be watching. He'll wait for us to call them and he'll wait until they leave – laughing the whole way back to the barracks about how mental Sal and I are.'

'What did the inscription say?' Andy asked.

'*I still don't believe in karma. Let's go back to the harbour – back to where it all began. I'll wait for you –*'

'He's coming back.' Jen reached for her cigarettes. She didn't speak to either of them as she went out the back. She needed to think.

You're going to spend the rest of your life looking over your shoulder, Jen. You know that, don't you? You won't be able to let Danny out of your sight.

She could hear the sea from where she stood. She could feel its absolute might in the air surrounding her. The briny smell of the waves hit her and she could feel the salt on her lips. It had all come full circle. It was only a matter of time before he came back. He had won, again. *If you let him.*

Sal was not in the room when Jen returned.

'Andy, can you check on Dan, please?'

She was alone. She picked up the book and she could feel his presence. It was the strangest of strange feelings. She opened the cover and read his message to Sal – the voice she hadn't heard in a long time was crystal clear as though she had summoned him right there. She listened for a moment. Three voices drifted down the stairs.

She pulled out her smartphone and googled the German international dialling codes. She punched the number with the code into her phone. Her heart raced as her finger hovered over the call button.

Andy and Sal came back in and Tess was the topic of conversation. Jen hit the save button and slipped her phone back into her bag. The book was where Sal had left it. Jen topped up the wineglasses.

'Are you going to speak to her?' Sal looked at Jen.

Jen knew by her face she too was having a hard time digesting the information about how Tess had played a crucial and really cruel part in the aftermath which had affected them all so greatly.

'I'm going to see her later,' Jen said. 'I need to know why she betrayed us like that.'

'Do you want me to come with you?'

'Yeah, thanks, Sal. That would be great.'

Andy looked at the pair of them. 'I don't know if that's a good idea. You don't know what the story is. Maybe I should go with you?'

'No – you can give Doc a shout and take him out for a beer. We'll go down and corner her when she's on her own. He has no idea what's going on, I wouldn't think, so you need to sus him out. I don't want them to have a chance to compare notes.'

Andy shook his head and laughed. It was a mirthless one, and it grated on Jen's nerves.

'How the hell am I supposed to get a recovering alcoholic out for a beer, Jen? And, Danny is here. We can't both go out.'

'I'm going to take Dan to my parents for the night. Just until we have sorted all this out.'

Jen knew Sal could feel the tension escalating between her and Andy.

'Did you contact him, Sal?' she asked.

'I did in my arse. No way! Creep! I want nothing to do with him. When I go back to Berlin, I'm moving in with Abe. Why would you even ask that?'

Jen picked up the book and stomped over to the stove. The heat hit everyone as she flung open the glass doors and chucked the book into the flames.

'Why did you do that?' Andy ran over beside her in a feeble attempt to salvage it from the fire, 'What have you done?' Sal was behind Andy, willing him to rescue it.

'I didn't want that fucking thing in my house. It proves nothing and the number is probably a dud.'

'It proves he was in my apartment, Jen. You had no right –'

Jen looked at her friend. 'He's going to come back here anyway – it's only a question of when. We will go to the Sergeant in the morning. In the meantime, I want nothing of his in my house – do you hear me?'

She knew they could hardly believe what she had just done – it was a stupid move but she hoped that little display would be enough to throw them. She knew what needed to be done and she was the only one that could do it.

'We could have given the number to the Guards.'

'Yeah, like that's going to work, Andy.' Jen closed the cast-iron door and watched through the glass insert as the book was devoured.

Chapter 33

The gentle sound of the breeze in the trees and the smell of dew on grass was a stark and welcome contrast to the smells and the seediness of Kurfurstenstrasse where I had spent the 24 hours in Berlin. God Bless Europe and its distinct lack of morals.

Weybridge Estate. Home sweet home. It never failed to impress me, particularly at night. I rarely walked the avenue, having no cause to, but I wanted my arrival to be a surprise. My hire car was parked in a laneway down the road. The trees had been well maintained, even in good old Arthur's absence, and I rather hoped the gardens had been looked after to his standard while I was away. The drive gently curved to the left and it took me ten minutes to stroll the length of it. I was, again, suitably impressed as the house came into view. The ground-floor rooms were lit up and the warm buttery glow spilling out the windows illuminated pansies, lavender and violas. Yes, I had no shame in the notion I knew the names of all the plants — that's what happens when you grow up in a stately home with absent stately parents and only a gardener for company.

There wasn't a car outside the front door, a fact I welcomed. I needed her to be alone. She would be incredibly surprised to see me as I'd not told her of my return. Yes, she knew I was still alive and well, living the high life as she thought in Morocco. I had given little or no thought to what she had been doing in the interim. I imagined alcohol and men featured heavily. She was a whore – a mignotta – and old habits die hard. She deserved to die – she was past it after all. Surely her beauty had failed her by now? It was her only bargaining chip and without it she was only fit for the knacker's yard. That made me chuckle – the vision of her as a mangy old brood mare ready for slaughter then rendered down into something useful like glue.

All in good time. I was getting ahead of myself. All the possibilities of how this night would end began to flood my mind and my younger self conjured up images of my father. He was a good man. Better than she ever deserved – she got herself pregnant with me only to trap him. She wanted money. She bled him dry. It eventually led to his suicide. But she had killed him, slowly, over the years. I recall the arguments and the raised voices. Funny how I couldn't remember the content of said conversations but the last one before he swung from the end of a rope had been particularly vicious. He accused her of being all sorts. A crook, a whore, an embezzler and a criminal. I was more than pleased to hear him call her these names, I had been trying to convince him for years. Some of the stories I told him were the absolute truth of course – the others, well, let's just say they were embellished. *Mignotta*. The bile rose in my throat. I hadn't felt that for some time. It was the Livia effect. Perhaps I would be lucky and she would announce she was dying of a terrible disease. That would be fun. I would, of course, stay with her until the bitter end – as any good son would do and I'd watch as her body imploded on itself and disease ravaged her. Perhaps all this oxygen from the trees was making me giddy. My imagination was on overdrive. It was delightful. Rather than knock on the door like some peasant seeking permission to enter, I made my way to the side of the house and into the walled garden. I stayed in the shadows as I wanted to pinpoint exactly where she was and what she was up to. The drapes were closed tight in the drawing room. I imagined her sitting in an embroidered chair, swigging brandy and allowing her evil eyes to rest. Perhaps she would pop a pill or two – the old muscle relaxants were her favourite drug of choice. I should know, she stuffed them down my throat enough times when I was too afraid to go to sleep or I demanded a bedtime story. *Shut up, you stupid silly little boy, are you blind to the fact I'm entertaining? No one wants you downstairs. Stay here or you will be locked in the stable.* The peasant brogue always came out when she was angry – two minutes later I'd hear her, all sweetness and light, calling to the staff to replenish the guests' drinks. *Mignotta.*

I couldn't delay the inevitable any further. I was looking forward to the look of shock and surprise when I walked into the room to greet her. I wondered would it be possible for our last conversation to be a pleasant one? I doubted she was even capable of it. She was a terrible mother and all my success was purely down to my own brilliance and survival instinct. I was lucky – I was strong and intelligent. Not many would have survived her insanity.

I let myself in through the back-kitchen entrance. It was quiet. For the last couple of months, Mother Dear had closed Weybridge Estate to the public. It was a move that surprised me but, on reflection, I realised she couldn't maintain the management of the place without my input. Shame. But there you go.

The kitchen smelled like it always did. It's universally acknowledged all homes have their own distinct smell. I wouldn't give Weybridge the title of home. And the smell? I didn't particularly like it. I was faced with the choice of taking the door to the left which led up a small flight of stairs into the dining room, beside which the drawing room was located, or I could take the door to the other side of the kitchen and take the long way around. I chose the latter. It would be interesting to see how the house had changed since I last stayed.

I was impressed. The house had been maintained in my absence and several long-overdue improvements had been made. The rooms and corridors were free from dust, implying she had kept on at least a couple of staff members. The kitchen too had given me this impression – it felt industrial and in the adjoining mud room a number of lockers remained locked.

I felt nothing as I walked around my home. 'Home' – don't make me laugh. I wandered towards my mother's bedroom and pushed in the heavy oak door. The room was in darkness but the unmistakable scent of her perfume oozed out at me like pus from a sore. I switched on the lights and took a look around. I knew where she kept the photo albums. They were buried in the back of the large fitted wardrobe and hadn't seen the light of day in years. She wasn't exactly a candidate for showing them off to guests round the dining-room table. I wasted no time in locating them and didn't bother with sentimentalities. I wondered what it felt like to be a person who loved nothing more than look at their parents' wedding album or have a whole sideboard stuffed with volumes of albums spanning the years. Perhaps it would have been nice to belong to that kind of family, where Father – now whitehaired and wearing bifocals – spent every waking hour cataloguing his lifetime collection of photos. Smiling happy children. Smiling happy adults. Neighbours and the local fairs. We were never that kind of family. Who am I kidding, we were never a family full stop. I was a meal ticket.

I located the picture I was after without much trouble. It was one of my father and me on a fishing trip when I was about sixteen, taken by the man who sold us bait. It was on this trip he told me he was leaving my mother and I was going with him. The world was our oyster and that fishing trip was the last time I saw him happy.

Our great escape never happened, of course – she was a persuasive woman and Father was weak – she always managed to sink her claws back into him when she needed to. She killed him. Whore.

I put the picture in my wallet and threw the albums back into the wardrobe. I had waited long enough. I wanted to see her. I wanted to tell her what I was going to do and I was looking forward to seeing her face as she realised I could do it. I hated her. She deserved to die. I needed to move on with my life. Start again and cut all ties. The clean-up operation. As I mused over starting my new life, I wondered if Sal had picked up on my hints. Would she come back to Ireland? And, if she did, would she come here or go to Wexford first? She should really be on the way. Perhaps I would ring the gallery and enquire? Mother would be pleased about that at least. She liked Sal and was impressed with the scale of her talent.

Back downstairs I felt the overwhelming urge to sing in the corridor. It was all coming together. I had returned from that hellhole unscathed with plenty of money and the freedom to go wherever I wished. The icing on the cake would be to have Sal there with me. She was mine – not his. I checked the disposable phone again. Nothing. It had only been 24 hours. She needed time to think. No news is good news.

'Hello, Mother Dear, I'm home!' My words echoed around the long expanse of hallway, buffeted by dark wood panelling. I was sure she would hear me – the heavy doors and the panelling weren't completely soundproof, and sounds carried better through the evening air. Moments later the door of the drawing room opened. I was right. I knew she would be in there. The crackle of burning wood drifted out from the room.

She stood in the light and exhaled smoke from the cigarette in her hand.

'The Prodigal Son returns! Scottie darling, do come and join me for a drink.' She clicked her fingers at me and dipped back into the room.

I wasn't expecting her to be so, well, calm.

I followed her into the drawing room and, sure enough, a decanter of her poison of choice sat alone at the end of the sideboard. The fire was lit and the drapes were drawn. How cosy. Her balloon glass balanced on the edge of the marble hearth beside a mobile phone, and cigarette smoke hovered in the air.

'Have a brandy, dear.'

'I'll pass, thank you.'

'Why the long face, Scottie? You got out of jail free after the mishap in Marrakech, did you not? You should be counting your lucky stars. That was a dirty business.' She sashayed across the deep-pile carpet, sat in an armchair by the fire and picked up her glass.

I was perplexed. What was she talking about? She knew nothing about Marrakech.

'Mother, you are drunk and talking rubbish as usual.'

'And you, my darling, are a stupid and silly little boy.'

I felt my shoe connect with the bones of her fingers as I kicked the brandy glass clean out of her hand. It smashed in spectacular fashion against the grand surround of the fireplace. The bile was rising and the red mist had started to descend. She didn't flinch. She was very close to me throttling her. I needed to relax. I had time.

'Get me another drink, Scott. It's going to be a long evening and we need to have a good old chinwag, dear.'

She knew how to grate on my nerves.

'By the way, darling, be a dear and pour a couple of fingers for our two guests. They will be with us shortly. We have been expecting you.'

'What are you talking about? You had no idea I was going to be here. No one did. Why would I care who your damn guests are?'

I was pacing. She remained calm. That woman had the same effect on me, every time – me assuming the role of son and somewhere in the recesses of my brain feeling accountable to her. This whore who sat in front of me did not deserve the title of 'mother'. She was a nothing – a feeble insect that needed to be squashed underfoot. *So why are you still standing there, you stupid silly little boy?* I rubbed at my temples and noticed the perspiration on my forehead. She was too calm – she *had* been expecting me. I didn't like it.

I changed my mind about the brandy. How I would have loved to lace her drink with my poison but I had none and, if these guests really were arriving, I couldn't do it. I was curious to see who was joining her. I reluctantly poured for her as well and handed her the glass.

She swirled the amber liquid around and around, the fire the object of her interest. She looked strained – not that I particularly cared – it was merely an observation.

'You have hated me all your life, haven't you?' She looked directly at me and flinched as she noticed the deformity on my cheek.

'Hate implies a strong level of emotion. I would like you dead. You mean nothing to me.'

'We are more alike than you think, dear boy.'

I laughed heartily for the first time that day. Who was she trying to fool? Her tolerance levels for the liquor had clearly reduced with age.

'I'm nothing like you. You are weak and pitiful. I am not.' My voice was measured and I was in control.

'You have no scruples, Scott. No morals and no conscience. Your father, God rest his sorry little soul, was a weak man. His conscience and his morals made him so. You and I do not have that affliction.'

'Father was a good man. You tricked him into marrying you and you killed him slowly over the years – while, of course, spending all his money.'

'You are correct. Yes, I did trick him into marriage and the most effective way to do that in this little pozzo nero of a country was a pregnancy. Followed swiftly thereafter by a wedding. No questions asked.'

'You were a worthy inhabitant of this wretched country then.'

'I paid the price for my subterfuge. I knew that there was something a little bit unbalanced about you from the day you were born. I tried to feel this famous maternal instinct for you, but it did not come. I was very fond of you, of course, but that bond was not there.'

I didn't like listening to this. I knew it all but she was finally confirming it. She hadn't moved from the seat. I remained standing.

'I was always a resourceful woman. Coming from my

background to where I am today is testament to that. What you have overlooked, all these years in all your accusations, is why I needed the money so badly. Why, why, why is the question.'

I wasn't going to gratify her with the enquiry. I couldn't really care less as to why.

'You are not as intelligent as you think you are, Scottie. Arrogance and ego are your enemies. When you were younger, it was manageable, but over the last number of years, as your alcohol and cocaine intake has increased, you have become a liability.'

She shunted herself to the edge of the chair and used the two high armrests to push herself into a standing position.

'Mother, I am here to tie up loose ends. I have come back to address a number of outstanding issues and then I am leaving this – to use your words – this *pozzo nero,* this cesspit of a country once and for all.'

'Do you remember when you first went to Trinity?'

'Yes.' Her ramblings were beginning to bore me now. I glanced around the room and spotted a beautiful and heavy brass poker. That might just work. Alternatively, I could simply smother her.

'You fell in with a crowd very quickly and before long you had started to sell the cocaine you loved so much to kids all over the city. You adapted quickly and you were making quite the profit while moving up the chain of command.'

'How do you know that?' I was intrigued now. She was correct in her assessment – I was a genius. In the space of about six months, I had eradicated my competition. I rather naively at first thought I was a one-man operation – before I realised I was a link in a much bigger chain. That suited me. Not long thereafter, I had met the Boss and, by the time I finished college, I was earning more than the lecturers there. It continued that way and, well, the rest is history.

'Again, dear boy, you never asked yourself the important questions. Your inflated sense of self blinded you. You never asked yourself *why* you were chosen – out of all those students – why you? Why did the organisation reach out to *you*?'

'The why is not important, Mother.'

'That's where you are wrong.' She held up her hand to silence me and cocked her head to one side like a dog. 'Our guests have arrived.'

Her demeanour changed instantly. As she made for the door she stopped, appraised me for moments and then spoke to me in a tone I can only describe as her trying to be genuine.

'Scott – I have tried all my life to protect you in my own way. I continued to do that since you left for Spain. His ears are now deaf to my pleas. He is volatile – remember that and tread carefully when you speak with him.'

'What the bloody hell are you talking about? This is ludicrous. I'm not afraid of one of your disgruntled boyfriends.' It had become exasperating – the woman was talking in riddles. I truly thought she had lost her mind.

She shook her head and her eyes were heavy with sadness. The elaborate chimes of the doorbell summoned her and she dutifully answered the call.

A stab of fear hit me in the gut and I once again scanned the room for something a little easier to brandish than the heavy brass poker. I was amused at my mounting of a defence against the faceless bogeyman. Notwithstanding, I chose my vantage point, slipped the poker in behind the sideboard and placed myself within three strides of both the weapon and the adjoining door into the dining room. I could hear two new voices – one male, one female. I strained to hear what was being discussed but couldn't make out the words. Ghosts of the past floated past me and I realised the last time I had stood in the room waiting for guests was the night Andy and the rest of them were here. The night it all began to come apart at the seams.

The voices came closer and a vague hint of recognition came into my mind.

He had entered the room before the penny dropped. A woman walked in with him, and Mother followed on their heels like an obedient dog.

He smiled at me.

Mother made the introductions in a flat tone.

'Scott – this is Lucy.'

The young, very attractive woman blinded me with a smile and shook my hand. I had her evaluated in seconds even though my mind was racing ahead of me. She was a force to be reckoned with, without doubt, and she was sleeping with her companion.

I didn't respond as my brain was trying to catch up with what had just happened. That man – he shouldn't be here. What was he doing here? What was the connection? How did he find me? I was trying to make sense of it in my head and he damn well knew it. He was smug, as always, and watched me like the vulture he was.

'No need to introduce you to Ivan.' She pronounced it as E-vhan.

'Scott – I have been looking for you!' His jovial tone was forced.

My spine stiffened and the muscles in my chest constricted.

'Evening, Boss! It's nice to finally know your name.'

He stepped forward and shook my hand. He placed his other hand on my shoulder, applying just enough pressure for it to be uncomfortable. I reciprocated by tightening my grip. He broke from the handshake and helped himself to a drink from the dresser.

'Livia, my dear. You're holding back. Go on, do tell him.'

When he turned around, drink in hand, he sneered at me – I had heard that tone and seen that face before – usually before he had someone shot. My mother's eyes darted from him to me, to Lucy and to the window as though she was planning an escape route. Panic lit up her face like a neon sign, and cigarette smoke escaped from her lips.

Then she spoke and her voice cracked with fear. 'Ivan is my brother.'

Chapter 34

'Your brother? My uncle? Bullshit!' I looked at my mother and him in disgust.

'That is no way to address your mother or your uncle, Scott.' He laughed in my face and raised the glass in salutation. It was then I noticed he was wearing a gun in a holster under his arm. *Fuck.*

Lucy touched him on the arm as she walked to the sideboard and poured a drink for herself. She clearly wasn't that good in the sack — he didn't even pour the woman a drink.

Uncle? What was going on here? I studied him and my mother. It was undeniable — of course, *now* I could see the similarities — when it was pointed out to me. I laughed out loud. The Family Business — I resisted the urge to quote Marlon Brando and do a Godfather impression. It wasn't the time for humour. This changed everything. It began to make sense in my head. I knew I had pushed the boundaries with the Boss on more than one occasion but I was a businessman — assuming the risks was what entrepreneurs did. I had seen men shot for less, but somehow I managed to dodge bullets. Now I understood. No one had spoken since the big reveal. I needed a drink.

'Scott, you have been a very bad boy.' His face was smiling but his voice held no gaiety.

Lucy was hanging on his every word. Mother was paling by the second.

I walked past him, just close enough for him to have to take a small step backwards. I poured a drink, turned around but stayed beside the sideboard.

'It isn't registering with you at all, is it?' he said.

'What isn't registering?' I took a large sip and it burned the back of my throat. Swallowing a cough, I eyeballed him.

'I'm here to wind up the business. Before that, you need a history lesson.'

By now, Mother was on her second cigarette – the half-smoked one lay dying in the ashtray. She was trying to communicate something to me through the look in her eyes – had we had any form of close relationship, I'm sure I would have picked up on the nonverbal clues, but we didn't so I ignored her.

'I have been Head of Operations here in Ireland since your departure to Spain.' Lucy spoke in a refined Dublin accent and had a real sense of self-importance. 'The channel you opened down in Wexford remained that way, even with the absence of two key players. We took a different approach and recruited again. After your episode that night, we had an in. We needed it after the mess you created.'

'Darling, there was no mess,' I said. 'And no one was lifted on my watch – Doc was your error, not mine. Who's your contact?'

My mind was reeling. I didn't like her tone and I began to feel that this evening would not end with a family get-together around the fire.

'We needed Fran out. He was the one who pulled you off the beach and he was the only one who knew you were alive. It worked to our advantage how low his IQ actually is and how much he loves his mammy!' She spat the last few words out –

clearly disgusted by Fran's lack of virility.

'So why not just get rid of him?'

'He wasn't worth the effort and in the end he proved more resourceful than we had first imagined.'

'Yes – Fran did prove very resourceful.' I laughed. 'He was feeding you information the whole time and he ultimately double-crossed all of us. Isn't that right, Boss?'

The Boss still hadn't contributed to the conversation, instead he circled us like a shark.

Mother was now in the chair with her hands in a position of prayer.

He finally spoke. 'Fran will be taken care of. He is back in the harbour and I'll be sending someone down there to tie up all the loose ends.'

'We need to back up here a little.' I looked at the Boss. I couldn't call him Ivan – it was alien to me. 'Where did all this begin? I feel like I'm missing out on a crucial piece of information here.'

'Let me tell you a story and a half, Scott. You're going to love this.'

I always had him pegged as a prick, now I was sure. His voice dripped with condescension as he approached a wingback chair and lowered himself into it. He handed the glass to Lucy. She handed it back replenished. His posture was that of a man used to having an audience and he was in no rush to expose the information for my benefit. I waited as he cleared his throat and stuck his nose into the glass. Quite the showman, he was. Lucy looked interested too – judging by the half-smile, she felt she was about to be let in on the family secrets, implying intimacy. The girl had a lot to learn about men like the Boss. I estimated she was around thirty-five or so. Classy. Her clothing was tailored and her perfume expensive. Her well-groomed mane of chestnut hair framed an expertly made-up face.

Ivan removed the gun from under his jacket, laid it on the arm of the chair and crossed one leg ever so casually over the other. He smiled at his audience and, with a flourish of his hand, began to speak.

'Let me take you back to Ireland in the early 1970's. The drug scene in the cities was small and backward – just like the Irish. Cannabis and LSD were the popular choice with perhaps a handful of medical students experimenting with amphetamines. The students and the hippies. Heroin wasn't on the streets and cocaine was associated with Americans and film stars. Ireland was a gap stop for drug imports to the United Kingdom and fear of the Irish Republican Army deterred most from thinking about a life of crime. The Irish police had it very easy. The odd raid on a pub and colleges and apartments connected with frequenters of pubs allowed them to pat themselves on the back. They had cleaned up the streets, as they thought. Over that decade things began to change. By the 1980's heroin had found its way into the country, but still no cocaine.'

I poured another drink and gestured to the others, inviting them to have a refill. We were going to be here for quite some time. My interest was now piqued by his delivery – as I've said, quite the storyteller.

He nodded in gratitude as I poured him a measure.

'Now, let me take you to Italy in the 1970's. It was a very different story. We were more advanced and organised in the supply and the consumption of drugs, mainly thanks to the Mafia and their connection with the Colombians. Our close proximity to the coast of Africa was a major influence.'

'Okay,' I said. 'This is a wonderful economic comparison between two countries in the seventies, but I'm more curious about my part in all of this?'

'Patience, Scott, patience. You are always in such a hurry to get to the punchline – it's a weakness of yours and causes you to be sloppy.' The venom was back in his voice. 'Your mother Livia and I were born very close together into a large family in the Campania region. We were poor and in our village prospects were limited. The older siblings had flown the nest and the country was in quite a mess – as was the rest of Europe in the years after the war. Father was a fisherman and mother a cleaner for a wealthy family in the village – the Cutolo family. And then beautiful Livia arrived and by the time she reached the age of ten, we knew she was something special. The voice of an angel and the village loved her. The Cutolo family took a real interest in her and paid for private lessons. Our family became part of theirs, spending all our time together, eating together, parties, family gatherings – all together, all the time. We loved them like our own, even though we all knew of their involvement with the oldest Mafia organisation in Italy. Surely you have heard of the Camorra, Scott?'

I nodded. Who hadn't heard of the Camorra?

'It was only natural then, as we got older, that we worked for them. I don't need to explain what we were doing. We had never seen so much money and we loved that family like our own. Livia was sent to study in the Teatro di San Carlo in Naples and I was their most trusted delivery boy.'

Mother had never told me about her history prior to her training in Naples. She was vague with the details of her upbringing. Father had paid for elocution lessons for years – another of his long-suffering attempts to turn her into something more polished than she really was.

'Our opportunity came when the Theatre sent out a travelling opera troop – your mother of course was the star of the show, and I her chaperon. We travelled all over Europe to perform for the season and our last stop was Ireland.'

He gazed off into the distance and didn't speak for a few moments. Mother was lost in a world of nostalgia and Lucy looked bored.

'Ireland, of course, reminded us of home. Sleepy fishing villages, the adoration of Our Lady and the money and wealth shared by a very small section of society. It became clear to me, very quickly, that there was a market for cocaine. I had the connections, I had the money and I had the balls to do it. We also had the perfect ruse – the theatre company. We travelled in convoy, no questions would

245

be asked if more vehicles were added to that. Initially, I brought it in through my own contacts at home but it proved to be costly and I didn't like the large percentage my own boss was creaming off my hard work. We needed to source another beneficiary – someone who had contacts in Ireland but who would be easily controlled. And, as if by the grace of God, we found both in your father. It was love at first sight when he met your mother and, after a few months courting, of course she got pregnant. Being the decent man he was, he married her without hesitation and we now had a home too. It was marvellous. The business grew rapidly. The appetite for cocaine was ravenous once the drowsy Irish got their first taste. I established a supply line from Colombia through Spain and, the beauty was, we were surrounded by water. I was bringing it in everywhere with no competition. Your father, unknown to him, was suppling the capital and the warehouse. He continued to work hard, like all decent folk, and your mother and I ran the enterprise from here. Do you not remember me living here when you were a bambino?'

'No. I don't remember.'

'Eventually, you grew up and you were recruited. And, wow – what promise you showed before you got too big for your boots. By then I had moved to Spain and ran the operation from there. It was the convenience of being located on mainland Europe, and again the proximity to the coast of Africa. We were building the empire and it would have been passed to you.'

I didn't know what to say in response. I felt as though my life had been controlled and orchestrated from before the time of my birth. How did my father not know that his wife and his brother-in-law were drug barons? He couldn't have. He was a good man, with morals and conscience. He really didn't stand a chance against my mother and him. I felt a heaviness in my heart for him. Another victim of drugs, simply in a more indirect manner.

'Your father was a good man, Scott, but naïve. His love for you and your mother completely blinded him to what was going on, right under his nose. Your mother was a good businesswoman and at first glance everything appeared above board. But your father eventually began to suspect something and threatened to blow the whistle on the whole operation. He had no idea how big and indeed how dangerous we were. Your mother and I killed him, you know, and we made it look like a suicide.'

An animal sob escaped from my mother and when I looked at her she was weeping. I could not believe my ears. My legs began to shake and black spots appeared before my eyes – not from sadness, but anger. I would kill both of them. My father was a good man and he was good to me. They manipulated, robbed and used him all his life and then they killed him.

I looked at Lucy and something had settled on her face too – a realisation that this was not a game and perhaps she too was now in too deep.

'And you, my dear,' he turned his attention to the young woman, 'you have become sloppy too. Your pal Tess seems to be becoming wary of you. She doesn't seem to trust you any more. I wonder why that is?'

'What has Tess to do with any of this?' I had to ask. This was getting interesting.

'Good grief. If you can't figure that out by yourself, I'm not wasting my time telling you. Fool.' He shook his head and drained his glass.

'Ivan, please,' said my mother. 'Let's just forget about all of this. Go back to Spain – forget about business here. We are too old for this now.' She was pleading with her brother and had taken his hand in hers as she stood beside his chair.

I felt like time was speeding up. My mother had aged. The atmosphere cracked with electricity.

Lucy had taken a step towards me and my uncle's face had darkened. I had come face to face with evil. Blood of my blood. My roots. My family. He was going to kill me. My nine lives had run out.

The poker was still where I'd left it. Its presence was no comfort to me.

'You were played, Scott, from the moment you were born.' He was rather amused by this idea and his laughter had the same effect on me as a whining child. 'Your arrogance and your inability to play by the rules has cost me a lot of money. Your disappearance out of Marrakech reflected badly on me and my crew now think I am losing my touch. You have put me in a very difficult position. You have also brought heat to me now that your sidekick, Fran, has gone home. He knows too much and now there is a trail straight back to me. We are pulling out and winding business up.'

'I made you a huge amount of money and you know it.' I'd had enough by now. 'We are businessmen. Business is risk. I opened the channels all over Morocco, Tunisia and Algeria. That's big business.'

'You opened a can of worms with your other business and the death of that little junkie from the bidonville. Your reckless behaviour in that harbour with that woman and her son destroyed your anonymity in Ireland and the death of her husband's first wife was linked to you. You are no good to me here now.'

'You would be nothing without me.' Then, despite the situation, I felt a surge of happiness as the phone vibrated in my pocket. Only one person had that number.

'You are a chip off the old family block, boy. Blood is thicker than water. You are the same as me – a carbon copy almost. But you have become volatile and sloppy. It's time to tie up loose ends.'

He lifted the gun and fired.

Chapter 35

Jen came out of the shed in her father's house with a bag of wood for the fire. She slipped the other bag she had hidden underneath it into the boot along with the firewood and walked back to the driver's side of the car.

'I'll see you in the morning for school, Dan. Love you!'

Jen's dad called to her as she was getting back into the car. 'Jen, love, tomorrow is Saturday. No school.' He laughed as she shook her head and got into the car.

Sal was on her phone, texting furiously as Danny and her father waved them off. Andy had walked down to the Gale to meet Doc. He confirmed, in passing, that Tess was at home catching up on accounts for the evening.

'Who're you texting, Sal?'

'Don't bother getting paranoid around me now, you. It's Abe.' She proffered the glowing phone to Jen. 'Read them if you want.'

Jen shook her head and stepped on the accelerator. They were headed back down in the direction of the harbour.

'What are you going to say to her?' she asked before dropping the phone back into her handbag.

'I'm going to rip her head off. She knew, Sal. She knew he was alive.'

Jen was thumping her hand against the steering wheel and with each thump the foot on the accelerator got closer to the floor. Her breathing was coming in rasps and Sal had to put her hand on her arm and command her to slow the hell down.

The lights of the village lit up the darkness. It looked like any sleeping fishing village in Ireland. A couple walked hand in hand in the direction of the beach. Teenagers. It didn't take too much of a stretch of the imagination to figure out what they were going to get up to. The remainder of their little group sat, swinging their legs on the wall of the post office, pushbikes abandoned against the streetlamp. They all lifted their heads out of their phones as Jen's car screeched to a halt beside them. She leapt out of the car with Sal in pursuit.

'Where the hell are you going?' Sal shouted after her as she tried to keep pace.

'I need to speak to Fran!' Jen shouted over her shoulder.

The teenagers sniggered and whispered as the women ran past.

By the time Sal caught up with her, Jen was already banging on the door.

Fran answered it, with a dressing gown on over his clothes and a distinct smell of weed oozing from every pore.

'Hi, Jen. Howya, Sal?' Fran looked really surprised to see them.

Jen got straight to the point. 'He's still alive.'

'Horseshit.' Fran stood back from both of them, as though he could get away from the news, and the front door began to close.

Jen kicked it open and it hit the wall with such force she expected the glass to fall out of it. He stood back, arms swinging in the breeze, and it took his hazy weed-filled brain a few seconds to respond. She filled him in on the story as Sal pleaded with them to keep their voices down. The teenagers on the opposite side of the road were getting miles out of this.

'I'll talk to Joe,' he finally managed to say.

'Do. And if you hear anything, you better bloody ring me first. Give me your phone number.' She slipped her hand into her back pocket and pulled out her smartphone. She was impressed at the speed he recalled his number – maybe he wasn't that stoned after all. She dialled the number and she could hear a phone trill in the background.

'Grand.'

'Do you think he's coming back?'

'What do you think, Fran? Of course, he is. He's coming for me – and for you.'

She turned on her heel and walked away from the door. Sal and Fran were speaking but she couldn't hear what they were saying. She didn't care. Tess was next. She felt good after kicking that door in – maybe she should have kicked him too. Her rage was growing, but she was in control. For the first time, ever, she could clearly see Scott's face. She felt anger, not fear. That was good. She needed to be ready.

Sal caught up with her and she had barely managed to close the passenger door as the car lurched out of the carpark.

'Calm down, Jen. You're acting like a demon.'

That made Jen laugh, but the laughter was a bitter and spiteful. 'It's about time, Sal. I'm done with being nice.'

'You need to pull yourself together. You go in there like a raging bull and you're not going to get the story out of her. Calm down. We need her to think we're down for a visit because I'm home. You need to be calm, okay?'

Jen took a couple of deep breaths. Sal was right. She needed to tread softly here. Tess was clearly involved in this mess still and they needed to be careful in their approach.

'Okay, you're right.'

Tess looked immediately suspicious when she opened the door to them. She hid it behind hugs for the pair of them and, by the time she had ushered them through to the lounge, she had composed herself. Jen watched her like a hawk. It was the first time Jen had been in the new house – it was much smaller than the old one and there was no indication that a married couple lived there – it was all Tess, in this room at least. There wasn't a hair astray. Hugh's schoolbag sat neatly against the armchair. He was in the chair, hooked up to headphones and buried in his phone. He didn't even look up until his mother tipped him on the shoulder and told him to go upstairs. He went to say something to her but spotted she had company and left without even acknowledging them.

'Sorry about that,' she said as she straightened the cushions on the floral-printed couch in front of the open fire. 'Here, sit down.'

They small-talked while she flitted to and from the kitchen with mugs of coffee and biscuits and Sal dodged the question when she enquired as to why she was home.

Tess joined them and sat on an armchair opposite the couch. Jen felt like it was a panel interview.

'Tess. Fran is back.' Jen watched for a reaction and she got one.

Tess, in an attempt to place her mug on the table, missed it and spilled coffee all over the carpet. Apologising, she stood up and said she was going to fetch a cloth.

'I know what you did,' Jen said.

She froze and looked over their heads in the direction of the bay window.

'It's not what you think.' She sat back down in the chair.

Sal remained silent but Jen knew, by the act of her placing her hand on her arm, that she could feel the rage pulsating from her. She remembered what she had said in the car, and took a deep breath.

'Enlighten me,' she said.

Tess sat and gazed into the fire. She remained silent for quite some time.

Then Sal's mobile vibrated against something metallic in her bag. None of them moved.

'It was the morning after you were attacked on the strand.'

'You mean the morning that everyone was searching the water for the man who'd tried to murder me and my eight-year-old son?'

'No one knew he was still alive at that stage. No one except Fran.'

252

'He told me the story. I don't need to hear it again. I want to hear where you fit into this whole fucking circus.' Jen was sitting forward on the couch, her hands clasped and her voice dangerously calm.

Sal sat like a poker beside her.

'Livia called me. I hadn't slept all night and I was worried about you.'

'What a great friend you are, Tess.'

Tess ignored the jibe and continued.

'I thought she had called to enquire about you and maybe about the search. The Guards had been to her house at first light and informed her what had happened. She seemed, I dunno, very calm on the phone for someone whose son had gone missing and was presumed drowned.'

Jen and Sal didn't take their eyes off Tess. They watched as she shrank into the chair, her voice devoid of the strength it usually carried. If she was the criminal mastermind that Jen had pegged her as, she deserved an Oscar for the performance she was giving. The tears began to fall and her voice was meek.

'She did enquire about you and was relieved to hear that you were both okay. Then she mentioned Scott and the money he had invested in the pub.'

She reached a shaking hand out for the coffee. She seemed surprised that the mug was empty. Sal stood, picked it up and went into the kitchen.

Tess smiled faintly at her when she placed the refilled mug in front of her. She continued her story.

'Livia told me that I was in a very awkward position and, if I couldn't help her out, then she would not help me. All I had to do was go down to the harbour and convince Fran to leave. She didn't care how I did it, but I had to make sure he would go. She told me if I didn't she would see to it that Hugh would end up under a car one evening when he was out on his bike. She also told me she would make sure I ended up homeless and without the pub. She told me that if Fran was still in the harbour in 24 hours, I would pay the price and then she hung up. At this stage, I had no idea of Fran's involvement or more importantly – Doc's.'

The two women were like statues, listening to her every word.

'It was only after the conversation we all had, when you came from hospital, that some of the pieces of the jigsaw began to fit together. Firstly, Fran's involvement in the drug operation and later, when I went to his house, he admitted to helping Scott. Livia knew and was trying to buy him time. Fran was the only link and she needed to get rid of him. She rang me the following morning again and told me that she needed me to do another job for her once everything cooled down. She threatened me again about Hugh and the pub. I still didn't know about Doc.'

'Why didn't you tell us?'

'I couldn't. She's fucking evil and I had that 80-grand debt to them hanging over my head. Then it all went quiet and I thought she was going to leave me alone. Eventually she rang me one day and asked me to do something for her. I refused. The following day Doc was arrested. A couple of hours later, she called me and told me next time her target would be Hugh. She was behind my husband getting locked up.'

Jen and Sal looked at her in amazement. If this was fabricated on the spot, she was a genius. If it was the truth, Tess had continued to live the nightmare too and couldn't tell any of them.

'She constantly threatened me all the time Doc was in prison. She told me if I didn't do what she said, he would suffer inside.'

'What were you doing for her? What was it?' Jen couldn't believe her ears. It was a tall tale to say the least but too strange not to be the truth.

'She continued to run the drugs into the harbour. Even though Fran and Doc were out of the picture, she kept that channel open and now I was the one storing them in the Tea Room. She made me sell the pub to pay back the debt and her solicitors altered all the paperwork to make sure it went through. The Tea Room is all a big front and I'm the one with the gun to my head all the time.'

'And then Doc was released, taking the pressure off you? She knew she'd lost some of her leverage then.' Jen could see exactly where this was going. Poor Tess.

'Yeah, you're right. She found another way of keeping the thumb-screws on.'

'Lucy,' Jen said.

Tess nodded.

'I went to pick Hugh up from school one day and he was outside, sitting on the wall. She was there, sitting beside him. It was that easy for her to get to him and as I left she told me, next time, he'd be nowhere to be found. She moved down to the harbour as soon as Doc told me he was going to be released. She watched me like a hawk and even that day I called over to you, she was there. I wanted to tell you — to spill my guts and come clean. So many times, I wanted to tell the truth but I couldn't.'

Jen buried her hands in her face. Sal stood and went over to the fire.

'All this time, he played all of us.' Sal's voice caught on the lump in her throat. She fired a log into the flames.

'I'm sorry for everything. Will you let me tell Doc myself? I will go to the police station too.'

None of them knew what to say or what came next. It was a nightmare — a full-on nightmare.

Jen eventually broke the silence. 'We need to keep this between us for now. Tess, if you go to the police, you'll be locked up.'

Tess was crying. She looked at the two women and sat forward in her chair.

'I'm relieved, now you know, and now I can do something about it.'

'You can't do anything about it until we know where he is, Tess. That's what we need to figure out and that's what we need Lucy for. She knows where he is.'

Jen didn't like the look of doubt that passed over Sal's face.

'Sal. We need to sleep on this. We will find Lucy in the morning and then we will go to the police — all of us together. Andy and Doc need to stay calm as well. If they think he's in Ireland, the first place they will go is to Weybridge. We can't let them. It's too dangerous.'

Sal nodded but didn't say a word.

Jen felt like she was having an out-of-body experience. It had all become very clear in her head: exactly what needed to be done. And soon.

'I'll text Fran and tell him to keep his mouth shut,' Jen said. 'Scott is not getting away with this a second time. This has to end. Are you both okay with that?'

They nodded.

Jen picked up her coat off the back of the couch and Sal followed suit. Tess remained seated, staring into the fire. They let themselves out.

Jen texted Fran as she was leaving.

Chapter 36

Lucy slumped to the floor – eyes open, her face frozen in a mask of surprise. The single shot had pierced her heart and a dark stain covered her breast. I had never been so close to death by gunshot before. The noise punched my ears and made me dizzy. My mother was saying something – she was shouting, I think, but I couldn't hear her with the ringing in my ears. Where was the gun? I looked at him. He had rested his weapon on the arm of his chair and resumed his affair with the glass.

'What the fuck? What did you do that for?' I had spilled the drink all over my hands with fright.

'She knew too much. I fired her.' He chuckled and looked at Mother.

For now, I was safe. After all, the gun wasn't pointed at me and he had shot her first.

Mother walked over and draped a throw over the woman who lay dead on her drawing-room floor.

'What are we going to do with that?' She stood over the shroud and looked at her brother.

It was surreal. My mother did not react in the way a person who had never been witness to a murder would. No screaming, no shouting, no fear. This was not her first time.

'We'll bury her on the grounds. Now the next question is what we do with him.' Ivan's voice was perfectly calm.

Mother didn't look at me. She advised him that all the people in the harbour who had any connection back to any of us needed to be taken care of. That was exactly what I was going to do for them, and then I would disappear — never to speak of or be involved in family business again. That suited me just fine.

Ivan's gun still sat on the arm of the chair and he continued to drink brandy. Eventually he roused himself and told me to go find a couple of shovels. Laying the offending gun on the sideboard, he bent down and whipped the blanket off the body. He checked her pockets and her purse, pocketed the cash and threw her wallet on the fire. Her phone was stripped of its SIM card — that too was burned. The device was smashed under the heel of his leather shoe.

The plan was simple enough. The body into her jeep. Drive the dirt track that ran from the back of the stables into the woods. Dig a grave. Body gone. As long as we were working together, I was in no fear for my own safety. We had the advantage of seclusion on Weybridge. He wanted the back of the jeep covered with something — a shag-pile mat from the hallway would suffice. The evening had taken on the feel of a tragi-comedy. While he was busy moving the mat, I at last had an opportunity to check the phone.

'I'm back where it all began — I'm in the harbour. Are you in Ireland or still in Berlin? Xx.'

I knew she would come back. I knew she would figure it out. And I knew it was her. I would recognise her Irish mobile number anywhere. It was a source of amusement to both of us. Her number ended in 666.

'Ireland. I knew you would come.'

I dashed into the front room while they were still at the jeep. A quick text came back.

'**I've missed you, so much. I want out of here, with you. Fran is back. They all think you're dead. Xx**'

I knew it. That crusty boyfriend of hers was no competition to me. Sal could never resist me. I should have got in touch with her sooner – but never mind.

'**We were good together. You've just proved you deserve to be with me. Let's go tomorrow.**'

'Okay. Where will we meet?'

'**I need one last trip to the harbour. I'll text you.**'

The phone vibrated again. She was quick with her comebacks.

'**Karma has brought us back together, Scott. Xx It's meant to be.**'

'**I don't believe in karma. I brought us back together. X**'

Ivan and my mother came in as I slipped the phone into my pocket.

My mother was quiet. However, her eyes were alert and she watched our every move. I was relieved to see he had left the gun behind as we made our way out to the vehicle. She again tried to communicate something to me non-verbally – I didn't know what.

The jeep's door clicked shut and I looked out at the gardens in front of me.

We didn't drive for too long before turning onto a smaller track under the cover of chestnut trees and Scots pine. The air was crisp and clean but the night was dark. The dipped lights of the jeep marked the spot, and we set to work. Of course, my mind wandered back to Marrakech and the last time I had embarked on a task of this nature. Fran had been there and now he was less than an hour away – holding hands with his mammy dear and watching shit TV. He had no ambition and had turned out to be a country bumpkin. Such a disappointment. I would see to him first and I would take pleasure from it.

I should have brought water with me. It was thirsty work. We dug a hole four-foot deep. It took longer than I had estimated, thanks to the roots of trees getting in the way but it would suffice.

'Let's get her out of the jeep and in there. I want to get the hell out of here.' He made his way to the vehicle.

I was impressed by his physical strength – I was still struggling to unlock my muscles and catch my breath.

It took my brain a few seconds after the boom to figure out what had happened. I was rooted to the spot as, in slow motion, Ivan's legs crumpled and he went down in a heap, head slamming off the front of the jeep. He fell, face down in front of the tyre on the driver's side and he wasn't moving. I couldn't see the shooter. All I could make out was him. His shirt had been torn clean off his eviscerated back. The icy grip of fear clawed at my innards and I dropped to the ground.

Chapter 37

I looked up as the figure came out of the darkness. The shotgun was still trained on Ivan and a steady hand held it. I could not believe my eyes.

'He always carries a second gun – concealed probably in the driver's door.' She pulled open the driver's door of the jeep and produced a handgun. 'He tricked you into a false sense of security when he left the other one on the sideboard.'

I got up onto my knees and I wasn't sure if I wanted to laugh or expel the contents of my stomach onto the ground in front of me.

'You are my son, Scott. I told you earlier I have tried to protect you in any way I could. This was the only way.'

She dropped the shotgun beside her brother and turned to face me. I didn't even want to ask where she had learned how to use a shotgun so proficiently. I never had her pegged as the outdoorsy type but father was an avid hunter – perhaps he had shown her.

This was something I thought I would never see and it gave me the strangest feeling. She was in control.

'Help me with him.'

It took a massive effort to move him from where he lay into the hole he had dug himself. We rolled the body in and went to the jeep to retrieve the other one. It was all surreal. The smell of damp earth and clay added to my feelings of perplexity. I hoped the grave wasn't too shallow for two, she face down on top of him, like lovers – wouldn't do to have foxes or stray dogs to dig them up. This was not how I imagined my evening would pan out.

Filling the grave in took no time at all. I wanted to get out of there and I worked with a speed I didn't think I could muster. Mother helped and once the earth was put back from where it came from, we covered the mound as best we could with foliage. The ground was uneven but it didn't stand out too much. We were on private property and no one ever came walking on this side of the estate. The lake was more of an attraction to picnickers and trespassers. That thought had crossed my mind, too, but it was safer here.

Words were sparse. There's not much to say in a situation of that magnitude. I was grateful to her – she was right. He did have another gun and it was a case of kill or be killed – he came here to kill me. My mother did the killing instead. The more I thought about it, the more I realised that I wouldn't have got out of there alive. When Ivan was heading back to the jeep it was to get the gun, not the body. It was going to be me in that hole with Lucy. Mother had saved my life.

We returned to the house and sat in the drive. We had the problem of getting rid of Lucy's jeep. Burning it out or abandoning it would draw too much attention. We decided on hiding it in the largest of the stables. The doors could be locked and it would be forgotten about. We drove it straight down there.

We entered through the back door of the main house and removed our shoes and clothing, replacing them with dressing gowns from the mud room. Burning our clothes was the sensible choice. The fire was still ablaze in the drawing room and we burned the items one by one while drinking brandy. The clock in the hall chimed – informing us it was ten o'clock. What an evening – it felt so much later than that.

I texted Sal again.

'Plans have changed. Meet me in the harbour before sunrise. 5am.'

A response came quickly.

'I'll meet you at Andy's boatyard.'

'You need to leave the country.' My mother's voice intruded on my thoughts about Sal and our romantic reunion.

'I will.'

'Stay out of the harbour. Get away from here. You brought this to my door. I want you gone.'

'You brought this to your own door, Mother.'

The fire cast shadows across her face. Anyone else looking at her would say her beauty was striking. To me, she looked like the old crone from my childhood nightmares. *She* was my childhood nightmare.

'It's over now. Enough. It was he who killed your father. Whatever you think, I did love him – he was a good husband and a good father. I ruined his life and he killed him. It's no wonder you turned out the way you did. You never stood a chance. I am sorry. Now please go.'

'You're right, I never did stand a chance but you are wrong about him killing Father – you both did, from the moment you clapped your peasant eyes on him. You're pathetic and I hope you die a slow and painful death, alone. You have never been my mother and it will be my pleasure to never clap eyes on you again.'

I didn't have to kill her with my hands. I hoped my words would do that instead.

Chapter 38

The minute Fran entered the Gale and clapped eyes on the pair of them, Andy could read his face. He looked like a man who wanted to run back out the front door and never come back. But he didn't. Instead, walking like a man who's waiting for a knife to be plunged into his back, he made his way to the bar. Several of the locals pointedly turned away from him as he approached. News travels fast in a small town.

Andy had let go of the anger much like he had done with Doc, and as soon as Fran turned around again he caught his eye and motioned for him to come over to their table.

'Sit down.'

He sat on the stool opposite Andy.

'Doc. How's it goin'?'

'Howya, Fran.'

Doc and Fran had no bad blood between them – Andy was the common denominator. They had both wronged him. Andy watched the creamy head on his pint pick a valiant battle with gravity. It was inevitable. Gravity always won.

They didn't speak for a while – instead, amused themselves by watching old Paddy. He was as old as the hills and no one ever dreamed of taking his seat at the bar. That was his throne. There was always a collective chuckle if a tourist swaggered in and took Paddy's perch, looking as though he couldn't quite believe his luck to find a free stool in such a busy bar. It was never too long before the man himself would rock up and roar a mouthful of abuse at the poor unsuspecting visitor. Their fate was in their own hands. If they were nice to the staff, they would be warned in advance – if they were rude, Paddy was payback.

Doc tried to make himself look small and turned his back to the bar. Fran kept his head down and made eye contact with the table.

'Are you uncomfortable here, Doc?' Andy looked at the miserable faces he was caught between and wished he was at home watching shite telly.

'If Paddy spots me, he'll be over to give me a hiding. He has been talking about it for months – you know how much he loves Tess.'

Andy looked at him and burst out laughing. Fran just stared into space.

'You're out of the clanger and you are afraid of an old fella like Paddy? Jesus, Doc, you are a gas man. He'll be grand – look,' he nudged him and smiled, 'he has a full pint in front of him and a Jameson lined up. You've a good twenty minutes before he turns around to beat you to a pulp.'

Andy laughed again. Fran's attention was back in the room and he too couldn't supress a smile. Paddy was the King of this Castle and well they all knew it.

'Jen called in to me.' Fran spoke into his pint as he raised it to his lips.

Doc wasn't yet privy to the conversation that had taken place with Fran, Andy and Jen – Andy had been working up to telling him.

Andy's phone sat on the table in front of him like a beacon. He picked it up twice, in a short space of time, and texted Jen to check in on her.

'What's going on, lads?' Doc wrapped his hands around his sparkling water and sat up straight in the chair. 'You look like you've seen a ghost,' he said to Andy before turning his attention to Fran, 'and you look like you're about to bolt out the door.'

The other two looked at each other. Andy cleared his throat and Fran made his excuses, heading in the direction of the men's room.

Andy gave Doc the short version of events, bringing him up to speed. Doc's slack jaw and pale face was indication enough he was hearing all this for the first time. He had no idea – Andy was relieved for that small grace. He had thought about it on the walk down to the pub. It would have been too much to endure had Doc been in on the big cover-up as well.

'You mean to tell me she knew all that time and didn't say a word.' It wasn't a question. 'Nah, man, you've got your wires crossed. There's more to it. It's Tess, like. My Tess. She's not that …' he hesitated and searched the air around him for an appropriate word, 'evil. No. Something is wrong. I told you she was acting weird, man.'

Andy didn't respond. He watched Doc's grip get tighter and tighter on the flimsy glass, afraid it was about to smash in his hand. He released his grip when Fran returned then he stood and went in the direction of the bar. His face was like thunder. Andy willed him not to do what he might be about to do. He watched and waited. Doc returned with more water and Andy breathed a sigh of relief.

'I can only tell you what Fran here told me, mate, and Sal. The girls have gone to speak to Tess.'

Doc slammed his hand on the table and a couple of the regulars looked around.

Andy raised his hand to the audience, reassuring them that things were fine. They turned back to their pints.

'So! You hatched a plan to separate us, get me down here – the women would accost my wife and you would establish what kind of criminal master plan we were running from the house?'

Fran looked like he wanted the ground to open up and swallow him. Andy had known he wouldn't be good in a situation like this and, as the conversation wore on, his nerves were fraying.

Fran drained his pint and left. Just walked out, without saying a word.

'It wasn't like that, Doc,' said Andy.

Neither of them even acknowledged Fran's departure.

'Jen had a right to know and wanted to speak to Tess and, yes, we did want to see how much you knew — but branding you as criminals and going on a witch hunt as you are implying is not how it happened.' Andy never raised his voice once. He outlined the facts as they were.

The pub was still busy. It was early enough but another hour and the place would be empty, bar Paddy holding court as the lonely barman cleaned up, trying to eek out his hours.

'I need to go home. I need to know what's going on — I should've seen this coming — but I've been so caught up in my own recovery, I didn't pursue it — I *knew* something was up. She's in trouble, man. There's no way she'd have acted like this if they didn't have some kind of hold on her and now you tell me he's still alive? I need to get home *now.*' In his haste to get his coat on, Doc knocked over his drink and shards of glass skittered across the floor.

The barman, ready for action to alleviate the boredom, was at the table in moments — ready for a fight.

'All good here, lads, yeah?'

They both apologised over the broken glass and, as Doc scrambled to pick up the detritus, the barman, exerting his authority, insisted for health and safety purposes he leave the clean-up to him. The yellow sign with the ridiculous cartoon on it materialised out of nowhere and he scurried away to get a dustpan and brush.

The phone lit up on the table. Luckily for Andy, the slosh of carbonated water had sprayed in the other direction. The screen told him it was from Jen. They were headed home. Tess was in trouble too and Doc needed to go home to talk to her. He told Doc and they didn't waste any time heading out front. Doc waited with him while Jen arrived to pick him up.

'Man, just go home and talk to her. Find out what's going on and we can all get together in the morning to figure this one out. We need to know where he is too.'

Doc stuck his hands in his pockets and examined his shoes.

'If only we had known what was in store for all of us. Me in prison, Tess a mess, you and Jen deciding not to have children, you giving up your life at sea and Sal running away to Berlin. All because of that prick.'

Andy frowned. 'What do you mean me and Jen deciding not to have children?'

'Just what she told Tess.' Doc looked confused. 'Tess told me you and Jen had made the decision. You discussed this, right? '

Andy stood in front of Doc and felt like his stomach had fallen out and through the floor. He'd had his suspicions Jen was hiding something and now he knew. He didn't speak as the tightness in his chest and throat wouldn't allow him to. Eventually he pushed out a few words.

'No, we didn't as a matter of fact – she was reluctant – but we didn't *decide* on anything.'

Doc looked uncomfortable. 'You know what women are like, man, they say a lot of stuff in conversation. Maybe Tess picked her up wrong.'

'Maybe.'

Andy wasn't sure if it was the tears or crushing disappointment that blurred his vision. Too much was happening in one day – information overload. He would speak to Jen but not tonight. *You knew she didn't want to have more children as long as he was still alive. You knew she felt like she had failed. And you kept pushing. Don't pretend this news comes as a shock to you.*

He recognised the headlights of the car making its way up the hill.

'I'll ring you in the morning, man. I'm going to see the

Sergeant too. We need to know how to handle this.'

'I'll call you then. I want to speak to Tess and we'll take it from there.'

They shook hands and, as Jen and Sal rolled into the carpark, Doc walked across the road, lost in his own thoughts.

Andy climbed into the back of the car. He couldn't quite bring himself to look Jen in the eye when she turned around to greet him.

She gave him a quick synopsis of what had transpired in Tess's. He noticed how upbeat she was and strangely detached from the whole conversation – she didn't sound like it was their circle of friends she was discussing.

He couldn't look at her as the feelings of rage and sadness swirled and danced in the pit of his gut. All those months she feigned disappointment as her period arrived, all those nights they spent together, him thinking he had the chance of being a dad. It was all a lie. She had no intention of giving him that.

She lied to you, Andy. She lied. What else has she lied about? But is now the time to be thinking about this? There's a madman on the loose and you are offended over this? Yes, but she lied. When this is over, you need to leave her – while you still have time. If she loved you – really loved you – she wouldn't have tricked you like this.

Sal was speaking to him too but he hadn't heard a word of it. She had turned to look at him and her face was full of sympathy.

'Are you okay, hon? You're miles away there?'

'I'm fine.'

He was glad the conversation had to come to a halt. They were pulling into the drive. He wouldn't allow himself to think about that for now. *It's her body, man, her choice. Her body, her choice. What about my fucking choice? She should have told me. I have rights too, you know.*

They were in the kitchen by the time he followed them in. The bottle of wine remained on the table from earlier on – he picked up a half-full glass and drained it, then refilled it and drained it again.

'Steady on there, Andy! What's up? What happened in the pub?'

Jen had come over and put her arm around him.

He wanted to scream at her to stay the hell away from him. He felt betrayed and cheated. Confusion fell on him like rain and he couldn't quite find words in his head that didn't involve screaming at her.

Sal had taken a fresh bottle of wine from the fridge and put it on the table on her way over to the record player. She removed her shoes and took a seat back at the table. Jen rubbed Andy's back before walking away and sitting beside her friend.

'Should we ring the Guards, Jen?' Sal asked.

'No, we shouldn't. We'll go see the Sergeant tomorrow – all of us, together, okay?'

Andy remained silent as Sal looked at him, begging for an answer. She was frightened. Sal could never hide her emotions and this one was etched all over her face. Something else was registered there too – but he couldn't quite put his finger on it. Andy knew that his silence was making her edgy and that wasn't fair on her.

'Joe will know what to do, Sal,' he said.

'What time in the morning?' she asked.

'Does that matter?'

'No, I don't suppose it does. What do you think they'll do?'

'The usual, I suppose,' said Jen. 'Watch the ports, watch the airports. I dunno. We don't even know if he's in the country yet. Maybe they will search the mother's house and, after all that Tess has said, they may bring them all in for questioning too.' She took a sip from her glass.

'God, it's mad to think we all got caught up in such a big thing,' said Sal. 'All about drugs and money. It's unbelievable. For a while I thought I loved him. Jesus.'

'Yep, well, there you go. You think you know someone and they are hiding things from you, right under your nose.' Andy noticed how his own voice had become detached too – like all of this was happening to someone else.

He looked at his wife and he couldn't tell why she looked so different to him. Was it because of what he had learned about her or because she had finally come to terms with the fact Scott was still alive? He supposed, now she knew for certain, she could prepare herself for what was to come.

They drank the second and then a third bottle of wine. Andy was drunk as the night came to an end. Even in his inebriated state, he noticed how sober both Jen and Sal were. Usually when she and Sal were together, it always ended with him putting the pair of them to bed. How things had changed.

Chapter 39

Scott's text about the change of plan had been a blessing in the end. She was ready for this and knew, either way, it was a new beginning for them. She moved quietly. The house was known to her, she didn't need the lights.

From Danny's room across the landing she could hear Andy snoring – it was a running joke with all of them. He wasn't a big drinker, but when they were all together and he did hit the wine, his snoring would wake the dead but he himself was impossible to rouse. Through the open door the child's nightlight cast images of stars and half-moons across the wooden floor and skirting-board. She imagined the little boy and his mutt curled up on the bed in the depth of the night in his grandparents' house, snoring gently and dreaming about taking over the world together. She wondered would she ever see the little boy again or sit down with the family and eat a meal.

Her heart was heavy at the prospect of what the morning might bring but she needed to do this. She needed to put her friends first and listen to her gut. It was a betrayal but the only way to guarantee everyone's safety. A calm acceptance had settled in her head and her soul. There was no other way. She was protecting all the people she loved. She wanted to do that for them and she was the only one who was in a position to do it.

She tip-toed down the stairs, blowing a kiss to the door behind which the greatest friends she ever had lay sleeping. They would understand, in time. This had to be done – there was no other way.

In the kitchen, save for the glow of light from the tiny lamp on the mantelpiece, darkness spilled over everything. Dawn was yet to breathe its magic into a new day. The landscape was free to breathe under the cover of darkness – it did not yet have to stand to attention, taking on its form for another day. The kitchen felt peaceful. Homely. That's the way she wanted to remember it, without his evil tainting the air and breathing fear into the walls. Three coats lay abandoned across the back of the chairs and the empty glasses still sat on the table, like they were reluctant for the party to come to an end.

She could have just gone back up the stairs, got back in the bed and rung the police – they could have cleaned up the mess – but she wasn't willing to take that chance. She needed to do this for all of them. She had planned this from the moment she knew he was alive. It had to happen.

She left the letters propped up against an empty wineglass. She had taken her time over them. Maybe he wouldn't come and the notes would remain sealed but she wanted to be ready. The hardest one to write was the one to Danny. To the little boy and his mutt. The rest, well, they would see where she was coming from and why it had to be this way.

The picture on the shelf over the record player beckoned to her. It was a black-and-white of the whole group of friends. Friends and loved ones who had seen too much pain and sadness at the hands of one man. The picture encapsulated love, joy and all the good things friends and families wish for each other in a lifetime. Joy, happiness, peace and love. Maybe after today, people would find that again.

She arrived at the shelf with no memory of walking there and looked at each of the smiling faces. She took the picture from the frame and put it in her pocket. Its presence gave her the strength to keep going. The clock told her it was a quarter past four. Plenty of time. Still time to back out.

She sought out the car keys. She thought of what was in the boot of the car. She needed that for the plan to work. Slipping out the front door, she held her breath as the sound of the central locking punched the dark stillness. The bag looked inconspicuous and banal lying in the boot of the family car. She took it out and slung it over her shoulder. She went back inside and the front door lock clicked quietly back into place. She took one last look around the kitchen. Determination was her motivator and she took a deep breath as she slipped out the patio door and headed in the direction of the strand before she could change her mind. What was done now, was done.

She walked quickly across the headland. The wet seeped in through her boots and the thought of buying a new pair crossed her mind before she stopped herself thinking about anything further than what was to be done.

She kept her head down as she came up the lane at the side of the post office. She wanted to cut across the small beach but the tide was in and part of the way was inaccessible. She needed to get there and didn't want to lose time picking her way over stones on the edge of the water in the dark. No one would be out – too early for anyone heading home from parties and not late enough for people heading to work. Anyone who was heading out to sea would be either on the trawlers by now on the way out, or waking up in bunks getting ready to cast off.

She stayed in the shadows and passed the church, the community centre, the other pub, the ice cream parlour, and the shop with stacks of newspapers outside, wrapped in plastic and string, waiting to assail the readers with sadness and misery from the four corners of the globe. She wondered what tomorrow's papers would say.

Her hands were stiff from clutching the big bunch of keys. She checked her watch. 4:38. He would be here soon.

No one was around as she turned the silver key in the padlock and slipped the bolt back.

The smell of diesel made her feel weak and Andy's face flashed in front of her. He was a good man and he was loved dearly. She felt guilty using his place for this, but there was no other choice. It was the only way. By suggesting to him to meet in Andy's place, she hoped his arrogance and belief he was getting the upper hand would weaken him.

In here, she could afford to turn on the light over the work bench. A torch showed her where the switch was and, as the light cast a gentle sodium glow over well-used tools and the hefty wooden bench, she laid the bag down on the floor and unzipped it. It was the only way. She had no choice. Her heart hammered in her chest and she reminded herself that fear was just adrenalin — the body's way of keeping itself safe. She hadn't been safe for a long time and fear had become as normal to her as breathing. She was ready. All she had to do now was wait.

Chapter 40

I wasn't sentimental enough to either wake Mother or give a final farewell to Weybridge. I had said my goodbyes and my leaving was done in spectacular fashion. I showed all of them. I even drove my own dear mother to kill a man in defence of her wonderful son. Now that was impressive. I filled my lungs with air as I walked down the avenue in the darkness. I regretted parking the car away from the house – I hadn't factored the ten minutes into my journey time but at this time of night it would be easy to make time up on the motorway

The hire car was where I left it. As soon as the windshield had cleared, I turned on the small road and pointed it in the direction of Wexford and the harbour. I didn't need maps, I knew my way. It was less than an hour.

Many considerations flashed into my mind as I made the last journey to the harbour. It had always been my intention to come back and show them what a real winner looked like but seeing Sal had changed things. Jen knowing her best friend had chosen me over her meant I had won again – and knowing that our reunion was going to be at the boatyard made me chuckle. I didn't need to finish what I had started – Sal had done that for me. It would've been careless of me to even attempt to make contact. I was retiring. Things had escalated in the last while and I, for one, needed a holiday. After all the hassle that I had been through because of the imbeciles I found myself surrounded by, I deserved a great holiday.

On reflection, the shine I had for my beloved Andy had tarnished too. He wasn't the man I thought he was. He was happy to settle in that one-horse town with Jen and her rug rat. The sheer thought of that existence made me feel queasy. No ambition. No strategy. I never believed in compromise or karma for that matter. That made me smile – karma. Perhaps I should start believing. Did karma bring me back to Sal? Did karma have me on this road now, making the journey to the harbour? Oh, all this procrastinating and surmising was making me tired. I had won, they had lost. End of story – move on with the girl and they all live happily ever after.

I was positively upbeat by the time I turned the last bend on the approach to the harbour. There was little activity in the village save for the odd bedroom light popping on. Weary mothers attending to snotty noses or a tummy bug, sleep deprived and constantly chained to a clock, all the time being pushed further and quicker towards Zanax and cheap red wine. The same thing in every hick village, in every hick town in Ireland. The humdrum, the routine, the *ordinariness* of it all. Skivvies in their homes being shouted at by lazy husbands and children so consumed by technology they thought they were on a battlefield even in their own homes. Why, oh why, would anyone choose to live that way? Travel the world, dance, make love, take drugs. Responsibility was for mediocre people. The bores and the rats on the wheel.

I never had myself down as a romantic but my heart skipped a beat as the pier and the boatyard came into view. I drove into the carpark opposite, parking behind a lorry with the local fish factory logo emblazoned across its side. I watched for some time and scanned the area. It was no trick. There were no hidden police cars, no choppers waiting for me to step out of the car. As I got closer to the boatyard, I realised the door was unlocked and light was seeping out. She was in there, waiting for me. She was mine, not his. I wondered if she would let me send the dreadlocked fool a sympathy card. Sorry, mate, I won – I always do.

Keeping a steady pace and my head down, I circled the boatyard, just to make sure she was alone. I could barely see through the grimy window but I made out a figure. Too small to be Andy. It was her. It was Sal. Maybe I would take her right there on the bench. I felt like it. I wanted her, so bad.

I wiped my slick palms on a handkerchief and pulled open the workshop door. This was the beginning of a new chapter for me and one that I deserved so much.

Chapter 41

The door opened and he sauntered in. She watched from a distance, grateful to be at the far end of the room with the chair between them. It took a couple of moments for his eyes to adjust to the light and for them to focus on her. A breeze blew the scent of his aftershave down the workshop and her heart lurched, strangled by memories of the past — her resolve waning with his advancing footsteps. She moved her feet slightly apart and straightened her back.

He walked towards her before stopping short. Then he burst out laughing. Looking around, he realised he was in the middle of the floor. She knew by the look on his face that that made him nervous. The workbench was out of his reach. No man's land, that's where he was.

'Well, well, well.' He stood tall and slowly raised his hands up in front of him. 'What is it lately with the women in my life pointing shotguns at me?'

'I was never your woman.' She didn't take her eyes off him and was reassured by the fact her hands didn't shake. She was in control for the first time and this was going to end her way.

'I underestimated you. You're more intelligent than I gave you credit for. That's a nice little stunt you pulled. But why do you think it's going to work, my dear Jen?'

'Because this time, my dear Scott, I have nothing left to lose. You have sent my family to hell and back and now it's my turn for payback.'

He went to take a step forward and she raised the gun up to her shoulder while resting her chin on the butt.

'Do you see any tears in my eyes, Scott? Do you see any tremors in my hands? I have waited for this moment for a long time.'

'How did you pull it off? Where is Sal? Did you threaten her with a gun too?'

'She arrived in my house last night after your little show back in Berlin. Did you honestly think the crappy quote and your declaration of love was going to make a difference to her? She loves Abe – he's more of a man that you will ever be and when she came to my house last night we fell around the place, laughing at your pathetic attempt to woo her. Andy nearly got sick laughing. You are pathetic, Scott, you are a stupid, silly little boy.'

'Careful, Jen.'

She knew she was goading him and it was getting to him but that's exactly what she wanted. She had waited so long for this and telling him what she thought of him while she had the power of a shotgun in her hands was better than the weeks and months of therapy she had paid for. It was all coming out of her, all the forgotten words and all the things she wished she could have said long ago. The only problem was – she knew she was running out of time. It needed to happen soon.

'It was so easy to get you in the end. Sal gave Danny her phone when she moved to Berlin – so they could stay in touch. I kept credit on it for him. I just took the number off the book and then burned the damn thing. For someone who claims to be superior to all of us, Scott, I tricked you quite easily.'

He threw his hands up in the air and laughed again.

'You're playing a dangerous game here.'

'Like I said, I've nothing left to lose. Once you're dead, my family is safe — if it means me going to prison or dying too, that's a sacrifice I'm willing to make.'

'You'll never pull that trigger. You are too weak.' He had put his arms back down by his side and his eyes were trained on her face. He didn't seem intimidated by the gun pointed in his direction.

She knew he had underestimated her again.

The door of the workshop was flung open.

'Jesus Christ, Jen. What the hell?' Sal was out of breath.

She was looking at the shotgun. It took a second for her to see him. 'Scott?'

Scott's face lit up and he turned around to see her.

'Don't *fucking* move, Scott! Sal, close that damn door, and come over here beside me.' Jen still had the gun pointed at him.

'I knew you would come, Sal. I'm glad to see you. How did you know we'd be here?'

Scott was still facing Jen. She didn't take the gun off him while he talked over his shoulder to Sal.

'Jen, put the gun down.' Sal walked slowly towards the workbench. She picked up a small lump-hammer and turned it over in her hands. 'You just couldn't move on, Jen, could you? You wouldn't leave sleeping dogs lie?'

'That's it, Sal, you tell her. Let get out of here, shall we?'

Sal walked over to Scott, smiling.

'What are you doing, Sal? Get away from him.' Jen steadied herself and adjusted the gun against her shoulder.

Scott smiled at Sal before turning his gaze back to Jen.

'I always win, Jen, always.'

'I've been looking forward to this,' Sal said.

She swung the small lump-hammer and he fell to the floor.

Jen screamed at her. Scott was dazed but coming to. Sal grabbed a cable tie off the bench, pulled his hands behind his back and slipped it around them.

'Are your *fucking* insane, Jen?' Sal ran to her friend.

Jen still had the shotgun raised. It was still pointed at Scott.

'I ran the whole way here. I couldn't fucking wake Andy and Fran wasn't answering his phone.'

Scott had managed to get up on his knees, even with his hands behind his back.

'Come on, Jen, shoot me, you crazy bitch! And fuck you, Sal. Clara was a better lay as well.' He spat blood out onto the floor.

'Put the gun down, Jen – I'm ringing the Guards. He's going to prison.' Sal's words were falling out of her mouth and her eyes were wild with terror. 'If you shoot him, he wins. Let him go to prison. That's what he deserves. *Stop!*'

'Sal,' Scot said, his words slurred, 'I really thought we had a future together – yet here you are being Miss Righteous. I have to admit, I'm disappointed.'

'*Shut up, Scott!*' Sal roared at him. 'Jen, put the gun down – we're ringing the Guards.'

'No, no, we're not. This is the way it has to be. Go home and let me finish this. I'm going to kill him.'

'Do it, Jen!' Scott shouted. 'Shoot me, you *cunt!*'

'*Shut up!* Jen, please – this is crazy.' Sal raised her hand onto the barrel of the shotgun. 'Put it down, Jen. This is what he wants – he wants to turn you into a killer like him. He'd rather die than face up to his crimes. Don't give him the satisfaction.'

Jen looked from Scott to Sal and back to Scott again. The barrel trembled.

'I'll ring the Sarge.' Sal took her phone out of her pocket.

'You're no killer, Jen.' His voice was stronger now. 'The thought of that is absurd. But it's in my blood.'

'*Shut your mouth, Scott!*' Sal screamed.

'I watched my own mother shoot her brother last night after he shot his girlfriend Lucy – you met her, didn't you? Yes, she's a friend of good old Tess. Sounds rather hilarious when I put it like that, doesn't it? We buried the pair of them under the trees on the estate. You remember that beautiful lake and cliff, don't you, Jen?'

She nodded. He was completely off the rails. How many more people would he hurt if he walked out of here?

'Well, darling. The trees are close enough to the lake – I didn't get the chance to take you all into the woods when you were there. A few minutes in the jeep and we had them buried like offal from a good hunt. Mother dear, she's a steady hand with a shotgun. I rather hoped the shock would kill her in the end but to no avail. The old crone still lives and breathes.'

Sal hung up the phone and tried the number she had called again.

Scott was rocking back and forth on his knees. Sal was pacing.

The rifle was heavy. Jen's arms ached. She hadn't taken her eyes off Scott.

The superciliousness of his tone ignited her anger. Flashes of Danny popped into her head from that night on the beach. It played out like a movie in her head, the snippets of conversations with friends, the therapy, the fear, the lies. All of it pressed against her heart like a tidal wave. He was here – right in front of her and all she had to do was pull the trigger.

Sal was on the phone. She was speaking to someone. Rapid-fire talk.

'Just give me Sal and I will leave you alone, Jen. She's mine – not his. If you get her to come away with me, I won't bother you or your family again.'

She pulled the trigger.

Sal dropped the phone and screamed. Time slowed down.

She wasn't even sure what was in the barrel of the shotgun but, whatever it was, it was fucking loud and it had hit him. She stumbled backwards with the recoil and a fierce pain told her she had dislocated her right shoulder. She felt her upper arm slip back into place but the muscles and ligaments were torn. The pain. That old familiar pain. It took her out of the workshop and back to the beach. He had laughed at her then and he was laughing again now. She staggered forward and fell over the chair. The shotgun fell from her hands and hit the floor with a dull thud. She looked at him and saw the blood. It was coming from his upper arm — or what was left of it. She had missed.

Sal was frozen like a statue at the back wall. Fear had made her grey in the face. Scott was trying to sit up and was laughing.

That laugh was too much for Jen. It embodied everything in her life that had gone wrong and that was evil. She wasn't going to give up this time. She needed to pick the shotgun up.

'Sal, help me.' She looked at her friend. Sal didn't move. Jen pulled her arm in to her body and hauled herself up, daggers of red hot pain shooting down her arm. He had dislocated her arm that night on the beach. It hurt like hell.

He was lying on his side now and the colour was draining from his face. All the while laughing.

'Come on, you little bitch! Finish what you started!'

Sal snapped out of her frozen state. '*Jen! Don't!*'

Like lightning thoughts came to Jen — her family — Andy's first wife and all the people Scott had killed or hurt along the way. She thought of all the women he had hurt. She focused on them and the pain lifted. She was alive. They weren't. He needed to pay and she was the one that was going to exact revenge for all of them.

She picked up the shotgun awkwardly with her left arm and sat down on the chair she had first stood behind. He was still laughing, but it was weaker now.

'You know, Jen, I really enjoyed myself on the beach that night.' His words bounced off the floor and up towards her. 'And all the times I used that picture of you and your boy to trick all those women into trusting me. I got such a kick from that. It was like punching you all over again.' He was trying to get up off the floor but he didn't have the strength. 'My only regret is not taking you on your kitchen table that day. How I would have loved forcing myself into your screaming face, pushing open those legs of yours and leaving myself all over your sexy little scars. I regret that now, but there will be other opportunities. I'll make that little bastard son of yours watch. Andy too and then I will gut all three of you.'

Sal, without a word, walked over to where Jen sat struggling to balance the shotgun on her right thigh. She stood to her right, and looked at her before lifting the barrel of the shotgun.

'Fuck you, Jen, and you too, Sal. I hope you both rot in hell.' He closed his eyes.

Sal nodded and Jen pulled the trigger. The second round from the shotgun hit him in the centre of the chest, the recoil this time absorbed by the chair and her stronger shoulder

Silence enveloped them.

Jen closed her eyes to the carnage. Sal took the shotgun from her and laid in on the floor at her feet. She knelt beside her and held her hand.

The silence was glorious. It was done.

Chapter 42

Jen kept her eyes closed. The smells of death hit her full force and she swallowed the sick feeling. Her eyes opened and she saw his feet. She allowed her gaze to travel as far as his chest. It had been torn apart. He was perfectly still.

Sal was still kneeling beside her, the shotgun in front of them.

'How did you know I was here, Sal?'

'Something woke me. I went downstairs for water and spotted your notes. I couldn't wake Andy. The car was still outside and the keys for the boatyard were gone off the hook. I knew you'd come here.'

Jen's mind wandered back to the days before Scott, to the days of freedom. The walks on the beach with her little boy, the fun with Sal and all the magical moments with Andy. She thought about Tess and Doc and how they had all been so close. It seemed like a lifetime ago and in those still moments she wondered if she could ever get those days back. What would happen next? The pain in her arm was immense. She felt as though she were just the witness to her own life. She could see herself slumped in the chair, her arm limp at her side and not enough energy to open her eyes.

Voices came. The door was opened. Someone stepped in.

Silence first and then a whistle of incredulity. A second voice. She knew now how her future was going to be. She would go to prison for this.

The two men came to her side.

'Jen! Sal! Are either of you hurt?'

Sal shook her head but pointed to Jen's arm.

'I think she's dislocated it.'

She watched as the Sarge ran his hands over Jen's body, checking for other injuries.

'Jen, can you hear me? It's Joe. We haven't got a lot of time. *Snap out of it.*'

His harsh voice in contrast to his gentle touch brought her back into the room. Fran stood in front of her, blocking her view. He was as white as a sheet and was looking at her like she was a creature from outer space. Sal was standing behind her chair.

Joe felt the top of her injured arm. 'It's not dislocated,' he said.

'It did slip out but went back in again,' Jen said weakly.

Joe had picked up the shotgun and was cleaning it with a cloth. He was wearing gloves.

'Who owns this?'

'Dad.'

'He never had a shotgun, Jen, do you hear me?'

She looked at him, confused.

'Do you hear me, Jen? Your dad never had a shotgun.'

Jen nodded.

'What did I just say?'

'Dad never had a shotgun.'

'How did you get him down here?'

'I helped Jen kill him,' Sal blurted out. 'It wasn't just her. We both did it.'

Joe repeated his question and Sal gave him the short version of the Berlin events. Jen picked up at the part where she took the number and burned the book because she didn't want anyone else to be able to contact him. Sal's old phone had been in Danny's room. She'd used that to organise the meeting.

'Where's that phone now?'

She handed it to him. He scrolled through the phone, deleting all messages. He went over to Scott and took his phone out of his pocket. He slipped it into his.

'Fran – bring the van up to the entrance.'

Fran nodded and left.

Joe picked Jen up and carried her to the door. Sal followed.

Fran pulled up, got out and opened the passenger door. When Joe sat Jen in, she cried out in pain. Sal sat in the cargo hold in the back.

Joe looked into the back of the van. 'Sal, where's your car?'

'I walked over. It was quicker. And I had been drinking last night – I didn't want to drink and drive.'

Joe laughed at the irony.

Jen looked at the Sarge. 'He said his mother killed his uncle last night and a woman was killed too. He said they're buried on the grounds of his house. The woman was Lucy who lives in the village. She was helping them blackmail Tess. Joe, he said he was going to kill Andy and Danny too. I had to protect my family, Joe. I had to protect my boy.'

His face was kind. 'Jen. You were never here. Leave it to me. That goes for you too, Sal. You were never here.'

Jen nodded again. She didn't know what else to do.

Sal put her head in her hands and nodded her assent.

'Fran, take them home. Tell all of them to stay put and keep their mouths shut. *They never left that house, do you hear me?* Find out what route each of them took on the way over here – check for cameras and find out if they met anyone along the way.'

It was hard not to notice the first shoots of light beginning to move across the sky, bringing with it a blazing, climbing wall of red. Red sky in the morning – sailor's warning. The sun wasn't quite ready to poke its head up over the horizon. But when she did come, it would be the dawn of a different era.

Chapter 43

Jen sat numbly in the van as Fran sat into the driver seat. He drove slowly back to her house, consoling her and telling her everything was going to be okay. When he established the routes they had taken, he told them over and over that they'd never left the house. When he got to Jen's front door, he turned her key in the door and called for Andy.

Andy came down the stairs, bleary-eyed and wearing only sweatpants.

Sal slipped in past them and went, in silence, to the kitchen.

The moment Andy saw his wife, his eyes filled with terror.

'Scott is dead,' Fran said. 'Joe is taking care of it – I'm going back down to him now. He said to tell you you need to sit tight and not say a word until we're back. None of you left the house tonight, got it?'

'Dead? How?' Andy looked shell-shocked.

'Never mind that. Did you hear what I just said? *None of you left the house.* Right?'

289

Andy nodded.

Fran strode back out to the van.

Andy helped Jen shuffle into the kitchen and eased her into a chair by the stove. She found a position for her arm to rest where the pain was manageable. Painkillers and rest were all she needed. She couldn't go to the hospital as she would have no way of explaining the shotgun-butt-shaped bruise that was sure to appear.

No one had spoken. Their eyes followed her as she, rather awkwardly, got up out of the chair and made her way to a kitchen cabinet. The foil on the blister pack crackled as she forced out two capsules with her thumb. Andy watched as she washed them down with the dregs of the wine.

Sal broke the silence. 'Jen.' Her voice was brittle and ricocheted around the room. In the distance, Jen's alarm went off on her phone. 'There's blood on your coat.'

Jen looked down and saw the splatters. She chucked papers and firewood into the stove and left it to light. She tried to take the jacket off and couldn't manage it. Andy took it off for her and put it in the fire. Her dress and shoes went next. Sal came back into the room with a blanket and handed it to her.

They sat there, holding a vigil around the fire — watching the garments burn. Eventually Andy stood up and hovered over the two of them. Sal was holding Jen's hand, both staring into the flames.

'Now that we're all complicit in whatever just happened, you need to start talking, Jen.' Andy folded his arms and stared at her.

She had never seen that look on his face before. She couldn't place it. The haze of codeine had started to descend.

'Scott is dead. I killed him. With Dad's shotgun — I took it from his shed last night.'

'We killed him, Jen,' Sal said. 'We're both guilty.'

Jen was calm but wondered if she would ever feel guilt or remorse. They often talked about that on the radio when reporting on murders — how the assailant felt overwhelming remorse and regret at taking someone's life. She felt neither. She felt relieved.

She glanced across at her best friend. Her face had become a mask with neither fear nor disgust near it. Instead: acceptance. She had played her part too.

'I got him to come down to the harbour with the intention of killing him. Sal tried to stop me but I didn't listen. He's gone and he can't hurt us any more.'

'How did you get him down there, Jen?' Sal asked. 'You burned the book with the number on it.'

'You went to the bathroom and I sent Andy to check on Danny. I put the number in my phone and burned the book so you couldn't give it to the Guards. Scott thought he was meeting you. I pretended to be you when I texted him from your old phone.'

'You had this planned from before the time you went to Tess's house, didn't you?' Andy shook his head. 'You're unreal, Jen. You had no intention of letting him get arrested. From the moment you burned that book – that evidence – you knew what you were doing.' He stared out the kitchen window.

'It's a shame I didn't lure him down sooner. Two people were killed on Weybridge Estate last night, though not by him he said. One was his uncle – the other Lucy who was living in the village – she was blackmailing Tess. He and his mother buried them both.'

Andy looked at Jen as though he had never laid eyes on her before. His bare feet squeaked on the floor as he shifted his weight from one foot to the other. The news about the other deaths seemed to wash over him. He made no comment.

Jen stood with her back to the stove. The heat was comforting and helped to relieve her pain.

'The Guards could have arrested him – yes – he'd have done time and then he would have been released. What *then*? He would have come after us again – that's what. I wasn't going live with that. He told me he would gut all of us. I had no choice. There was no other way. And I'm glad. I'm glad he's dead, Andy. He can't hurt us any more. It's over.'

Jen was surprised at the calm in her own voice. She thought she might be in shock but everything was clear to her in that moment. She would wait for Joe to arrive and then she would know what the next step was. Maybe she was going to jail for a long time but it was worth it, knowing he was dead. Danny was safe from now on.

Then Andy was nearly on top of her, heaving with rage and grief and fear.

'You're in a whole world of trouble, Jen! All of us are. What are we going to do? All this nonsense about Joe taking care of it – what does that even mean? He can't make a murder go away!' The wave of fear overwhelmed him and he fell to his knees in front of her, his body wracked with sobs.

She laid her hand on his head, almost afraid to touch him, afraid to taint him.

She looked at Sal again. Her friend nodded. It will be okay, the gesture said, it's okay, Jen.

'I need to have a shower.' Jen side-stepped around Andy. 'I need to clear my head. We'll wait for the Sergeant to get here and then we'll see what happens. I need to ring Dad.'

'Why?'

'To see how Danny is.'

Andy's mouth dropped open. 'How can you act like nothing has happened?' He stood up from where he knelt.

Sal moved closer to Jen. For a moment, she thought Andy was going to hit her or shake her. Jen put up her good arm to stop him and Sal stopped in her tracks.

'Andy, I always ring Danny first thing when he's on a sleepover. For now, it's a normal morning. I will tell Dad I'm too hungover to collect him this morning and I'll be over later.'

She picked up her phone and dialled. Always the early riser, her father was up and only delighted Danny was staying until the afternoon. He informed her that they had already had breakfast. The sound of her father's voice washed over her like summer rain. For a second, she forgot about it all and just listened to his voice. She could hear Danny's trainers squeaking across the lino in her parents' kitchen, and she could hear her mam telling him to put on his coat and scarf and take Mr Cassidy for a walk. 'Love ya, Mam!' came the shout from the background. She swallowed the lump in her throat, told her dad she loved them all and hung up.

Something was rattling around in her brain. What exactly was Joe up to and what did it all mean?

'Where is Scott now?' The question passed Andy's lips like an afterthought.

'In the boatyard.'

She didn't stay in the room long enough to see his reaction.

Chapter 44

The knot in Jen's stomach was getting tighter, and tighter and tighter. She sat beside Sal and listened to the tick-tock of the oversized clock on the wall. The seconds dragged into minutes, then an hour, then another. They didn't move from the kitchen – they drank tea and jumped at every little sound. Andy worried about the boatyard. It should be open. It would look odd if it was closed. How would he explain that?

The *Ten O'Clock News* came on in the background. Jen tuned out from it – its only relevance was the time. It had been about four hours and they had heard nothing.

A gentle rap on the door boomed around the kitchen. Andy looked out into the hallway.

'It's Fran.'

She heard the door open and click closed again. Fran came in, followed by Joe and Andy.

Joe spoke first.

'You were never out of this house, Jen. Have you got that? You all got up this morning, hungover after Sal's surprise visit. You had a catch-up over a few bottles of wine last night. Andy – you took the morning off because of your hangover and your plan is to go in this afternoon – it's Saturday after all. Your diary is quiet today. Where's Danny?'

'He stayed with Mam and Dad last night.'

'Great. That adds to the reunion and wine story.'

He looked around the kitchen and pointed to the glasses.

'Good,' he said.

He walked to the bench and filled the kettle from the tap.

Fran sat on a chair, took a notebook from his pocket and laid it on the table.

'What's that?' Jen asked.

'We'll tell you in a minute,' Joe answered for him. 'Here's what's going to happen.'

He sat down and fixed his eyes on Jen.

'Right. You and Sal called around to your friend Tess last night to catch up. Sal and Tess hadn't seen each other for a while. You had a coffee and let Tess get back to the paperwork she had been doing when you arrived. In the meantime, the men went out together to bury the hatchet. They had a beer and then went their separate ways. Andy was anxious to get back here for a drink with you two and Doc didn't want to be in the pub alone. Fran didn't hang around when the other two decided to leave. He left first and went home. Doc went home to his wife and you three drank it out here. You woke up when the alarm went and you rang your father to keep the boy until the afternoon. I have been in touch with your father, told him the shotgun had been stolen from his house, it had showed up in a bag with his initials on it and the best thing he could do was pretend he never owned that unregistered shotgun. It never gets mentioned again. That clear?'

She nodded.

'You have been here, drinking tea and chatting ever since. Jen, your shoulder injury came from slipping on spilled wine last night.'

It all sounded so simple so far.

'Sal, did you tell anyone about what happened in Berlin? '

'No.'

'Are you sure?'

'I'm certain.'

'Okay. Keep it that way.'

The kettle clicked and Fran was the one who responded. He made tea.

It was the random normal gestures that were beginning to make Jen feel so bizarre.

Andy stood on the far side of the room. He couldn't look at any of them.

'In about two hours' time, the closest station to Weybridge Estate is going to get a call from Livia Carluccio Randall reporting a terrible series of events in the preceding hours.'

No one in the room seemed to breathe.

'A body will be found in the lake – a male – in the boot of a jeep. Shortly thereafter, a further two bodies will be found in the woods – one male, one female.'

'*This is all bullshit!*' Andy roared at Joe. '*What* two bodies? *Where* are all these bodies coming from?'

Jen spoke up. 'I already told you. His uncle and that girl Lucy were killed last night.'

'Oh! That makes it all right then, *does it?* What are *we* going to do? Just drive up there, fire Scott in the boot of a jeep, drive it off the cliff into the lake and then magic up another couple of bodies? They could be anywhere. It's not fucking Hollywood we're living in. This shit is serious. We need to go to the *actual* Guards rather than *Clint Eastwood* here and tell *them* the real story. They will understand once we explain how he has terrorised us for so long.'

'Sit down now and listen to me, Andy.' Joe stood up to his full height and the tone of his voice quietened all of them. 'If we do that, we are *all* going to prison. Every one of us, including me. Jen will get locked up for murder – and Sal will be her accomplice. Jen planned this. She lured him down here and shot him dead. Sal helped her. That's murder and, mitigating circumstances or not, she's going down for *murder*. She won't survive a life sentence – she'll probably come out in a box. You think your friend Doc had a hard time in Wheatfield?! That place is like a holiday camp in comparison to where Jen would end up.'

Andy couldn't listen any more but he couldn't go anywhere. He was hopping from one foot to the other as he searched all the faces in the room.

'Am I the only one who thinks this is crazy?'

No one responded to his question.

Fran pushed the notebook across the table to Jen. She picked it up and looked at the neat handwriting. A list of names – all women and all different nationalities.

Andy was the one to ask what it was.

'It's the names of all the women he sold to traffickers in Marrakech. They are probably all dead now – all fifteen of them.'

Jen dropped it out of her hand. The thought of what those women had gone through made her sick to her stomach. Those were the women he had lured to their death using a picture of her and her beautiful innocent son.

'How did you convince his mother?' Sal asked, shrewdly realising how it went.

'It didn't take long to put the workshop back together thanks to the drains in the floor and the power hose. I drove his car back to Weybridge and Fran followed in the van. Livia recognised me as a Guard straight away and she knew Fran's face from the original news reports when Scott disappeared – his associate, as they called him. She sang like a bird and gave me nearly forty years' dirt on herself – the criminal mastermind that she was. I told her I could make it all go away. All she had to do was alter the story a bit. She was the victim in this when her criminal son and her criminal brother just happened to cross swords in her house. She had no idea of what they were up to so it would be unlikely that she would go to prison. Mention money and good name to someone like her and she will look after herself. She hid her double life from her own husband. She will tell this story and walk away from it too. There may be part of her that wants to atone for her son's sins – who knows – but she will stick to the story. She doesn't have her brother there any more to protect her from the competition.'

'Why are you doing this, Joe?' Sal's voice was thick with emotion.

'In this village, we are a tribe. The village takes care of its own – come hell or high water. That's our way and has been for generations. I have watched all of you grow up. I went to school with your parents and, when I started this job, I did it so I could take care of my own. I never wanted to marry and I never wanted to leave the harbour. Over the decades, the people of the harbour were my family and I looked out for them. It worked for a long time. The roughest time in my life was at the hands of that man and he slipped out of our net. I watched how his actions affected everyone here and ruined the lives of many families I cared about. I swore, by hook or by crook, when my chance came, I would make him pay for that. I knew he would be back and I knew that Tess was involved – I had been watching her and I knew she was storing drugs there. I didn't touch her – she was the only connection back to the whole operation. I was so focused on him, I dropped the ball and I didn't look further – perhaps if I had, I would have guessed about the mother and traced him that way. When Doc and Fran came back to the village, I was certain he would eventually show up to settle the score, and I watched and waited. You beat me to it.'

'Are we supposed to just act like this never happened?' Andy's voice was strained.

'Yes, that's exactly what I'm asking you to do. Fran will be brought in for questioning at some stage, considering he came back. I have taken a statement from him and, the last he knew, Scott was dead in Marrakech. The rest of you will pick up the pieces and get on with your lives.'

Jen stood at the patio door and blew rings of smoke out at the sky.

'There is no justice in this world and the law does not work on the side of the good guys,' Joe continued. 'After all you've been through, do you think it fair for Jen to go to prison for murder, Andy? If you do, make the call now and I will tell the authorities how I took over and did the rest.'

No one moved.

'He's dead. He has finally paid for all the evil he inflicted on the world. That in my book is justice – good riddance. I am going to pay Doc and Tess a visit now. They will forget the part of the story about what brought Sal back from Berlin in exchange for me 'forgetting' about Tess smuggling drugs into her business. It's over.'

They gathered round the table – lost in their own thoughts. Fran made more tea while Joe gathered up cups. Fran handed the notebook to Joe who assured them all he would hand it over. The girls' disappearances would be investigated and hopefully they would show up somewhere but he didn't hold out too much hope. He advised Andy to have a good clear-out and a spring clean of his workshop and he told Jen to take plenty of painkillers and keep ice on her shoulder for a few days. There was no need for her to visit the hospital.

'What about Dad's gun?'

'What gun, Jen? Your dad never owned a gun, remember?'

The two visitors placed their cups in the sink and made their way to the door. Jen walked out with them and Andy followed. Sal stayed put in the kitchen but they could hear her tidying up – as friends do.

Chapter 45

Livia Carluccio Randall glided into Weybridge Garda Station in a haze of Chanel and hairspray. Her heels tapped softly on the lino and her deep-purple woollen coat stood out against the beige walls of the tiny rural station. Her bracelets chimed louder than the bell she had just tapped on the counter.

She kept her gloved hand over her nose while she stood at the frosted-glass hatch. The whole place smelled of mildew and boredom. She could hear him huffing and puffing behind the glass before his large bulk appeared and slid back the lock.

She had never seen him with reading glasses before and he was definitely wearing more clothes than he was during their last little rendezvous.

She smirked at him as he tried to hide the red spreading all over his face.

'No need to be coy, Seamus, dear. This is not a social call.'

She thought he looked somewhat disappointed but, under the circumstances, she really didn't care.

'Right. Hello, Livia. How can I help you today?' He stood with his pen poised and ready over a notebook.

'I'd like to report a triple homicide on the grounds of my estate.'

'A triple –' He looked up at her. 'I'm sorry – *what?*'

'Sergeant Dempsey, I'd like to report a triple murder on the grounds of my estate.' She removed her gloves to reveal perfectly manicured nails.

'I understand what *homicide* means, Livia.'

He was acting like a petulant child. She put it down to shock. It's not like the village was a hub of crime-fighting. He pulled himself together by adjusting his tie and pulling another pen from his shirt pocket.

'You are here to report a triple murder on your estate, and how do you know about these alleged murders, *Mrs* Carluccio Randall?'

'Because I bore witness to two and committed the third one myself. I would like to turn myself in and give you a statement of the facts.'

By now the sweat was out on the sergeant's forehead.

Livia looked at her nails again.

'You'd better come through.'

He opened the flimsy wooden door. The corridor between reception and the back office was so narrow, the bulky sergeant had real trouble turning around to lead her down. She waited patiently while he got flustered, did an about-turn, and pulled himself together. His shirt strained to cover his shoulders and the blue of the cotton began to darken in small patches.

Her designer heels continued to tap the lino tiles.

He made a right turn onto another small corridor and to her immediate right was a room that served as a cell. The small cot in the room was covered in boxes of paperwork and the room seemed to double up as storage for cleaning products.

Once in the back office, he spent a few moments clearing stacks of paperwork from the chair in front of his desk. She wondered where all this paperwork was coming from before noticing how organised and clean the little office was.

'Take a seat, Livia.'

'Thank you.'

Once he sat down into his own seat he became more relaxed and in control of the situation.

'Livia. I am going to take your statement first and then I'm going to put in a call to District HQ. They will send their sergeant and two detectives. They will be in charge and it will be taken from there. Okay?'

'Yes, that's fine.'

'Righto. We're going to start the interview now and I'm going to record it also.' He couldn't keep the excitement out of his voice.

In fairness, this was no doubt the most action he had seen in years – she'd allow him a bit of drama.

He fumbled around with the machine, watching the green spike on the display as he repeated the word 'testing' over and over.

'Righto – are you ready?' He looked at her expectantly as though he was about to settle down and listen to a radio play.

In one sense, she guessed that's exactly what the recording would become. She nodded and turned herself in the chair ever so slightly in the direction of the recorder.

'Sergeant Seamus Dempsey, here and present with Mrs Livia Carluccio Randall on this day, September 30th 2016 at 14 hundred hours,' he announced in a voice he must have learnt from TV cop shows.

Livia stifled a snigger. Clearly it had been a long time since he had interviewed anyone.

'Livia, in your own time, please proceed.' His voice had returned to normal.

'I would like to report a triple homicide on the grounds of Weybridge Estate, last night, September 29th 2016. I witnessed the first two murders and I committed the third.'

'Are the three victims known to you?'

'Yes. The first victim was my brother's *fancy woman*. Her name was Lucy something-or-other, the second victim was my only brother, Ivan, and the third was my son Scott.'

'Jesus Christ.' The comment slipped out of the sergeant's mouth before he could stop it. He coughed before advising her to tell him in her own words the exact movements that led to the crimes.

'Yes, Sergeant, but could you be so kind as to get me a cup of coffee first. I'm rather thirsty.'

People never said no to Livia Carluccio Randall.

'Certainly. My apologies for not offering one sooner.' He hauled himself up out of the chair and, as an afterthought, he looked at the recording machine. He spoke to it and told it the interview was suspended.

Before long he was shouting down the corridor enquiring whether or not she took anything in her drink. Black with two sugars, she advised.

The coffee wasn't bad, all things considered, Livia thought, and he had produced a packet of biscuits. How very odd.

'Interview resumed at 14.15. Okay, Livia, please proceed.'

By now she had a tissue balled up in her hand and her eyeliner had begun to bleed from the tears she had squeezed out. He looked uncomfortable and avoided eye contact by rummaging around in the top drawer of his desk. He handed her a half-empty packet of Kleenex.

'My brother and his fancy woman had come to see me. They arrived at the house very unexpectedly last evening. I was delighted to see them of course but I wasn't prepared to entertain guests. I had only met Lucy on one previous occasion, and was looking forward to getting to know this young lady my brother seemed so taken by. We decided on dinner in town. Once my darling guests had freshened up, we had pre-dinner drinks in the drawing room. We were really enjoying ourselves and reminiscing on our childhood. Without warning, my son Scott showed up to the house and he was like a lunatic. I haven't seen my son in two years – you do know the story there, Seamus?'

Seamus nodded and gestured for her to continue.

'He came into the drawing room where we were and you can only imagine my shock and fear when I saw a gun in his hand – it was like something from a film. I was, by now, very frightened but, as his mother, I thought I could reason with him. I never stopped loving my dear son, Sergeant, even though I knew he had grown up to be such a bad man.'

At this point she allowed another couple of tears to escape. She watched as he reached out across the table to pat her hand, changed his mind and put his hand back down on the desk. She, on cue, held the tissue to her nose before reaching for his hand. He took hers and they sat in silence for a moment.

She smiled apologetically and slid her hand away. Sympathy and compassion wafted from the sergeant like the scent of summer from honeysuckle. Poor fool. Putty in her hands. She continued.

'He was shouting about how Ivan, my brother, had betrayed him – how he had stolen from him and how he was there for his money. He was shouting and roaring and then Ivan joined in. He started shouting back and telling him that he was sick of being in business with him and he wanted out. He wanted to retire – and that the girl Lucy would take over in his place. When he said that, Scott shot the girl. Just like that. I tried to go to her and help her but he wouldn't let me move. She was dead. I was so scared. Ivan didn't seem too troubled by the dead woman on the floor. I think to protect myself, I became very detached. As if I wasn't really there. That helped me to establish the facts – Ivan, my only brother, was a drug baron with a huge business somewhere in Spain, and Scott worked for him – as did the girl. It all made sense. Scott then forced us to put the girl's body into her jeep. He made Ivan drive at gunpoint and I was in the passenger seat. He took us to the woodland on the east side of the estate where he made Ivan take the woman's body out of the boot and dig her grave.'

Livia looked up at the sergeant. He was *hanging* on her every word – sitting forward in his chair with his hand over his mouth.

'He left me in the passenger seat while he stood over my brother with a shotgun. I noticed there was a whole box of cartridges on the back seat. I was too frightened to move. I couldn't help my brother – when he had finished digging the grave, Scott fired the shotgun and killed him. He then put him in the grave with the woman and filled it in. He brought me back to the house and sat with me in the drawing room. He made me scrub that woman's blood off the floor while he sat in the chair and drank. He was angry and threw a glass full of brandy against the fireplace.

After a couple of hours, he drove me to the lake, not too far from the woodlands and told me that he was going to hang me from the tree from which his father had killed himself. It was my husband's favourite spot, you see. It was on a height overlooking the lake below. That's where he took his own life. Poor Scott had always blamed me for his death.'

Another dramatic pause and the rustle of plastic as she extricated a tissue from its packaging.

'We drove up the steep hill to the cliff and he parked the jeep. He went to the boot and I got out of the passenger seat. He was bent over the boot doing something. He wasn't looking at me – too arrogant – he always thought I was stupid. The shotgun was on the back seat. I picked it up and reloaded it from the box of cartridges.'

She looked up again. The sergeant's face was lit up with excitement from the drama of it all. Good.

'I'm no stranger to guns, you see, Seamus. My husband and I used to hunt on the grounds on a very regular basis.' She waited for a reaction. She got a nod from him and then continued.

'Once the gun was loaded, I went to the back of the jeep and pointed it at him – my hope was to engage him in conversation long enough for him to see the light and turn himself in. He was calmer at that point than he had been all evening. I told him we could afford good lawyers, things would be okay. And then I saw what he was doing.'

Her voice broke. Seamus spoke to the recorder and then scarpered to the kitchen for a glass of water for her. He was out of breath when he returned.

'Thank you.' She took a long draught and put the glass down on the table.

'When you're ready,' he said.

She nodded. He switched on the recorder and said his piece.

She continued. 'He had a long length of rope and he was fashioning it into a noose. He turned to face me and told me that he hated me. I was the source of all his pain and I had killed his father. He told me he was going to take pleasure in hanging me from a tree and listening to the sound of my neck breaking before he left me swinging, covered in my own excrement, for all the world to see.'

'Interview suspended.' Seamus paused the tape. 'Livia, would you like to take a break for a moment? I can get you another coffee?'

Perfect. She blew her nose loudly and told him she would like to continue and that his support was making her strong enough to tell him the whole truth.

'I shot him twice. First in the upper arm and the second shot to the chest. The rope fell from his hands and he slumped into the boot of the car – the force of the shotgun drove him backwards.'

She pulled her blouse to one side and showed Seamus the bruise that had started to form on her shoulder – from the shotgun she fired.

'I panicked, threw the gun into the lake, closed the boot, took the handbrake off and let the jeep roll down the slope, over the edge and into the lake. The gun he used to kill Lucy was in the footwell of the car.'

'Good grief, Livia. What time was all this at?'

'He shot Lucy and Ivan somewhere between eight and nine. I'm not sure how long he held me hostage in the house but I think it was around five when we went to the lake. It was still dark. After, I went back to the house in a daze and tried to fathom what had happened. I knew I had to come in to see you. I'm sorry I didn't come in first thing this morning.'

'That's understandable, Livia. You're here now – that's what matters.'

The poor fool. He was delighted with the outcome – imagining himself as solving three murders so easily and handing it over to the big boys in district HQ with a big ribbon on it. They would all clap him on the back and tell him what great work he had done. She seized her opportunity. This was the only part of the plan where she had any real control.

'Seamus – what happens now?' She made her voice sound like that of a scared child.

He spoke in the tone of a concerned friend. 'Remember what I said to you about HQ? A team will come out from Wexford to question you again and then the scene will be investigated. You will need to get a lawyer. What happens after that depends on a lot of things but, for now, we'll just concentrate on today.'

'Thank you, Seamus.'

'You did the right thing, Livia. The truth always wins. I'm going to make that call now.'

She held up her hand. 'Before you do that, can I ask you one last favour?'

'Yes, of course.'

'Can we please go to Weybridge. Let me show you where the bodies are and let me say goodbye to my home and family one last time. I want to do that with you, Seamus, not some strangers.'

'Livia, please, don't put me in this position – it's not exactly protocol.'

'Please, Seamus,' the tears flowed freely now, dropping off her chin onto her blouse, 'I came here of my own accord. No one knew about the murders – you can trust me. The detectives can take me from the house. Please, Seamus!'

He picked up his coat from the back of the chair, the recording device forgotten in the stress of the moment.

She parked her car outside the front door and got out. The Sergeant pulled in beside her. She watched him struggle with his seatbelt before he got out of the squad car.

'Who owns the Beemer?' He pointed to the slick black car parked on the other side of the drive.

'Scott. I presume he hired it.'

He took out his notebook and scribbled something in it before opening the passenger door to his own car and gesturing for her to get in.

'Righto, Livia. In your own time, you can direct me to the woods.'

Seamus was a decent man and they'd had a couple of trysts over the years but today it was all about the story. She directed him round the side of the house and out onto the dirt track leading to the woods.

He could see for himself where the fresh mound of clay was. To her, in the daylight, it looked so much smaller. Her brother was in there – she swallowed the lump in her throat and for a split second she believed the story she had spun. It was safer to be the victim.

He reversed back out onto the dirt track before getting out of the car and opening the boot. He marked the entry into the crime scene with the only thing he had in the boot. A hazard triangle.

They drove up the hill by the lake and Livia was impressed with how the Toyota handled the bumpy tracks. She would never have dreamed of coming down this route in anything other than a 4X4 but they were still moving.

When they arrived she steered him in the right direction. She pointed to the tree her husband had swung from and then to the tyre marks on the land from where the jeep had gone into the lake.

Seamus bent down and picked up a rope with a noose on the end. He dropped it again as though it had burned him.

Livia removed her coat and hung it on the peg beside the back door. She removed her shoes as they were wet and covered in mud. Seamus followed her in and they made their way into the kitchen. The house was empty – she had rung the cleaners and had given them the day off. The breakfast dishes sat on the worktop beside the Belfast sink.

'Shall I make you a coffee, Seamus?'

He was on edge, knowing that any minute the big brass would arrive out from town and his part would be pretty much over.

'Yes, thank you,' he answered nevertheless.

She filled the kettle and sat it on the range.

'I did love my family, you know, Seamus. From the moment I arrived in Ireland, I loved it and thought it would be a new life for me. But I was never really free. In the end, I've always had to do what I was told.'

She stopped herself from saying any more. Seamus was too on edge. He wasn't listening and the hiss of water dripping from the kettle onto a flame on the cooker seemed to be making him all the more nervous.

She handed him a coffee and put sugar and milk in front of him.

'This village is lucky to have someone as honest and righteous as you are. I hope this whole process is over with soon. Thank you for being a friend over the years, Sergeant. You are one of the few decent men in my life.'

This made him blush.

'Don't be talking like that now, Livia. Have a cup of coffee and we'll take the day as it comes.'

She pointed at her dainty little feet and her trousers. The fabric was wet at the ends – the grass from the woods.

'May I go upstairs and get changed before they arrive?'

'Yes, you may, but please be quick about it. I'd rather you were down here under my supervision when they get here.'

'God bless you, Seamus.'

She gave him a hug which he clumsily accepted and reciprocated.

She walked slowly and purposefully down the hall. He was standing at the kitchen door watching where she was going. When she was halfway up the stairs, he went back to his coffee. She could hear the crunch of tyres on gravel and knew she didn't have long. It didn't matter. She had everything ready. She opened her bedroom door and locked it behind her.

She made straight for the bed. The photos were laid out on her wedding dress, beside it the only memento she had of her life in Italy: a silk scarf she wore for luck when she performed.

The melody of her favourite opera song began to play in her head. It made her smile – it was a tenor's aria – and the most famous one of all.

The doorbell rang. She imagined detectives in suits standing at the front door, already resenting the occupants of the sprawling mansion. Mad men and mad money, they would think – not really caring about the family or the lives behind that enormous door. She pressed play on the CD player on her bedside locker and Pavorotti's voice seduced her from the speakers.

'*Nessun dorma! Nessun dorma! – Nobody shall sleep! Nobody shall sleep!'*

She thought she could hear boots on the stairs but she wasn't sure. All she cared about was the music. She sang, quietly at first, but louder with every line.

Ma il mio mistero è chiuso in me, il nome mio nessun saprà! – But my secret is hidden within me, my name no one shall know!

She always loved translating this song from her native tongue to English – for her, the English translation sounded all the more beautiful.

She thought of her young self and the wonderful man she fell in love with. For a while they were happy – before she became a pawn, just as much as her future husband would become. Ivan was the marionette master. For decades. With everyone who had ever crossed his path. She wanted to be a mother and a wife. She really did. Oh, how it had all gone so wrong!

Il nome suo nessun saprà ... e noi dovrem, ahime, morir, morir! – No one will know his name and we must, alas, die, die!

Dilegua, o notte! Tramontate, stelle! Tramontate, stelle! All'alba vincerò, vincerò, vincerò! Vanish, O Night, Set, stars, set, stars! At dawn, I will win, I will win, I will win!

She wondered for the briefest of moments what they made of the singing coming from the bedroom. As the music faded, she could hear them banging on the big oak door – demanding that she open it and come downstairs.

She clutched the picture of her husband with their newborn baby in his arms to her breast.

She hit repeat on the CD player, unwrapped her little gun from the silk scarf, held it to her temple and closed her eyes.

Chapter 46

As Danny played upstairs with Mr Cassidy, the three friends sat round the television in the sitting room. Images of Weybridge Estate assaulted them and they held their breath waiting for the news. The reporter gave out the details of a triple homicide on the grounds of the sprawling mansion and launched into the history of the place, Scott's disappearance, the father's suicide and their connection to many politicians and businessmen. The public were assured that Gardaí were following a definite line of enquiry.

Jen's phone rang as the television screen flickered with pictures of crime-scene tape and technicians in white boiler suits. Andy answered. He said very little to the caller, instead nodded and grunted.

He hung up the call and sat down.

'That was Joe.'

The others held their breath and waited for him to speak.

'Livia walked into the police station early this afternoon. She sat with the Sergeant and told him a story of what had happened the night before. She gave her statement, including a confession that she had killed her son, and it was recorded. She then took the Sergeant out to the house to show him where the bodies were. Detectives arrived as she was in her bedroom getting changed. They could hear operatic music from her room. She had locked her bedroom door. She sat on her bed, put a Colt 1908 vest-pocket pistol to her temple and pulled the trigger. It took the detectives half an hour to break down the antique oak door. She's dead. They are not looking outside of her confession. It's over.'

Justice had been served. None of them would weep for Scott. He was a monster and had caused untold damage to all of them. Equally, they could not bring themselves to weep for the woman who had bred that monster. They were two of a kind and she had as much blood on her hands as he did. Their secrets and the lengths they were pushed to would go to the grave with the mother and son who had tried to ruin their lives. Justice had come to both sides. Karma had seen to that.

Epilogue

One year later

The sun burst in through the stained-glass window behind her, casting a rainbow of colours over the faces looking at her. Jen was running one of her all-day workshops the result of rigorous training from her close friend Dr Norval. The classes were designed to be a safe place for people to come where they were given the tools to unlock their creativity and maintain their own positive mental health.

It was rare that people didn't get something from the group but there were one or two that didn't come back after their first visit. To each their own, she thought. She couldn't save them all. Not that she wanted to – that was up to themselves.

'Just before we break for lunch, I'm delighted to tell you my greatest friend, Sal, is coming in today with her partner to give you a masterclass in life drawing – she's en route from Berlin to New York and it's a real privilege to have her here. Anyone who's not interested, the reading room and/or the gym is available. We'll meet back here for the last session of the day then – okay?'

Lots of nods and smiles in her direction. By now everyone was hungry and the main priority was lunch. As usual, Tess was inside in the little kitchen, cooking up a storm. Everyone filed out and made for the restaurant. Jen walked down the corridor instead.

She knocked lightly on the door. A riot of sound answered her and she walked in. Doc was at the top of the room. When he had finished his Addiction Counselling course, he'd begun to look into how he could use his inherent skill of playing music and song-writing as a tool to help older children and teenagers. Music therapy was where it was at and he was a natural. Danny and Hugh had joined the class in the early days – Danny struggled with the actual playing of his guitar but loved it anyway. Hugh followed in his father's footsteps both as musician and teacher – he had a natural ability to get through to the kids his own age and, before long, the chords and the circle of fifths were understood by all.

'Doc, lunch is ready. You all good here?'

He nodded and gave the kids a list of instructions.

Jen walked on. She passed by the restaurant window, making hand-signals at Tess – I'm going outside for fresh air, she mimed, too warm in here. Tess nodded to the fridge – her lunch was in there.

Crossing the road outside the community centre she took the set of steps down onto the small beach. She descended the steep, loose stone steps with the confidence of twenty odd years' experience.

The strand was quiet and she made her way down to the kissing stone close to the water. Glancing at her watch, she had a good fifteen minutes before Andy arrived into the centre to meet them for lunch. Him, Fran and Joe had been out with a tour to the islands that morning and would head back out to collect them around three or so.

To her left was home. She couldn't see it from here, the way the headland curved, but she could feel it and to her right was the harbour mouth and the marina. The gentle lapping of the water kissing the shore soothed her and the gulls cried out and greeted her. Flagpoles whistled and banged in the breeze and the odd shout from the working folk on the pier blew in her direction.

She kicked off her sandals and buried her feet in the damp sand. Taking a couple of deep breaths, she pulled the worn letter out of her pocket and began to read it.

Dear Jen,

I hope this letter finds you well. You do not know me but I know of you. My name is Leigh Pelser and I write to you from Walker Bay, South Africa. It has taken me some time to put pen to paper and compose a letter to you but, all things considered, I felt compelled to – in short, you saved my life.

Nine months ago, I was removed from a brothel in Marrakech by an international police operation. I had been there for some time, being beaten and forced to sell my body. No one knew where to look for me as I was travelling alone. I will not go into detail of how I suffered as I know you too have had a very difficult time.

A good friend of mine has been living in Dublin for the last few years and we stayed in touch. There was an Irish girl there too, who was freed at the same time, and when she returned to Ireland it was reported on, of course with the back story of Scott's demise, and the earlier report of your assault. My friend sent me on all the links to the papers and it was there I recognised you and your son.

The notebook your friend gave to the detectives in Ireland led them straight to where we were held and finally home. Some of the girls weren't so lucky. The search continues for them.

To summarise, I want to say thank you to you and your friend for saving my life. I was told you made many follow-up calls on behalf of the girls and you pushed them to keep looking.

I wish you all the love in the world, Jen. I imagine from your photographs that there is plenty of that in your life. I do not want or expect a reply to my letter as I think we both need to move forward and forget about the ties that bind us.

I think the words of our own famous Lucy Schreiner are appropriate as I sign off.

'And so, it comes to pass in time, that the earth ceases for us to be a weltering chaos. We walk in the great hall of life, looking up and round reverentially. Nothing is despicable — all is meaningful; nothing is small — all is part of a whole, whose beginning and end we know not. The life that throbs in us is a pulsation from it; too mighty for our comprehension, not too small.

And so, it comes to pass at last, that whereas the sky was at first a small blue rag stretched out over us and so low that our hands might touch it, pressing down on us, it raises itself into an immeasurable blue arch over our heads, and we begin to live again.'

Yours, in gratitude,

Leigh

Jen didn't need to read the words — she knew it off by heart, especially the quote from *The Story of an African Farm*. She was glad the woman didn't want a response but it was a letter she was grateful to have received. The initial shock, of course, saw her in Dr Norval's office in tears, retraumatised by all of it. But, as she had done with everything, she worked through the emotions and moved forward. She held no remorse or guilt for her actions or for the fallout after the fact. They had got on with it and moved on. They deserved that and he deserved what he got too.

Home, family and community were the most important things in life. The tribe. When all was said, and done, Jen knew she was surrounded by love. Her family and her home were part of the community that had looked out for each other over generations and would do for generations to come. Secrets were always buried within the fold, celebrations were celebrated, a new life would always be welcomed and the loss of a community member would be mourned — the person, never forgotten, living on in blood and in memory. Breed, seed and generation are the ties that bind and they can never be broken.

She bent over and picked up a beautiful rock that lay on the sand. The stone was as white as snow and as smooth as marble. Standing up, she glanced up and down the shore — she still had the beach to herself. She held the letter to her chest and thought about Leigh. She wished for her nothing but happiness and love too. Wrapping the letter around the stone, she twisted the paper tight and the package took on the appearance of a comet. The time had come for her to sever the last tie that bound her to her past, to the sadness and to the devastation that twisted man had wreaked on many lives. It was time to let go and today was a good day to do that.

She walked to the edge of the water – the cold licking her toes. She kept walking until the sea began to swell over her knees. She let the little comet fly out of her hand and watched as it splashed and sank beneath the surface. The last weak tendrils of the past unwrapped their hold on her heart and slipped away into the surf.

THE END

ALSO AVAILABLE FROM

POOLBEG
CRIMSON

THEY ALL FALL DOWN

CAT HOGAN

Ring-a-ring o' Roses . . . How far would you go?

Jen Harper likes to play it safe. She is settling into life on the outskirts of a sleepy fishing village with her little boy, Danny. Life by the sea – just how she wanted it.

When she meets Andy, she feels the time has come to put her baggage and the scars of the past behind her. Then she is introduced to Scott, Andy's best friend, and is stung by his obvious
disdain for her. Why is Scott so protective of his best friend? What is the dark secret that threatens all of them?

In her attempt to find answers, Jen must confront her demons and push her relationships to their limits. By digging up the past, she puts Danny and herself in danger. Will she succeed in uncovering the truth before they all fall down?

Raw and energetic, They All Fall Down *is a fast-paced and addictive novel exploring the depths of flawed human nature, the thin line between love and obsession and the destructive nature of addiction.*

ISBN 978-178199-864-9

ALSO AVAILABLE FROM

POOLBEG
CRIMS●N

THE LAST LOST GIRL

MARY HOEY

Unravelling the past can be dangerous . . .

On a perfect July evening in the sizzling Irish summer of 1976, fifteen-year-old Festival Queen Lilly Brennan disappears. Thirty-seven years later, as the anniversary of Lilly's disappearance approaches, her sister Jacqueline returns to their childhood home in Blackberry Lane. There she stumbles upon something that reopens the mystery, setting her on a search for the truth – a search that leads her to surprising places and challenging encounters.

Jacqueline feels increasingly compelled to find the answer to what happened to Lilly all those years ago and finally lay her ghost to rest. But at what cost? For unravelling the past proves to be a dangerous and painful thing, and her path to the truth leads her ever closer to a dark secret she may not wish to know.

'A haunting, mesmerising first novel with a chilling secret at its core. It will grip and surprise you to the very last page' *RTÉ Guide*

ISBN 978-178199-8311

ALSO AVAILABLE FROM

POOLBEG
CRIMSON

THE OTHER SIDE OF THE WALL

ANDREA MARA

When Sylvia looks out her bedroom window at night and sees a child face down in the pond next door, she races into her
neighbour's garden. But the pond is empty, and no-one is answering the door.

Wondering if night feeds and sleep deprivation are getting to her, she hurriedly retreats. Besides, the fact that a local child has gone missing must be preying on her mind. Then, a week later, she hears the sound of a man crying through her bedroom wall.

The man living next door, Sam, has recently moved in. His wife and children are away for the summer and he joins them at weekends. Sylvia finds him friendly and helpful, yet she becomes increasingly uneasy about him.

Then Sylvia's little daughter wakes one night, screaming that there's a man in her room. This is followed by a series of bizarre disturbances in the house.

Sylvia's husband insists it's all in her mind, but she is certain it's not – there's something very wrong on the other side of the wall.

ISBN 978-178199-8328

If you enjoyed this book from
Poolbeg why not visit our website

www.poolbeg.com

and get another book delivered straight
to your home or to a friend's home.

All books despatched within 24 hours.

Free postage on orders over €20*

Why not join our mailing list at
www.poolbeg.com and get some
fantastic offers, competitions,
author interviews, new releases
and much more?

@PoolbegBooks

www.facebook.com/poolbegpress

*Free postage over €20 applies to Ireland only